LITTLE LADY, BIG APPLE

This Large Print Book carries the
Seal of Approval of N.A.V.H.

LITTLE LADY, BIG APPLE

HESTER BROWNE

WHEELER PUBLISHING

An imprint of Thomson Gale, a part of The Thomson Corporation

Detroit • New York • San Francisco • New Haven, Conn. • Waterville, Maine • London

THOMSON
GALE

LIBRARY OF CONGRESS CATALOGING-IN-PUBLICATION DATA

Browne, Hester.
  Little lady, Big Apple / by Hester Browne.
    p. cm.
  ISBN-13: 978-1-59722-495-6 (hardcover : alk. paper)
  ISBN-10: 1-59722-495-2 (hardcover : alk. paper)
  1. Dating services — Fiction. 2. London (England) — Fiction. 3. Manhattan (New York, N.Y.) — Fiction. 4. Large type books. 5. Chick lit. I. Title.
PR6102.R695L59 2007b
823'.92—dc22   2007001559

Published in 2007 by arrangement with Pocket Books,
a division of Simon & Schuster, Inc.

Printed in the United States of America on permanent paper
10 9 8 7 6 5 4 3 2 1

LITTLE LADY, BIG APPLE

ONE

My name is Melissa Romney-Jones, but between the hours of nine and five you can call me Honey.

That's when I'm at work, running the Little Lady Agency, London's premier freelance girlfriend service. During office hours, I'm Honey Blennerhesket, queen of scruffy bachelors and scourge of slacking domestics. The Little Lady Agency, my very own business, is the first port of call for hopeless single chaps who need to borrow a woman's expertise for the afternoon. You'd be astounded how many of them there are.

It's not, I should stress, as racy as it sounds, but it has completely changed my outlook on men, in more ways than one.

As it says on my business cards, I offer — or, rather, Honey offers — every girlfriend service a man could need, except sex and laundry. Aside from that, I'll tackle anything, no matter how random or daunting, and it certainly keeps me busy. In the last year, for instance, I've advised on the purchase of hundreds of suits; put a couple of would-be grannies right off the idea of grandchildren; helped break off five engagements and assisted nine marriage proposals; salvaged three flats after three wild parties; bought stacks of godparent gifts; sent thousands of roses to spouses, secretaries, sisters, and secret girlfriends; and generally acted as the invisible woman most men need to keep them on the straight and narrow.

You're probably wondering why I can't just do all this as Melissa. Well, there are several very good reasons for that.

First of all, if the name Romney-Jones seems familiar, it's because my father, Martin, is the only Member of Parliament to have survived no fewer than four separate political scandals (two tax, one sex, and something murky involving an EU cheese producer in Luxembourg that I've never quite gotten to the bottom of). When I started my business, I didn't want him to find out what I was up to, and now that things are working out rather well, I don't want him cashing in.

Secondly, if I'm being honest, in real life I'm a complete pushover, ground down by years of merciless advantage-taking by Daddy and the rest of my horrendously self-ish family. So I found that creating bossy, supergroomed Honey sort of gives me permission to put my foot down where I'd normally fear to tread. Honey has much better shoes than I do, for a start. Most of them are stilettos, to go with the fitted pencil skirts and devastating bombshell sweaters I wear for work, and Honey's not afraid to stamp those stilettos when she needs to get results. Rather hard, too, if the situation demands. Sometimes I don't even notice the blisters till I get home.

Plus, to be honest, there's something kind of sexy about being Honey. She never rounds her shoulders to hide her ample cleavage or worries about how she looks from behind. And I never realized that wearing stockings for work would have such startling effects on my out-of-office life. . . .

Ahem. Anyway . . .

Thirdly? Well, everyone likes to be able to clock off at the end of the day, don't they? When you've spent hours ironing out endless male problems, it's nice to be able to walk away from them. And I do walk away. In dress-down Melissa's comfortable flats.

Quite apart from the delicious wardrobe, I absolutely love my work. No one can sack me, for one thing. Up until I started the agency, my CV comprised five personal assistant positions in five different estate agencies and one unfortunate spell working for my old home economics teacher, who, *as I found out at my own expense,* wasn't quite the lady I thought she was. Let's just say that when *I* escort a man to dinner, I don't expect to be the pudding course. But ironically enough, it was wearing Mrs. McKinnon's prescribed corset (and the blond wig I used as a disguise) that unleashed the straight-talking, wiggly walking force of nature that is Honey Blennerhesket, so I suppose I have something to thank Mrs. McKinnon for. I like to look on the bright side like that.

And, despite what my father might sneer about mummy's boys and hand-holding, I get a tremendous sense of job satisfaction from my work. There's something so gratifying about taking shambolic bachelors and revealing their inner foxes — rather like tarting up derelict houses that no one can bear to move into, only to see them besieged with buyers the next week. Some of my clients do need an element of structural repair, as well as cosmetic improvement, but that's even more rewarding to sort out. Besides, Honey likes a challenge.

For a while I didn't think Melissa would ever be able to compete with Honey, who was just so much more . . . colorful than me. More confident, more dynamic, more everything, really.

But then the weirdest thing happened. We met — I mean, *I* met — someone: Jonathan Riley. He was tall, charming, courteous, with perfect teeth and a very handy fox-trot — in short, a proper, old-fashioned gentleman. He was also running the Chelsea estate agency I used to work at and looking for a human shield to protect him from the London dating market while he got over the breakup of his marriage.

Posing as Jonathan's girlfriend in smart restaurants and glamorous cocktail bars all over London wasn't exactly what you'd call work. The hard part was trying to keep my professional distance at the end of each date. Well, that and keeping my wig straight. Just as I was miserably sure he was falling for Honey the blond bombshell, he told me he'd fallen for me — frumpy old Melissa underneath! Only he didn't think I was frumpy. When I'd gotten over being amazed, I was very, very happy.

And I still am. Quite *extraordinarily* happy.

The three best things about Jonathan are that he's a real grown-up *man:* he has properly tailored suits; he can order food in three languages; he buys his own moisturizer without a shred of embarrassment; and he never, ever, leaves the bathroom door open when I stay over at his enormous house in Barnes.

He's also strong enough from all the squash and running that he does to sweep me into his arms and make me feel tiny and fragile. And once he's swept me into his arms, he's also very good on the, ah, follow-through, if you know what I mean.

And thirdly, Jonathan actually listens to me. We have lovely weekends away in the English countryside (he's been too busy for us to have a proper holiday), trailing round stately homes while I recycle all the useless facts about moats and knights from my history lessons and he nods in apparent interest. He asks me where I want to go for dinner, or how my day was, *and then remembers what I said.*

Bonus: he's not afraid of my ghastly father.

The only negatives about Jonathan are that he's very busy and doesn't always get my jokes. My best friend, Gabi, would add that he also has bright red hair, but frankly that's a positive for me, since we both have to keep out of the sun.

He is, in short, a complete dreamboat.

■ ■ ■ ■

However, being practically perfect during working hours didn't mean I wasn't still prone to lateness and snagged tights in the mornings. I was already seventeen minutes behind schedule, and since Gabi was supposed to be helping me on my first job of the day, I had no doubt that those seventeen minutes were about to double.

I was running late because my flatmate, Nelson, had phoned our local radio station to add his considered opinion to a heated debate about recycling and had insisted on my hanging around to record his contribution on the kitchen radio.

Gabi was running late because there was a sample sale in Hampstead, for which the doors opened at 7:00 a.m.

At 8:33 a.m. we were both scuttling down the street toward the agency, knowing full well that Tristram Hart-Mossop would be waiting for us outside Selfridges at 9:00 a.m. on the dot, and I wasn't anywhere near ready for that.

"I don't see why we can't just go straight to Oxford Circus!" panted Gabi.

"Because I need to get changed! Come on, we're nearly there." I walked briskly down Ebury Street. My old boarding school was the type that encouraged brisk walking.

"Jesus, Mel, you move fast for a big girl. What kept you, anyway?" she gasped. "A morning quickie with Dr. No?"

"Certainly not!" I should explain that Gabi worked part-time in the estate agency that Jonathan managed, and she had great trouble seeing him in a nonmanagerial role. He had a rather "results-oriented" management style. While Nelson tended to refer to him sarcastically as Remington Steele on account of his all-American, clean-cut jawline, the girls in the office — *apparently* — liked to call him Dr. No.

Jonathan, I might add, rarely said no to me.

"He likes to get off quickly in the mornings," I added. "He's usually ready to go by seven."

Gabi snorted dirtily. "That's what I meant."

I looked at her, baffled. "No, I thought you were asking me if we'd —"

"Forget it," she said. "Your kind of innocence should have a preservation order."

Gabi and Nelson were always baiting me with double entendres. I never got them. With a family like mine, one grows up habitually looking the other way.

"Nothing wrong with having an innocent mind," I said, unlocking the door and pushing it open.

There was the usual stack of interesting-looking mail, but I didn't have time to check through it. Instead, we bounded up the stairs two at a time, past the frightfully discreet beauty salon on the ground floor, where Chelsea wives snuck off for their Botox and electro-tweakage, and into my office.

I threw my huge handbag on the leather sofa and handed Gabi the bunch of ranunculus I'd bought on the way.

"Right," I said, peeling off my cardigan. "I'm going to get changed. Stick these flowers in water, would you?"

"Okay," said Gabi, looking round for a vase. "God, this place is comfy. I've seen less cozy houses."

"That's the point."

My office was a little second-floor flat: The main room was my lilac-walled, calming consultation space, with a tiny bathroom, an even tinier kitchen alcove, and a small second room, in which I kept spare clothes, supplies, and a fold-out bed in case of emergency.

Leaving the door open so I could chat to Gabi, I slipped out of my floaty summer skirt and hunted about for my garter belt. There weren't that many businesses where you could spend hundreds of pounds on Agent Provocateur underwear and charge it to office furniture. As I slid the first crisp new stocking over my toes and carefully smoothed it up and over my leg, I started to feel, as I always did, a little bit more confident. More put together. More in charge.

"Do you want coffee?" yelled Gabi.

"Please!" I fixed the stocking in place and quickly rolled on the other. I'd got quite adept at this. There was a knack to it, a little flick of the finger and thumb, which was really rather satisfying to acquire. I could imagine Jane Russell doing it. After my stockings came the black pencil skirt, which skimmed over the curve of my tummy. It was a high garter belt, with a decent flattening capacity, but it could only do so much.

Something about stockings made me stand up straighter. I hunted through the hangers to find a clean blouse.

"Biscuits?" yelled Gabi.

"In the barrel. Homemade. Nelson knocked some up for me."

Gabi let out a gusty sigh of admiration. Nelson made famously light shortbread.

I slipped into a fresh black shirt and buttoned it over my rose satin balconette bra. Not that clients ever got to see my spectacularly glam underpinnings, obviously, but it made *me* feel better, knowing they were there. My fingers hesitated over the third button, where my shirt parted precariously close to the delicate lace of my bra. I left it undone.

It promised to be a warm day, after all.

Finally, I wriggled my stockinged feet into a pair of high-heeled stilettos, pulled back my shoulders, and I was ready.

Honey Blennerhesket. Five feet eleven inches of woman.

Out of habit, my hand reached for the finishing touch, the final piece of the Melissa-to-Honey transformation: Honey's long blond wig, currently sitting on top of the filing cabinet like a religious icon, its caramel curls spooling lusciously around the antique porcelain head.

I stopped. No. That was the one thing that Jonathan *had* said no to. No more wearing the wig as part of the "stand-in girlfriend" service. I think he was worried that other men might fall under its spell as he had, but frankly, he had nothing to worry about on that score.

Still, it was so lovely. And it made me look so glamorous. The wig had only been a disguise, but somehow it had unleashed a whole side of me that I'd never really known was there.

I took a step nearer and stroked the real hair.

Not that I minded giving up something so small for Jonathan, but I'd never felt so gorgeous as I had when I'd been a slinky blond. Would it hurt just to try it on for a moment, just to get me in the . . .

"Here you go, milk, no sugar . . . Jesus Christ!" blurted Gabi as she stepped into the room with the coffees.

I sprang back from the wig guiltily.

"I never get used to how different you look in the whole Honey getup," she marveled. "Look at that tiny waist! You sexbomb, you."

I flapped away the compliment. "It's all tailoring. You should —"

"Yeah, yeah." Gabi was more of a designer jeans girl. She nodded toward the wig. "So, you going to put that on?"

"No," I said firmly. "I don't wear that anymore."

"Ever?"

"No. Jonathan and I agreed that I wouldn't."

"Not even in the privacy of . . . you know?" Gabi twinkled naughtily. She was

18

shameless sometimes. If you asked me, she got away with a good deal under the guise of straight talking. "He doesn't ask you to do any . . . role playing?"

I blushed. *"No."*

Between you and me, I did still like to put it on now and again. When no one was around. Just swishing all that hair about was so sexy and confidence-inspiring. Nelson, who never tires of teasing me, claimed it had voodoo powers, like something out of a spooky novel. The Wig That Flounced on Its Own.

Actually, in my middle-of-the-night panic moments I sometimes wondered if Jonathan secretly preferred me when I was Honey the blond. He was a very successful estate agent. He drove a Mercedes that cost more than Nelson had paid for his flat. And his ex-wife, Cindy, was a real blond, unlike me. And again, unlike me, she probably hadn't been drummed out of the Pony Club for overfeeding her horse (out of love, not carelessness).

There was something about the thought of Cindy that put the fear of God in me, on many levels. I suppressed a shudder.

I hadn't actually met her, and so probably shouldn't be drawing unfair conclusions. Of course if I *had* met her, then maybe I wouldn't be haunted by my vivid imagination.

"No," I said more firmly. "He doesn't like me wearing it at all. Says he's had his fill of blonds for now."

"More fool him then," said Gabi, offering me the mug and gulping from her own. "Come on! We've got three minutes, and that's if we can find a black cab." She blew on her coffee, then added, "Mind, dressed like that, I doubt you'll have a problem on that front. Not that you ever do."

"Don't rush," I said. "No point in scalding yourself."

She thrust her watch in my face. "Look at the time!"

A strange calm had descended over me. "Tristram can just wait. We'll get there when we get there."

Gabi gazed at me with something approaching admiration. "Blimey. That's what I call power dressing."

"I think better in high heels," I replied. "You've got the camcorder?"

"Check."

"Wonderful," I said serenely and sipped my coffee.

We made it to Selfridges by five minutes past. That was the beauty of Honey: She was never exactly late, but she knew the value of keeping men waiting for a minute or two.

Tristram Hart-Mossop looked less than thrilled to see us nonetheless, and I hurried him up to the menswear department as fast as possible, trying to keep Gabi away from the lure of the perfume hall. With the benefit of hindsight, I realized she might not have been the ideal choice of sidekick for this particular job.

When the three of us were safely upstairs, I took a deep breath, marshaled my thoughts like a midget gymnast about to perform a complicated series of flick-flacks and piked whatnots, and launched into full Honey mode.

"So, you see, Tristram," I trilled with an expansive wave of the hand, "you've got one thousand pounds to spend on clothes, and I'm going to help you spend it!"

Then I turned to Gabi, who was filming me on my office camcorder, and added, with a smile so broad it made my cheeks hurt, "Because I'm Honey Blennerhesket, and I'm 'Making You Over!' "

Gabi, to her credit, didn't laugh when I said this. Which was good of her, because I heard some passing shopper snigger behind me and someone else say, quite distinctly,

"Who?"

"Tristram," hissed Gabi as the awkward pause stretched out, "say something!"

Tristram Hart-Mossop, the textbook illustration of "awkward teenager," shuffled self-consciously, shooting nervous glances in every direction. I couldn't decide whether he was terrified of being separated from his computer for an hour or just terrified of being seen out in the company of two women. He was hopping from foot to foot as if he was desperate for the loo, and I was already feeling more like a warder than a makeover queen.

Gabi coughed and pointed at the camera, which sent him into another spasm of twitching and glancing.

I prodded him discreetly and whispered, "Just pretend you're at home. On a family video!"

Tristram let out a strangled squawk of mortification that hinted at its own story, then managed to croak, "That's great! Um, yuh, cheers. Right."

I nudged him to look at the camera, and he managed to haul his eyes up for a second, before his gaze darted wildly first to a pyramid of socks, then over to the trousers, and then onto a man changing a shop-floor model.

"So," I finished with another chuckling smile, "without further ado, let's get on and *make you over!*"

"And cut!" said Gabi. "That was great. You're very good on camera, you know, Tristram."

I gave her a quick "don't build your part up" warning look, and she raised her eyebrows in fake innocence. It wasn't, I must say, very convincing. Innocence wasn't one of Gabi's natural expressions.

"Still don't remember entering this competition," Tristram mumbled poshly, shaking his head of shaggy brown hair as I hustled him toward the lambswool sweaters like a sheepdog, keeping my eyes fixed on possible escape routes. "And, y'know, I watch a lot of TV and I don't remember seeing this program on MTV, like you said —"

"That's because your mum entered you, as a surprise!" I caroled gaily and slid my arm into his. "And you haven't seen it before because this is a pilot. Isn't that exciting? You're the first one! Now, let's go and find you some new clothes. . . ."

We weren't really filming a makeover show for MTV, needless to say. I was using stealthy means to get the allegedly fashion-allergic Tristram into a new set of clothes that wouldn't make him look like he'd covered himself in glue and cartwheeled round the storeroom of a thrift shop. His mother, Olympia, had tottered up to my second-floor office in Pimlico in a state of utter despair, having heard about Honey from a friend of hers whose son I'd cured of nail-biting. (Seventeen surprise phone calls a day soon ambushed him out of it.)

"Tristram simply refuses to buy new clothes. Refuses!" she wailed. "He's so self-conscious about his height, but also, I think, it's because he has the oddest shaped *knees.*" She stopped herself. "Not that I've ever told him that. But he takes any comment about his appearance as a personal criticism, for some reason, and just slobs around in the same two T-shirts all the time. He won't listen to a word I say. I mean, he's got university interviews coming up, and they're going to think he's some kind of drug addict!"

Looking at Tristram now, towering uncertainly over a display of boxer shorts as if he wasn't quite sure what his gangling limbs might do next, the only drug he seemed to be on was some kind of growth hormone.

I'd calmed down Mrs. Hart-Mossop as best I could with a plate of shortbread and

24

promised to smarten Tristram up to the point where his own father wouldn't recognize him.

"You'll have a job," she'd said, forgetting herself sufficiently to start dunking her biscuit.

The one helpful thing Mrs. Hart-Mossop had been able to reveal was that Tristram was a rabid telly addict and absolutely loved reality television shows — to the point where he rarely left his room to experience reality itself. And so here we were, in Selfridges, pandering sneakily to his secret (or so he thought) addiction to *Queer Eye for the Straight Guy* and, in the process, introducing him to the world of linen.

Gabi really was filming too, even though I'd asked her to pretend and keep the camera turned off. I could already imagine the hilarity that would ensue when she played it back at home for Nelson, who never missed a chance to have a good laugh at my expense, particularly when it involved my having to fib. Given my family background, I am an incomprehensibly bad liar. Nelson has an annoying habit of shouting "Ding!" whenever he spots me, well, *bending the truth,* shall we say.

"Turn it off!" I hissed while Tristram

toyed curiously with cuff links, as if he'd never seen them before, then shot a panicked glance over his shoulder at an invisible store detective.

Gabi shook her head and stepped out of my reach just as Tristram turned to me.

"Are these, like, fabric nose-studs?" he asked, holding up a cuff link to study it more closely.

"No." I took it from him and replaced it in the huge bowl. "That's advanced dressing. We'll get to that later." I upped my encouraging smile. "So, Tristram, where would you like to start?"

His face went dark with reluctance. "The computer department."

"No!" I laughed rather grimly, now that I could see what an uphill battle this would be. "I mean, shall we start with a smart suit, or with casual wear?"

He looked at me like a giraffe peering down on a broom-wielding zookeeper, then swung his gaze toward Gabi, who was zooming in lasciviously on a very lifelike dummy modeling tight jersey briefs.

"Is that thing off?" he demanded, biting a long finger.

"If you want it to be," I said soothingly. "Gabi? Could you give us a moment? Fingers out of your mouth, please, Tristram."

With the camera off, Tristram sounded dejected, and he started fiddling with the iPod in his pocket. At least, I hope it was an iPod. "Look, can't I just have the money? Nothing's going to fit. Nothing ever does. Even when Mum pretends it looks okay, I just look like a freak."

"No, you don't," I said bracingly. "You just need the right clothes!"

"I like the ones I've got." He shot another frantic series of looks around the menswear department, then bit his thumb. "Poppy Bridewell, um . . . This . . . girl I met at a party said I looked artistic in T-shirts."

There was a fine line between artistic and autistic. I wondered if it had been a loud party.

"Is she your girlfriend?"

He shook his head, scattering dandruff on the cashmere pullovers. "Don't have one. Never meet girls."

"Well, Tristram, just think how many girls will be watching this!" I said conspiratorially. "And when they see you looking great in new clothes, clothes that really make the most of those lovely shoulders you have . . ." I lifted my eyebrows. "I'm sure you'll soon be *fighting* them off!"

I could hear Nelson "ding"ing in my head, but I crossed my fingers. Nothing enhanced

27

a man's confidence like knowing his shirt was working for him.

"You think?" grunted Tristram, but his face looked more hopeful, and he even managed a shy glance from under his eyelashes toward Gabi.

"Just come with me," I said and propelled him toward the changing rooms. I'd phoned ahead and asked the personal shopper to put aside some bits and pieces just to get us started. "You're already very good with layers, Tristram," I said, nudging him into a cubicle with some buttery-soft cotton T-shirts and a cashmere pullover. "You just need to upgrade them a little. Now pop these on, and let's see what they look like . . ."

Gabi reappeared, viewfinder to her eye, and Tristram shuffled compliantly behind the curtain, only hitting his head briefly on the rail.

"It's amazing what people'll do if they think they're going to be on telly, isn't it?" whispered Gabi, shaking her dark curls as if she herself wouldn't do exactly the same thing. "I was in Brent Cross shopping center this weekend, and this camera crew was there, and I . . . What?"

"You said you'd cut up your credit cards."

Gabi shrugged guiltily. "Yeah, well. You'll

never understand about me and my credit cards. They're like you, and your . . . wig."

"Let's drop the wig, shall we?" I said breezily.

Her generous mouth twisted into a naughty grin. Gabi was petite, and cheeky, and had the sort of long, dark eyelashes that always looked as if she was wearing full liner and mascara, even when she wasn't. "You can't Honey me, Mel," she said. "I work with women much posher and much stroppier than you."

Technically, Gabi and I didn't have much in common, what with me being what she generically termed a "Chalet Girl Princess" and her being the Queen of the North London Shopping Centers, but since my first day at the Dean & Daniels estate agency, where she'd ripped her skirt doing a very cruel impression of our office manager, Carolyn, mounting her Vespa, and I'd stitched it back up for her with the sewing kit I always kept in my bag, we'd been bosom buddies. The best friendships are like mobile phones, I think — you can't explain exactly *how* they work, but you're just relieved they do.

"Shh!" she said before I could say anything. She pointed at the cubicle. "Clothes are appearing!"

29

I looked over to the cubicle and saw reject clothes being tossed petulantly over the curtain. Oh, no. If Tristram thought he could just run through the lot in five minutes and pretend nothing fit, he was sadly mistaken. I glanced about for the tailoring man to pop in and get his measurements for a decent suit.

Tristram slunk out of the changing room, scratching his armpit and squinting in a frenzy of self-consciousness. The T-shirt was too short, and riding at half-mast, revealing some not-unattractive abs, and the sweater was shoved up around his elbows. The jeans, though, fit perfectly. He looked like the Incredible Hulk mid-transformation, but still about ten times better than when he'd gone in.

"Honey," he began in a cracked whine, but I cut him off before he could start.

"See?" I said to the camera. "Doesn't Tris look fabulous! Don't those colors bring out his huge brown eyes? Now, try on these jackets!" I pushed some jackets at him and made a mental note to find a sales assistant so that I could discreetly ask if they had some in longer lengths.

"Are you in for dinner tonight then?" asked Gabi dreamily. "Nelson says he's making something with fresh trout. He's a really excellent cook, you know."

I gave her a level look. I *knew* Nelson was an excellent cook. I'd known he was an excellent cook for the best part of the twenty-odd years I'd known *him.*

When I'd moved into Nelson's slightly shabby-chic flat behind Victoria Coach Station five years ago, it had just been me and him, and we'd been very cozy, in that way that only old, *old* friends can be. Our fathers were at school together, and Nelson and I had grown up fighting over who'd hidden Monopoly money under the board, and sending each other Valentine's cards to make sure we each got at least one. I'd rather gotten used to our unmarried, marital lifestyle — him bossing me about, criticizing my parking but helping me with my accounts, while I generally added some female fragrance to his lifestyle. Nelson sailed a lot on weekends with his mate, Roger. Now that summer was in full swing, the flat was beginning to smell like a marina, but without the champagne and suntan lotion.

However, since my sister Emery's wedding at Christmas, Gabi had been sort of seeing Nelson, and much as I wanted both of them to be happy, I couldn't help feeling what Jonathan would call *conflicted.* Gabi was my best friend, and Nelson — well,

Nelson was like my brother. The first night Gabi stayed over without giving me time to make myself scarce, I gobbled three Nytol and slept with my head wrapped in the duvet, just in case I heard something I shouldn't.

"So, are you in tonight or what?" asked Gabi again.

"Um, yes," I stammered. "Actually, no. No. I'll . . ."

"You think Nelson would wear these?" she asked, holding up a pair of red silk shorts.

"Definitely not!" I said without thinking. "He's always going on about he hates that swinging free feeling and how he's constantly thinking he's about to catch himself on something . . ."

We stared at each other in mutual horror.

Fortunately, at that moment, there was a yelp, and Tristram's face reappeared round the curtain, looking both panicked and affronted. I snapped back into Honey mode without even thinking.

"This chap's just told me to take off my trousers!" he howled.

"He's only measuring you for a suit, Tristram," I said briskly. "Nothing to worry about. Let the nice man get the measurements, and then all you have to do is choose a color!"

Tristram opened his mouth to protest, saw the stern expression on my face, and withdrew his long neck.

"Blimey," said Gabi, impressed. "I've never really seen you doing this Honey thing before. It's quite scary, isn't it?"

"Is it?" I wasn't sure what to make of that.

"Are you wearing stockings?" Gabi did a suggestive shimmy, and I blanched. "Or did Jonathan knock that on the head too?" she enquired. "I know he's not happy about you carrying on with the agency, not now you're meant to be a respectable estate agent's girlfriend and all that."

I looked suspiciously at the camcorder. Did that red light mean it was on or off? Things had also gone very still inside the cubicle, so I dropped my voice discreetly. "Jonathan's fine about the agency, for your information. He just doesn't want me to pretend to be anyone's *girlfriend* anymore. What I do with the rest of my time is my own business. If you must know, he's very proud of me for being so entrepreneurial. End of topic."

"Oooooooh," said Gabi. "Touch-eeeee."

"Not in the least. I'm going to get Tristram into a suit," I announced, to change the subject.

As I said this, Tristram stepped out of the

changing room in a black jacket and a really cool pair of dark jeans. He looked pretty good, if I said so myself.

"Oh, wow!" I swooned, clapping one hand to my bosom. "Tristram! Look at *you!* Don't you look gorgeous?"

The beginnings of a shy smile began to tug at the corners of Tristram's mouth, despite his best efforts to look cool and don't-care-ish. The clothes made a difference, but what really finished it off was a touch of confidence.

I went over and put my arm around him so we were both facing Gabi's camera. I hoped she had it on steadicam, because her shoulders were twitching with barely suppressed laughter.

I, on the other hand, was taking it very seriously, because Tristram obviously was. I felt him flinch, and his fingers went up to his mouth automatically. Discreetly, I placed one of his hands around my waist and hooked the other into his belt loop.

"So, how do you feel, Tristram?" I cooed. "That jacket fits you splendidly! You've got such lovely broad shoulders, you know!"

"Um, yeah, um, I . . . cool," he mumbled. That was about as articulate as most public schoolboys got, but from the way he was sufficiently emboldened to start some tentative groping, I chalked it up as a win and subtly removed his paw from my rear.

Tristram, Gabi, and I had a very nice cup of tea downstairs in Selfridges, next to the computer department, before Gabi and I sent him on his way, promising to let him know the moment we had a broadcast date. I thought I saw the salesgirl wink at him on the way out and realized that bribing the odd assistant might be a good confidence-boosting strategy to employ in the future.

"You realize that Tristram had his nose practically down your cleavage at the end?" said Gabi, peering at the flickering playback screen.

"Did he?" I blushed and poured myself some more tea.

"Any closer and he'd have been talking to your navel. You want to see?" she offered.

"God, no!" I shied away. I hated seeing myself in pictures. The images never quite matched the vision I had in my head. The vision that was usually played by a young Elizabeth Taylor.

"You know, we *should* send this tape to MTV," said Gabi through a mouthful of raspberry cheesecake. "You could get your own program. *From Geek to Chic.* You think?"

"No, I don't think." I looked on enviously. I only had to breathe near cheesecake and I put on about five pounds. I had that sort of figure. Gabi called it voluptuous, but Marks & Spencer's called it size 12. "Shouldn't you be saving yourself for supper?"

"Not a problem." She squished the last few crumbs down on the back of her fork and popped them in her mouth. "Got the fastest metabolism in London, me. 'Swhy I think me and Nelson are just fated to be together. Fast as he cooks it, I eat it!" she added with a cheeky wink.

Funny. Gabi's last boyfriend, Aaron, had barely had time to phone out for a pizza, but he'd made money as fast as she'd been able to spend it — almost — and she'd nearly married him.

I pushed aside these unworthy thoughts. It was the end of a very long week, and frankly I was looking forward to spending the rest of the evening in a soap-opera-related trance, ideally with Nelson rubbing my feet.

Then I remembered that it was dinner for two and gooseberries for one at our house that evening, and the blissful image abruptly shattered.

Oh, don't be so selfish, I told myself. *Pull yourself together!*

Gabi was a good friend, and I should have been thrilled she'd found someone as decent as Nelson. "Thanks for giving up your day off to help me out," I said. "It was really sweet of you."

"No problemo." Gabi finished off the last of the tea. " 'Sides, it's not my day off. Carolyn thinks I'm having a root canal. She's not expecting me in till Monday at the earliest."

"Gabi . . . ," I said reproachfully.

My phone started ringing in my bag. I have two: a normal one for myself, and a swanky black one for work.

But this was my own line, and the number displayed made my heart sink, right into the pit of my corseted stomach.

"Hello?" I said as brightly as I could nonetheless.

"Melissa!" barked Daddy. "Get yourself home at once. There's a family crisis. Your mother needs you."

Then he hung up.

Well, I thought, trying to look on the bright side, that sorted out one of my immediate problems, at least. There was little or no chance of having to avoid public displays of affection at my parents' house.

"Congratulations," I said to Gabi. "You and Nelson have got the place to yourselves

37

this evening!"

"Thanks, Mel," she said with a wink, and I felt pleased, guilty, and slightly sick, all at the same time.

TWO

I drove to my parents' house in a state of consternation, not helped by the stream of messages arriving on both phones.

Even if Nelson hadn't been such a home-made policeman, lecturing me incessantly about hands-free car kits, I wouldn't have wanted to check the messages anyway, in case they'd contained even more pleas to fit appointments into my bursting schedule and/or updates about whatever this emergency was at home. When it came to my father, ignorance was usually bliss. Which was just as well, because as far as he was concerned, "the truth, the whole truth and nothing but the truth" were three entirely separate levels of information.

The other members of my family weren't much better. They rarely bothered to explain their crises in advance, on the grounds, I think, that if I'd had any inkling of what I'd have been letting myself in for, I'd simply have driven in the opposite direction.

I pulled a reflective face in the mirror. That said, things had been quite peaceful in the eight months since Christmas, when my younger sister Emery married William, a sports-mad, ultracompetitive, thrice-married solicitor. Peaceful by Romney-Jones standards, at least, since they'd spent most of those eight months moving to Chicago and therefore removing themselves from immediate contact; although Emery was so vague that she could easily be on the verge of childbirth by now and not thought to mention it.

There had been nothing in the paper about my father for months — although Parliament was out of session at the moment.

My mother was, the last time I called home, resident in the marital manor house and not shacked up in some seaweed spa in the west of Ireland, or, worse, in some discreet ranch called Serendipity in Arizona having her liver holistically massaged. Though that, again, might have been connected in some way with Parliament being out of session.

My other sister, Allegra, was in Sweden, where she lived with her husband Lars, an art and antiquities dealer specializing in prehistoric arrowheads and other more arcane stuff that I didn't like to ask about.

And Granny . . . I turned up my Julie London CD, which reminded me of her. Granny was the one redeeming feature of my family: She was glamorous, amusing, and the only person I knew with sufficient self-confidence to rattle my father. She had friends in higher places than him, coupled with a mysterious private income, which meant that he couldn't crack the financial whip at her either.

I loved Granny more than anyone, but if there was some crisis afoot at home, she was almost certainly on a camel tour of Egypt or similar, charming all and sundry from beneath a diaphanous veil.

I made it back to the family pile in a very decent two hours, and when I pulled up in the drive there was a full complement of cars outside. That never boded well. Family crises seemed to escalate exponentially the more Romney-Joneses joined in. And from the chewed-up state of the gravel, all the cars had been parked with some rage. Mummy's mud-splattered Mercedes station wagon still had a dog in the back that she'd obviously forgotten to let out in her haste to get in. Daddy's Jag was blocking in Emery's old lime-green Beetle, left there since her wedding, and an enormous black BMW X5 was halfway across the ornamental flower-bed in the center, looking not so much parked as stalled and abandoned.

I peered at it. It was brand new. God knew who that belonged to.

I parked my own Subaru well out of the way, next to an ancient hydrangea, and checked my face in the rearview mirror, taking three slow, deep breaths to prepare myself for the onslaught. When that failed, I had a couple of squirts of Rescue Remedy. Then another, for good measure.

The gardens were deceptively calm in the warm August evening, and I could smell the tall box hedges, which ran around the perimeter of the house, mingling with the musky roses climbing up the front wall. I wondered, hopefully, whether I'd be able to deal with whatever it was in time to be back for the date I had with Jonathan on Saturday night. He was taking me to a dinner dance, but he wouldn't say where: he wanted it to be a surprise. I sighed happily. Jonathan's surprises were always pleasant ones. Which was more than I could say for my family.

I drew back my shoulders. The sooner I got it over with, the sooner I'd be drifting round the dance floor in my best Ginger

Rogers frock.

Jenkins, Mummy's oldest basset hound, leaped up at the window of her car as I approached, barking his head off with excitement, and I helped him out. He was getting on a bit and sometimes needed a hand over the dog shelf, as his back legs were somewhat arthritic and his undercarriage tended to ground him like a barge.

"Hello, old man!" I said, wobbling his big ears and trying not to get my face within reach of his toxic breath.

He snuffled gratefully at my bag as I made my way inside. Already the echoes of a family row were bouncing off the parquet tiles like so much distant cannon fire. I adjudged, from the level of shrieking and bellowing, that the row was taking place not in the kitchen, as usual, but in the drawing room, which indicated that it was quite a high-level argument. In the intimidatingly formal drawing room, my father could take full advantage of the uncomfortable antique sofas, which he liked to stalk around then lean over, aggressively, without warning, to bellow in the ear of the occupant. My mother much preferred to argue in the kitchen, where she had improved access to plates and knives, not to mention "cooking sherry."

"Have you taken leave of your senses entirely?" Daddy was yelling at some unfortunate — my mother, I guessed, since he asked her this question more often than anything else. "Do you think the world revolves entirely around you?"

I paused at the door, temporarily paralyzed by the sheer hypocrisy of this comment, coming from a man who refused to read the morning paper if someone else had gotten there first and "spoiled the pages."

"No," said a low but equally piercing voice. "I imagine the world revolves around Art. Which is better than imagining it revolves around money, like you do."

Oh, God. Allegra. What was she doing here?

Jenkins whimpered, turned tail with surprising agility, and skittered across the parquet and down to the kitchen, out of harm's way. I was tempted to join him, especially since it was village fete time and I knew Mummy would have cleaned out the cake stalls with her usual inability to stop at four fruit scones.

"Don't be so bloody precious!" roared my father, who had no time for Allegra's artistic nature, or, indeed, Lars's art gallery, oddly profitable though it was. "Even Melissa doesn't come out with claptrap like that, and she doesn't know the difference between shorthand and streetwalking!"

Charming. The "real" nature of my agency, as understood by Daddy, was something of a running joke. Or it would be, if it had been funny.

"Martin!" screeched my mother. "Do not use my Meissien dish as an ashtray!"

I gave Mummy or Allegra ten seconds to leap to my defense, then, when no one did, I barged in before they actively joined in with slurs of their own.

"Oh, Christ, what now?" Daddy bellowed by way of paternal greeting. He had apparently forgotten that it was in fact he who had summoned me there in the first place.

"Hello, Melissa," said my mother, through tight lips. I mean they were tight lips, literally. Her whole face seemed unnaturally taut, and she was wearing her shimmery blond hair much more forward than usual. "I'm so glad you're here. I know you can talk some sense into everyone, darling. You always do."

"Hello, Mummy. Hello, Daddy," I said, shrinking, like Alice in Wonderland, back to my nine-year-old self. "Hello, Allegra, how lovely to see you at home! I thought you were in Stockholm at the moment."

Allegra was quite something to behold in

the chintz of the drawing room. She seemed taller than ever, in a long black kaftan-type thing that would have made me look like a funeral parlor sofa but draped over her willowy frame like couture. It might well have been couture, come to that. Her long dark hair — about the only thing we had in common — rippled down her back, and her face was unmade-up, apart from her lips, which were a bright matte scarlet. I couldn't take my eyes off them.

"I've left Lars," she announced, red lips moving in a hypnotic fashion amidst all the black and white. "I have Come Home."

"God alone knows why you have to come back to this one," interrupted my father. "You've got a perfectly good home of your own on Ham Common."

She shot him a poisonous glare in reply and turned back to me with a pained expression. "It's over. All over, Melissa."

"Oh, no!" I said, feeling terrible for her. "You poor thing!" Allegra and Lars were notoriously tempestuous, as befitted artists, but she'd never actually left him before. That was, she'd explained, the whole point of having two houses in separate countries. It cut down nicely on the togetherness. "What's happened?"

A dark look crossed Allegra's pale face. "I

46

can't talk about it."

"Is it too painful? Give it time," I urged. "When Gabi split up with Aaron, she couldn't —"

"No," said Allegra. "I mean I really can't talk about it. I have to speak to my solicitor first."

"A solicitor?" My hand flew to my mouth. Was it that bad? "Oh, Allegra! I'm so sorry!"

She nodded. "I know. He's on his way over now."

Now? I frowned. "But surely it can wait until you've had a chance to sleep on things a little, you know, calm down? . . ."

Allegra made a zipping gesture over her lips.

My mother let out an impatient sigh, but Daddy shushed her with his raised hand. "That's my girl," he said with a ghastly smile of pride. "Always make sure you're on firm legal ground before you get the kicking brogues laced up. Aren't you glad now that I made the pre-nup in England and not in Stockholm? Hmm?"

Allegra tossed her head scornfully.

"I always think there's a touch of *art* in a really clever contract," he concluded.

"But, darling, why can't you go back to Ham?" asked my mother. Her hands twitched automatically for her cigarettes, but she was obviously on one of her annual giving-up kicks, because I didn't see her familiar gold cigarette case around. Instead, she reached underneath the sofa and pulled out an embroidered bag with a kitten on the front. To my astonishment, she withdrew a shapeless hank of knitting and started clicking away, lips pressed firmly together where her cigarette would normally have gone.

Daddy tapped the ash from his cigar ostentatiously into the fireplace.

"I wonder what will kill you first, Martin?" she said, shutting her eyes. "Tobacco or me?"

"You, I'd hope, my darling," replied my father easily. "I'm on the board of at least two tobacco importers — shame to cast a shadow on business."

He whipped back round to Allegra. "Answer your mother's question, Allegra — why can't you go back to Ham? Perfectly good house you've got there. What's happened? Lars changed the locks?"

"Lars has not changed the locks," snorted Allegra, flapping her long black sleeves huffily. She and Daddy were practically nose-to-nose on the carpet now. "That's *my* house!"

"So why can't you go and boil with rage there, instead of cluttering up my home?"

48

he demanded. "Your mother and I went through this when you were a teenager. We don't need to have another round of midnight phone calls and dead cats in the garden."

Dead cats? No one told me anything, even then.

"Not that we don't love to see you at home, darling," added my mother, clicking furiously. "It's lovely to see you."

My father wheeled round on his heel. "Are you off your head, Belinda? Of *course* we mind her turning up here! Not only am I a busy MP, I am now serving on no fewer than two Olympic subcommittees!"

"Are you?" I asked, temporarily distracted. "I didn't know that."

"Yes, well, I've been invited to join a couple of select committees for the London 2012 business. Taking up a lot of my time, involves a tiresome amount of meeting and greeting and so on. . . ." He sighed as if he didn't spend half his life trying to find junkets to skive off on.

"Really?" I said, impressed all the same. My father, involved with the Olympic spirit! "Congratulations!"

He brushed it away, but he was unable to hide his preening. "Well, lots of opportunities floating around right now. For the right people . . . if you know what I mean."

Unfortunately, I did.

"So what sort of committee are you on?" I asked, intrigued.

"Oh, this and that . . . I can't really talk about it," he said. "Very hush hush just at the minute, but it's very high level. Very high level." This seemed to bring him back to reality, because he swung back to glare at Allegra, who had arranged herself along a sofa like a militant end-of-the-pier crystal-ball reader.

"So you'll appreciate that I don't need all these amateur theatricals going on when I have work to do. If I want to see *Phantom of the Opera* I'll have a night out in the West End. You're welcome to stay here tonight, Allegra, but you can't just land here and treat this place like a hotel. You have no idea what plans your mother and I have for entertaining this week, for one thing."

A look of dread passed across Mummy's face, and she knitted faster. She spent most of her time organizing dinners and cocktail parties for Daddy's constituents and contacts and, with what time was left, writing notes of apology and explanation to cover any untoward consequences.

"I can't go back to Ham because it's covered in POLICE LINE DO NOT CROSS tape!" Allegra roared.

"What?" I gasped, but no one was listening to me.

"Oh, don't be so hysterical!" snapped Daddy dismissively.

I stared at her, my skin crawling with panic. Mummy looked less concerned by this news than she had about Daddy's weekend plans, and as for Daddy and Allegra, they seemed to be positively reveling in the drama.

"There are forensic policemen from three different countries swarming all over my beautiful home, and I am not allowed to go back, all right?" Allegra spat, with no small relish. "You don't think I'd put a foot over your Godforsaken threshold unless I absolutely had to? I've left my husband, not had some kind of mental collapse, for Christ's sake!"

Mummy made a choking sound and scrabbled around in her knitting bag. I wondered if she had a whole other set of knitting patterns for serious stress, but instead she pulled out a medicine bottle, wrenched off the cap, shook out a handful of pills, and swallowed them.

"Valerian," she lied unconvincingly, seeing my shocked face.

"Valerian, Vicodin, Valium . . . ," mused

51

Daddy, puffing on his cigar. "What's a couple of letters between friends when you're working your way through the narcotic alphabet?"

"Right up to Viagra," spiked Allegra.

"Enough!" roared Daddy. "I will be in my study. Working. At the job that twenty-three thousand sentient voters have elected me to do." And with that, he hurled his cigar butt in the fireplace and stalked out.

Allegra, who had risen momentarily to argue, threw herself back on the sofa and glowered at the open door. "I thought age was meant to mellow bastards like him."

"It doesn't," said Mummy, who was suddenly much more serene now that Daddy was out of the room. Her knitting, however, remained jerky. "It just intensifies them. Like those really stinky cheeses."

Since no one was going to offer me any, I helped myself to a cup of stewed tea from the tray on the mahogany side table. There were many questions I was burning to ask Allegra, but I fished around for an easy, nonconfrontational opener. Which wasn't as easy as it sounded, believe me.

"So . . . how long are you planning on staying, Allegra?" I asked. "In England, I mean."

"God knows." She let out a theatrical sigh

and kicked off her shoes so she could tuck her bare feet underneath her. She had enviably ruby-red toenails. "Until I'm deported, I guess."

"Oh, darling, it won't come to that, will it?" murmured my mother. She paused, then asked more seriously, "I mean, will it?"

I looked on, aghast.

"That depends what that little shit Lars has been up to," Allegra hissed. "And believe me, when I find out, it won't just be Scotland Yard he'll be scuttling away from."

I sipped my tea and thanked God that I, at least, had a morally upstanding and thoroughly responsible boyfriend in Jonathan. The dodgiest thing he was liable to do was send his secretary out to feed his parking meter.

"Allegra," I began, carefully. "Why *have* the police taped up your house? No one's been . . . hurt, have they?"

She cast an imperious look toward the door to check that Daddy wasn't lurking. Clearly she was hoping to keep him out of the picture for as long as possible — why, I didn't know. Power games, presumably. "Lars has been implicated in some international smuggling ring. I don't know what. Cocaine, I assume," she added airily, "and there was some mention of rhino horn. And antiquities." She paused and twisted the large gold rings on her right hand. "Such an *idiot.*"

"Gosh," I said, shocked. "I never thought Lars —"

"And arms," she went on, with a flick of her long white fingers. "Some other type of drug too, but I can't remember what . . ."

"Allegra!"

". . . and possibly money laundering, but for God's sake! Is there any need to be searching *my* house for evidence?"

As there was no polite sisterly response to this, we sat in silence for a moment while Mummy's needles clicked hysterically. I couldn't work out what she was meant to be making: It looked like it could be anything from a matinee jacket for Jenkins to some kind of ceremonial hat.

"Mummy, why are you knitting?" I asked, because I had to know, imminent Interpol raid or not. "Emery isn't pregnant, is she?"

"Not as far as I know, darling," she said. "I just enjoy it. It gives me something to do with my hands. Some lady at one of the Women's Institute fairs recommended it for giving up smoking. She was smoking forty a day, she said, and now she knits entire king-size blankets in under a week. Plus," she added, "I can fantasize about shoving these

54

needles up your father's ghastly nose at times of stress."

"No plans for your wedding anniversary yet then?" asked Allegra. "Thirty-five years in September, isn't it?"

Mummy knitted faster. "That's weeks away. Don't buy a card just yet."

"So what are you going to do?" I asked Allegra, to change the subject. "Have you, er . . ." It was delicate, talking about money. I hated it. "The police haven't done anything awful, like freeze your bank accounts, have they?"

Allegra's head swiveled over to me, sending her curtain of jet-black hair swinging. "How the hell did you know that?"

"Oh . . . just a guess." I wasn't stupid. It had happened to Daddy twice.

She sighed. "Well, yes. That has happened. And I refuse to ask that bastard for a loan."

"Which one? Lars or Daddy?"

"Daddy. Though Lars owes me."

"Just as well, darling," murmured Mummy, "because I don't think he'd give you one."

"No," I agreed. "And there are always conditions."

I knew that from personal experience. Daddy's loans made Mafia money-lending look like some form of charity handout.

55

What you didn't pay in interest, you paid in favors owed.

"I can give you enough to tide you over," offered Mummy, "but . . ."

"No, no," said Allegra, placing her hands firmly on her knees. "I'll just have to get a job. That's what you did, wasn't it, Melissa? When you couldn't find a rich husband?"

I stared at her in shock. On so many levels.

"Just joking," Allegra said. "I mean, how hard can it be? I don't need that much to live on in London. I reckon about fifty thousand would be enough. Where's the *Times?* Don't they have an Employment section?"

I narrowed my eyes slightly. I sincerely hoped *this* wasn't what Daddy had wanted me to come and sort out. I was a problem-solver, not a white witch. "Allegra," I began, "have you thought about, er, what skills you'd be able to offer? Because there really aren't that many jobs that pay that sort of money for so little experience . . ."

The phone rang on the side table. Mummy stared at it for a second, as if trying to place the sound, then picked it up. "Hello?"

"Your lipstick is smudged," Allegra informed me. "You should either wear lipstick with panache or not at all." She paused to let this information sink in while I fiddled self-consciously with my compact, then added, "Have you thought about plain lip gloss?"

Mummy put the receiver to her chest and looked at me sympathetically. "It's your father, calling from his study. He says can you pop in to see him, please? He'd like a word."

"And that word will doubtless be *cash*," snorted Allegra.

"Allegra," said my mother weakly.

I got up, startled by the novelty of actually wanting to escape to my father's Study of Doom.

I only had to get within thirty feet — yelling distance — of my father's study to feel my stomach begin to knot and my palms begin to dampen: Virtually every difficult conversation of my childhood had taken place within its book-lined walls. Most of those difficult conversations had been about the cost-effectiveness of educating me at a series of very expensive schools — I'm afraid my grades made Princess Diana look like Stephen Hawking — but there had been some other delights thrown in for variation, like the time he'd explained we'd all have to go and live in France to avoid a tax scandal, and then there was the one about our au pair's horrendous court case in which my Snoopy pajama case had played an embarrassingly central role, and . . .

However, when in situ in his oak-paneled study, Daddy still had the ability to reduce me to jelly, even after a year of asserting myself through Honey's no-nonsense persona. These days I could just about tell Emery to buy her own curtains rather than have me "run some up" for her on my sewing machine, but Daddy was a whole other kettle of fish.

The decanter was already on his desk, and he'd poured himself a large Scotch by the time I walked down the corridors that led to his bit of the house. When he heard me knock, he swung round in his chair like a Bond villain and steepled his fingers. I hated it when he did that. It usually meant he knew something I didn't and wasn't going to tell me straight away.

"Ah, Melissa," he said, gesturing toward the chair as if I'd turned up for an interview. "Do sit down. Take the weight off your feet."

I tried not to take that personally.

"It's a while since we've had a little chat, isn't it?" he mused, sipping his Scotch. "I think the last time, if I remember rightly, was at your sister's wedding. When you told me all about your escort agency."

The wedding I'd organized, I might add. All by myself.

"It's not an escort agency," I replied hotly, rising to the bait despite myself. "It's —"

"Yes, yes . . ." He flapped a hand at me. "So you say. Anyway, how is business? Booming? Hmm?"

"It's going well," I said cautiously.

"Making lots of contacts?"

I eyed him, not sure where this was going, but certain it was going somewhere. Somewhere I would almost certainly not want to end up. "Ye-e-e-es."

He frowned in what I think he imagined was an understanding manner. "Or is that awfully dull boyfriend of yours laying down the law about what you can and can't do? Hmm? I imagine he's got some pretty strong views about, ah, a few of your sidelines, eh?"

How did he do that? Did he have some kind of telepathic hot wire into my deepest secrets? I went hot and cold.

"No," I insisted, for what felt like the millionth time. "Jonathan's very happy for me to carry on the agency. I mean, I'm mainly sorting out people's wardrobes and arranging their parties these days, but I'm sure if I wanted to take on a client who needed me to . . ." I slowed down, realizing the untruth

59

of what I was saying. But I was committed now. ". . . deal with more lifestyle issues, he'd understand."

"Ding!" went Nelson's lie detector in my head.

Damn.

Daddy tipped his head to one side and smiled at me, as if I were a very stupid little girl. "Well, that's nice. It would be a shame to let such a clever business idea go to waste."

I was thrown by this unexpected turn of events. Last time we'd discussed the Little Lady Agency, he'd accused me of working as a hooker and dragging the family name into disrepute.

"Anyway, Melissa, since you're doing so well, you must be run off those great big feet of yours, no?"

"Well . . ."

"Come, come, either you're doing well, or you're not?"

"I'm doing well."

"So you can give Allegra something to do." He pushed himself away from the desk with the air of a job well done and started flicking through his Rolodex of cronies by the phone. "Keep her busy. Out of our hair."

I stared at him. "You *are* joking now, aren't you?"

Daddy looked up from his address book. "Does Allegra's divorce strike you as anything to joke about?"

"Well, no, but . . ."

"You do seem to be remarkably uncaring about your sisters," he observed reproachfully. "I practically had to twist your arm to help out with Emery's wedding. Is it because you're feeling the call of the old maid's apron, eh? There's always volunteer work, you know. Spinsterhood isn't the end of the world any more, my dear girl."

"But I can't *give* Allegra a job!" I wailed. "There isn't enough for her to do, even if I wanted to help out. Which I do. Of course I do. But wouldn't she be better working in an art gallery, or something like that? She's got lots of experience of . . . um, art."

I didn't want to say that Allegra could wipe out my client list in about seven phone calls. She had the interpersonal skills of a grave robber, and most of my clients were ridiculously sensitive.

Daddy peered at me patiently. "I realize that, Melissa. Allegra would be an asset to any gallery."

My eyes boggled at this outrageous fib, and he had the grace to drop his gaze momentarily.

"But, thinking as a protective father," he

went on smoothly, "it would be quite stressful for Allegra to reenter the job market at
—"

"*Enter* the job market," I corrected him.
"She's never actually had a real job."

"Quite so," agreed Daddy. "Even more
reason why this isn't the time to open
herself up to the strain of interviews and
possible rejection."

"And she's also under investigation by the
police," I added.

"I *know*," said Daddy. "And, well . . ." His
voice trailed off discreetly. "The press are
ghastly, prying creatures. And I know you
girls have always suffered the pressures of
being the children of a prominent politician."

He looked at me beadily over his fingers,
and the penny dropped. With a clang, right
in my eye.

"You want me to give Allegra a job at *my*
office because you don't want her showing
you up in someone else's!" I said.

"Right the first time," said Daddy, shuffling some papers on his desk, as if the
interview was nearing a close. "We don't
want some nosy HR woman poking around
in our business, and I don't want Allegra
getting on the front page of the *Sun* for

downloading porn or taking drugs in the loo or whatever else she's liable to do."

"But I can't afford to pay her anywhere near what she wants," I protested, thinking of Allegra's exorbitant ideas about salary. "I don't even pay myself that sort of money!"

"Oh, I don't expect *her* to scratch around on nothing," said Daddy. "I'm happy to, how can I put it, supplement her income?"

I stared at him, trying to see where the scam was. There had to be one. Daddy was not a "free money" sort of businessman.

"And I can put a little something your way too," he said generously. "I'm going to need some guidance on international etiquette, with so many meetings with dignitaries in my Olympic diary, and who better to guide me than London's premier etiquette expert?"

If I was reeling before, I was knocked off-balance by this, and Daddy seized on my uncertainty like a hawk spotting a field mouse with a gammy leg.

"Wouldn't that be *wonderful*, Melissa?" he demanded. "Not only working on an internationally significant project, but helping your father at the same time! And promoting your business! And getting paid! And," he added as an afterthought, "maybe meeting some nice young man!"

63

"I have a nice young man, thank you."

Daddy sniffed. "Well, an American one, yes. So, can we agree on this? Between us? Hmm?"

I knew there was something I was missing here, but I couldn't put my finger on what it could be. "And what if I say no?" I hazarded bravely.

Daddy drained his Scotch. "Don't make me answer that, Melissa. Bottom line is she can't hang around here like some kind of very high maintenance vampire bat, and that's the long and short of it. I have things to be getting on with. I'd be most upset if I had to add Allegra — and you — to that list."

"Er, I'll think about it," I said. What option did I have? "I'll do my best."

"Good, good . . ."

He picked up the phone and gave me a ghastly smile, showing all his teeth, old and new.

I excused myself and went down to the kitchen for something to calm my nerves.

THREE

Needless to say, the next day I didn't get back to London in time to dance away my cares with Jonathan and several bottles of Krug champagne. Mummy, Allegra, and even Daddy each accosted me to insist that I stay for dinner to "stop Daddy/Belinda/ Allegra from saying something silly" — an impossible task — but when I managed to call Jonathan, I discovered he'd been trying to call me.

"I've been trying to get hold of you since last night. Where've you been?" he demanded in his gorgeous American accent. "I've been worried!"

I shivered with pleasure. Jonathan had the sexiest voice — the sort you hear on upmarket American legal dramas, where the lawyers are all impassioned and terribly expensive. Luckily he thought my posh English accent was equally sexy, so we spent quite a lot of time just talking utter rubbish about the weather, then falling into passionate embraces. And I must confess it was rather nice to have someone worry about me, too.

"I'm at home," I explained. "In the country. The mobile phone reception is frightful, I know . . ."

"I *tried* home. It's constantly engaged." I could imagine him sticking his hands into his thick red hair as he talked, and my skin tingled at the thought of how he angled his head to one side when he did it, showing the butterscotch freckles on his neck. "I've left about five messages but no one got back to me." His voice softened. "Hey, Melissa. Say frightful again."

I went pink. "The reception is frightful," I said in cut-glass tones. "And my family is *ghastly.* They're having another crisis, that's why I'm here. But, stop it, I need to talk about tonight."

Jonathan sighed. "Promises, promises. I need to talk about tonight too. I can't make it, I'm afraid."

"Oh, why?" I asked, seeing the light at the end of the tunnel go out.

"I'm in New York — I got a call yesterday and had to fly straight out. I've been trying to get hold of you since then."

"Work?" I asked tentatively. The estate

agency that Jonathan worked for was based in New York. As was Cindy, his ex.

There was a pause. "Yes, for work. And . . . tying up some other stuff. Listen, I've just stepped out of a meeting, so I can't really talk, and the longer I talk to you the worse I'll feel for missing tonight. But listen, I'll be back first thing Monday, and I'll make it up to you, I promise. You want me to bring anything from New York?"

"Just yourself," I said, trying not to let my disappointment show too much.

"Okay, honey," he said. "I have to go. Take care of yourself. I'm thinking about you."

"I'm thinking about you," I said quietly, and then my sister stormed into the room, followed by my father and the dogs, and I had to ring off to break it up.

I drove home on Sunday in a state of exhaustion, my brain teeming with all manner of crushing things I could have said to my father had I only been able to get my brain in gear.

He was right, I thought remorsefully, crawling through a traffic jam on the M25. I should maybe have thought about how I could have helped Allegra in her moment of need. She was my sister, after all, and much water had passed under the bridge since we were children. We might have had things in common now, if only I'd looked hard enough. I'd have had to look very hard.

The moment I opened the door to our house and breathed in the mouthwatering aroma of a full roast chicken dinner, my heart swelled with gratitude for the little things in life, like having a flatmate who made his own gravy.

I'd phoned Nelson to let him know about my weekend drama, and also about Jonathan's cancellation, and he'd come up trumps, as usual. Nelson knew me well enough to rustle up a comforting evening meal on the weekends I went home, and this smelled like the works: applesauce, chicken, and roast potatoes. I sniffed the air. Was that bread and butter pudding? My stomach rumbled gleefully. My favorite. And he usually insisted I lavish it all with homemade custard, too. My curve-enhancing lingerie wouldn't have been half so tight if Nelson hadn't been such an ace cook.

God, I was so lucky to have a flatmate like Nelson, I thought for the millionth time. It was like being married, but with none of the worries about not "communicating properly" or letting your leg hair grow over your ankles.

"Hi, honey, I'm home!" I yelled, dumping my bag in the hall. I couldn't help noticing that none of Gabi's designer belongings were hanging on the coat pegs, and my mood rose a little higher.

"Hi, Mel." Nelson appeared at the kitchen door, wiping his hands on his blue-and-white-striped professional home chef's apron.

We might have behaved like brother and sister, but we didn't look alike. Whereas I was brunette and, um, *well-built,* like a water spaniel, say, Nelson was tall and dark blond and reminded me, in many ways, of a golden retriever. Reliable, handsome, happy to help blind people and children. Slightly smug.

Actually, that's not fair. Nelson never made a big deal about helping people — he worked in fund-raising but never forced me to buy Fairtrade chocolate or lectured me about driving the sort of car that single-handedly destroyed seventeen trees a year. He was just one of those naturally good chaps.

I know, sickening.

He had a dreadful singing voice, though, which took the edge off the perfection, thank God, especially at Christmas.

"Smells like a big dinner," I said, popping a sprout in my mouth and hunting around for the corkscrew. "I am so ready for a night in." I bestowed a broad smile on him. "And if you want to watch that marine archaeology DVD, I promise I won't talk through it. Just as long as you do my feet at the same time . . ."

Nelson didn't respond to this generous offer with the enthusiasm I'd hoped, and I paused, wine bottle in hand, to examine the confusing mass of emotions playing across his normally very simple-to-read face.

"Um, that's really kind of you, Mel," he said. "But you really don't have to. Did you have a good time at home? How were your parents?" he asked oddly.

"Oh, still alive," I said.

"Even your mum?"

I poured Nelson a glass of wine, then a large one for myself to fortify my spirits. "She's in a bit of a state, actually. And for once Daddy isn't the reason. Do you want to guess?"

"Melissa, I really couldn't," said Nelson heavily. "Whatever I guess isn't going to be insane enough. Just tell me."

I was rather surprised that Nelson was giving up so easily; normally he was happy to bait me about my family for hours. Still, maybe he was tired.

"Allegra's left Lars," I said. "He's been busted for drug smuggling. She's moved back home and isn't allowed to go to Ham because there are forensic teams dusting her house for evidence."

"No!" said Nelson. He didn't sound very surprised.

"I know! Isn't it awful!" I sipped at my wine. "I never did understand what it was that Lars actually did."

"To be honest, I think you were the only one who didn't, Mel."

"Well, yes. Thinking about it, they did seem to have an awful lot of money for a pair of artists," I mused. "When I got there, there was a great big BMW in the drive and we argued for ten minutes about who it belonged to before Allegra remembered it was hers. She'd bought it when she flew in. With *cash*."

Nelson grunted.

"Anyway, apart from the BMW, she says she's completely broke, back at home, driving them up the wall, and now Daddy wants me to give her a job," I went on, less cheerfully. "He's on an Olympic committee, you know. Who'd have thought that, eh? Daddy, doing something sporty?"

"Tell me he's not handling the ladies'

beach volleyball team."

"Gosh, no! I think it's administrative."

Nelson goggled at me, as though I'd missed a joke. "I just hope he's not sitting on the committee handing out the supply contracts. It would be mortifying, and yet entirely predictable, if your father, the man with stickier fingers than Nigella Lawson, was caught with his nose in the trough." Then a funny look passed across his face. "Still, if he's out and about on Olympic business, your mum will be lonely, won't she? All on her own in that big house. No one to talk to."

I got the feeling he was driving at something here, but I couldn't see what.

"Well, no, not with Allegra . . . Nelson, let's not talk about my family." I got up and started to help him transfer the supper to the table before I could start picking at it. "Let's talk about, um . . ."

Our eyes met over the hob, and we both looked down. I didn't really want to talk about Gabi, and I could tell he didn't either.

There was an awkward pause, and then I said, "Sailing!" at the same time as he said, "Shoes!" in the same bright voice.

"Ah, well, yes, I'm glad you mentioned sailing, actually," he said rapidly. "Because there's something I need to talk to you about."

"Go ahead," I said as he heaped food onto my plate. "I'm all ears."

"Um, don't wait for me," said Nelson, gesturing toward my dinner. "Tuck in. I made all your favorites . . ."

"I know," I said happily, loading up my fork. "I can see."

Then the mists started to clear. This was an elaborate supper beyond a mere weekend home. This was cupboard love at another level. The butter-roasted sprout turned to ashes in my mouth.

"What?" I mumbled, trying not to look concerned as my mind raced through a series of unworthy horrors, each of which made me feel more guilty than the last: Gabi was moving in. Nelson was selling the flat. Gabi and Nelson were getting married.

I swallowed the sprout with some difficulty and had to chase it down with an unwise mouthful of wine.

"Are you okay?" asked Nelson solicitously.

I nodded and spluttered. He was being a bit too nice now.

"You sure you don't want me to punch you in the back?"

"Quite sure," I gasped.

"Okay, well," he said, picking up his knife

and fork with studied casualness. "The thing is that I've finally got a place on a training tall ship."

"A what?" Relief returned, along with the feeling in my throat. If it was just sailing . . .

"A tall ship, you know, an old-fashioned sailing ship." I must have looked blank, because he sighed impatiently. "You know, masts, scurvy, sails, crow's nests . . . that sort of ship. Anyway, it's a charity that teaches underprivileged young people how to crew and run the ship, and I've got a place on the volunteer staff. You know it's something I've wanted to do for ages . . ."

Indeed I did. The opportunity to sail while ordering people around *and* doing good was something Nelson couldn't possibly turn down.

"And I've got some time off work to go and do it. They let us do that, you see," he added. "Take time off to pursue charitable projects. The young people on the ship come from very different backgrounds. Some are disabled."

"There's no need to look so smug," I protested, riled by his sanctimonious expression. "You're not the only one helping the less fortunate. Only this week I saved a teenager from five years of enforced celibacy, just by getting rid of his trousers."

"That was very generous of you," said Nelson seriously. "Did you charge him extra?" Then he suppressed a snigger and spoiled the trendy vicar effect.

I studied his face for clues. I assumed this was some kind of rude joke. Straightening up my back, I looked him in the eye to show I wasn't going to rise to whatever bait he was dangling.

"I charged him the normal wardrobe consultation fee and knocked a bit off because he took us out for tea afterward. If you must know. So how long are you going to be away playing Jack Sparrow, then?" I asked, getting back to the matter at hand. "Do you want me to use the time to redecorate your room?"

Nelson helped himself to the remaining chicken leg. "Ah, well, that's the second part of my, er, news. You know I had that builder over to check the flat for the insurance company?"

I nodded.

"Well, according to him, the whole flat needs rewiring and the bathroom needs moving. Apparently, it's a death trap. So I thought if we're going to have the plumbing done, I might as well have it repainted. And if it's going to be repainted, then I might as well look into new carpets, and . . . I'm going to have to ask you to find your own accommodation for a while, I'm afraid."

My face froze.

"I'm going to be away for three months, you see, until the end of October, and the place will be like a building site, and I'm not sure what the insurance situation would be, so . . . Mel?"

I wasn't listening. I was a couple of steps ahead of him.

"Where am I going to live?" I demanded.

Nelson had the nerve to look disapproving.

"Oh, no," I said, cottoning on. So that's why he'd been so concerned about my poor mother's lonely existence! He was hoping I'd move in there for the interim! "Oh, no, Nelson, I know what you're thinking, and the answer is categorically no. Weren't you listening? Allegra is in residence, and she's making the place look like Dracula's castle. She and Daddy are already at loggerheads, and I honestly don't want to get involved."

Nelson threw his hands in the air. "But Melissa, you can't stay here. I'm really sorry. It just makes more sense to get everything done at once. It's not going to be for long."

"How long?" I was really trying to be brave now, but the mere thought of going home . . .

"A month?" he tried.

We both knew this was a complete guess.

"Right," I said, bravely stabbing three sprouts onto my fork and larding it up with applesauce. "Well, if that's the way it is."

"Can't you move in with Jonathan for a while?" he asked. "You've been going out for months now, and you're always going on about how great it is, dating someone with two spare bedrooms and a guest bathroom."

I bit my lip. As usual, Nelson had hit straight on my weakest point. "I don't want to pressure him. I mean, Jonathan's divorce only came through at Christmas. I don't want him to think I'm pushing him into anything —"

"For God's sake, Melissa, he's an estate agent! Ask him if you can arrange a sublet on one of his spare rooms. He'll cut you a deal, I'm sure."

I chewed miserably on my sprouts. What were my options, after all? Home? Moving into Gabi's tiny studio in Mill Hill?

There was always the tiny spare room at my office. But that was full of boxes and dry-cleaning bags and about ninety pairs of shoes. And I spent enough time there as it was.

"I don't know why you're making such a big deal about it," he huffed. "I thought you were meant to be Miss Dynamism these days. I thought wimpy old Boo Hoo Melissa was a thing of the past. I thought —"

"Okay, okay," I snapped. He was quite right. I needed to pull myself together. It wasn't like he was moving out with Gabi, forever. "I'm just concerned about, um, how it'll affect my work."

Nelson smiled smugly. "That's more like it."

I glared, annoyed at myself for falling straight into his trap.

"Three months at sea," I said, suddenly realizing how much I'd miss his company. "That's ages." I could always find somewhere to sleep for a month, but without Nelson's solid presence around the place, roaring in disgust at the news, it wouldn't be the same.

"Well, yes," he said. "But I'll have access to text and e-mail and stuff. Come on, I'll be back before Bonfire Night."

We looked at each other over the roast chicken.

I swallowed. Nelson was going to sea!

"You'll text me, won't you?" he said. "And you'll let me know if anything, um, untoward happens?"

"What? Like me and Jonathan getting married?" I asked, trying to be jolly.

"I was thinking more of any blackmail or legal actions arising from your business, really," said Nelson, helping himself to more roast potatoes. "But that sort of thing too."

I was touched, although I didn't let it show. Nelson and I had an unspoken agreement that at moments of high emotion, all affection was to be demonstrated only by rudeness. So instead, I said, "You'll text me too if you sink the boat, won't you? Or if the disabled kids get so sick of you patronizing them that they make you walk the plank?"

"Cheers. I've put Roger in charge of distributing my effects," he said drily. "So don't think you're getting the DVD player."

We munched through our heaped plates in companionable silence for a moment or two.

"How's Gabi taking it?" I asked.

Nelson had the grace to look a little uncomfortable. "I haven't told her yet. I thought I should tell you first so you wouldn't hear about your impending homelessness from someone other than your landlord."

"Thoughtful of you." Homelessness. I sighed again, so hard that the bills on the table all lifted and fluttered back down again.

"Tell you what, I'll pay the phone bill this month," offered Nelson. "Gesture of good-will."

"Thank you," I said and mentally put the money aside for spending on earplugs — if I had to go home — or, failing that, a very cheap hotel room.

Still, I let him watch his dreary underwater archaeology DVD, and he rubbed my feet until I fell asleep.

FOUR

On Monday morning, I arrived in the office, and I was pleased to see four new messages on the answering machine already. Weekends could be trying times for my clients. Families, as I knew myself, presented all kinds of problems.

I made a pot of coffee and settled in behind my big desk, kicking off my stilettos for comfort and allowing myself an indulgent gaze at the framed photograph of me and Jonathan, positioned next to the phone, where I'd see it the most. It was my favorite photograph: me and him in black tie, taken at a dinner dance at the Dorchester the previous November when I'd still been pretending to be his girlfriend and he'd still been pretending to be hiring me for convenience. That was the night I really fell in love with him, I think. I hadn't realized that beneath the starchy exterior was a man who could dance like Gene Kelly and make me glide like Cyd Charisse.

Sometimes, looking back over the oily parade of lounge lizards and Sloane Square no-hopers that made up my romantic past, I wonder if they were just some kind of trial I had to undergo so I could end up with Jonathan Riley. Like an army assault course, only with three times as many mud slides and an estate agent at the end of it.

Jonathan was so far out of my usual league that since we'd started going out officially, I'd gotten into the habit of taking lots of pictures of us together, just so I'd believe it was true. He was thirty-nine, worked as a CEO or COO or something at Kyrle & Pope, the big international estate agency that now owned Dean & Daniels, and he had a real old-fashioned film-star polish. Gabi disagreed, on account of his "obsessive-compulsive time keeping," but he did something to me that I can't really explain. He literally swept me off my feet every time I saw him.

I'm a sucker for men in well-cut suits, but there was something going on underneath Jonathan's businesslike exterior — a sort of naughtiness — that melted my insides whenever I caught a glimpse of it. Not that I was complaining about the exterior: He had sharp gray eyes and perfect square teeth, and when he smiled, his whole face turned from serious to boyish in one delicious instant.

Obviously, I didn't want to jeopardize this apparently perfect relationship by moving into his plush pad in Barnes prematurely. I still wasn't convinced that Jonathan knew exactly what he was going out with. He might have thought he'd stopped paying for Honey's professional perfection in favor of my own more ramshackle charms, but the reality was that I was spending just as much time and effort on being a supergroomed, superorganized version of Melissa as I'd ever done tarting myself up into Honey.

Sometimes I wondered nervously just how long I could afford to keep up this level of waxing.

The phone rang. Composing myself into a more professional frame of mind, I picked up the heavy Bakelite receiver. "The Little Lady Agency? How can I help you?"

There was an infinitesimal pause on the other end. "Mmm," said Jonathan, appreciatively. "Say that again?"

Butterflies fluttered up inside my stomach.

"I could say, 'Hello, it's Honey'?" I suggested huskily.

Jonathan spluttered something I didn't catch, then said, in a very grown-up voice,

"Oh, it's good to be back in London. I'm wondering if you're free for lunch?"

"Absolutely!" I said, my accent intensifying until I sounded like Elizabeth Hurley. "What time?"

"How about one o'clock, at Boisdale on Ecclestone Street."

Oooh. Scottish steak.

"That would be delightful," I said. "I'll look forward to it!"

"Mmm, just one more time? The 'delightful' bit?" he said, but fortunately his PA, Patrice, came in with some papers before we could get into trickier waters.

I went back to work with a much lighter heart and skimmed through a list I was making of appropriate presents for children of all ages. It was one of those ironies that the less marriageable the bachelors on my client list were, the more suitable their friends seemed to deem them as godparents, despite their having no experience of children whatsoever. It was all to do with available cash flow, Nelson informed me; the more puking, howling babies they saw, the less likely they were to want any of their own and therefore the more cash they had to spend on the godchildren.

As I was checking the Hamleys website for teddy bear prices, the phone rang again, and when I picked it up, I knew it was Nelson's mate, Roger, even before he spoke. He had a distinctive way of breathing.

"Roger Trumpet!" I said cheerily. "How's tricks?"

There was a surprised squelch as Roger cleared his sizeable nose. "Shouldn't I be asking you that? Eh? Eh?"

That sounded like a dig. I ignored it.

"If this is about Nelson's trip, I'm afraid I can't talk him out of it," I went on, sending my list to print. "Anchors aweigh, and all that."

"I wasn't ringing about Nelson, actually," said Roger, though I could tell by the sulky tone that had entered his voice that I'd struck a nerve. "I need to book your services. Your professional services."

"Oh, good!" I said, pulling my appointments book nearer. I liked a challenge, and since Roger combined astonishing assets *on paper* with some of the worst social graces I'd seen outside a monkey house, he was a big one. "What for?"

"Well, you remember that party of my mother's where you pretended to be my girlfriend?" he began.

"Mmm," I said sympathetically. It had been memorable, for many reasons, not least the unexpected rush of female attention Roger had enjoyed afterward. "Is she still trying to set you up with your cousin Celia?"

"Yeah." Another wrenching nose clearance. Honestly. I made a note to mention it tactfully at a later date. "Only this time it's the Hunt Ball, and Celia's running the show and won't take no for an answer. She's taken up women's rugby recently, and, you know, I don't like to, er, let her down . . ."

"Roger, have you considered telling your mother that we're in the twenty-first century now and that it isn't compulsory to get married by the age of thirty anymore?"

"I have, but she's making her *will*. I'm getting the grandchildren guilt trip. Who's going to get the cider interests. What will happen after she's gone. I keep telling her that she didn't marry my dad until he was forty-three, but what can you do?"

"You don't need to talk to me about parents," I said heavily.

"Yeah, well, I knew you'd understand. So if you wouldn't mind popping along in one of your nice tight dresses to the old Hunt Ball next month, that would be splendid. Third Saturday in September, Hereford. No funny business, obviously, but just let her know that it's all back on with you and me. Wear the wig if it helps."

My pen hovered over the date, then sadly I clicked the cap back on.

"I'm really sorry, Roger, but I can't. I don't do those girlfriend dates anymore."

"What?" The panic in his voice was audible. "But Melissa, I *need* you to do it!"

"Roger, I'm awfully sorry. Um, I can try to find you a nice girl to meet, though — maybe take her out for dinner beforehand, and ask her if . . ."

"No, no, no," Roger interrupted impatiently. "No, that's not the same thing! I need someone temporary or not at all. What do you take me for? Some kind of sleazebag?"

"I'm sure we can work something out," I soothed. "Leave it to me."

Roger harrumphed and hung up.

I looked at the clock. It was twenty-five past twelve. That seemed like as good a point as any to call it a morning and walk slowly to lunch with my real boyfriend before any of the other needy males in my life phoned the office.

As Roger would have figured out had he been sensitive in any way, the fact that Jonathan and I had met while I'd been pretending to be his girlfriend was a major reason why I'd discreetly removed it from my advertised services.

The funny thing being, of course, that Jonathan was the only client I'd ever had who hadn't actually needed my services at all — an irony that occurred to me yet again when I saw him sitting at our table in the elegant surroundings of the Boisdale's courtyard garden, a vision of immaculate summer style.

Jonathan's working wardrobe comprised lots of impeccable suits and sober ties, but today he was dressed down, and it made my heart skip with nervous lust. He was wearing a pair of navy trousers and a soft periwinkle shirt that brought out the silvery gray in his eyes. The sunlight bounced off his hair, making the waves gleam like licks of flame.

The casual effect was slightly undermined by the fact that he was busy making notes about something into his Dictaphone, but he always did that, even for grocery shopping, so I forgave him.

I allowed myself a moment to enjoy the novelty of ogling my own boyfriend, then made my way over.

"Hello," I said, almost shyly.

"Hello, yourself." He leaned over the table, put one hand lightly on my arm, and kissed my cheek. It was a warm day, and I could smell the cologne rising off his skin, which sent a secondary shiver running through me. He wore Creed, like Errol Flynn. Jonathan wasn't a man given to public displays of affection, which suited me fine — I found the polite restraint he showed in public actually rather sexy. Knowing his private displays of affection as I did, if you know what I mean.

"You look absolutely beautiful," he said seriously.

I swatted away the compliment, but I had put some effort into my outfit: a neat fifties-style print sundress with a little vintage cardigan, pinned together with one of Granny's old diamanté brooches. And some stiletto sandals that I'd slipped on outside the restaurant, while my flats had gone into the enormous bag I toted everywhere.

Looking lovely in London in the summer took some effort, especially since I wasn't what you'd call a summer person. Pale skin, tight corsets, hot sun? Don't mix.

"Thank you," I said, examining the menu. "You're looking rather fresh yourself."

"I can get fresher if you want."

I looked up. "No, honestly, there's no need. You smell fine."

Jonathan let a little laughing breath out through his nose. "That wasn't what I meant, but . . . okay."

The waiter approached to take our drinks order. Jonathan smiled at me, then looked up and said, "Two glasses of champagne, please. No, you know what? Bring us a bottle."

I beamed. "Are we celebrating?"

"Yes, we are. On several counts."

"One, it's a beautiful day?" I suggested.

"Two, I have beautiful company."

I beamed, inside and out.

"Three," he went on, "I have good news."

"Oooh," I said. "What?"

"All in good time," he said playfully. "Four . . ."

My stomach lurched as he arched his eyebrow suggestively.

"Four?"

"Four, this morning, I brokered a deal on the most enormous house you've ever seen," he finished, as the frosty champagne flutes arrived. "It had a carport you could fit three Range Rovers in."

"Oh." I'd have preferred something more romantic, but that was Jonathan — very work focused. Which wasn't unattractive.

"And how about you?" he asked, letting the waiter pour the champagne, then raising his glass in a silent toast. "How was your weekend in the country?"

"Awful," I said, chinking his glass. "And I had some bad news at home too. *Home* home, I mean."

"I'm sorry to hear that," said Jonathan. "Nothing too bad, I hope?"

I sighed. "Well . . . it depends. Tell me your good news first."

"Okay." He coughed and said, "They're restructuring the company — which was why I had to fly back to New York — and I've been promoted to a new position in charge of International Sales and Relocation." He widened his eyes, as if this should mean something to me.

"Oh, wow!" I said. "Well done! That's great news!"

"Yeah. Yes, it is."

"You're such an international man of mystery, Jonathan," I teased, only half-joking. At least Cindy hadn't been the reason he'd had to fly back at such short notice. "I didn't know you were going for a promotion."

"Well, I didn't, really . . ." He moved the salt and pepper around the table. "It was a surprise to me, too, but once things start moving, they move fast." He paused. "Thing is, it's going to mean more traveling, and . . ."

"What?" My stomach was rumbling as I

perused the menu. I fully intended to stick to steak and a salad, but I'd heard such good things about their haggis that it seemed bad business sense not to try it out for future recommendations. I was, after all, supposed to be an authority on date restaurants. "Have you had haggis yet, Jonathan? It's a Scottish speciality. Sheep's innards in . . . a sheep's stomach. I know it doesn't sound very appetizing," I added hastily, "but my auntie Moira swears by it."

Jonathan pulled a face. "I'll pass, okay? Listen, it'll mean I'll have to travel more," he repeated slowly. "And spend more time in New York. Starting right away."

I looked up as I realized what he was saying. "Oh."

We were both silent for a moment. My appetite shrank.

"So go on, what's your bad news?" he asked. "We can package it up with my having to travel more and make one bad news bundle."

I bit my lip. Suddenly it was more of a stack than a bundle. "Oh, Nelson's going on some sailing expedition, and he's getting the builders in to overhaul the flat. I have to move out for a month while they pull the place to pieces."

"He's getting someone reputable, right?"

queried Jonathan, looking concerned.

"I think so."

"Because you know what some of these cowboys are like. You end up spending twice as much fixing the damage they do. Listen, I have a great contractor . . ." He reached into his jacket pocket for his Dictaphone.

"That's kind of you," I said faintly. Priorities! "But I still have to move out."

Jonathan's hand froze. "I know, honey. But I was just thinking, how can we make this as painless as possible?" He reached over and took my hand. "So where are you going to go?"

"Well, actually, I was wondering . . . ," I began hesitantly. Then I stopped as a new awful thought struck me. What if "I'll have to travel" really meant "we should cool things down"?

I stared, panic-stricken, into his gray eyes and wished I could tell the difference between amusement and seriousness in Jonathan's expression. Sometimes he played his cards a little *too* close to his chest.

"Come on," he said, "where are you going? I need to know where I can get hold of you. You don't get away that easily!"

He stretched his other hand across the table and circled my wrist. "Not when you were so hard to get hold of in the first place," he added in a soft undertone.

"I don't know *where* I'm going," I admitted. Tingles ran across my skin as Jonathan discreetly stroked the inside of my wrist with his thumb. "I really don't want to go home — I mean, I couldn't, it's too far to commute into my office — Daddy won't let me have the keys to his London flat because he reckons he needs it, Gabi doesn't have enough space for all her shoes, let alone me . . ." I looked up with an appealing expression. "I don't suppose you've got a room in your house you could sublet to me?"

I tried to sound jokey. But I wasn't joking.

"When's Nelson kicking you out?" asked Jonathan, getting his diary out of his jacket pocket.

"In about a fortnight's time."

Jonathan's brow furrowed, and he flicked back and forth between pages. They were all covered in his very small, neat American handwriting.

The waiter, who'd been hovering patiently, pounced as soon as I raised my head. I plumped for the haggis, though I didn't feel up to eating anything very demanding now. Without looking up from his diary, Jonathan briskly ordered a steak and some fries, a salad, and a bottle of mineral water.

"A fortnight?"

"Yes."

"Well, you can't stay in my house," said Jonathan. "I have some old clients staying there as a favor while they look for property in London. I have to go back to New York pretty soon, to settle some deals, meet people, see how these changes will impact our basic company infrastructure. But there's one very obvious solution."

"What's that?"

He gave me his tiniest smile, the one that hid genuine excitement. "You'll have to come with me. Come and live with me in New York for a month. Kills two birds with one stone. You'll have somewhere to live, and I won't have to miss you like crazy."

I stared at him. "But I can't!"

"Why not?"

"Well, I can't leave the agency for a *month!*" I stammered. "I've got appointments, and people booked in. I mean, I'm meant to be organizing a . . ."

I was aware that my phone was ringing in my bag. My work phone. I struggled to ignore it.

"I have to organize a . . . a . . ."

Jonathan raised an eyebrow. "Your cell phone is ringing."

"I know!" I said brightly. "But I'm ignoring it. No, what I meant was that I have to

95

arrange . . ."

Then I remembered who it was likely to be. The internal struggle increased, until I was forced to grab for my handbag.

Jonathan rolled his eyes.

"I'm so sorry," I said to him, stabbing at the buttons. "Hello? Gerald? Please tell me it's not the dishwasher again, or . . . oh, dear. Duvets aren't meant to go in your washing machine. You have to take them to . . . oh, no!"

Recently, I seemed to have acquired a whole crop of freshly divorced, fifty-something clients whose wives had "callously abandoned them" by running off with the Pilates teacher after thirty years of domestic service. The result was a rash of flooded laundry rooms, minor iron-related house fires, and embarrassing scaldings all over South West London.

"I'll call the plumber," I said firmly, as one of London's foremost tax accountants confessed that he'd not only flooded his flat but also shorted out the power in his neighbors'. "No, don't worry, I'll deal with it. And we'll run through the whole laundry routine again later, shall we? Righty-ho. Yes, I'll make you some prompt cards, if you like. Calm down, Gerald. Yes, I'll ring you later on."

"You think of everything." Was that a note of terseness or admiration? Given Jonathan's quest for ultimate office efficiency, and his slight antsiness about my more hands-on agency work, it could have been a bit of both.

I pulled a face as I turned off the cell phone. "Sorry. But, you see, I can't just up and leave. Much as I'd love to go to New York with you," I explained, "God knows what would happen."

"Indeed," said Jonathan drily.

Our food arrived, and I gazed sadly at my plate. My appetite had vanished. One did need a certain amount of appetite to tackle a good haggis. That or a total ignorance of the ingredients. "Anyway, do these clients of yours need a housekeeper?" I suggested, breaking it up with my fork.

"Melissa, I'm offering you a month's vacation in New York." Jonathan sounded confused. "It's a city you've never visited, something which surprises me, actually, and I'd love to show you round *my* town, like you did for me. But, hey, if you'd rather stay here and *work* than be on holiday with me? . . ." This time he made his voice arch, but not quite enough to hide a flicker of hurt.

"That's not fair!" I protested, my face

turning red with confusion. "It's not a question of what I *want*."

"It is."

"But, Jonathan . . ."

He attacked his steak methodically, slicing off the fat like a surgeon. "You call me a workaholic, but I'm not the one who carries two cell phones, both of which are permanently switched on. And don't deny it," he added as my jaw dropped, "I know you have your work phone on vibrate when we go out. Not even my grandmother needs to go to the bathroom so many times in one evening." He looked up at me from his steak autopsy. "I mean, don't get me wrong — I love that you're savvy *and* polite. Most businesswomen I deal with would just take the calls at the dinner table. I just wonder where I fit into all this. Whether, ah, whether I had higher priority when I was a client?"

"Is this about the wig?" I asked. "Because . . ."

"No!" He laughed. "I don't want to have the wig conversation again, Melissa. All I mean by that is that I'm really proud that you're my girlfriend. And I want you to be my girlfriend when you're at work, as well as at home. Not pretending to be someone else." He shook his head. "Besides, I can't risk you running off with someone else, can I?"

Such was Jonathan's innate adultness that he was able to say all this without sounding whiney.

But it really wasn't fair of him to suggest I didn't put him first. If he only knew how much effort I put into looking casual and effortlessly organized in my own time; when I was being Honey, brisk sauciness seemed to spring forth naturally.

Anyway, my business *depended* on me. It wasn't like I could just get a temp in.

"Jonathan, I can't believe you think that! I mean, you are the first priority in my life." And that was true. "And I'd *love* to go with you, you know I would —"

"Then come." Jonathan held my gaze, and I got the distinct impression that this was something that had been bubbling under the surface for a while. The huffs when I was late because of clients running over. The raised eyebrows about my more, um, *fitted* office wear.

I wriggled in my seat. He couldn't honestly think I'd run off with someone else, could he? *Me?*

"You're asking me to choose between the two things that mean the most to me," I said in my brave little soldier voice. "I can't just —"

"It's not a *choice.* You need somewhere to live. You also need a holiday. Plus, being totally selfish for a moment here — I need to have you around." He smiled, and as he said that, I felt something swell in my chest, and my heartbeat quickened.

Jonathan took my hand in his again, playing with my signet ring. Almost, I noticed, as if he was trying to work out what size it was. The blood rushed from my head. "Quite apart from anything else," he went on, "it makes good business sense. I wouldn't get much done if I had to be on the phone to you all the time, would I?"

"Well, that depends . . ."

"No, it doesn't. So, you'll think about it?" asked Jonathan, as if he already knew what my answer was going to be.

"I'll think about it," I managed to gasp as he raised my palm and kissed it, holding my gaze over the top.

"Good," he whispered.

Honestly, sometimes I felt like the only thing missing from our romance was the Busby Berkeley dance routine and the big band hidden from view in the bushes.

"Run this by me again," said Gabi, from

beneath a large pair of black sunglasses. "Mr. Perfect wants to take you to New York to live in his bazillion-dollar condo for a month while you're homeless, and you don't want to go . . . why?"

"Because I hate letting people down," I repeated. When she put it like that, it didn't sound so convincing. In fact, it sounded ridiculous.

Gabi made her feelings clear with a dramatic clearing of her nose. "Mel, the only person you're letting down here is me. Do you not understand how much cheaper Kiehl's skincare is in America? I'm economizing these days, you know."

We were sitting on a bench in Hyde Park, eating ice creams and watching people pour out of offices, tearing off their clothes to catch the last of the parching London sun.

"I'll really miss him," I said mournfully. "I should have known it was too good to last. And I notice it's not like he's putting *me* in front of his career, is it? Hasn't stopped *him* taking a job that 'requires more traveling.'"

Gabi snorted. "Christ on a bike, Mel, I don't understand you. He's not asking you to move out there! He's just offering you somewhere to live while Nelson does his bloody sailing sainthood!"

I looked at Gabi and could tell she was

scowling beneath her huge shades. Evidently she'd discovered the downside of dating someone with a nobility complex.

"He told you, then?"

"Yes, he told me. And he didn't offer *me* a go in his hammock either. No stowaways allowed, apparently."

"Well, no. You don't have knotting skills."

Gabi's eyebrow rose above the frames.

"I don't want to know, thanks," I said hurriedly. "But, listen, I just can't up and leave the office. It's not that easy. Even if I did leave it all behind, like Jonathan wants me to, I'd have Nigel Hendricks on the phone every three minutes, worrying about whether his personal trainer was coming on to him again, or . . . or Inigo Blythe — you remember him?"

"The guy who would only talk to women through the medium of his Kermit the Frog glove puppet. Yes," said Gabi heavily, "I do remember him. That was a *long* cocktail party."

"So what on earth am I meant to do? I can't just abandon these people!"

She pulled down the shades to give me the full benefit of her sarcastic look. "Will London really grind to a halt if you stop telling overgrown schoolboys not to tuck their shirts into their boxer shorts?"

"Well, not *as such,* but Jonathan's obviously got it into his head that I think my clients are more important than him, which they *aren't,* obviously, but if he catches me checking up on whether they're all right he'll just see it as proof that —"

"Okay, if he's making such a big deal about choosing between him and work, how about this — tell him you'll definitely go to New York. No question. Jonathan, you are my lord and master and I can't bear to be separated from you for ten of your earth minutes. But, really, plan to go for a *fortnight,*" suggested Gabi. "I mean, it's not unreasonable for you to take a holiday — people expect it now and again. If you get ahead of yourself with the preparation stuff, all you'd have to do would be to check your answering machine and get your e-mails. And you can do that from Jonathan's place."

"That's true," I said slowly. "And I don't need to tell him I'm checking. I could do that while he's at work."

"Exactly. Then, after a fortnight, if you're still gagging to come home — though I can't imagine why on *earth* you would be — you can make up some excuse about your family having a crisis that requires your immediate intervention, nip back, deal with anything that needs dealing with, then nip back again for however long you want." She cut me a sideways look. "Chances are you'll get summoned back to sort them out anyway."

"You make it sound like going up to Leeds on the train," I said, though actually it wasn't such a bad idea.

"Aaron and I used to go to New York for shopping breaks all the time," shrugged Gabi. "It's no big deal."

We licked our ice creams companionably.

"You're not scared, are you?" asked Gabi suddenly.

"Scared?" I bluffed. Gabi had a disconcerting ability to see into my head, and then see things even I hadn't spotted. "What of?"

"Of living with Jonathan. Him seeing you less than perfect without your makeup." She looked at me significantly. "Maybe meeting all his ball-breaking friends and relations. And his ex-wife. Things getting serious."

"Don't mince your words, will you?" I protested. But there was no point in fibbing to Gabi. She knew me too well. "Um, yes, there is a bit of that, I suppose. It's just been going so well, and —"

"Stop worrying," she said firmly. "Anyone can see Jonathan's mad about you. And you've already met some of his friends, haven't you?"

"Well, two of them — Bonnie and Kurt Hegel."

"And they liked you!"

"Um . . . after a fashion." That had been quite a ghastly evening. Jonathan had still been dating me in a professional capacity, and it had been the first time he'd seen any of his and Cindy's mutual friends since their separation.

"Pshuh!" said Gabi. "You told me you were all bosom buddies by the end of the evening. Didn't you end up shipping hand-made fishing flies over to Kurt?"

"Well, yes, and Bonnie was rather sweet about . . ." I clapped a hand to my mouth as a new thought struck me. "Gabi! They'll have told all Jonathan's friends I'm blond! And called Honey!"

Gabi flapped her hand dismissively. "Tell them you dyed your hair. Main thing is, you've met them, haven't you? And they liked you, and they'll have let everyone else know how you and Jonathan make the cutest couple since Lady and the Tramp." She peered at me. "*Everyone* else. So what's to worry about? Think about it — summer sales in the shops, proper ice cream, Jonathan pulling out all the stops to show you a good time . . ."

American ice cream. Mmm.

Not to mention Jonathan showing me a good time . . .

I wrenched my mind back to practicalities. "What about the office? What about the mail? What if people try to turn up and leave things?"

"Look, if it makes you feel better, I'll call in and look through the mail for you," said Gabi. "Get your messages. Put your freaks on hold."

"Would you?" A plan was forming in my mind. One that involved Allegra working at my agency without actually shutting it down before my flight landed at JFK.

"I *do have* office experience," Gabi huffed. "But I'm making you a list of things to bring back from Bloomingdales, all right?"

So as not to waste any time, she got a notebook out of her bag and started on it then and there. I gazed round Hyde Park and was surprised to feel rather excited.

FIVE

Jonathan greeted the news of my decision by taking me out to dinner and plying me with Manhattans in the American Bar at the Savoy until I was more than happy to walk the entire length of the Embankment in high heels, holding hands and listening to him telling me all the things I would love about New York, starting with the subway and working upward to the Empire State Building.

"And the very, very best thing," he said finally, twirling me into his arms beneath the string of lights that ran alongside the Thames, "is that you'll be there with me." He paused, tipping his head to one side thoughtfully, as if to look at me better. "Although your company would make pretty much anywhere perfect."

Between the drinks, and my heels, and the glorious romance of the warm summer evening, I nearly lost my balance, but Jonathan tightened his grip around my waist and said nothing. I gazed up at him, and my heart melted like chocolate at the tender expression in his eyes.

"And if I do as good a job of showing you New York as you did showing me London," he went on, leaning closer to me, so I could make out the first faint glints of gingery stubble on his smooth cheek, "you won't ever. Want. To leave."

"Ever?" I managed weakly as his lips came tantalizingly nearer and nearer and his hand slid down onto the small of my back.

"That's the plan," Jonathan whispered, his lips a breath away from mine. "At least, not without me."

Then he kissed me for a long time, while a police barge went by on the river behind us, and I let all thoughts of agency-related chaos drift right out of my head.

I drove Jonathan and his collection of suit carriers to Heathrow myself, to make the most of our last few hours together. We'd said our good-byes the night before, since we were both allergic to those gloopy displays you often see at airports, and to be honest, if he'd said good-bye the way he had the previous night, we'd have been thrown out of the business class lounge.

I didn't rush back to the house, even though it was Sunday evening, which I usually reserved for armchair detective dramas and the week's ironing. Nelson, being Nelson, had insisted that we start "going through the flat" in advance of his departure. I'd have preferred to blitz it in one awful go, with gallons of coffee and the promise of a takeaway at the end, but he'd booked space at the Big Yellow Storage Place and was determined to fit everything into the space he'd arranged. And not a box over.

"We need to weed out some of this junk," he insisted, forcing me off the sofa, where I'd slumped, still playing back Jonathan's last, long kiss in my head. "I've got boxes for storage, boxes for thrift shops, and boxes for the dump. And when I say dump, Mel, I do mean dump."

Nelson stood back with his hands on his hips and surveyed with some desperation the general detritus of several years' domestic bliss. "I mean, we can just ditch all those magazines, can't we?"

He gestured toward the stack of lovely glossy mags holding the stereo speakers off the floor.

"Well, no . . ." I *needed* those. I looked into my half-drunk gin and tonic and wished I had the energy to mix up another.

"Can't we start in the kitchen instead?"

But there was no stopping Nelson once he got started on "household tasks." His father, who was a military enthusiast, had run their family like a sea cadet unit, using a series of whistles to indicate "task time." Even now, Nelson and his older brother Woolfe got twitchy whenever soccer matches were on television.

"You realize how much you could have saved over the years if you'd just read those stupid things in the hairdresser's?" he added for good measure, lifting up the speaker so he could start piling the magazines into a dump box. He brandished a fistful of *Tatler*s in my direction. "There's over a hundred pounds of idiocy and shampoo ads in this stack alone."

"I think you'll find that half of that pile includes your *Practical Boat Owners*," I observed. "But you're right — go ahead and chuck it all out. They're just taking up space."

Nelson's packing action abruptly stopped. "Well, in that case, maybe we should do some *selective* chucking."

The doorbell prevented me from responding in a way I'd have liked.

"That'll be Roger," he said with some

relief. "He said he'd come over to give us a hand."

My face fell, and I gripped my warm G&T harder. "Roger? Oh, come on, Nelson. It's Sunday night! My boyfriend's just flown back to New York! I've got a hard week coming up. The last thing I need is Roger Trumpet and his Personality Vacuum coming round here to punish me with small talk."

Nelson gave me a reproachful look. "Don't be mean. Roger's nowhere near as bad as he used to be. Mainly because of your sterling efforts. You should be proud of him."

"I am," I said, pulling a desperate face. "But not on a Sunday night when we only have one more Sunday night left here!"

"The flat isn't going anywhere! You're just moving out for a few weeks, for heaven's sake!"

"But I was going to iron!" I wailed. "I thought we were going to make a curry and watch *Inspector Morse*!"

Heavy footsteps were now audible on the stairs leading up to our first-floor flat, and already I could feel Roger's enervating presence begin to drain me of sparkling chitchat. He did that to a girl. Ten minutes with Roger Trumpet, in a bad mood, was like inhaling chloroform.

"How did he get in?" I demanded. "Is the front door open?"

Nelson's brow furrowed. "Now that *is* a good question."

We didn't need to wonder about Roger's means of entry for long, because there was a brief knock on the front door and then Gabi appeared, with Roger in tow.

"I met him outside," she explained, wiping the mascara from where it had smudged under her eyes.

Roger nodded at everyone by way of greeting. He wasn't wiping his eyes, but he wasn't exactly looking thrilled either.

"I didn't know Gabi had a key!" I exclaimed, a bit too brightly. "Nelson?"

"Um . . . ," said Nelson. "Yes. I was going to mention that to you."

"Were you?" I said, still very brightly.

Gabi sniffed. Her nose was red, and her hair wasn't as perky as usual. It honestly wasn't like her to be so downcast about a man. Whenever Aaron had gone away on business, she was on the phone to me within minutes, planning where we could go for cocktails. Still, Nelson was different, I supposed grudgingly. He was less a boyfriend, and more a lifestyle. We'd all miss him.

My heart went out to her poor, sad face.

"Gabi, would you be a sweetheart and go and put the kettle on?" I suggested. "I'm gagging for a cup of tea." And gratefully, she vanished into the kitchen, where loud clattering started up.

Roger, Nelson, and I stood there in the middle of the floor. Nelson realized he was holding a stack of *Cosmopolitan*s, the top one of which was last year's Ho-ho-holiday sex special, and he quickly put them into a dump box.

"So . . . how are you, Roger?" I asked, grasping the conversational nettle. "Looking well!"

Roger pulled a face, which I guessed was meant to indicate some kind of response. For a young man in his early thirties who was the heir to a substantial cider-and-sparkling-pear-juice fortune, who lived in Chelsea, and who was in possession of all major mental faculties apart from dress sense, Roger cut a very unprepossessing figure. He'd gone through a more urbane phase, when I'd taken him in hand rather rigorously, but since I'd been spending more time at work and with Jonathan instead of at home on the couch with Nelson and Roger, he'd regressed. Badly. Tonight he was clad entirely in shades of porridge and didn't appear to have shaved for about

113

four days. It might have passed as a style statement on a more put-together man, but not on Roger.

Communicating in shrugs and grunts was where I'd picked up, not left off.

"Roger!" I said more emphatically.

"I'm very well, thanks, Mel," he said. "Not much going on, but even less going on for the next three months." And he shot a wounded glare at Nelson.

"Roger," said Nelson evenly, "if you wanted to crew on this tall ship, you should have applied. Stop acting like such a girl."

"I'm thinking of doing some sailing in the *Maldives*," he informed me. "One of my friends has got a *Nicholson 42* that he needs to bring back to England."

"Roger . . ."

"So I might do that."

Gabi reappeared with mugs of tea, one of which she gave to Nelson. "Organic skimmed milk, three sugars," she said, and bit her lip.

"Good timing, you two!" I said before she could ask to keep the mug to remember him by. "We'd just got started!"

"Yes!" Nelson piped up in the same "that's right, Melissa!" tone. "*This* box is for the charity shop, *this* one's for keeping, and *this* one's for dumping. I'm going to set my

114

stopwatch for one hour, and then we'll go out for dinner, okay?"

"Okay!" I said.

Honestly. We sounded like a couple of children's TV presenters. Or parents.

"Fine," said Gabi, staring morbidly at a bookshelf. "Are these your books, Mel? *I Do, or Die? Why Men Marry Some Women and Not Others?*" She looked inside. "To Melissa, Merry Christmas, love from Mummy and Daddy."

I grabbed them from her and dumped them in the charity shop box. "No need for those any more! And I never thought I'd be sitting here saying that." I beamed with delight. "You know, when I think of the time I wasted on men like Orlando . . ."

Nelson looked up from his stack of CDs. "*I* never thought I'd be happy that you'd taken up with an American estate agent, but after Orlando von Borsch, I'd have given Jack the Ripper a chance."

"Nelson!" I said. "He really wasn't as bad as you made out."

Nelson hated all my ex-boyfriends. Particularly handsome, year-round-tanned, slip-on-shoe-wearing ones like Orlando.

"He was, Melissa," agreed Roger. "Definitely. He was a slimy creep. Don't you remember how he made you collect his dry cleaning?"

"And never gave you the money for it?" added Gabi.

"And twice it included a strapless, backless ball gown?" added Nelson.

I paused. Orlando had had a lot of dry-clean-only clothes. At the time I'd thought it was terribly chic, but now I wondered if he'd deliberately just sent everything there so I'd pick it up for him — and pay for it. Sometimes I even wondered if he *wanted* me to see the dresses.

"Well, that was the old me," I said confidently. "I was pretty dim in the past, I admit, but not any more. No one takes advantage of Melissa Romney-Jones now."

"Ding!" muttered Nelson, wrapping one of his model battleships in an old copy of the *Telegraph*, but since we were all feeling rather overemotional, I didn't pull him up on it.

We packed and stacked in companionable silence for a few minutes.

"Be ruthless with clutter," intoned Nelson. "There's going to be no room in the new and improved flat for knickknacks." He looked up. "And I mean that, Melissa."

"Like this, you mean?" grunted Roger, waving an elaborately wrapped explosion of net and hand-folded paper doves.

116

"Emery's wedding," sighed Gabi. She looked at Nelson, who had suddenly become fascinated by a box full of old contact lenses. "It's so sweet you kept it. Don't you remember, Nelson? That was the night . . ." Her voice trailed off in another uncharacteristic wobble.

I swallowed as a pang of missing-Jonathan-nostalgia hit me. *We'd* gotten together at Emery's wedding too.

"Oh, for pity's sake," moaned Roger. "That's all it ever is round here — snog, snog, snog. It's like being trapped in a high school disco, hanging out with you lot. Don't you ever think what it's like for the rest of us? The ones who aren't completely out of their heads on Love's Young Dream? Eh?"

"If this is about the Hunt Ball, Roger . . . ," I started.

"It's not!" he snapped.

Nelson looked at me. "Shall we all go out for dinner now? Maybe do some more when we come back?"

"I think that would be a good idea," I said firmly.

With my flight booked and all my possessions bar the ones I needed to take to New York checked into Nelson's Big Yellow Storage Place, I thought it would be prudent to pop home, just to ensure that nothing was about to erupt while I was away. It would be absolutely typical for Daddy to turn up on CNN, accused of embezzling the entire Olympic fund, at the exact time that I was trying to impress Jonathan's supersmart friends.

The upside of Daddy's new position of power, according to my mother, was that he was AWOL when I arrived, and, as I found out, she had no idea whether he was engaged on parliamentary or Olympic business, nor did she know when he was going to be back. Not that she seemed unduly concerned.

"Oh, he's got a new secretary, darling," she said vaguely, keeping her eyes glued to her knitting needles. "Got to keep the Olympics and the parliament stuff separate and all that. One, two, three . . . bugger!" She thrust the knitting at me with an imploring look. "Have I dropped a stitch?"

We were sitting in the kitchen, which was the coolest room in the house in the summer. Jenkins was sprawled in his basket, near her feet, panting.

"I don't know, Mummy, I don't knit," I said.

She took it back and frowned. "Christ, it's

so hard to tell with mohair."

It wasn't surprising that she was dropping stitches, since her hands were shaking as if she'd been sitting on a washing machine, but I didn't say anything.

"Daddy's got a new secretary?" I asked suspiciously. Daddy went through secretaries like most men went through shirts. "Just for his Olympic business?"

"Oh yes, um, Claudia, I think she's called."

"Right."

How convenient, I seethed. I could see it now: Daddy probably e-mailed his secretarial requests along with his office requirements — blond, under twenty-three, very good at dictation . . .

Mummy looked up, her face suddenly wreathed in serenity. "Don't worry, darling. I sent Claudia a little note, in private, just to tip her off about Daddy's weak heart." She smiled. "Any overexcitement and he could drop down dead. You know, too much to drink, too much . . . stimulation of any kind." The needles started clicking again. "She wrote straight back to reassure me she'd keep an eye on it. So thoughtful."

I swallowed. "That's not entirely true, though, is it?"

"No, darling. Well, not as far as we know.

But then, who's to say, with your father?"

My mother did a good impression of being ditsy, but sometimes she amazed even me. And when it came to her relationship with my father, frankly there were things it was best not to know.

"You know he's got me researching international etiquette?" I said. "I'm rather enjoying it."

Mummy looked pleased. "How nice for you, darling. At least that's one assistant he can't be accused of employing for her looks!"

Charming.

"So, anyway," I said, changing the subject, "I'll be away for a fortnight, to begin with. I'm staying with Jonathan in his apartment in New York!"

Mummy traced a shaky finger along her knitting pattern and cast a longing look at the big silver box on the welsh dresser that used to contain her Marlboro Lights. Then, with an effort, she wrenched her attention back to the pattern, which for a fluffy hippo.

"And what about work?" she asked tightly.

"Gabi and Allegra are going to answer the phones for me while I'm away," I said, "but I am going to come back, so don't let Daddy get any ideas about this job for Allegra being permanent."

Mummy sighed and bashed her needles together. "Oh, darling, once you see New York, you won't want to come back."

"I will," I insisted stoutly. "My life's here. People depend on me. *Clients* depend on me."

She peered at me over her knitting. "If you want your relationship to work out, Melissa, you should think about what's best for Jonathan, instead of *other men.*"

"Mummy!" I protested. "You make that sound . . . awful."

"Well," she said. "It's true."

"Anyway," I went on, blushing, "Nelson's here, and Gabi and . . ."

"That's another man," Mummy observed, clicking away. "You should think about soft-pedaling that too. I'm sure it must bother Jonathan, knowing another man sees you in your bathrobe every morning."

"He's my *flatmate,*" I exploded. Honestly, I was so sick of telling everyone there was nothing going on with me and Nelson. "The fact that he *does* see me in my bathrobe should tell you that there's nothing going on." I rolled my eyes as my mother raised her perfectly shaped eyebrows with as much sarcasm as someone with maximum Botox could manage. "Honestly! We're just

121

friends."

"Who's that? You and Nelson?"

I swiveled round as Allegra swanned in, swishing her long chiffon house-kaftan behind her.

Great. That was all I needed.

"Shut up, Allegra," I said on a wave of crossness, then immediately felt scared. Telling Allegra to shut up was second only to telling my father to get lost, and third only to putting one's head into a crocodile's jaws.

"I mean," I added quickly, as she opened her mouth and widened her eyes so the whites were visible around the kohl liner, "I don't think you see it quite the way I do. How's the investigation going?"

She snapped her mouth and eyes shut, so that two thick black lines and one bright red line appeared on her otherwise white face.

"Don't ask," said my mother quickly. "We've had Simon here three times this week."

Simon was my father's barrister. He was the heavy artillery, brought out only for High Court actions and anything that might get into the papers. He was also my god-father, for he'd spent more time with my father over the years than my mother had.

"So," I said brightly, "shall we talk about

my trip to America then?"

"Oh, God, if we must," sighed Allegra. "How are you flying? Cattle?"

I bridled. "Do you mean economy?"

"Allegra," said Mummy reproachfully. "Melissa isn't married to a wealthy business-man. She's self-employed."

Allegra snorted and opened the fridge door to see what was in there. It seemed to be full of bottles of algae and urine samples, which I assumed were her health drinks. Then again, one never knew with Allegra.

"I'm flying economy because there were very few seats available," I informed her. "It's a popular time of year, and if I'd gone business it would have cost more than I earn in a month."

"Poor you," said Allegra.

I didn't bother to get annoyed. I was proud of earning my own money. Better to travel cattle and pay for it myself than fly first on someone else's credit card, I thought — although obviously I didn't actually say so. That would have been asking for trouble.

"Well, if you must be a martyr about it, you'll need these," said Allegra, reaching into her bag.

"Allegra . . . ," said my mother warningly.

"It's perfectly innocent," she snapped, throwing me a little brown bottle.

"What is it?" There was a prescription label in Swedish, but oddly enough it wasn't made out to Allegra Svensson.

"Melatonin. Helps you sleep on planes. Knock back a couple of those with a glass of red wine and you'll be out like a light until JFK. Get yourself into first, ideally, drop off, and they'll never be able to shift you." Allegra helped herself to a handful of Mummy's expensive salted caramels and swished toward the window. She peered out, opened a window, made an obscene gesture, then slammed it shut, sinking dramatically onto the window seat.

To her credit, Mummy refused to acknowledge any of this performance.

"I wish that police protection man would bugger off. He's making a complete dog's breakfast of the rose garden. I mean, what can they do? Send hit men in? I can't believe Lars knows anyone more dangerous than Stockholm's worst dentist."

"I should make tracks," I said, suddenly longing for the relative sanity of Nelson's now-echoing flat.

"Do you want some jam to take back, darling?" asked Mummy, waving vaguely in the direction of the kitchen cupboards. "I've got one or two extra jars."

"Ooh, yes, please," I said. The local Women's Institute made seriously good raspberry jam; it was one of Daddy's perks as regular fete-opener that he got first pick of the preserves stall. "Is there any raspberry?"

"I think so," she said, peering at the mass of mohair skewered on her needles. "Have a look."

The cupboards in our kitchen were very old and reached from floor to ceiling, a relic from the days when three parlormaids, a cook, and a scullery maid staffed the place. I swung open the cupboard where the jam and breakfast cereals normally lived and gasped in surprise.

Five of the six shelves were crammed with a gleaming array of jam jars: strawberry, raspberry, loganberry, apricot, black currant, blackberry, marmalade, and various other permutations. There must have been over a hundred cotton-topped jars in there, stretching back into the dusty depths.

"God almighty!" I exclaimed.

"What? Nothing you fancy? I think there might be some lemon curd, if you look, darling," said Mummy, apparently unperturbed.

"Mummy! I thought you'd got the shopping thing under control," I said reproachfully. "You promised. No more binges."

She put down her knitting and looked a

little sheepish. "Well, it's the WI markets. I have to support them as the local MP's wife. And there are so many! You can't just patronize one — they find out, these ladies! Anyway, it's such good jam. And it always comes in handy, you know, for gifts. And when I'm giving people tea."

I looked at her suspiciously.

"Like the other day," she said defensively. "I had a journalist round from *Country Life*. I made her a lovely English cream tea, with four different sorts of jam. It made a lovely photograph. I knew those silver preserve boats would come in useful eventually."

She picked up her knitting again.

"You didn't tell them you made it, did you?" I asked carefully.

The needles clicked quicker. "I didn't say I *didn't*."

I sighed. Still, how could I get hoity-toity with her when my whole business was built on pretending to be someone I wasn't?

I helped myself to a jar of raspberry jam and a couple of lemon curds.

"Oh, I nearly forgot," said Mummy. "Daddy left a letter for you on the mantelpiece in the drawing room. It must be a business thing — he wouldn't tell me what it was about."

"Plus ça change," said Allegra in a ridiculously outré French accent, just in case we'd forgotten she was still lurking about, "plus c'est la *même* bloody *chose!*"

How I was looking forward to having that in my office. It would be like having Harold Pinter manning the phones, but without the light relief.

I wandered through to the drawing room. The envelope was tucked behind the marble clock, amongst a crop of formal invitation cards.

I opened it and read the note card inside. Beneath the family crest, in my father's unhelpful handwriting were the words: *Allegra's blood money to be paid into your account, take off 20% of same for your etiquette advice, first of month. Will be in touch. Pls shred. MRJ*

Twenty percent? Of how much? It was typical of my father not to commit salient details like that to paper; he was notoriously shred-happy, after an unfortunate incident with one of those dreadful bin-stealing tabloid investigators. It wasn't so much the tax details he was unhappy about as the shopping list with twelve bottles of Scotch and his prescription cortisone cream listed for everyone to see. What made it much worse, in my eyes, was the fact that he'd implied that the Loving Care had been

Mummy's.

Anyway, I thought, tucking the card into the pocket of my linen trousers, I had other things to worry about. Knowing Allegra, she'd have negotiated her own wage direct with my father, and twenty percent of whatever she was getting was bound to be decent, if not adequate, compensation for having her around.

Back in the kitchen, Mummy was trying to make her hippo stand up on the table. I had to swallow a gasp of horror — its head was the same size as its body, none of its limbs were equal in length, and it appeared to have a fin. She didn't seem perturbed and carried on trying to make it stand with a childlike patience.

Because of its grotesquely misshapen head, it looked as if it was trying to do some kind of yoga headstand.

"That hippo's got five legs," observed Allegra from the window seat. "Unless you've made it very anatomically correct? In which case it's positively disturbing." She flicked some more V-signs out of the window at the hydrangea bushes.

"Oh, damn," sighed Mummy. She tried one more time to coax it into uprightness. It flopped over. She looked crushed.

My heart went out to her. Poor Mummy.

"He's adorable!" I said, wanting to cheer her up. She got so little encouragement from anyone. "Can I have him?"

"Really?" Her face illuminated with pleasure. "Of course, darling. Please do. You can give it to Jonathan, if you like?"

"Um, I'll just keep it for myself," I said quickly. In a box. Under the stairs. "Right, I'm off. I've got packing to do." I turned to Allegra and tried to look stern. "Don't forget you're coming in for a briefing at the office before I go."

"I hadn't forgotten," lied Allegra.

"Well, please don't forget. It's important."

"Yadda yadda yadda," she replied, gazing out the window. "Don't forget your jam."

I put the jam in my handbag, making a mental note to buy *Country Life* to find out exactly what Mummy had said about her preserving skills.

"See?" said Allegra, turning back to bestow a wintry smile on us both. "I'm totally cut out for this lifestyle advice thing. It's just nagging, isn't it?"

"No, not really," I replied hotly. "It's a bit more than that, actually, it's . . ."

Then I realized that Allegra was giving me her special sarcastic look. The one that had actually made Lars cry at their wedding reception.

I pulled back my shoulders. "We'll talk about this later, Allegra," I said with as much self-control as I could muster, and I stalked out to the car.

Six

There were times, sharing a flat with Nelson, when it was hard to remember that I was living in the twenty-first century and had the vote. Seeing him off on his voyage of educational smugdom was one such occasion, made worse by Gabi's insistence on behaving as if she were starring in her own historical miniseries, minus the crinolines and extras with false warts.

Heaving bosoms, though, were very much on the menu. But then they always were with me.

With military precision, Nelson loaded up my car with his sailing gear, Roger, Gabi, and then me, so we could drop him off, then wave him away at the docks, where his ship was being stocked up with rations, and sails, and crew. I was pretty impressed with the *Bellepheron*: It was a real tall ship, with three masts decked out with beautiful white sails and a saucy figurehead on the prow. If it hadn't been for the boxes of microwave porridge going aboard, you'd never know you weren't in some BBC costume drama.

"Will you write, Nelson?" said Gabi, scrunching her handkerchief.

"Gabi, we've been through this before — I won't have time," said Nelson impatiently. "But we've got the most modern satellite navigation and communication equipment known to man, and we're docking as often as possible to let people on and off. It's not like I'm going to come back with scurvy and one eye."

"How about a beard?" she asked hopefully.

"I might manage a beard," he conceded wearily. "A small one."

"And a parrot?" I suggested.

"Don't push it, Melissa."

Roger slapped his arm. "Be safe, mate," he said. "If you fall overboard, I'm having your new cricket bat, okay?"

"Okay," said Nelson. "But not the cup."

He punched Roger's shoulder.

"Too small, mate," said Roger, and he feigned kneeing Nelson's groin in return.

Honestly, you wouldn't think they'd known each other for over twenty years. Or maybe you would.

"If you two have quite finished . . . ," Gabi

piped up meaningfully.

Roger and I turned to her in surprise.

"I'd like to say good-bye to Nelson," she went on. "Alone."

A funny sensation swamped me, and I had to force myself to smile to stop it from showing on my face. Roger, who lacked any social graces, didn't bother to disguise his surprise at the new pecking order, and he dropped his jaw in outright sarcasm.

He drew breath to make his feelings known, but before he could say anything, I said quickly, "Of course. Come on, Roger," and hauled him away to an ice-cream stand.

I was quite happy to turn my back on whatever scene was playing out while I got us both mint choc chip cones. When I turned back, however, Roger was staring unashamedly, and I almost felt sorry for him.

Gabi was hanging off Nelson's neck — inevitable, really, since he was well over six feet and she only scraped five feet two if she was wearing heels — and they seemed to be kissing, sort of. Or Gabi could have been giving him a lecture a few centimeters away from his mouth.

Nelson, I'd noted, didn't lecture Gabi the way he lectured me. Maybe because he couldn't get a word in. She was the only person I knew who could override him when he was in full eco-warrior mode.

"Is this what it's going to be like from now on?" moaned Roger. "Watching those two carrying on, like . . . like . . . Bollocks."

I turned my head in time to see him engulf his entire scoop of ice cream in one terrifying downward mouth movement.

"I hope not," I said with multilayered sincerity.

He disengaged himself with a slurping sound, leaving a perfect peak on each side of his ice cream.

"Roger," I said, "please don't do that again. It's troubling."

"All in the tongue action." He winked at me. "Chicks dig it."

"No, they most certainly do not," I said with a shudder. Things really had slid. "Where are you *getting* all this stuff?"

If anyone thought he was getting it from me, my business was ruined.

"Books," he said vaguely.

"Roger," I said sternly, "I think I need to take you in hand again. And with a very firm grip."

Roger choked on his cone, spraying molten ice cream everywhere.

"What?" I demanded. "What?"

Roger was saved in his spluttering by Nelson yelling, "Mel! Over here, Mel!" in a voice that could carry through fog.

We looked up to see Nelson waving me over in his best kindergarten manner. Gabi had disengaged from his neck and was busying herself checking her mascara.

"At least you're wanted," said Roger somewhat sourly.

I went over and gave Nelson a hug. "Take care," I said. "No showing off to the children."

"Of course not." He hugged me back, and I buried my head in his broad chest. Nelson was great to hug. He had hugged me through many crises already. "And you take care too, in America." He pushed me away so he could look into my face. "And if anything happens with Remington Steele . . ."

"I'll let you know," I promised. "I'll send a pigeon or something. But, honestly, nothing's going to go wrong. I know it won't."

"You e-mail me," he repeated, squeezing my shoulders. "I'll turn the ship round and come and get you. I mean it."

"Okay," I said, slightly embarrassed by the intensity of his look. "If you sink, let me know. And if the little children stage a mutiny with table forks or something."

"I'll fall on my Swiss Army knife first.

135

Now, I've left a list of all the things you have to lock before you leave, all right? And the details for the builders and the electricians. I've made a very specific plan of action which Gabi's in charge of implementing, and I've asked my brother if he'll pop over and . . ."

"Nelson," I said firmly, "we are all perfectly capable of carrying out your every wish."

"I know. Well . . . okay, I know." He looked over my shoulder, then dropped his voice. "I haven't told Gabi, but this is my emergency number, if you really need to get hold of me." He hugged me again and slipped a piece of paper into my jacket pocket.

I bit my lip. Even though I was secretly glad he'd given me the number and not Gabi, I still felt a bit awful. It wasn't much fun trying to work out where we all stood these days.

"In case the workmen blow up the house, right?" I said.

"Er, yes," said Nelson. "That sort of thing. But, seriously, Mel . . ."

A loud whistle from the ship interrupted the rest of the conversation.

"I've got to go," he said. "I'm meant to be organizing the crew." He straightened his shoulders. "In fact, they're giving the wrong whistle. I need to get that sorted out before there's a terrible misunderstanding."

Roger, Gabi, and I stood on the quayside as Nelson self-consciously walked up the ramp onto the deck.

"Ship ahoy!" shouted Gabi and waved her hankie. It had clumped where she'd blown her nose into it.

I reached into my capacious handbag and discreetly passed her a fresh one.

"Au revoir!" she bellowed, undeterred by the curious looks we were getting from other crew well-wishers. "Bon voyage, Nelson!"

"Come on," said Roger, tugging at my arm. "Before people start thinking she's got some kind of Lady Hamilton complex."

"Bye, Nelson!" I yelled and waved.

He waved back, then vanished below-decks.

Gabi stood firm.

"Gabi," I said patiently. "It's not like the *Queen Mary*. It's not suddenly going to slide down into the dock while someone crashes a bottle of champagne over it."

"Won't it?" She looked surprised.

"No. It could be ages yet before they go. They get a little tugboat to . . ." I trailed off, seeing she was still gazing up at the portholes. "Didn't Nelson make you watch his tall ships videos?"

She nodded and sighed. "I wasn't really concentrating on the boats, though."

"Gabi," I said, sliding my arm through hers, "let's go home, have a pot of tea, and watch *Upstairs, Downstairs.*"

As we moved toward where my car was parked, I sensed a disheveled presence on my other side.

"Can I, er, can I come back as well?" mumbled Roger. "I forgot to go shopping this week and, er . . . You know."

I put my arm through his too. "Of course you can, Roger. Nelson left us all a shepherd's pie to remember him by."

And so the three of us made our way back to the now very empty flat and settled ourselves in for comfort eating and comfort viewing. When no one muted the television in order to point out the historical inaccuracies in the scullerymaids' uniforms, it felt emptier still.

There was only one other task I had to get out of the way before I could fly to New York and into Jonathan's open arms, and I was looking forward to that even less than I had been to waving Nelson good-bye.

I had to hand over the office to Gabi and Allegra.

The one bright spot, though, was the fact that Gabi's moping around the place lasted exactly as long as two episodes of *Upstairs, Downstairs.* By the time she turned up at the Little Lady Agency for her debriefing at lunchtime on Monday, she was almost back to her normal pre-Nelson self.

By which I mean she arrived carrying two bags from Topshop and proceeded to spend an hour dunking my chocolate biscuits in her tea, while divulging the most appalling gossip about the tabloid editor whose house was being sold through the estate agency.

"Right," I said, checking my watch for the sixth time, "let's make a start, shall we? No point in waiting any longer for Allegra — she's obviously decided she's got better things to do. So. These *red* files are for wardrobe shopping trips —"

"Just tell me where the wig is," wheedled Gabi. "I promise I won't use it."

"No!" We'd been in the office for an hour, and the more I thought about the prospect of leaving Gabi, let alone Allegra, to run free among my confidential files, the more I was beginning to think I shouldn't actually go at all. "The wig is strictly — and I mean *strictly* — out of bounds!"

Gabi pouted. "But I only offered to do this because of the wig."

139

I looked at her imploringly. "Please, Gabi. I'm relying on you here. I'm about to put my livelihood into the hands of an egomaniac with the social graces of an underfed tiger, and only you can keep her from decimating my client list. Please. At least wait until I'm out of the country before you start going through the drawers."

"Okay." Gabi tapped her French manicure on the arms of her chair. "But if she's not here in the next ten minutes, I'm going to have to go. Selfridges isn't open all night. And," she added beadily, "I want you to know that I wouldn't spend two weeks' bonus holiday on anyone else but you."

"I know. I am grateful beyond words. So is Nelson," I added in a shameless appeal to Gabi's weak spot. "More coffee?" I suggested. "You'll need to know how the coffee machine works. Especially if Allegra's going to be in."

At that point the door opened with a theatrical flourish and Allegra herself shimmied in, bearing three shopping bags from Peter Jones, a venti iced latte, and a parking ticket.

"I can't believe the traffic wardens in this country," she spat by way of a greeting. "They're evil! Evil!" She slammed the ticket on my desk, rattling the Bakelite telephone in its cradle. "Can I get petty cash for this? Business expense."

"You're an hour late," said Gabi. "Unless you're here for a different appointment?"

Allegra swiveled in surprise.

Actually, I did too.

"And you are?" she demanded.

"Gabi Shapiro," said Gabi, extending her hand. "Pleased to meet you. We'll be working together."

Allegra turned and looked at me with an interrogative raise of her Paloma Picasso eyebrows.

"Gabi is my, em, usual assistant," I fibbed quickly. "She's very familiar with how the agency operates, so I've asked her to come in while I'm away. To show you the ropes, as it were."

"Are you saying I can't manage?" demanded Allegra. "Are you implying I might need . . . supervision?"

"No!" I protested, my resolve melting in the force of her personality. "But, you know, Allegra, it's very delicate, some of what I do, and it really helps to —"

"Delicate how, exactly?" asked Allegra, checking my desk ornaments for price labels. "Just giving a load of slack-jawed Mummy's boys a kick up the arse, isn't it?"

"No, it isn't!" I objected as my heart

plummeted.

"Yes!" said Gabi. "That's about the size of it."

I spun round and regarded her with horror. Honestly, I could *feel* the blood draining from my face.

"Sit down, Mel!" insisted Gabi before I could disabuse her, pushing me cheerily into one of the comfortable leather library chairs I kept for clients. "Relax! Now, you can tell me and Allegra exactly what you'd like us to do while you're away. *Can't* you?"

I swallowed.

"Yes, do tell us," drawled Allegra, temporarily looking up from the desk. "Then you can tell me what you thought you were doing when you bought this revolting pen holder . . . *thing.*"

I looked at the pair of them. I was leaving my business with these two? I must be mad.

"Right," I said, getting a grip on myself, "take some notes, please."

They both stared at me.

"Notes." I nodded toward the antique roll-top desk. "If you look in there, Gabi, you'll find notebooks and pens. Okay. First of all, daily routine. First thing you do in the morning is check the messages. Phone and e-mail. I tend to get a lot of people phoning during the night. In crisis. Phone them back first, and let them know I'm not here, but I'll be back in —"

"We have to wait until you're back?" said Allegra. "Where's the fun in that?"

I fixed her with a look. "Allegra, this isn't a *fun* situation. This is *work*. And, yes, you *do* have to wait until I'm back. I'm only going to be away for a week or so."

"Fine," said Gabi brightly. Too brightly. She looked as if she had a plan, but I couldn't imagine what on earth it could be, and that worried me.

"So, yes, check the phone messages, then the post. There might be some bills, in which case they go into the pink bill file. There might be some checks, in which case they go into the green check file. There might be some invoices which go into the blue —"

"Invoice file," chorused Allegra and Gabi.

"Well, quite," I said, discomfited.

"This office work business seems pretty straightforward to me," said Allegra, stretching out her long legs. "I should have done it years ago. Piece of cake. The fuss you make, Mel, I thought you'd be *slaving* away . . ."

"What do you want us to do if anyone phones up wanting an appointment?" asked Gabi quickly.

"Look in my appointments diary, which is

right in front of you on the desk." I didn't mention the fact that I'd already photocopied it three times, just in case of an accident. "I've made a list of how long each standard service takes — wardrobe consultation, general date coaching, that sort of thing — but if it's anything more complicated, then call me."

"Call you? What if you're in the middle of a romantic moment with Dr. No?"

That was a good point. I'd more or less promised Jonathan that I'd be taking a holiday. And I knew he was getting tetchy about "my work priorities."

On the other hand . . .

"Text me," I said. "Keep it brief, and I'll let you know roughly how long it'll take, then book them in for when I get back."

"Right." Gabi made a note.

"But remember we don't do any of that pretend girlfriend stuff anymore," I added. "You have to be really firm about that. I still get about three calls a week from people and some of them can be quite pathetic, but you just have to be firm." I paused. I had one slightly masochistic client who thought the refusing was all part of the service. He'd bombarded the office with literally hundreds of red roses until I'd abandoned diplomacy and gotten Nelson to phone him up, pretending to be the police.

They'd *both* enjoyed that a bit too much, actually.

I shook myself. "The right *kind* of firm, obviously. It, er, just encourages certain people, but I'll leave it up to you."

"What else?"

"Don't forget to get some fresh flowers every other day — Nelson lets me budget for that in my accounts. Whisk a duster round this place, because it's really important to keep it clean for people coming in. Check the diary for birthday and anniversary reminders — clients get three reminders, one a fortnight in advance, one three days in advance, and one the day before to leave time to send flowers if they've completely forgotten. If they've completely forgotten," I added, "offer to send the flowers for them. And be delicate with the anniversaries. You never know when they might have . . . hit a rough patch."

"You mean, when they've split up?" growled Allegra with a toss of her dark hair.

"Well . . . yes."

"Fine," said Gabi. "In which case I'd just put a new set of details for the mistress in the diary, right?"

I blinked. Gabi's relentless practicality might be more of an asset than I'd reckoned.

145

"Well, yes," I said again, "but for God's sake, be nice. You have no idea how much this business depends on being firm but *nice* to people."

I swung my most beseeching gaze between Allegra and Gabi, two women known for their firmness but not necessarily for their niceness.

Gabi looked affronted. "You don't have to tell me that, Mel. I'm the soul of discretion."

Gabi knew as well as I did that this was an utter fib. However, since Allegra didn't — *yet* — I let it go.

"So, apart from checking your diary, answering your phone, and buying flowers, that's it?" said Allegra. "And for this, you're going to pay me . . ."

"No!" I said quickly, before she could reveal her astounding Daddy-subsidized wage to Gabi. "No, er, of course not! That would be awfully dull for you. Um, there are lots of birthdays and September weddings coming up, and with your combined shopping experience, I'm sure you could handle buying some presents, couldn't you?"

Gabi's eyes lit up.

"Check with the client first," I went on, "and get them to make you a wish list, just

146

to get an idea of how much they want to spend. Between the pair of you, there shouldn't be any problem finding some really wonderful gifts!" I said hurriedly. "Just make sure you put a note in the purple present file of what you got, who it was for, and how you sent it, then I won't accidentally send them something similar next year."

Allegra smiled patronizingly. "I doubt it, Melissa. I don't think you and I have very similar tastes."

I was about to remind her that it wasn't about our tastes so much as the gift-givers' when the phone rang and saved me.

"Now, listen," I said, putting on my tortoiseshell glasses. "This is what I want you to do."

They both rolled their eyes, which wasn't the response I was after at all.

"Hello, the Little Lady Agency," I said, mentally picturing a cup of hot chocolate. My old home ec teacher had taught us that tip for projecting a really enthusiastic phone manner. "How can I help you?"

"Mel, it's Roger."

A skin appeared on the hot chocolate and I had to make a real effort to keep my voice alluring, more for Gabi and Allegra's benefit than Roger's.

"Hello, Roger, how are you?"

"Fine. Look, I know what you said before, but I really do need to talk to you about this Hunt Ball. I *cannot* go with Celia. My eczema's come back just thinking about it. I'm begging you, just put on that lovely blond wig and —"

"I'm sorry, Roger," I said, pushing the spectacles up my nose. "As I explained before, I don't offer personal services like that anymore."

Gabi and Allegra sniggered.

I ignored them.

"Not even for a mate?" Roger demanded huffily. "Nelson's not here. He'd never know."

"It's not *about* Nelson . . . look, Roger, I'd love to help you, but I can't. I just can't. We'll talk about this later, all right? I'm sure we can come to . . ."

Roger put the phone down.

"Honestly," I said. "He needs a girlfriend, as soon as possible. And a real one at that."

"What did he want?" asked Gabi. "Fumigation recommendations? Or a dentist?"

"He wants me to go with him to a Hunt Ball. As Honey," I said, rearranging the papers that Allegra had riffled through on my desk. "And did you see how I said no?"

"Tsk. I could have done it," said Gabi.

"Just give me the wig."

My head shot up. "No, you could not. No!" I said, raising a warning finger. "*No, Gabi. Before you even *think* it. It's not on.*"

"I don't see why not," said Allegra. "If it's okay for you to do it, what's the difference? It's just like a franchise."

I gave both of them a very firm stare, the sort I used on clients who resisted my attempts to chuck out their "favorite" Thatcher-era boxer shorts. "It was okay when I did it. But now? I no longer do it. So no one does. The subject is closed," I said. "Now, let's talk about cleaners."

SEVEN

Naturally, with Nelson's advice about planning ahead ringing in my ears, I'd been rigorous in my to-do lists, up to and including having my big toes waxed, but — of course — I hadn't planned for the traffic jam on the M4, which left me exactly ninety seconds to get from the taxi drop-off to the check-in desk for my flight from Heathrow.

I sprinted through the terminal as best I could in my chic upgrade-me-please mules and tried not to notice everyone staring at me. I absolutely didn't want to be one of those dreadful arguers you see on airport documentaries — the ones who turn up late, then claw wildly at their faces and shriek at the check-in staff that they can still see the plane on the tarmac — but neither did I want to miss my flight.

Panting, I slapped my ticket down on the desk and smiled as charmingly as I could.

"Hello," I said. "I'm on the twelve-fifteen

flight to New York."

The check-in girl took my ticket silently and jabbed at her computer.

I waited, breathing slowly to get my heart rate back to normal. "Oh, what great nails you've got!" I observed. "How do you keep your manicure from chipping when you're typing all day?"

She looked up, and a faint "don't bother" smile crossed her face. "I'm very sorry, madam, but the flight's overbooked. We don't have a seat for you on this particular flight, but I can —"

"Sorry?" I stared at her. "But that's impossible. I booked my ticket ages ago."

She pointed her chip-free nail up at the clock and spoke very slowly, as if I were completely stupid. "Yes, madam, but you're checking in very late. And it's industry policy to overbook flights, but on this occasion everyone has turned up. I'm afraid you'll have to wait and see if anyone takes a voluntary bumping."

"Oh," I said, feeling foolish. "But I really do have to go on this one. My boyfriend will be waiting for me at the other end, and . . ." I stopped, realizing how lame this sounded. Behind me was a gray-faced mother with two children and a baby in a carriage, and two students. The baby was emitting a shrill grinding noise that I didn't know human beings could make outside horror movies, and the students were having a frantic argument in a language I didn't know, but it seemed to involve their visas, which they were shoving under each other's noses.

I turned back to the check-in girl. "They're overbooked too, aren't they?"

She nodded.

"And they're ahead of me in the voluntary bumping line?"

She nodded again. "But if we have to bump you, you'll get compensation."

I tried not to think of the romantic welcome Jonathan probably had waiting for me. He was so good at those end-of-movie moments. I could see it now — a bunch of flowers, that discreet but teasing half smile, probably a car waiting to whisk me off to his fabulous apartment . . . No compensation would make up for spoiling that. "I'll take a seat," I sighed.

Now, in my position, I knew Gabi would have pulled every string she could think of — from my business, to my father, to Jonathan's frequent flyer miles — but I hated doing that sort of thing. I never sounded convincing, even when it was true. So much for those tips in *Glamour* about letting your clothes ask for your upgrade.

I wandered off to get myself a coffee and a newspaper, and when I came back, the check-in girl was negotiating furiously with the students.

I hovered, not wanting to butt in, and suddenly felt a large hand smack me on the bottom.

"Melissa!" boomed a voice behind me.

I spun round.

Looming up behind me like a pin-striped drainpipe was Harry Paxton, a business acquaintance of my father's for whom I'd done some Christmas shopping last year. I'd been recommended on account of my extreme discretion apparently (doubtless by my father), which was just as well, since he'd seemed to have a suspicious number of "goddaughters" on his list.

"Hello, Harry," I said, extending my hand for him to shake.

He went for a kiss. "Melissa," he mumbled into my knuckles. "And what brings you to Heathrow? Business or pleasure?"

"Oh, I'm flying to New York. Or, rather, I was, until I was bumped off the plane." I pulled a face. "It's rather inconvenient, but I suppose I'll just have to get a good book and make the best of it."

"Can't have that!" exclaimed Harry.

"What nonsense! Come with me."

He bustled off in the direction of the first-class check-in and walloped the counter hard until an airline representative appeared. She looked significantly more eager to please than the one at the economy desk.

"Now, see here," he said. "I've checked myself into first class, but my assistant has been bumped out of economy by some minion of yours. Should have booked herself in with me, silly girl. False economy in this case, what? Ha-ha! Now we need to deal with a fair bit of business before we land at JFK, so I'd be obliged if you could take a look at your screen or what have you, and see if you can't pop her into first with me."

"Of course, Sir Harry," beamed the airline lady, clicking rapidly.

Blimey. I'd forgotten he was a Sir.

"There you go!" said Harry, with a stagey wink that showed off his false teeth nicely. "Give the lady your passport. That all you're traveling with?"

"Um, yes!"

He beamed. "Very small clothes, eh? Excellent!"

"Well, no, just clever packing," I murmured, handing over my passport. I saw her expression flicker when she checked the back. Having an Honourable Granny on my contact details, as well as Daddy's official MP title, often raised a few eyebrows.

"Jolly good," boomed Harry jovially. "Now, how about a quick snorter while we wait for the cattle to load? Rather good lounge here, actually."

I cast a guilty glance back at the economy check-in, where the mother was practically banging her head against the desk, while her children stuffed crayons up each other's noses.

I turned back with a big smile. "I'll see you there in two shakes! I just have to . . . make a quick call."

He patted my bottom again. "Don't be too long. I need to have a little chat with you about Margery. She's packed in the singing and is insisting on learning the damn cello now. Sounds like we're running a slaughterhouse in the conservatory. Need some tips to nip it in the bud, what?" And he tapped his nose.

Great. I'd had chapter and verse about Harry's wife's desire to become a leading light in the local operatic society all through last Christmas, and I wasn't sure there was much more advice I could offer beyond the purchase of undetectable earplugs. Cellos weren't easy, or cheap, to sabotage. But it was a small price to pay for a seat I could fit my whole bottom in.

And maybe there was something else I could do to help.

When I was sure Harry was out of sight, I walked quickly back to the economy counter and muttered discreetly to the check-in girl that I recognized the woman with the baby from a BBC consumer affairs show and that I was sure I'd seen her filming secretly in the loos. Something about an exposé.

I suppose it must have worked, because ten minutes later, the woman was pushing her suddenly angelic kids into the first-class lounge, followed by two very surprised students.

First class was a new experience for me. The seats were so far apart that Harry had to lean over to talk to me. And talk to me he did, right through the safety demonstration, right through the explanation of the films on offer, and right up until the flight attendant came round and he broke off to order his first Scotch.

From long years of cocktail parties at home, and then office parties at work, I was used to making conversation with men like Harry — not that it involved much actual conversation on my part. Nodding, humming, and twitching my eyebrows were about the limit. Still, men were always telling me what a good listener I was.

We'd run through various anecdotes about his time as chairman of the local Neighborhood Watch committee when he leaned over even further and said, "Do you fly a lot, Melissa?"

"Oh, yes. Holidays and so on," I nodded.

"Are you a member of the, ah, Mile High Club?"

I racked my brains. Was that something to do with Air Miles? Gabi was obsessed with how many she got on her credit cards and claimed that spending a small fortune on shoes had actually saved her a small fortune on flights. Gabi Maths, she called it.

A light went on in my head. Maybe if I was a member, I wouldn't get kicked out of first class when they realized I only had an economy ticket.

"Yes," I said, nodding harder. "Yes, I am. Have been for ages."

"Good!" Sir Harry grinned so hard that his eyes almost disappeared. "Excellent! Well," he went on, dropping his voice discreetly, "I'm just off to the little boy's room now . . ." And he winked slowly, on account of the whisky, I supposed. "I'll see *you* in a moment."

"Wonderful!" I said, and as soon as he'd

gone, I motioned to the flight attendant for a glass of champagne and the headphones, and I settled down to watch the latest Harry Potter film on my personal video screen.

Half an hour passed very pleasantly, and I'd moisturized twice with the complimentary Jo Malone face cream when I realized that the seat next to me was still empty. Where had Sir Harry gone? I looked round the cabin in case he'd table-hopped to someone more interesting, but there was no sign of him.

Oh, dear. I hoped something hadn't befallen him in the loo, like a sudden deep vein thrombosis. I'd read they could be nasty.

"More champagne?" The flight attendant leaned over with another mini bottle, and I seized my chance.

"Um, I'm rather concerned about my, er, colleague." I felt myself turning pink with the effort of fibbing and being discreet simultaneously. "He's been gone from his seat for quite a while now, and . . ."

"That's no problem at all," she smiled. "I'll make sure he's okay."

"Would you? That would be so kind," I said gratefully and settled back into my comfy seat.

I watched her walk down the aisle toward

the lavatory, knock once — I couldn't hear, since I had my state-of-the-art headphones back on — then recoil backward from the door in shock. For a horrible moment I wondered if poor Sir Harry had died in there, but he came bustling out almost immediately, adjusting his clothes, nearly pushing past the poor woman as he stumbled back down the aisle.

Turbulence, I assumed. Or constipation. It happened a lot to men his age, if their confided medical histories were to be believed.

He glared at me when he sat down, but I smiled sunnily and removed one ear of my headphones. "I ordered you some cold water," I said. "You should try to rehydrate if you're drinking at altitude, according to my facialist! It would be such a shame to have a vile headache when you land, wouldn't it?"

He muttered something I missed as I was replacing my headphone, and when I turned back to tell him about the hypnotherapist I'd just remembered about in Parson's Green who could cure his wife's knuckle-cracking, I was startled to see that he'd donned one of those blackout eye masks that practically covered the whole face. It was like discovering an Elizabethan executioner in the next seat.

Still, it meant that I could enjoy the business-class luxuries undisturbed by conversation, and I spent the remaining five hours toying pleasantly with a number of romantic reunion scenarios, most of which seemed to take place in black and white and all featured me and Jonathan dancing like film stars.

I'd often daydreamed about my first trip to New York with Jonathan, pretty much since our first meeting. I was usually bundled up in some adorable fur-lined hood, clutching heaps of beribboned Christmas presents while a fine dusting of snow fell around us and groups of rosy-cheeked youngsters sang carols on street corners. And a yellow taxi came to pick us up and sweep us off to the ice rink, where Jonathan would skate with casual skill, and we'd stop for hot chocolate and enormous cupcakes.

As Nelson liked to point out, most of my fantasies have a significant food element.

Obviously, I knew it wasn't always Christmas in New York, in much the same way that London wasn't populated with chimney sweeps and dancing flower-sellers. But as I stood in the queue for immigration, my clothes starting to cling to my damp skin in the sticky humidity, I did start to question Jonathan's insistence that everywhere was air-conditioned to the point where I'd need a good warm cardigan to go *inside* buildings, rather than one to put on when I went out.

God, I thought, peeling my trousers discreetly off my legs, *maybe two bags of clothes won't be enough.* Such had been my concern about having the right clothes with me for every possible occasion that I'd even phoned my sister Emery in Chicago for packing advice.

"Take nothing at all," she'd insisted with uncharacteristic certainty. "Nothing!"

I'd rolled my eyes at the phone. "Well, what am I going to wear?"

"Wait till you get there to decide. Go shopping. See what mood you're in. But take something squashy in your hand luggage, in case it's hot."

Emery, I should point out, was one of those annoyingly waiflike girls who could float around braless in designer rags and look ethereal, rather than like an escapee from the chorus of *Les Misérables*.

"Mmm. The weird thing is," she'd gone on, "I find New York is just like those Scottish castles we used to go to on holiday . . . it's kind of spooky, actually. It can be really hot outside, like . . . *tropical* . . . and yet inside . . . everything's freezing. I don't know how they do it. It must be the stone floors, don't you think? Bizarre."

I'd stared at my own reflection in the mirror over Nelson's phone table. *How* were we related?

"You don't think it's the air con, maybe?" I'd suggested.

"You know me, Melissa, I don't talk about politics," Emery had said firmly.

Now, of course, I wished I hadn't taken Emery's advice, because I'd packed the bare minimum of clothes and then sucked all the air out of my luggage with Gabi's special vacuum packer. In practical terms, the only outfit I could slip into without exploding my whole carry-on was a slinky silk jersey dress that I'd only packed in my handbag at the last minute because you could screw it into a little ball without fear of wrinkling it.

The fact that such slinky minimalism required several complicated Pants of Steel elements went without saying, but with the humidity rapidly reaching tomato hothouse levels, pretty soon I wouldn't have much choice. I refused to meet Jonathan with sweat stains and a shiny nose. It was hardly Jackie Kennedy Onassis. But then neither was shuffling forward slowly in a queue

162

while my hair slowly slumped.

Oddly, Sir Harry had vanished off the plane the second it had landed, before I'd even been able to thank him properly for wangling me such a lovely flight, so I'd been left to find my own way out as best I could. Once they'd taken my fingerprints and I'd squinted into the security camera, I scuttled into the nearest loo for emergency renovations.

A year of turning myself in and out of Honey Blennerhesket at short notice meant I was pretty good at tarting myself up under pressure: a splash of cold water on my wrists, mouthwash, fresh mascara, and some red lipstick, and I looked almost human. Once I'd wriggled into my slinky dress, I really did look as if I'd traveled over in first class. For the final effect, I slipped on my shades and strode into the corridor, a whole new woman.

At the arrivals gate, whole families were blocking up the doors in massive group hugs, waving raffia donkeys and pushing vast taped-up cardboard boxes full of God knows what.

I scanned the crowd for Jonathan's red hair.

He wasn't there.

My heart sank.

There must have been hundreds of people out there, waiting for passengers! I hovered at the door, not wanting to walk past him in case he was hidden behind someone else. Honestly, he could wave or something, I thought. I mean, there's reserved behavior and there's plain unhelpful.

Just as my mood was sinking from disappointment into despair, a small woman with jet-black hair and a neat twinset approached me.

"Ms. Romney-Jones?" she said, putting out a tiny little hand to shake. "I'm Lori? From Mr. Riley's office? I've been sent to pick you up."

"Melissa, please!" I said.

"Mr. Riley apologizes, but he's been called away on some urgent business," said Lori, smiling. "May I compliment you on your outfit, by the way? You look just like a film star!" Her face dimpled when she smiled. It gave her a very pretty, Russian-doll look.

"That's very kind of you," I said, trying not to sound too disappointed at the news of Jonathan's unavailability. Even though I was. Awfully disappointed.

Why couldn't he be here? What was more important than my arriving in New York for the first time?

"He's very sorry not to be here to meet

you himself, but he asked me to take you to his appointment and he'll take you home from there," said Lori. "I have a car waiting outside. Are these all your bags?"

"Yes, yes, that's all," I said, letting her take my big wheelie case while I wheeled the other, with my big handbag digging into my shoulder. I followed her through the concourse and outside, where the hot air hit me like a wall.

"Gosh!" I said, unable to stop myself. "It's so hot!"

"I guess so," said Lori amenably. "But it's been much hotter than this. This isn't too bad compared with last week!"

"Really?" I said faintly, and sank gratefully into the air-conditioned limo she magicked out of nowhere. For the first time ever, I understood Jonathan's obsession with cars that had powerful air-conditioning as well as seat position memory functions.

"We're going through Queens now," Lori informed me as the car swept down the fast lane. Soon the swooping bridges and Manhattan's skyline of tall buildings started to rise out from behind the billboards and off-ramps. I couldn't stop staring. Everything was so familiar, from television and films, and yet — there it was! Real!

I'd had a very similar experience when

Gabi and I had visited the *Coronation Street* set in Manchester.

"Kind of amazing, isn't it?" said Lori proudly as the driver lurched impatiently from one lane to another. Fortunately, the car was so enormous that I didn't even feel the swerve.

"Absolutely," I said, trying to take everything in and not sound like a total bumpkin. I failed. "It's . . . amazing."

Before I could think of anything more profound to say, Lori's mobile phone rang. "Would you excuse me?" she said politely.

We carried on into Manhattan, with me getting progressively more excited and fluttery at the thought of seeing Jonathan, and Lori getting more and more calls on her mobile, which she dealt with in a courteous undertone. I kept hearing the words "Mr. Riley" and "schedule" and "impossible."

The streets narrowed into grid patterns, dotted with thrillingly familiar high American traffic lights and green street signs, and even I could tell we were heading into seriously upmarket territory.

"This is Park Avenue," whispered Lori as we pulled up outside an impressive apartment building with a long green canopy and a doorman who held the door for us as we went in.

"Right," I breathed.

"If you'd like to wait here, Mr. Riley will be finished in a few minutes," murmured Lori in suitably hushed tones as we entered the lobby. "I'll go and get you a coffee and something to eat, if you'd like?"

I was quite happy to sit and refresh myself in the discreet splendor. The lobby of this apartment building was more lavishly appointed than most London hotel bars: oak paneling, brass light fittings, vast green plants. It also had bone-chilling air-conditioning, which was raising all the hairs on the back of my arms in a most gratifying manner.

"I'd love a cup of coffee," I murmured back. "And a muffin or something, if you think they wouldn't mind me eating in here," I added, partly as a joke. Just partly, though.

"I'm sure that won't be a problem," murmured Lori deferentially, and it dawned on me that the reason she was treating me like some kind of visiting royalty was that I was Jonathan's guest.

I blinked. What with Gabi and the whole Dr. No business, it was easy to forget that Jonathan was a very big cheese at Kyrle & Pope.

"That would be kind," I said with a smile.

"Thank you."

Lori backed out of my presence and went up to the concierge to murmur a few more words to him. I was left sitting on the huge velvet sofa, appreciating the fine art and the immense explosion of fresh flowers in the grand marble fireplace.

While I was pondering how much an apartment in this building must cost, I heard footsteps on the parquet floor behind me and a few low-spoken words of conversation. I knew it was Jonathan, winding up his business with some clients, and a shiver of anticipation ran over my skin. Not wanting to turn round and gawk, my ears twitched all the same, and I picked up the words "board meeting . . . personal references . . . cats on leashes . . ."

Then there was some manly well-wishing and backslapping, the doorman was thanked in an undertone, and after a few tantalizing seconds, the smell of Creed came closer, and closer, then I felt warm breath on my skin, and then a soft kiss on the nape of my neck.

"Hello," Jonathan whispered into my ear, his breath tickling my suddenly hypersensitive neck. "How very nice to see you."

Every hair on my body pricked up and tingled, but I made myself turn round very

168

slowly in the manner of Rene Russo in the *Thomas Crown Affair.*

When I did, it was worth it. Jonathan was looking heart-stoppingly businesslike in a sharp, navy blue linen suit, with a creamy shirt and a liquid gold tie. His hair was perfectly groomed, and he showed no signs at all of the raging heat outside.

He looked a little tense, but then he was at work, after all.

"Let me see you," he said, taking my hand and making me stand up. "You're telling me you've just gotten off a five-hour flight? I don't believe you. You look wonderful!"

I glowed. Jonathan wasn't fulsome with his compliments, like some of my more sleazy exes had been, but when he gave them, the look in his eyes said about a thousand times more than his actual words did, and I knew he really meant it.

"Thank you," I beamed. "It's just a little something I found in my handbag."

He leaned forward and kissed my cheek, lingering long enough to smell my scent and for me to smell his cologne. I knew he wasn't going to pull me into a Hollywood embrace in front of the concierge, and for some reason that sort of discreet kiss was even more exciting.

Jonathan could be very Rhett Butler when

he wanted to. It was positively knee-buckling.

"Thank you for coming," he said right into my ear, so no one else could hear. "I can't tell you how wonderful it is to see you."

I wanted to be equally mature and restrained, but I couldn't. "I've missed you," I said impulsively, unable to hold it in any longer. "It's felt like ages!"

"It's felt like a very, *very* long time," he agreed. "I'm five hours behind you, too." And for a moment, he looked as if he was struggling with his own restraint.

Lori coughed behind us, and we jumped.

Well, I jumped. Jonathan just turned round and took the coffee and a small bag from her with a quick thanks, then handed them to me. She smiled, nodded slightly to him, then opened her mouth uncertainly, only speaking when he raised his eyebrows in encouragement.

"Will you be going back to the office this afternoon, Mr. Riley?" she enquired. "Because I can have those papers sent over to you this evening if you want to look at them before tomorrow's board meeting? And I have the references for the Grosvenor apartment."

"Right," said Jonathan, shooting out his

cuffs to adjust them as he thought aloud. "Okay, cancel everything for the rest of the day, and have whatever you think most urgent sent over to me tonight. I'll take a look at it. And, Lori, thank you for picking up Miss Romney-Jones from the airport. I appreciate your time."

"Yes, thanks very much," I added. "I'd never have found my way here by myself!"

Lori smiled until she dimpled up, nodded shyly, and then excused herself.

"You want a cup for that?" asked Jonathan when she'd gone, nodding at my Starbucks cup.

"No, no, it's fine," I said.

"Go on, I know you like a proper cup for your coffee."

"No, honestly, don't worry about it," I said, confused. Where was he going to get me a cup?

"Listen," he said, his face perfectly serious, "why don't we go upstairs and borrow a cup and saucer from the apartment I've just viewed?"

I stared at him, then laughed. "Oh, don't be silly! You can't do that!"

"Would that be very unprofessional of me?" Jonathan gazed at me, all innocence.

Was he winding me up? "Well, yes," I spluttered. "Of course it would!"

"Melissa," he said solemnly. "I don't like to follow the rules all the time. Come on, I've still got the keys."

And he set off for the lift.

I trotted after him in a state of some confusion, my heels clicking loudly on the richly polished floor. I was surprised that the concierge didn't try to stop him.

"Listen, Jonathan, I really don't want to —"

"Sh!" he said, putting a finger on his lips.

"But I don't want you to —"

"Sh!"

He waited until the wrought-iron gates shut behind us, then leaned forward and gave me a long kiss. It was such a long kiss, and I'd been looking forward to it so much, that I barely noticed when we reached the tenth floor.

Jonathan, though, had better timing, and he stepped briskly out of the lift the minute it stopped moving.

"Now, which one was it?" he mused to himself, looking at the keys.

"Jonathan, please, don't," I said, straightening my dress and trying to get my breath back. "Can't we just get a cab home and . . ."

He pretended to try various keys in the forbidding oak door until one fit. "Ah, here we go," he said and lifted a foxy eyebrow in invitation. "Can I invite you in for a . . . cup of coffee?"

I had to admit that I was getting an idea of what he might have in mind, and although I was shocked to the core at the out-of-character naughtiness of it — well, perhaps that was what was so exciting.

"Okay," I said. "But you'd better find me a saucer too."

"Something saucy?" he enquired.

"No, a saucer."

"I'm sure I can rustle up something," he said and pushed the door open for me to go on in. I slithered past him flirtatiously, then stopped in my tracks.

When I say this was an apartment, I mean it was an apartment in the sense of a *state* apartment. Everywhere I looked was either oak-paneled, gold-plated, or draped with fabrics.

"Crikey," I breathed. "Is the owner still here?" I stepped into the hallway, which had ornate brass light fittings, converted, I guessed, from the originals. The smell of myrrh and cloves and beeswax polish floated through the whole apartment.

"No," said Jonathan, suddenly sounding quite brisk.

I wandered slowly through to the sitting

room, which was massive — bigger than Nelson's whole flat, I guessed. Long windows, hung with deep red velvet curtains, looked out onto parkland, and an old glass chandelier hung from the high ceiling, sending slanting diamonds of refracted light all over the crimson walls. The room was dominated by three huge leather sofas and some striking modern paintings.

The overall effect was stylish and modern but, at the same time, curiously empty. There were no bookshelves, or photographs, or anything personal at all. The sofas were grand, but they didn't invite you to get comfy on them. And the view was there to be admired, just as you were meant to admire the paintings — I knew I should have known who they were by, but I didn't.

I wasn't quite sure why Jonathan had brought me to this amazing apartment for our big reunion, but still, that kiss in the elevator had been a pretty big hint about what he had in mind.

"So," I said, turning back to Jonathan and leaning seductively against the doorjamb. "This is the sitting room. Are you going to . . . show me the bedroom now?"

He was staring into space, and he seemed to shake himself back to life when I spoke. A deep frown line had appeared on his forehead. "Yeah, yeah. A cup, right?"

And he walked through a doorway into the kitchen.

A cold chill of embarrassment froze me in place for a second or two. What? How had I gotten that wrong?

Hastily adjusting my dress, I followed him into the kitchen, trying to work out where that playful flirtiness had vanished to. And why? Maybe he was reminded of problems on the deal — maybe it had been a tougher meeting than he was making out.

The kitchen was like the interior of the Starship *Enterprise:* Everything was stainless steel and looked to be of professional quality. There were no visible handles on anything, and I could see our reflections in everything from the walk-in fridge to the matching dishwashers.

"Wow!" I said again. "Nelson would love this! Is the owner a chef?"

"No," said Jonathan, opening a cupboard. "The owner is a woman whose idea of home cooking was to put Thai fusion takeout on her own plate instead of getting a maid to do it."

Oh. I frowned.

He handed me a bone china cup and saucer with a fine band of silver around the edges.

"Thank you," I said, carefully decanting the contents of my takeaway cup. It wasn't like Jonathan to be so dismissive of his clients.

"Want a side plate for the muffin?" he enquired, offering me a matching tiny cake plate. "Never been used. Part of an eighteen-place dinner service, too. Look." And he swung open the cupboard door to reveal more china than I'd seen in one place outside the Peter Jones homeware department. "Never been through the dishwasher."

I took the plate, trying not to let my surprise show. "How do you know all this?"

Jonathan's mouth made a flat line. "It's my old apartment."

I blinked. "Sorry?"

"It's where Cindy and I used to live. She's been living here while I've been in London. I know, I know," he added, raising his hands, "she was meant to sell it as soon as the divorce went through, but the market's been slow. And now the . . ." Jonathan didn't often swear. He swallowed. "Cindy's put it on the market with Kyrle & Pope and wants *me* to broker the sale."

A heavy weight plunged in my stomach, like a duck being shot and falling vertically to earth. That explained everything. I put the cup and saucer down as if they were red-hot.

Cindy.

The mere mention of Cindy made me feel jumpy. And underdressed. And under-achieving, and, for some reason, cross. She'd behaved appallingly to Jonathan, and yet he'd put up with her shenanigans for years — so he must have really, *really* loved her. I'd never met Cindy, and he virtually never talked about her, but the few frag-ments I'd picked up were enough to paint a pretty disturbing picture: how she'd put her own secretary on the Atkins Diet, that sort of thing.

I'd only ever seen one photograph of Cindy, which I'd found by accident in a drawer at Jonathan's house. It had been taken at some very smart function; he was in a dinner jacket, looking tense, and she was wearing a long, straight, severe dress in crimson silk that emphasized her long, straight, severe figure. Also her long, straight, severe face, which could, as Gabi would have said, have done with a few pies. Her blond hair wisped around her head like a cotton-candy crash helmet. It wasn't fool-ing me, though — I knew, left to its own devices, it, too, would be long and straight.

My inner TV detective told me at once that she was the sort of cow who smiled sympathetically while she was sacking you and boasted about "playing hardball with the guys" while claiming her haircuts as business expenses.

Well, I didn't know that, to be fair. But who's fair about their boyfriend's ex?

Actually, the one major definite fact I knew about Cindy summed her up for me: She and Jonathan split up when she found out she was pregnant with his brother Brendan's baby. With whom she was now living.

You see? *Not* a nice woman.

Jonathan and I had had one shortish heart-to-heart about her. It had been triggered by the arrival of a birth card, announcing the Gift of a Son to Brendan Riley and Cindy Riley.

I hadn't liked to ask, but at that point he'd volunteered a quick rundown of their married life: They'd met at a formal dance when his New England boys' school had hosted her New England girls' school — that much I could sympathize with — and she'd won his heart by arguing with him all the way through a fox-trot. They'd then dated through university (Princeton for him, Brown for her) and married on graduation while Cindy was still called Lucinda, with the reception at the New York Yacht Club and the honeymoon in Antigua.

What with Jonathan being a career realtor and Cindy working her way swiftly up the ladder at an advertising agency, they'd had a series of nice apartments. I knew their final marital home had been pretty smart, but it was only now that I was standing in front of a twenty-thousand-pound kitchen range that I was starting to see the extent of what they'd had between them.

I gulped.

And the fact that she wanted *him* to sell it demonstrated, to me, anyway, just what a cow she was.

"I guess she wants to make sure I get the best price," he added. "She knows I don't broker sales anymore. But she told my CEO that only I could deal with it, or else she'd take it elsewhere. And," — he waved a hand around — "as you can guess, there's a pretty big commission on this."

"I can imagine," I said weakly.

Jonathan's mouth set into a lipless line again. "Obviously it's in my best interests to get as much as I can for it. But mostly, I don't want to give her the satisfaction of showing her that I care. If she's trying to make me feel bad about the divorce, it's not working. It's just an apartment to me. It's not like it has sentimental value."

The toughness in his words broke my

heart, because I knew he couldn't possibly mean it.

"Oh, don't say that!" I exclaimed. "That's not true! You *must* have had some happy times here."

He sighed, then held out his arms. I slid into them gratefully and squeezed him tight. I could feel his lean muscles beneath his thin shirt. We fitted together perfectly.

"Melissa," he murmured into my hair, "I have more happy memories of the year I rented that house in Barnes, when I first met you, than I do of six years of owning this place."

"Really?" My heart skipped.

"Yes, really." Jonathan traced his lips along my forehead. "That's when I knew how unhappy I'd been, because being with you made me feel like a different person." He held me at arm's length so I could look into his eyes and see how serious he was. "You woke me up. Those trips round town . . . You know I used to scour guidebooks, trying to find new farmers' markets and stately homes and umbrella shops I could ask you to take me to?"

"You did?" I pretended to pout. "And I thought you were interested in the history of London!"

"Well, yeah. That too. But I was more

interested in the tour guide."

I sank back into his arms, trying not to let all my elation show on my face at once. There wasn't really enough room. "It was a pleasure. Even the Masonic halls."

"So the least I can do is return the favor," Jonathan went on, stroking my hair. "Minus the umbrella stores, if you don't mind. But I have a whole list of other places to take you."

"Mm." Jonathan's fingers were now caressing the soft skin behind my ears, but somehow I couldn't quite relax into enjoying the sensation. There was something echoing and cold about the apartment, and it wasn't the air-conditioning. "Darling," I began tentatively, "not that I don't like this apartment, but can we go back to your new place?"

Jonathan paused, then looked at me quite seriously. "Listen, Melissa, I only wanted to show you this place because I wanted to show you what I'm leaving *behind*." He fixed me with his special, extra-determined look. "I want to move on with *you*."

My skin tingled. "Good," I said, trying to appear cooler than I felt. "That's . . . that's . . . good."

Jonathan looked at me, his head tilting to one side. " *'Good'?*"

I opened my mouth again, but I wasn't sure what I was supposed to say. Here was Jonathan, offering to chuck away this dream apartment so he could start a whole new life with me, the clammy, jet-lagged woman whose dress was sticking to the back of her thighs.

It was rather overwhelming — in a positive way, obviously.

"British understatement," I reassured him.

Jonathan's face relaxed, and he took my hand. "I think we've spent enough time in this place, don't you? Let's get a cab home."

Home. I liked the sound of that.

EIGHT

Jonathan summoned a cab out of the surging traffic with the merest twitch of his hand, and we set off downtown. It was as much as I could do to stop my eyes flicking from side to side at the array of familiar shop names and amazing buildings that I recognized from about a hundred films.

Jonathan, meanwhile, had gotten straight onto his favorite topic: houses, the acquisition and improvement thereof.

"It was the quickest deal ever, *ever.* I just fell in love with this property the moment I walked in the door," he was saying, his eyes shining. "It never even went on the market. You see that there?" He pointed out the window as we sped down Fifth Avenue. "St. Patrick's Cathedral. Gorgeous, huh? And that's Rockefeller Center, can you see the international flags? And, down there, on the left . . . Saks Fifth Avenue? The famous department store?"

My head swung from side to side, trying to take it all in.

"Anyway," he went on, "I was meant to be checking this house over for an old family friend, but as soon as I saw it, I just thought, I've got to have it! So I put wheels in motion right then and there."

"Really?" This opportunism sounded somewhat out of character for Jonathan — in fact, it rather smacked of my father's behavior — but my attention was temporarily distracted by steam coming up out of a subway vent. Exactly like in a film!

"I wanted something totally different from that Upper East Side apartment Cindy and I had," he went on. "Somewhere I could have a library, and a study, if I wanted, and not have to kowtow to the co-op board whenever I needed to have the plumbing fixed."

I'm not saying I wasn't listening, but there was an awful lot to take in, all at once. There were Gaps everywhere. Really *big* Gaps with underwear sections. I knew I should be getting more excited about the swanky stores, but frankly, Gabi's vehement speeches about how much better Starbucks was in America, and how Duane Reade knocked Boots the Chemist into a cocked hat (not her exact words) made me eager for more basic shopping. I just nodded and carried on trying to fit everything together in my reeling head.

"It's quite a different neighborhood too," he said as we sped past more blocks of tall office buildings, coffee shops, and drug-stores. "You know how you used to tell me that London was like a bunch of villages, all joined up? Well, this really is a village. Greenwich Village. It's kind of like London in some ways. Quick! See that?" he added, pointing out the window again. "It's called the Flatiron Building. It's shaped like a flatiron and . . . oh, you missed it. Listen, we'll take a bus tour, so you can see all this properly."

I turned to him and squeezed his hand tighter. We were holding hands in the cab — Jonathan and I shared the same strict rules about what was and wasn't acceptable on public transport. Anticipation is under-rated, in my book. "You're doing a great job."

"I'm finding it hard to concentrate on the scenery outside," he said solemnly, and for a moment he sounded almost nervous.

The neighborhood was definitely getting less citylike as the car weaved in and out of the traffic, until finally we rounded a large, tree-filled park, surrounded by some very elegant town houses.

"Washington Square," said Jonathan. "The Henry James novel?"

I nodded, as if I'd read it many times, but my attention was really fixed on the narrowing streets and gorgeous brownstone houses, which seemed elegant, but homey at the same time. If Jonathan had bought somewhere round here, he ought to be seriously chuffed. There were window boxes filled with cascading ivy and geraniums, and pretty shutters on the windows. People were walking dogs, and sitting outside at café tables, and generally looking more boho than they had been a moment ago. Boho in an expensive, Notting Hill way, though.

Jonathan indicated for the cab to stop outside a brownstone house with steps up to a dark green front door. It was second to the end of the street, near a cobblestoned crossroads, and it had a tall tree shading its front step, with ivy curling around the iron handrails winding down to the basement windows. And, rather prettily, instead of just being a number, the street had a name: Jane Street. I liked that.

"Here you are," he said. "Home sweet home. Whaddya think?"

"It's beautiful," I replied and squeezed his arm. "And it definitely looks like a home."

The hint of nervousness vanished from his eyes and he smiled back, showing his perfect white teeth.

"Good," he said. "I'm so glad you approve." He paused. "Like my classic English understatement there?"

While Jonathan was paying the driver, I peered out the window at the house, preparing myself to step back into the muggy air. Actually, on closer inspection, there was something slightly, well, less tended about this house, compared to its neighbors. The paint on the door, for a start, seemed to be bubbling, and the lion's head knocker was dull.

Jonathan got out and opened my door for me, then got my luggage. I followed him as he hoisted the bags effortlessly up the steps and turned his key in the lock.

"So," he said, stepping back to let me into the cool, tiled hallway. "First impressions?"

"It's . . . it's full of character," I said.

It was full of packing cases. And beyond the packing cases, I could see some delightful details — a big fireplace with lovely original tiles in the sitting room, between two long sash windows, and flower-petal moldings on the ceiling. But the packing cases were pretty much the dominant feature, in the hall at least.

Above that, though, was a light, airy smell of shaded rooms and old wood. It smelled of grandmothers and faded wallpaper and books and dusty lamps. Not an unpleasant smell at all, to my nose, but one that I knew was a sign that the whole place needed doing up. I hoped he wouldn't do it up too much. And there was another smell too, which I couldn't quite put my finger on but there was something familiar about it.

"Excuse the mess," Jonathan explained, his footsteps echoing on the tiles as he led the way through into the long sitting room, which I now saw contained a couple of distressed leather sofas and stacks of books. "Not everything's unpacked, because the designers and the builders wanted to see it as it was. It needs a lot of work, and I've been really busy, setting things up in the office —"

"Jonathan," I said, stopping him so I could put my arms around his waist. "Please tell me you've at least unpacked somewhere for me to have a nap?"

His tense face broke into a smile, then went serious again. "But of course. You don't think I'd have been so ill-mannered as to have invited a guest without clearing out a guest room?"

"That would be the polite thing to do," I

agreed, even though by now I was tingling all over with excitement. It had been quite a while since I'd seen him, if you know what I mean. Then I did a double take. "Guest room?"

"That's right." Jonathan nodded. "I even checked with one of your British etiquette books about getting the right flowers, the water vase, the selection of amusing bedside reading . . ."

For a moment, I wondered if he meant it. He did take my tips about etiquette extraordinarily seriously. I squirmed, not sure if I'd made the right assumptions. We weren't, after all, living together, and he was, in many ways, terribly old-fashioned . . .

"But in the end," he said, leaning closer so his lips were right over mine, "the master bedroom was the first room I got ready. And I think you'll prefer it . . ."

"I'm sure I will," I murmured, my eyes closed, totally forgetting how sticky I still was after the flight, as his familiar smell came closer and closer, and I felt his breath on my skin.

Just as he was about to kiss me, a frenzied howling and scrabbling tore through the air, making me jump so hard that I accidentally head-butted Jonathan's nose.

"What the hell is that?" I yelped as the

howling increased to a deafening pitch, accompanied by the sound of wood being attacked.

Jonathan clutched his face. "That's my new housemate," he said, with enough venom to be heard through his cupped hands.

"Your what?"

"Blame Cindy," he said heavily, and, taking my hand, he led me through the sitting room to the kitchen.

The howling got louder as we approached the back door.

"Jonathan, what on earth is it?" I demanded, mentally picturing a Labrador or a boxer, at least. So that's what I'd smelled: eau de hound.

"Stand back," he warned as he undid his cuff links, folding back his pristine cuffs to his elbows. Then he rotated his shoulders, braced one foot against the door, and turned back to me. "I mean it, honey. Get back behind the table."

"Oh, Jonathan, don't be . . . okay." Seeing the look on his face, I moved aside one of the dining chairs and stood behind the table.

"Right," he said, more to himself than me, then yanked open the door.

A flash of white shot out like a furry bullet. With superb timing, Jonathan managed to snatch it by the collar with one hand and by the rear end with the other, scooping it up into the air like a rugby ball.

I don't know who was more surprised: me or the dog.

On balance, probably the dog, since it stopped barking for three seconds, long enough for me to see that rather than being the Hound of the Baskervilles, it was actually a West Highland terrier roughly the size of my toiletries bag. And when it stopped barking, it forgot to put its tongue back in, which made it look exactly like the spare toilet-roll cover the matron had in the sick-bay lavatory at school. Pom-poms for its head and ears and everything.

"Good Lord," I said, trying not to laugh.

Obviously, it was one of those dogs who responded poorly to owner amusement, and it threw its head back and went into a deafening yapping of complaint.

"Shut up! Shut up!" yelled Jonathan help-lessly.

"What's it called?" I shouted.

"Braveheart!" shouted Jonathan, as if it pained him to say it aloud. "I didn't choose the name. Get the dog food out of the fridge!"

I opened and closed appliances until I came to the fridge. There wasn't much in there, apart from some milk, three bottles of rather decent champagne, and a plastic takeaway box.

"I can't see anything!" I shouted back over the sound of indignant barking.

"The box," yelled Jonathan. "It's the box of stuff."

I pulled out the plastic container, confused. "But this is takeaway, isn't it? There's pasta in here and everything. Are you sure it's not . . ."

"Braveheart has a dietician," he roared. "Now if you look in the cupboard next to you, there's a dog bowl."

I opened the cupboard. It was empty, apart from what looked suspiciously like a porcelain soup plate.

Now, I know my mother was a bit daft about her ghastly animals, but this was really ridiculous. It had a crest on it. In gold leaf.

"Jonathan, you can't be . . ." I stared at him as he and Braveheart tussled with each other. "Darling, stop shaking the dog," I added before I could stop myself. "It won't help."

"I'm not shaking him," said Jonathan through gritted teeth. "He's shaking me."

Braveheart turned his pom-pom head and snarled in my direction, as if to say, *Make it snappy with the food, woman.*

Hastily, I tipped the contents of the plastic box into the bowl and set it down on the floor by the huge stainless-steel swing-top bin.

Jonathan let go of the dog, and it catapulted itself across the kitchen floor, skidding only momentarily on the tiles, before sinking its nose into the dish of aromatic pasta verdi.

"It's Cindy's dog, she got him while we were still going to counseling, she thought it might bring us together," Jonathan explained rapidly, taking advantage of the temporary silence, broken only by the sound of slurping and a china bowl being scraped round the floor. "Other people have babies to patch up their relationship, but Cindy couldn't timetable a hospital stay into her development program at work, so we got a West Highland terrier, he's got a longer pedigree than I have and his ancestors belonged to Queen Victoria's mother's companion."

I felt my eyes widen in horror. I've never subscribed to the insanity of warring couples having a baby to "bring them together," but I didn't think getting a puppy was much better. Both required constant attention, peed everywhere, and howled during the night, guilt-tripping their way to getting what they wanted until both parental parties were simply too exhausted to argue anymore.

And, more selfishly, I wasn't sure I was ready to hear the entire history of why Jonathan and Cindy had or hadn't managed to start a family, condensed into the time it would take this evil little mutt to scarf up a gourmet meal.

"He's certainly a handsome thing," I said instead, trying to be positive. Because, to be fair, Braveheart was handsome. As small dogs went, he looked every inch the pedigree specimen, all perfect snowy coat and shiny black button eyes. And sharp little teeth.

"Typical Cindy to get a white dog in New York," said Jonathan, unrolling his sleeves with more of his usual wry humor. "He's ridiculously high maintenance. Braveheart has more staff than I do, and he costs about as much to run as Cindy's car."

"Do you like him?" I asked.

"No," said Jonathan.

"So why is he here? Did you get joint custody when the divorce happened?"

"Ah." Jonathan paused in putting his cuff links back in. "Well, no. Cindy wanted Braveheart as one of the disposable assets from the house, and I was happy to let her take him because I was in England." He pulled a face, as if to say, *Which I miss already,* then went on, "But then when Parker arrived —"

"Parker?"

"My nephew," deadpanned Jonathan. "Cindy and Brendan's baby."

Oops. I should have remembered that.

But, really, Parker Riley. Honestly. What sort of name was that? He was a baby, not a fountain pen.

"How, um, charming," I said, embarrassed.

"Yes, well, when Parker arrived, Cindy decided that Braveheart's hilarious table manners weren't so much hilarious as lethal, so she dumped him here."

I'm sorry to say that I couldn't stop myself snorting. "That's big of her," I said disapprovingly. "I hope she doesn't do the same thing to Parker when she gets sick of him."

"Now, don't you go getting the idea that Cindy doesn't care about her Scotch baby," he said, wagging a finger at me. "You'll find, if you open that drawer there, that she's made a list of all his needs so I can look after him properly."

I pulled open the drawer, which should have held assorted household debris. Instead it held a single laminated sheet and a state-of-the-art presentation bound folder.

"Important numbers," I read. "Braveheart's walker (Karen). Braveheart's walker (emergency). Braveheart's veterinarian. Braveheart's canine dietician. Braveheart's groomer." I looked up. "Does Braveheart have an astrologer?"

"Not yet." Before Jonathan could carry on with whatever he was about to say, the phone rang in the sitting room. "Ah, damn. I told them not to call me at home. Look, I'll just get that. If he starts acting up, get him into the vestibule and shut the door, okay?"

"Okay." I eyed Braveheart nervously.

My father, who was wrong about most things, was right when it came to dogs. He reckoned that a strict ratio of owner height/ dog size should apply. Anyone over five feet seven, according to him, should have Labradors or bigger; anything smaller than that looked camp. He would permit Jack Russells — a breed he secretly admired for their tenacious refusal to let go of trouser legs — as a supplement to a larger dog, like an Irish wolfhound or something. Dogs small enough to fit into a handbag, as far as he was concerned, might as well be cats.

Braveheart finished chasing the bowl

around the floor in his efforts to remove the last forensic traces of supper — as I would, had I been served that — and stared at me. I could tell he was spoiling for a fight. He reminded me of a diminutive Welsh estate agent at Dean & Daniels; two gin and tonics on top of his Napoleon complex, and he started getting pushy with men twice his size. I'd had to administer first aid more than once at office parties.

"Hello," I said, trying to be nice. Generally, I took quite a firm line with dogs, but this was Jonathan's dog. Actually, it was Cindy's dog, and by now I wouldn't have put it past her to have fitted him with a microchip voice recorder to find out what was really going on in Jonathan's life.

Braveheart growled, his teeth jutting over his drawn-back lips in a show of small-dog belligerence.

"Now, come on. I'm sure you're a lovely chap," I said, leaning over to stroke him. "No need for all this grumpiness! We're from the same country, practically."

Big mistake. He waited until my hand was millimeters from his wiry coat, and just as I was congratulating myself on charming him into submission, he turned with lightning speed and sank his teeth into the fleshy part of my hand.

"Bugger!" I hissed, not wanting to draw Jonathan's attention and lifting my hand up to suck it better. To my horror, Braveheart clung on, and I swear he narrowed his eyes at me.

With a superhuman effort I managed to disengage his jaws and sent him skittering across the kitchen floor.

My skin was unbroken, fortunately, but a series of cross little marks were now stamped into my hand.

"You little Scottish . . . bugger!" I hissed at him.

Braveheart panted back, unbowed.

In the sitting room, Jonathan was conducting a yes/no conversation with someone, and I heard his voice getting nearer.

He reappeared in the doorway, and I hastily rearranged myself into a semblance of normality.

"Sorry," he mouthed, then nodded to Braveheart, who was sitting, stunned, in the corner, preparing himself for his next attack. "Well done! He's never been so quiet!"

I nodded, hiding my hand behind my back.

"Won't be long," Jonathan finished and walked back into the sitting room. "We'll be there . . . Of course, I'll mention it. No, it won't be a problem . . ."

I sat down at the kitchen table and rubbed my eyes. All I really wanted now was a bath. A bath and a cup of tea, and a change of clothes, and maybe something to eat, actually, then I'd feel more like . . .

What was that faint growling, ripping noise?

I opened my eyes very slowly to see Braveheart with his nose deep in my handbag. It was, as I might have mentioned, a large handbag. It looked as if it was consuming him, slowly, like a Venus flytrap.

"Oh, no, you don't," I said in what I hoped were jolly, unthreatening tones, and reached over to pull it away from him.

The growling intensified, and Braveheart increased his purchase on the bag.

"Now, don't be silly!" I said, pulling harder.

He tugged the other way, getting his head looped under one of the handles.

I glanced over toward the sitting room. Jonathan was still talking, albeit in "winding up" mode.

"Give!" I hissed, pulling at the bag.

Braveheart's lips lifted again, almost in a smile, and he started to walk backward, so we were engaged in a very undignified tug-of-war.

"This is ridiculous!" I hissed and made a

lunge for the bag.

Of course, this just tipped the whole thing over, scattering the entire contents over the kitchen floor: lipsticks, tape measure, white handkerchiefs, my travel socks, mobile phone, purse, spare purse, change purse for tips, sunglasses, whistle, breath fresheners, mini manicure kit, keys, useful addresses written on business cards, compact, Nurofen, Allegra's bloody melatonin, the dress and underwear I'd changed out of at the airport, diary, notebook — all sent bouncing and rolling across the bare wood floor.

Immediately I fell to my knees, trying to jumble everything back into the bag before Jonathan came back in and saw what a bizarre collection of nonsense I'd carted across the Atlantic with me.

I was searching in vain for the missing Right Eye contact lens case when I realized that, once again, Braveheart's hysterical barks of triumph had gone quiet.

When I looked up, I saw, to my horror, that he was silent because he was licking something off the floor. I crawled nearer, on my hands and knees so as not to frighten him, and saw that the top had come off Allegra's melatonin bottle and Braveheart had one white tablet balanced on his tongue.

He also had my knickers on his head, an

ear poking jauntily through one leg hole with a frill of lace drooping over one eye. But I wasn't so worried about that for the time being.

I grabbed the bottle and slammed my hand over the remaining pills. How many had he taken? I looked so ridiculous that Braveheart forgot to put his tongue back in, and for a second I nearly managed to grab the pill. But then he swallowed it and snapped at my fingers instead.

"Oh, God almighty!" I breathed. This was all I needed. Dog poisoning. There was no way I could turn him upside down and shake it out of him, and definitely I wasn't going near those jaws again.

I grabbed my mobile phone and dialed my home number, praying that Allegra wasn't tying up the line quarreling with Lars.

It rang and rang. I kept my eye on Braveheart, who was now truffling round the kitchen for more food, howling to himself for amusement. When he passed the door out to the vestibule, I took the opportunity to shove him in and shut it. Immediately he set up a loud protest, but for the moment, as far as I was concerned, that was a good thing.

"Come on, come on," I muttered, turning

nervously to see where Jonathan had gotten to in his phone conversation.

"I've got nothing to add to my previous statement. I really can't comment further," said my mother's voice, very insistently. "I have *nothing more* to say on the matter. And neither has my husband."

"Mummy?" I said, moving out of the kitchen into what looked like a scullery of some kind.

"Hello, darling!" she said enthusiastically. "Where are you calling from?"

This was her discreet finishing-school method of working out which of her daughters was ringing, since she could never tell us apart on the phone.

"New York," I said heavily. "It's Melissa. Look, Mummy, that melatonin Allegra gave me — what would happen if, um, if a dog ate some? A smallish dog."

"How small?"

"About the size of a West Highland terrier," I said with a nervous glance toward the now silent vestibule.

"Oh, nothing, I shouldn't think," said my mother. "Might get a bit sleepy. I sometimes give the dogs Nytol if I have to take them up to Scotland in the car. They don't mind. I expect they feel as if they've been smoking dope. Probably gives them lovely dreams!"

"Mummy!" I said, scandalized. "You drug the dogs?"

There was a movement in the hall, and I heard Jonathan's voice coming nearer. ". . . I'd like the table in the corner? Yes, if you don't mind . . . and can you make sure that . . ." His voice faded discreetly as he walked away.

"It's all homeopathic," insisted Mummy. "No worse than feeding them tea and biscuits, like Mrs. Bleasdale does."

"So it should be fine?" I repeated. "To be absolutely sure?"

"Don't see why not," she said. "Just don't get him addicted. Valley of the Dogs and all that."

Relief flooded through my system, followed by awful guilt.

"Thanks," I said, then heard Jonathan wind up his conversation. "Look, I'll speak to you later, Mummy. But thank you."

I hung up and scuttled back into the kitchen. I opened the door to the vestibule and found Braveheart there, still chuntering to himself but in a more docile fashion. To test Mummy's theory out, I took my life into my hands and scooped him up.

He looked at me crossly, then settled himself in my arms like a baby and broke wind gently.

At this point Jonathan walked back in and practically did a double take.

"You're kidding me!" he said. "How in the name of God did you do that?"

"Oh, er, dog training tips from my mother," I mumbled.

"Really? Wow. You never cease to amaze me, Melissa," he marveled. "Is there anything you can't do?"

Braveheart managed to pull back one lip, exposing his teeth, and I knew I'd just stored up a whole lot of trouble for myself.

"Oh, um, I have many hidden talents," I said.

"Speaking of which," said Jonathan, taking Braveheart out of my arms. "I have an early table booked at the Rainbow Grill for seven, and I have this thing booked in with the walker at six. So why don't we put him in his basket and let him get a nap before Karen comes. I'm sure you could do with a nap too, after your flight?" he added, with a wink.

I nodded, not feeling very tired all of a sudden.

"In that case, why don't I show you to the master suite," said Jonathan, lifting my hair up so he could nuzzle the soft hollow of my neck, "and we can . . ."

He let his voice trail off seductively as he

kissed his way up to my ear, into which he murmured some rather outrageous things.

I dragged my guilty conscience away from the image of the dog walker hauling a semiconscious Braveheart round the park and instead let myself be led up to Jonathan's newly refurbished master bedroom.

Well, I say *led*. To be honest, I didn't take much leading.

NINE

My first night in New York was pretty fabulous, even by Jonathan's exacting standards of high living. He took me to a very smart restaurant right at the top of Rockefeller Center, where we ate lobster and drank champagne, looking out of the picture windows over the whole of Manhattan. As the dusk fell, the office windows glowed yellow, and the car taillights made red daisy chains along the straight streets beneath us.

"Happy?" said Jonathan, topping up my glass.

I could only nod. What with the gorgeous art deco building, and the incredible view, and the thoroughly adorable new shirt he was wearing that made me want to, well, get the name of his tailor at the very least, I'd run out of superlatives over the (divine) starter.

"Good," he said, twitching the corner of

his mouth into a smile. "That's all I need to hear."

On the way home in the taxi, I flaked out completely, and when my body clock jerked me awake again it was still dark, and I was lying in the crisp white sheets on Jonathan's huge bed, curled up inside the protective arc of his arms. He was holding me tightly in his sleep, and when I stretched out my leg, in case he was getting pins and needles, I felt his arms tighten around me, as if he didn't want me to go.

I lay awake for half an hour after that, just so I could enjoy how nice it felt.

By the time I woke properly, with warm rays of morning sunshine spilling through the slatted shutters, Jonathan was already out of bed and, from the sound of it, making breakfast. Not wanting to miss him before he left for work, I showered in a rush, pulled on his shirt from the previous night, made some emergency adjustments to my face, and went downstairs.

He was at the table, fully dressed, eating breakfast and frowning over some documents, but when I walked in, he looked up from his work, and a sweet beam of pleasure spread over his face.

"Well, good morning!" he said. "I was going to let you sleep in, let you catch up on your beauty sleep. Not that you need it."

I slid my arms around him from behind, resting my cheek against his. "Plenty of time to catch up tonight," I said. "I'm looking forward to one of those authentically ethnic takeaways that are so much better than London's, and an early night?" I kissed his ear. "Very early. About ten minutes after you get in from work, in fact."

"Ah," said Jonathan, reaching past the granola for his Blackberry. "I did tell you about Bonnie and Kurt, didn't I? Their Welcome Back party?"

I racked my brains. He *had* mentioned something about having drinks with Bonnie and Kurt, but then I'd had a lot to organize in the past few weeks. My heart sank as I caught sight of a formal invitation card on the windowsill. "I don't think you said *when,* exactly . . ."

Jonathan wagged his Blackberry at me. "I'll have to get you one of these if you're going to be a real New Yorker."

"But I thought you had a proper diary!" I protested, temporarily distracted. "I gave you a Smythson's diary for Christmas!"

"That's special," he said quickly. "For . . . backup. You can't synch paper. Anyway, don't look so shocked. We really don't have

208

to stay long. But they're so keen to see you again and welcome me back . . ."

I swallowed and battled down my rising panic. Bonnie and Kurt were nice people. They'd obviously gone to a lot of trouble. And even if it *was* Cindy's home turf, I was going to be there with Jonathan.

"Look, we can leave by ten. I can get the dog-sitter to call with a crisis we have to rush home for. Bonnie's met Braveheart — she knows he's gone through three walkers already."

I opened my mouth to protest, and a terribly unattractive whole-face yawn came out. I stifled it as best I could, but Jonathan immediately looked cross with himself. "Oh, you're exhausted. I guess I do so much traveling back and forth that I forget how much it takes out of you. I'm so sorry, honey. Listen, how about I call Bonnie and —"

"No, I'm fine. And I'm looking forward to it," I insisted. "It'll be lovely to see them again. Um . . . What time are you going to be home tonight? Because I don't really know what to wear, and I could do with your expert opinion."

"I really can't say till I get to work. I've got a busy day. But, sweetie, whatever you wear, you'll look like a million dollars." He smiled. "You always do."

"But everything I've brought with me is . . ." I trailed off. I didn't want to tell Jonathan that all my Honey clothes, the ones that made me look curvaceous and bombshell-y, required the sort of underpinnings that could stop bullets. I'd die of heat exhaustion within half an hour, and swooning into the canapés was a pretty drastic way of breaking the ice.

A deranged yapping at the door prevented me from explaining this to Jonathan. The yapping soon turned into dull thuds, suggesting that Braveheart was hurling himself against the glass like a football hooligan.

"Can you deal with Braveheart?" sighed Jonathan, finishing up his coffee and sliding his briefcase off the table. "I can't. You seem to have a knack with him."

I swallowed guiltily. Braveheart needed a dog psychiatrist, not a trainer, and I didn't have enough melatonin tablets to drug him for my entire stay, even if I wanted to. But Jonathan was beaming at me like there was nothing I couldn't do. "I'll try," I said weakly.

"That's my girl," beamed Jonathan. "I love that about you, Melissa. You're a can-do sort of woman. None of this 'We'll have to hire a dog behavior specialist' nonsense."

I smiled bravely and made a mental note to call my mother for dog tips. Ones that didn't involve turning them into junkies.

"Anyway," he went on, making his way to the front door, "please don't get uptight about this evening. It's just a very small informal party. You'll be among friends — Kurt and Bonnie already love you." He paused, then had an idea. "Hey, do what I do — go to Barneys and get one of their shoppers to pick something out for you."

"I could do that," I said slowly, thinking of the air-conditioning. And the sales. Maybe they'd have some magic American underwear that could suck in my stomach without giving me internal hemorrhaging.

"Look, whatever you wear, you'll still be the most beautiful girl there," said Jonathan seriously. "Don't forget that."

I blushed. "Oh, stop it."

"I mean it." Jonathan reached into his pocket for his wallet, picked out a card, and chucked it across the table. "But treat yourself — go to Barneys and charge it. Call it my welcome-to-New-York treat. Okay?"

"Thank you," I said. "I'll get something special."

"Nothing off the sale racks," said Jonathan sternly, then the thudding and howling started up again.

"I'll deal with that," I assured him.

"We'll be home by ten, I promise you," he said. "I have no intention of sharing you beyond then."

As soon as I kissed Jonathan good-bye on the front step, however, the howling and thudding stepped up a level.

Steeling myself, I went over to the utility room door.

"Braveheart!" I cooed in my best cajoling tone. I didn't want him running riot while he was in this frenzy. "Calm down. Calm down, and we'll have some lovely breakfast!"

In response, the yapping turned more outraged.

"Please?" I tried opening the door a notch, in case the fury was being caused by his imprisonment. I'd only edged the door open a tiny crack when the powerful force of a small dog shoved it, and me, out of the way.

His center of gravity was lower than mine, and my feet slipped out from under me as he shot past. I landed squarely on my backside, so hard that the glasses rattled in the dishwasher. After years of hockey I was used to falling over, but even so, I felt strangely embarrassed, as if Cindy herself had trained her dog to humiliate Jonathan's girlfriends.

When I turned round, Braveheart was sitting on the kitchen table, his tongue out, quite obviously laughing at me.

"Fine," I said in a cheerful, but firm, tone. My mother used to say it was all about tone with dogs, not words. "If that's the way you want to play it. I'm going to take you for a walk so long that you'll be too exhausted to mess around with me, you snotty little yap-dog. Let's see who's got longer legs then, eh?"

I might be perspiring from places I didn't even know had perspiraton glands, but I still had my pride. I wasn't going to let a dog that size get the better of me.

A quick call to Mummy revealed the magic secret of food bribes and firm looks, a tactic she assured me could be used on small dogs, medium dogs, large dogs, and all husbands.

To my surprise, it worked. Once I'd lured Braveheart onto his leash by shameless use of cold roast chicken breast, combined with a surprise attack-lunge learned from years of self-waxing, we set off down Jane Street.

Even though it wasn't yet nine, the air was already thick with heat, and I was grateful for the shade offered by the trees that lined the street. Really, I thought, admiring all the pretty shutters and brownstones stoops, you'd hardly imagine you were in New York at all, walking around here. It felt more like Bloomsbury, but with much nicer cafés.

Braveheart, despite his twice-daily dog-walker sessions, wasn't as submissive as I'd have liked on the leash, and it quickly turned into a battle of wills. Embarrassingly so, given how small he was. Every time we passed another dog and owner, he'd snarl and carry on as if he were some kind of Irish wolfhound. But at least apologizing to the various other dog walkers meant I could tell Jonathan I'd already chatted with to some locals.

An hour later, at home, as per Cindy's laminated instructions, I put Braveheart back in his box at home with some food and MooMoo, a disgustingly slobbered toy cow, and walked up to Barneys with Jonathan's card burning a hole in my purse. It was a bit of a trek, but the ever-changing display of shops took my mind off the distance I was covering. Plus, every calorie counted, when it came to the sort of clothes I knew I'd have to squeeze into.

I explained to the charming personal shopper, through the door of the enormous changing room, that I needed some under-wear that would reshape my body in the manner of plastic surgery and yet remain invisible beneath sheer clothing. Instead of laughing in my face and suggesting liposuction, Hanna (we were on very friendly terms immediately) nodded seriously, went off, and came back with an armful of what looked like skin graft. Then another armful of slinky cocktail dresses, and every five minutes, another three pairs of shoes.

Amazingly, within an hour, I had not only a whole new outfit but also a whole new body underneath.

I looked at myself in the flattering mirror. Even if I was jittery on the inside, on the outside I looked like I'd bought a confident new personality along with the skyscraper sandals. Hanna had found me a simple but beautifully fitted linen dress, which made my waist appear tiny but didn't, as was usually the case, make my hips look vast in comparison. It was a luxurious shade of violet that brought out my eyes, and she'd teamed it with a vintage-style cashmere wrap "for inside." What with the Jimmy Choos and my hastily inserted contact lenses, I was one hair appointment away from looking exactly like Catherine Zeta Jones.

"Don't try anything else on," said Hanna, shaking her head at me firmly. "You will *never* find a more amazing look. I *refuse* to bring you any more clothes." She tipped her head to one side. "Now, have you got a blow-out booked? No? Let me get you a number."

"I'll take it all," I said and handed over Jonathan's charge card.

Kurt and Bonnie lived in an apartment on the Upper East Side. New York isn't like London, where the street names give you a clue to an area's flavor — the more upmarket the Manhattan address, I was discovering, the more discreetly numerical it was.

"You really didn't need to go to this much effort, sweetie," said Jonathan, for about the billionth time, as we headed up Madison Avenue in a Lincoln town car.

"Oh, I didn't!" I insisted, shifting nervously in my seat so as not to wrinkle my dress. I'd spent longer getting ready for this party than I'd done for any event since Allegra's twenty-first birthday party, where we all had to dress up as eighteenth-century aristocrats with powdered wigs.

Jonathan, of course, was looking effortlessly chic in a fresh shirt and linen summer suit. He had the kind of expensive style that transcended meteorological intervention.

"Tell me again who'll be there," I asked, preparing my mental Rolodex.

"Bonnie and Kurt, whom you know already," he replied patiently, "Paige, who was at college with Cindy, David and Peter, who are realtors, Bradley, who's a friend from Princeton . . ."

"House!" I said excitedly.

"I'm sorry?"

"House! Isn't that where *House* is set? Princeton?"

"Are all your cultural references TV-based?" Jonathan's mouth screwed up wryly. "Well, yes. It's also one of the finest universities in the United States."

"Oh, yes, yes, absolutely," I said, but to be honest, since I saw the Princeton-Plainsboro Teaching Hospital on a more regular basis than my own local clinic, this fact was more significant.

"I went to Princeton," Jonathan reminded me, since I'd forgotten to comment. "And so did Bradley and Kurt, and a few others whom I think Bonnie will have invited. But don't mention any of that to anyone else there, because I think Bonnie went to Harvard, and it's rude to rub her nose in it."

I made yet another mental note.

When we arrived, a liveried doorman opened the door of our car for us and directed us under the long canopy into the apartment building. Jonathan announced us at the desk to another doorman, then we were allowed up in the stately elevator to the Hegels' apartment, where, finally, the door was opened by a man in a caterer's uniform.

Bonnie and Kurt were standing just inside the door, chatting animatedly while jazz music burbled in the background. Since they both waved their hands around to illustrate their points, it looked as if they were simultaneously signing the conversation for the deaf.

"Bonnie, Kurt," said Jonathan, shaking Kurt's hand and leaning forward to deposit a kiss on Bonnie's cheek.

"Hello!" shrieked Bonnie, throwing her hands in the air, then clasping me to her bony bosom. My upper chest was pressed up hard against a splendid blown-glass necklace. "So good to see you! But look at *you!* You dyed your beautiful hair!"

Kurt peered at me, his bald spot glinting in the soft lights. "You dyed your hair. Why did you do that, Honey? It was exquisite. Wasn't it exquisite, Bonnie? Didn't we say that you really did look exactly like a young Brigitte Bardot with that beautiful hair?"

I looked anxiously at Jonathan, who simply smiled and put his hand round my waist.

"I think she looks exquisite however she

wears her hair. And, ah, guys, I'd prefer it if you introduced Melissa as Melissa this evening, not Honey."

Bonnie tipped her head. "Don't tell me. Honey is your *special* name, right?"

"Exactly," I said, not wanting Jonathan to do all the talking for me. "I won't tell you what I call Jonathan."

Bonnie let out a cascade of tinkly laughter. "Oh, you are so funny! Let me get you a drink."

She waved at a waitress who was circulating with a loaded tray, then handed Jonathan a glass of white wine. "Chablis for Jonathan, as always, but what about you, *Melissa?*"

I looked sideways at Jonathan, who was already being dragged off in conversation by two other men, both clapping him enthusiastically on the back. "Welcome *back!*" one roared. "How're your *teeth* after a year in London, fella? Still there?"

Jonathan smiled broadly. "As you can see! It's great to see you, Kyle. Let me introduce you . . . Melissa, this is Kyle Barton, and this is Andy Petersen, both old friends from college. Guys, this is Melissa Romney-Jones." He paused. "My girlfriend."

The warmth in his voice when he said that made me forget my nerves temporarily.

"Hi, Melissa!" Kyle's large hand engulfed mine and pumped it up and down. "Great to meet you!"

"Thank you," I said, trying to imprint the names into my head.

"Kyle, I'm just going to say hi to some people here, and I'll be right over to you, okay?" said Jonathan. "Then we can catch up properly."

"Sure," said Andy and lifted his own glass to me. "Look forward to seeing you soon."

Jonathan gave me a happy little wink and turned back to Bonnie, who was looking approvingly at my new dress. "So, Bonnie. I hope you've got lots of great people for Melissa to meet."

"Everyone wants to meet Melissa!" replied Bonnie, offering me a glass of champagne. "I couldn't fit them all in. I've had to arrange lunch next week for a few girls who couldn't make it tonight . . ."

Argh. Did that include Cindy?

"You don't mind, do you?" asked Kurt solicitously. "I did tell Bonnie that your schedule would be full. Didn't I tell you that? You can't just assume she'll be free. I bet Jonathan's got her booked into events all over town, hey, Jon? How long are you staying, in any case, Honey?"

"Melissa," hissed Bonnie.

"Forgive me, *Melissa,*" said Kurt. "You'll have to have Jonathan synch your Blackberry."

I looked up at Jonathan. He was beaming with delight and making "Hi!" facial expressions over Bonnie's head, as people clearly tried to catch his eye across the room. He looked down at me.

"I have plans for Melissa, yes," he said with a squeeze of my underpinnings, which I'm sure neither Kurt nor Bonnie saw. "But I think I can spare her for the occasional lunch — so long as you don't tell her the camping story."

"It's a date," I said at once. "I need to hear the camping story. And I'll check my Blackberry," I added. "Just as soon as Jonathan explains how one works."

"That's wonderful!" Bonnie looked delighted. "Now, let me see who I want to introduce you to first." She scanned the crowd of gleamingly coiffed heads and gesticulating hands, with the odd flash of sparkle as jewels caught the light. There must have been about fifty or sixty people, but the spacious room barely felt full. Like Jonathan's old apartment, it was all wood paneling and chandeliers, although it felt decidedly warmer, in atmosphere as well as temperature. "We're all old friends tonight," she went on, grabbing my hand and leading me off. "With some new faces, just to mix things up."

As we set off in her enthusiastic wake, Jonathan whispered, "Bonnie knows *everyone*. She sits on every committee going, so she'll introduce you to some great people. She's kind of like you in that respect."

"Wentworth!" exclaimed Bonnie, before I could respond. "Look who's back!"

A sturdy man whose shoulders spoke of many hours invested in team contact sports turned and, on seeing Jonathan, broke into a delighted smile. "Jon! Hey! Great to see you back!"

"Melissa, this is Wentworth Carson," Bonnie went on, as I extended my hand. "Wentworth, this is Melissa Romney-Jones, Jonathan's girlfriend."

If Wentworth mentally added the word "new" to that description, his face didn't show it. "Hello, Melissa," he said, shaking my hand. "Very pleased to meet you."

"Will you excuse me a moment?" asked Bonnie. "I think Kurt's started telling his fishing story again . . ." And she shimmered off.

"So you're back in town for good, then, Jon?" asked Wentworth. He turned to me and added, "We missed having him around this last year. I have to tell you that the softball was nothing short of an embarrassment without his magic pitching arm."

"Really?" I'd had no idea that Jonathan played softball, but it made sense. "Why didn't you say, darling? You could have asked Gabi to enter a London office team into the Hyde Park league."

Wentworth clicked his fingers and pointed at Jonathan. "The Kyrle & Pope International — I like that. Can we fix a date for next year?"

"Wentworth manages our Manhattan rentals," Jonathan explained, keeping an amused eye on Wentworth. "You think I'm competitive, you should spend a day with him."

I smiled, but I noticed Jonathan hadn't answered Wentworth's question about how long he'd be back for.

"Have you spent much time in the States, Melissa?" Wentworth asked me, and I shook my head.

"No, this is my first time. It's all so . . ."

I hesitated over the right word, while Jonathan and Wentworth gazed expectantly at me, national pride already written over their faces. I didn't want to risk upsetting them with understatement, but I didn't want to sound like a dim tourist, either.

"It's all so . . . familiar and unfamiliar at the same time!" I said. "I absolutely love New York. I can't wait to get to know it better."

Wentworth beamed at me. "Well, if we can lure you away from the bright lights one weekend, you two should come out to my country place in the Hamptons, right, Jon?"

"We'd love to," said Jonathan, and I nodded.

"Jonathan!" Kyle had appeared at Wentworth's shoulder. "Sorry to interrupt. You got a minute? We need you over here."

"Will you excuse us a moment, Melissa?" asked Jonathan. "One of the things I love about Melissa," he added to Wentworth, "is that she is the queen of party conversation. I've seen her charm traffic wardens out of giving her tickets."

Wentworth opened his eyes wide. "Hey. Now that'll make a difference after . . ."

"Won't be a moment," said Jonathan quickly. "Grab Bonnie and ask her to introduce you — she'd love to."

I nodded and watched him disappear into a crowd of tall men, who were all obviously thrilled to have him back.

Bonnie was nowhere in sight, but it's a rule of mine never to stand around on my own at parties. Standing around worked for

Emery, who was inevitably "rescued" by men who'd been eyeing her up all night, and it worked for Allegra, who usually commanded an audience, but if I stood around for longer than five minutes, people tended to ask me for refills. In my experience, if you smile in at least one direction, someone will come over without you having to crash a conversation, even if it is under the impression that you're remembering a meeting they've forgotten.

As I was beaming unspecifically around the room, however, my attention was drawn to a conversation happening just behind me, in the corner.

I say "conversation." It was more a desperate attempt by one woman to extract more than two words from a remarkably sullen man.

He was wearing head-to-toe black, accessorized with dark shades, despite the fact that we were indoors, and an absolutely foul scowl. While the poor woman was trying to chat, he was shoving mini Cumberland sausage rings into his mouth as if he were in a timed eating competition, then using the cocktail sticks to pick gristle from between his teeth. From where I was standing, it was like watching a human cement mixer.

"So you're British!" she was saying.

The man grunted, and I inched closer to eavesdrop.

"Wow!" she said desperately. "I'd love to spend time there. Such a great country!"

"You reckon?"

"Oh, yeah . . . I mean, Tony Blair! I'm a big supporter of . . . his fair trade commitments!"

Crikey, I thought. She must really be scraping the bottom of the conversational barrel if she's onto Tony Blair already.

The man paused in his systematic consumption of the eats table. "He's an effing idiot."

The lady took a step back. "Oh, really? You think so?"

I narrowed my eyes. I might be very, very wrong, but this beast seemed oddly familiar. Something about the "effing" — it bespoke a certain type of Englishness; one I came into contact with pretty much every day.

And there was something else. Something I recognized from somewhere . . . My mental Rolodex flipped wildly. Was he an old client? Someone I was at school with?

"And that gobby hag of a wife!" Even with his shades on, I could tell he was rolling his eyes.

"Cherie? Oh, but she's a great role model

for professional women! Don't you agree?"

"Are you *insane?* Do you not have *eyes?*" he enquired. "What is *wrong* with this country?"

Now, I was no big fan of Cherie Blair, but if this was meant to be a Welcome to New York party for me as well as Jonathan, I simply couldn't stand by and let this buffoon do such an appalling ambassadorial job for the motherland.

As I took a step forward and prepared to launch myself into the conversation, to my horror, I heard him say, with a distinct nod toward her chest, "So, are those real then?"

"Pardon me?" she enquired.

"The girls there." He nodded, as if he were genuinely interested, rather than trying to come on to her. "Are they real?"

Silently, she clapped her hand to her cleavage. "I don't . . ."

That was the final straw. I couldn't stop myself.

"Pearls!" I said, intervening briskly. "Ah ha ha! He means your necklace! It's, er, cockney rhyming slang! The girls . . . pearls!"

"But I'm not wearing any," she said coldly. "These are sapphires."

I took a closer look. Indeed they were. About three apartments' worth too. "Gosh, so they are! What a gorgeous necklace! No, it's, um, just one of those generic terms! Means all jewelry. The girls, you know — what you keep in your jewelry box."

There was a brief moment while we all digested this nugget of information, broken suddenly by a dirty snigger.

"As in . . . pearl necklace!"

I glared ferociously, and he quickly shut up.

"How interesting language is." She shot the rude man a haughty glare. "For a moment, I thought you were being offensive. Would you excuse me while I . . . freshen my drink?"

She said it in a tone that clearly meant *go somewhere far, far away from you, you charmless oaf.*

"You've still got half a glass of wine there," he pointed out.

She paused, looked at her glass, then looked back at him. "I think I need something stronger." She flashed me a cold smile. "Excuse me."

I stepped aside to let her past and realized that I'd managed to leave myself trapped with him. And now he was peering at me, as if *he* recognized *me* from somewhere.

My mind whirred, trying to work out why this particular brute seemed so familiar — not easy when he was wearing sunglasses indoors. But that thick black hair, the consumptive complexion, the voice . . .

"Do I know you from somewhere?" he demanded, removing the sunglasses, and I knew at once who he was.

TEN

It was Godric Ponsonby.

Or, as he'd been universally called, when I'd known him for a few brief months in 1994, Oh-Godric.

A hot flush started in my forehead and spread rapidly down my body.

Oh-Godric and I had had a fleeting flirtation, and even more fleeting backstage tussle during the final night party of a school production of *A Midsummer Night's Dream*. My girls' school had had to borrow some men from the nearby boys' school, and Godric had been one of the few artistically inclined volunteers. I hadn't been acting, though — I'd been in charge of wardrobe, and pretty busy with it, too: the boys had constantly damaged their doublets and insisted on personal repair attention, usually while they'd still been wearing them. Godric had been the worst offender. He'd had a long list of fabric allergies too, and consequently, by the final night, we'd been on such intimate medical terms that snogging had been more or less inevitable.

I cringed at the memory. Even then, I hadn't been naive enough to believe I was Godric's first choice for drunken grappling. Emery, in the throes of her Goth Actress phase — she'd worn a lot of Rouge Noir nail polish and grown out her eyebrows — had been the star of the show and had had the male fairies following her around like geese. I suspected she'd given Godric the flick, and so, on the last night, he'd consoled himself with literally pints of punch and a quick roll around the props cupboard with me.

Actually, it would have been quite romantic if he hadn't had a "bad reaction" to the doctored punch, vomited all over Bottom's head, and broken out in hives. The matron had taken the night off, so I'd had to drive him to the local emergency ward, while he'd still been in his Marks & Spencer's opaque tights, still vomiting, and I'd never seen him again after that. Just as well, really, given what I knew about his, er, inside leg measurements.

Obviously he recognized me too, at exactly the same moment, and presumably suffered the same excruciating mental slideshow.

I wondered if he'd be discreet enough to pretend we hadn't even met so we could start again. After all, one doesn't like to start reminiscing about love bites and curaçao vomit at a smart Manhattan cocktail party.

"Melissa?" he said, peering at me, then dropping his line of sight a bit lower. "Melons?"

I ignored the Melons bit. Fine. There was no getting out of it. "It is!" I said. "Hello!"

"You don't remember me, do you?" The mixture of grumpiness and chronic shyness hadn't changed much in ten years. At least I knew he hadn't deliberately been rude to that woman. Godric never had had much in the way of social confidence. From my sewing chair in the wings, I'd noted that the other thesps had affected gloomy self-doubt, but with him it seemed painfully real.

Still, that didn't excuse much *now*. Good heavens above, no.

"Of course I do!" I protested. "It's Godric. Godric Ponsonby!" For a second, I moved forward to kiss him on the cheek, then thought better of it and put my hand out to shake instead. "What are you doing in New York? Do you know Bonnie and Kurt?"

"Who?"

"The hosts?" I raised my eyebrows in

Bonnie's direction, but she'd vanished into the throng again. "Um, well, do you know Jonathan then? Jonathan Riley? The party's in his honor."

"Who?" he grunted. "No. I don't know any of these tossers. Didn't even want to come. It's a crap party."

"Yes, you do! You know Jonathan," interrupted a small, dark woman, who'd appeared from nowhere. "*Jonathan* found you that awesome loft in Tribeca! Hi!" she said, grabbing his arm and looking up at me intently. "Paige Drogan."

"Hello," I said. "I'm —"

"No, *I* should do the introduction," scowled Godric. "Weren't you taught any manners? Paige, this is Melissa Romney-Jones, Melissa, this is Paige Drogan. She's my agent. Don't suppose you've got a job, have you, Mel?"

But I was still gawking from the previous revelation to rise to that. "Your *agent?*"

"Yeah, 'm an actor," he muttered.

"No!" I gasped. "A real one?"

Paige laughed prettily and smoothed back her short, coffee-colored hair. She was wearing a tortoiseshell-print wrap dress that emphasized her pepperpot curves, finished off with bright yellow shoes and a pair of black winged librarian glasses that frankly gave me serious spec envy. She reminded me of a wren.

"He's being very modest," she chuckled. "Ric's about to be huge over here. He's starring in a very significant film, which opens in a few months and is going to really launch him to the next level, but he already has a market presence with some very well-received television work. You may have seen him in *Grey's Anatomy*?"

I shook my head. "Um, we're rather behind you, I think."

"And he's working on some stage projects, aren't you, Ric?" She nudged him. "Ric?"

He nodded sullenly.

Paige put a little cupped hand to her ear and tilted her head to one side, birdlike. "I can't hear you, Ric, this party's awful loud. What was that?"

"I'm in *The Real Inspector Hound,*" he mumbled offendedly, as if she'd demanded to know his bowel movements. "It's not a very good production, and the director doesn't know what he's talking about, but, you know . . . at least it's proper theater. Not like wasting time with those film wankers who —"

"Ha ha ha!" laughed Paige in a transparent attempt to drown him out. "Ha ha ha! Ric, honey, can you go and get me and

234

Melissa drinks, please?"

"She's got a drink," he pointed out.

"Well, I'm sure she'd like another," said Paige firmly.

"Ungh," grunted Ric. It was a sound I heard about nine times a day on average — a combination of resentment and resignation — and he sloped off in the direction of the waiters.

"I saw what you did there," said Paige. "With Lucy Powell? Thank you for that. Ric's a sweetheart, but he's kind of unpolished!"

"Yeeeees," I said, wondering if unpolished was an American euphemism for barely socialized.

"So . . . anyway, let's talk about you — you're the famous Melissa!" She beamed at me with a scary intensity.

The famous Melissa?

I suddenly felt lanky and un-put-together, my new outfit, perfect hair, and bargain $15 manicure notwithstanding.

"Well, I'm not sure about the famous bit," I faltered.

She tipped her head to one side. "Ah, I've got my ear to the ground," she said. "I'm Paige with an *i*. I was at Brown with Cindy, but Jonathan and I go *way* back too. Like Ric said, I'm an agent. For actors."

"How interesting," I said, ignoring the flicker of panic that ran through me at the mention of Cindy's name. I really had to knock that on the head. It wasn't like she was *here.* "Anyone I know?"

Paige reeled off a list of clients, some of whom sounded vaguely familiar. "So. You and Jonathan, huh?"

What did that mean? I didn't know what to say, so I just smiled and nodded.

"So you're English?"

"Absolutely," I agreed, relieved to be on safe ground. "Many generations."

"Married before?"

"Um, no."

"Kids?"

"No!"

"Cool. Okay, I'm building up a picture here. What is it you do?"

I was starting to feel slightly interviewed. "I run a . . . a life management consultancy," I said defensively.

The upside of New York was that no one raised their eyebrows and snorted at this, as they would have done in London. Paige actually looked impressed. Though that may have just been a holding expression until she worked out what it was that I did.

"Really? Whereabouts?"

"In London? Victoria?"

She gave me a "more information?" look.

"Near Buckingham Palace?" I hazarded, economizing somewhat on the truth, I must admit. Well, my office *was* near Buckingham Palace. Compared to, say, its proximity to Brent Cross Shopping Center.

"Right," she said, arching her perfect brows above the frames of her spectacles. "And what type of client relationship is your specialty? I mean," she added before I could reply, "please God tell me you're not one of those terrible women who play with color swatches and tell men to floss!"

And she laughed one of those blood-chilling power laughs. The sort with no humor involved whatsoever, the sort that gives you a conversational deadline: Prove me wrong by the time this laugh dies away.

The temperature seemed to ramp up a couple of degrees at this point, despite the air-conditioning, and beads of sweat began to pool in the cups of my Lycra skin-graft bra. Suddenly, I felt as if I was at some kind of large-scale interview, where the whole panel was Jonathan's friends. And they knew a lot more about the job I was applying for than I did.

To my horror, even as I was wishing I could click my heels and be back in Nelson's comfy sitting room, I felt a familiar tingle up my backbone as my whole posture started to shift. My hips went slightly forward, pushing out my ample bosom, shrinking my waist and lengthening my back.

Honey. I dragged Honey's personality in front of mine like a riot shield. Even though there was already a little voice in my head telling me it probably wasn't a good idea.

"Actually, I run a life coaching agency," I said breezily. "I work with a variety of clients, mostly male, from a broad social spectrum."

Paige nodded more slowly but didn't look totally convinced, so I found myself plowing onward.

"It's terribly old fashioned, in some senses, but I find simply harnessing some of the more traditional aspects of etiquette is really rather empowering for many men." I smiled. "Providing them with social parameters from which they can build their own relationship bridges, on a professional as well as social level. And through positive role reinforcement from a feminine perspective, I'm able to encourage them to project and visualize an idealized version of their own persona, and guide them toward attainable targets."

Paige was nodding hard now. "Uh-huh. I

can see that, the way you handled that moment there with Ric. It was pretty slick. And you're doing that over here?"

"I'm on holiday right now," I hedged. Honestly, my heart was beating so fast. Where did all this stuff come from?

"But you could do your coaching work here, yes?"

By now, Jonathan was on the other side of the room, apparently deep in an anecdote with a couple of tall women and a priest. "Well, I don't see why not," I said, more to sound professional than anything else. "I'm sure American men have their own sets of hang-ups."

"Oh my God, yes." She nodded frantically. "And therapy isn't always the answer."

"Well, quite," I said, as if I didn't think therapy was a license to moan. "One can't blame one's mother for everything."

Paige threw her head back and cackled. Then she snapped it back to fix me with a fierce look. "Listen, Melissa, I could use your help."

My heart sank. The last thing I needed was to get involved in someone else's relationship. Especially someone who knew Jonathan. "Oh, honestly, Paige, I don't really know much about American men and —"

"It's not an American man," she said. "Can we meet for a coffee this week? I'd really love to talk with you."

I made demurring noises, casting my gaze around to see if Jonathan had moved into hearing distance. "Well . . . I am meant to be on holiday, and Jonathan isn't . . ."

She intensified her gaze until I could almost feel it on my face. At the same time I felt my will to resist evaporate.

How did she do that? I wondered. What an amazing trick. If she could teach me how to do that, I could have Braveheart eating out of my hand in seconds.

"Well, okay," I conceded.

Paige smiled.

That Sphinx-like smile was worth learning too, I thought, dazed. It just made you wonder what you hadn't noticed.

Fortunately Godric chose this moment to reappear, with four glasses of wine squashed in his hands, as if he was schlepping drinks from the bar at the White Horse.

Paige rolled her eyes. "Ric! I keep telling you. Just ask the waiter to bring you what you want! You don't have to carry them across the room like that! You're not a server!"

"Shut up," said Godric.

Not really wanting to get embroiled in

further conversation with either of them, I started to move backward in my patented party extrication method — inch away until you make sufficient corridor for other people to pass between you, wave hopelessly as if being swept out to sea, then leg it.

"Call me!" mouthed Paige.

I nodded in a way which I hoped conveyed yes, but within no definite time frame.

While I was still backing away, I managed to bump into someone, and when I spun round to apologize, I found myself standing nearly nose to nose with a statuesque blond woman with magically unsupported breasts and the most gorgeous smile I'd ever seen outside the beauty pages of *Vogue.*

"Oops! Hi!" she said, extending a beautifully manicured hand. "Jennifer Reardon. I'm a colleague of Bonnie's. And a friend too, of course!"

"Hello," I replied, fixing her name in my head. Jennifer. Breasts. Diamond hoops. "I'm Melissa. Melissa —"

But she interrupted me before I could finish my introduction. "Are you *British?*"

"Yes," I said. "I am. I'm . . ."

"Oh my God, I was *right!*" she said, clapping her hand to her chest. "My instincts are so good for these things? I saw you talking to Ric Spencer over there, so I figured

241

you must be the writer Bonnie was telling me about. The column in the London *Times,* right? Hi, I am so pleased to meet you! Now, call me nosy, but have you got any inside stuff on this new girlfriend of Jonathan's?" she went on, with a giggle. "I've been out of town for a while so I'm a little behind on the gossip. He's been really tight-lipped about her — which makes you wonder, huh?"

I opened my mouth to put her straight, but she didn't give me a chance to speak.

"She's British too, right?" she demanded gleefully. "I was at Cindy's for dinner earlier this week — you know his ex-wife? She might come along later, actually, if she has time — and she was telling me she heard he was dating this blond girl called Honey or Happy or something like that. Totally too young for him, and soooo rebound! I mean, it's an understandable reaction, after breaking up with your wife of all those years, but, eek!"

Jennifer pulled a face, then touched my forearm in an "oh, we're so awful, aren't we?" gesture. My stomach shrank. I knew I should say something before she dug herself any deeper, but my throat had suddenly gone tight with horror.

"And Cindy totally thinks it's because he's

242

cut up about her and Brendan, but listen, who wouldn't be? It's a terrible, terrible situation, but sometimes you've got to go with Fate, know what I mean? Their baby is the cutest, cutest thing. Parker? Isn't that an adorable name? I could eat him up! Not literally! A ha ha ha! He so has Cindy's eyes. Anyway, I must catch up with Jon in a minute because I need to give him a message from Cindy. Do you know if he's brought rebound girl along tonight?" She craned her neck around to see past my stunned face. "I don't see any teenage blonds in here. I guess she'd stand out, right?"

Jennifer was rattling on at about ninety miles an hour, and so probably didn't notice the silence falling around us. I've been there myself — you're so busy dishing out the gossip that you can't hear anything but your own voice. But since I hadn't spoken for what felt like an hour, to me the shocked hush was all too apparent.

So much for people claiming never to eavesdrop at parties.

"You know her, huh?" she said, seeing my crestfallen expression. "Oh, nuts. Have I put my foot in it?"

"Melissa," said Bonnie unwittingly, bowling up behind me with a tray full of food. "I had to show you these myself — aren't they darling? Jonathan's had three already." And she shoved a plate of miniature Yorkshire puddings filled with shavings of roast beef and wisps of horseradish under my nose.

She looked up when I didn't speak. Neither did the seven people immediately around us. I felt sick.

"Oh, now don't tell me you're low-carbing!" said Bonnie, taking my silence the wrong way. "Jonathan loves you just the way you are! He told me so! He says one of the things he loves best about dating you is that he can always order a starter and a dessert without feeling bad!"

I could almost hear the penny drop in Jennifer's head. It probably didn't hit much on the way down. A ghastly recognition slid over her face, and her eyes went glassy with embarrassment.

If I'd been Honey, or even Gabi, I might have made a scene and stalked out, but this wasn't my party or even Jennifer's. It was Bonnie's, and she'd gone to a lot of effort. I wasn't going to let someone else spoil it and make a show of myself in the bargain. I'd show them how well-brought-up British girls could rise above sticky moments. Even if we did want to sprint, sobbing, from the room.

"Oh, I can't stand women who go out for dinner and never eat! What on earth's the point?" I said, taking a Yorkshire pudding and racking my brains for the most outrageously untrue thing I could think of to break the crashingly awkward silence. "Now, tell me, is it true that all shopping is free for tourists on Sundays? I'm sure I read it somewhere."

At once, about seven different voices joined in with sympathetic denials and then suggestions for outlets that had such terrific values that it might as well be free.

Jennifer melted into the background, mumbling something about having a top-secret sample sale leaflet in her bag somewhere.

I managed to keep the tears that were rising in my throat at bay by frantically nodding my head and raising my eyebrows, hoping fervently that Jonathan hadn't overheard. I couldn't see him anywhere. I mean, it was very flattering that he was so confident about my social skills that he could just leave me to meet people, but it wasn't like this was your run-of-the-mill drinks party . . .

And then I felt a familiar hand in the small of my back and a sudden warm breath on my neck. Relief swept over me.

"Sorry, but I couldn't leave you alone a minute longer," murmured Jonathan in my ear. "I've been studying your rear view for ten minutes now, and I don't see why these people should have the monopoly on the front." Then, as I went pink, he put his arm around my waist and said in pretend formal tones, "Hello, I'm Jonathan, Melissa's boyfriend. Has she mentioned me? Oh, dear. Apparently not. Sorry, Anthony, you've been wasting your time — she's taken."

Everyone laughed, and Jonathan launched into the story of how I'd tamed the evil Braveheart in the time it had taken him to confirm a restaurant booking. "Just by using her accent!" he marveled. "I'm telling you, Melissa is an organizational miracle worker."

The lady standing next to Anthony (Was her name Blythe?) touched me on the arm and said, "Melissa, any time you want to come over to my house and organize our Weimaraner, you are more than welcome. Please."

Feeling slightly fraudulent, I accepted everyone's amazed congratulations, then made an excuse about getting a pen and paper to write down those sample sale details. On my way out, I had a quick glass of champagne to revive myself, then — since no one was looking — another.

My heart was still hammering, and not in a good way, as I splashed water on my wrists in the marble-lined bathroom. I reapplied my lipstick slowly in the huge gilt mirror and wondered forlornly if Honey would have handled the situation better. I always seemed to come out with better repartee when I was wearing that wig.

I pushed the thought away with a stern hand and smoothed my flicked-up brown 'do. I didn't need the wig to be polite. Manners, that was all I needed. Besides, Jonathan chose Melissa, not Honey. Of course his friends would be suspicious of any new girlfriend — it was only natural. And Bonnie and Kurt had been so kind and welcoming, and other people had been friendly. Even Jennifer, right up until . . .

But had they only been nice to me because he'd been standing there by my side? Jennifer's words seared across my brain. Was that what they were *thinking* — that I was just some rebound bimbo Jonathan was dating while he was still grieving over Cindy?

God. How I wished Nelson were here to give me a boot, or Gabi. I opened my bag and took out my mobile phone, then resolutely put it back. Gabi would be in bed right now, and Nelson would be . . . well, I wasn't going to phone Nelson at the very first inkling of trouble.

I took a deep breath. *You'll just have to show them how suitable you really are,* I told myself. Then I turned on my heel and strode back down the parqueted corridor, Mummy's dog training tips at the ready.

As promised, Jonathan swept me off at ten o'clock, and we left to promises of lunch dates, and drinks with Bonnie and the girls, and requests for advice on everything from neurotic dogs to clever birthday gifts for godsons. I think Jennifer must have either snuck off or hidden in the loo for the rest of the evening, because I didn't see her again.

"You were such a hit!" Jonathan squeezed my knee in the cab. "Bonnie was raving about how you were even nicer than she remembered, and how marvelous it was that you just circulated and talked to everyone."

"Isn't that what you're meant to do at parties?" I asked. I didn't want him to guess how much effort it had taken after Jennifer's bombshell. "Talk to people?"

Jonathan pulled a face. "Well, no. *Some people* like to get conversation buzzing by telling the hostess she needs to lose ten pounds, then pulling her outfit to pieces."

It had been bad enough having Cindy's presence hanging over me at the party, but I wasn't having her in the cab with us afterward. "They were terribly nice people," I said firmly. "Especially Bonnie and Kurt. It was kind of them to make me feel so . . ." Again, I hesitated over the right word. ". . . amongst friends."

Jonathan suddenly looked serious. "Listen, Bonnie told me about Jennifer's stupid remarks. I'm so sorry. You were very dignified, and she's grateful to you for not taking offense. If I'd been there . . ."

"Oh, that." He *did* know. "Well, I just did what any well-brought-up person would do."

"Well, Bonnie was mortified. She's going to speak with Jennifer. Set her straight. Jen's always had a big mouth."

"Well, at least she knows I'm not a blond bimbo now," I joked weakly. "Although it was flattering that the rumor-mill thought I was some teenage nymphet."

"Melissa." Jonathan put his finger on my chin and turned my head so he could look me in the eye. "Bonnie's going to tell her that I think you're the best thing that's ever happened to me. Blond, brunette or redhead. And she happens to agree."

"Oh," I said, looking down at my lap. My

insides glowed with delight to hear him say that, but — well, the whole evening had been somewhat overwhelming. "I'll bear that in mind. Anyway," I added, to change the subject, "apart from that, I had a lovely evening! I met some very interesting people. Like your friend, Paige? The actor's agent?"

"Paige? I didn't see her."

"Yes," I went on. "She was there with one of her clients, actually, an English chap. It was like being back at home for a moment, watching him pick his teeth and insult the guests."

Jonathan's face darkened, and abruptly I sensed I was on thin ice. "Honey, what exactly did you tell Paige about your job?"

"I told her I was a life coach. Of sorts. I'm not daft, Jonathan," I said lightly. "I didn't tell her anything that might, you know, be *embarrassing* to you, if that's what you're worried about. I'd never do that!"

Jonathan seemed to be summoning up superhuman levels of tact. "Darling, I'm very proud of what you do. I mean, yes, *obviously,* I don't think the circumstances of our meeting would . . . play so well, taken out of context, and while in years to come it'll make a great story, I just don't think, for now, it needs to, you know . . ."

Get back to Cindy, I thought, but I said

nothing.

". . . be discussed at parties," he finished. "You know how these things get embroidered. Plus," he added, with more of a smile, "this is meant to be a break for you! A vacation from work. Us time!" He took my hand in his. "You let Paige Drogan know how good you are at fixing up idiot men and she'll have you working twenty-four-seven for her client list. And you don't want that, believe me. I mean, don't tell me she didn't hint at it?"

"Um, not exactly." I didn't think it was the best time to mention the fact that Paige *had* asked me to call her. "Anyway, she mentioned that you'd already done a favor for this chap. Ric? You remember?"

Jonathan groaned. "Do I? Yeah, slightly. Paige made me spend an interminable day with that . . . that . . ."

"Oik?"

He clicked his fingers and pointed at me. "Good word. Oik. Jesus. I mean, sure, the guy can act but . . . euch. I don't know if he means to be rude, but I've never come so close to punching someone." His expression softened. "I only put up with him because he was from London and he kind of reminded me of you."

"Well, I'm touched. Funnily enough, I do

251

know him, vaguely," I admitted.

"Not a client? Please God."

"Do you *mind?*" I said. "You think I'd release something like that back into the community? He'd hardly be an advert for the agency. No, Godric and I . . . met briefly at school."

"Godric?" Jonathan looked amused. "Ric's short for Godric? Now, if I'd known that while I was putting up with his belly-aching."

"Family name. Some kind of inheritance issue, I think. Anyway," I said more emphatically, "forget all that. I need to make some kind of to-do list for the next week, and I'd like some suggestions, please."

He slid his arm around me, tipping my head onto his shoulder. "Melissa, I have plenty of suggestions, believe me. And," he added, under his breath, "some of them are tourist attractions!"

"Okay," I said happily. I had a feeling that Jonathan's suggestions could quite easily take up my entire stay.

ELEVEN

As it turned out, Paige didn't even allow me time to think of a reason not to call her, as she rang me so early the next day that I assumed it was some horrendous emergency unfolding at home.

Fortunately, Jonathan had already left for his 6:00 a.m. squash date and breakfast meeting.

"Hello?" I mumbled into my mobile. "What's happened?"

"Hi, it's Paige Drogan here!" She sounded unnaturally cheery. "Can we meet this morning?"

I fumbled around for a reason to say no, but my brain was still fuzzy. "Um, well, I have . . ."

"It'll only be for half an hour. Can we say . . . eleven o'clock?"

With a massive effort, I rallied myself into social fib mode. "Oh, dear, I have some appointments scheduled for today . . ."

There was an ominous pause. "I thought you said you were on vacation?"

Paige's voice made me feel uncomfortably as if she were in the room. "Yes, well, I am, but I'm meeting some people while I'm . . ."

"Then you're going to be around? Great! I'll text you my office address, and I'll see you at eleven. Thank you so much, Melissa. I look forward to speaking with you later!"

And the line went dead.

I stared at the phone in my hand. My eyes were still barely focusing in the half-light coming through the slatted shutters. I sniffed, suddenly conscious of the really quite awful stench of sleepiness hanging over the room. Despite the fresh white roses Jonathan had thoughtfully had delivered to put by the bed, it smelled as if a rugby team had bunked down on the floor overnight, still in their sweaty shorts.

Damn. I'd already failed in my intention to get up first every morning to make sure Jonathan saw me only in my fragrant state. But even Roger's flat didn't smell like this. It couldn't be *me,* could it?

I rubbed my eyes and sat up, at which point I realized that Braveheart was on the bed next to me, snoring gently.

No wonder Cindy and Jonathan's relationship had taken a turn for the worse. I knew a friend of my mother's who'd encouraged her smelly Great Dane to sleep on her bed for the express purpose of keeping her randy husband at bay.

"This won't do, Braveheart," I sighed, and scooped him up, getting a faceful of dog breath for my trouble, to return him to the kitchen. His crate showed all the signs of a breakout from the inside.

He sat in his luxury basket and chuntered as I made some breakfast. It was rather sad, I thought, that as long as Braveheart had some attention, he more or less behaved himself. He wasn't an evil dog. Just a histrionic one.

If I accomplished one thing while I was here, I thought, toasting myself a bagel, it was definitely going to be mastering Braveheart where Cindy had failed.

Karen the dog walker arrived to collect Braveheart while I was loading up my handbag in the sitting room — something he announced with a hysterical bout of rude barking.

"No!" I yelled, and he stopped.

"It's just me, you stupid dog!" chirped a voice from the kitchen. "Concetta, is the brute back on the meds? How'd you shut him up?"

"I couldn't possibly tell you," I said, gliding through. "Trade secret. Hello, I'm Melissa, Jonathan's girlfriend."

"Karen Herbert," she replied, shaking my hand and turning deep red. Considering the fact that she had farm-girl blond braids and the same sort of freckled skin as me, that was very red indeed. "Oh, my God, I'm sorry, I thought you were Mr. Riley's housekeeper. Um, I mean, I'm actually very fond of —"

"Don't. I quite understand," I said. "He's an acquired taste."

"I should have realized you were visiting," she confessed guilelessly, twisting a braid in embarrassment. "Mr. Riley's got Braveheart booked in for everything: shampooing, grooming, overnights . . ."

"Would you like a cup of coffee?" I asked suddenly, seeing a golden opportunity to find out more about not only Braveheart but also Jonathan's dog-care habits.

Karen's face lit up. "You have time?"

"Absolutely," I said and turned the spotless cappuccino machine back on.

Karen made gabby Gabi seem positively tongue-tied. Within twenty minutes, I'd learned that her middle name was also Melissa; she was actually a sculptor; she was

256

only doing the dog walking part-time while she worked on some project that I wasn't sure I'd heard right, since it seemed to be something to do with making cars out of dried lemon peel for some basement gallery; she did a little light ice sculpting for fancy parties on the side; her family in St. Paul thought she should be thinking about getting married now that she was thirty-one, but she was having lots of fun speed-dating; she was dating four men right now "but only three of them knew about the others"; New York men were only prepared to devote thirty-seven minutes a week to their relationship; and there was Someone Out There for Everyone.

"I know that," she added fervently. "My therapist told me, and so did the tarot card reader on Sullivan Street." She paused. "This is great coffee. You know, it's so nice to meet an owner!"

I drew breath feeling like I was on a roller coaster that had just stopped.

"Are London men so impossible to get hold of?" she asked suddenly. "I arranged to meet Sean — you remember, the accountant — for dinner last night, and he kept calling to say he was on his way, then he was in a taxi, then he was in traffic, and by the time he arrived, it was, like, eleven!" She rounded her huge blue eyes at me. "We had one drink, and he kept his Blackberry on the table the *entire time!*"

"How dreadfully rude," I said, disapproving. "I would have given him thirty minutes' grace, then left."

"Really?"

"Definitely!" Punctuality was one of my favorite hobbyhorses. "It's so rude! It suggests he doesn't think you've got anything better to do than wait around for him! In fact," I added, warming to my theme, "next time, say you can't meet him until ten. And don't say why. Go and have a massage, or call your mother. Just make him feel *you're* fitting *him* in. Then see what happens."

Her face brightened. "You know, I'll do that. Thank you! That's so smart!"

I glanced at my watch and realized we'd been talking for nearly an hour. "Oh, Karen, I'd love to stay and chat more," I apologized, "but I have a meeting in half an hour."

"Oh, my God, and I have dogs to walk!" she cried. "C'mon, Braveheart! Hey!" she said, looking up in surprise. "I didn't have to grab him to get his leash on."

"He's learning who's in charge," I said, clicking my bag shut and slipping on my shades.

■ ■ ■ ■

I headed for Paige's Soho office, rehearsing my array of polite refusals as I went. It took me a little while to find her office, since once I got into Soho, I found myself awfully distracted by the numerous pavement stalls selling gorgeous bargain necklaces and handmade bags and things that would make perfect Christmas presents.

Eventually, I found the bell for Paige's office: a trendy loft right at the top of an old cast-iron building. I straightened my skirt, smoothed my hair, and was directed into the elevator by the security men at the desk.

There were two other people in the elevator with me, both too cool to acknowledge any other presence, and when I stepped out at the top floor, I was surprised to find that the inside of the office was as modern and stripped back as the outside was elegantly old-fashioned. I swallowed as I pushed open the glass door and went in. It wasn't the "put you at ease" style I'd tried to achieve in my own office. It was the sort of place where you automatically wanted to walk straight out and buy entirely different clothes from the ones you foolishly thought were pretty snazzy when you got dressed that morning.

"Ms. Drogan is very busy this morning," the receptionist informed me, as if it was par for the course. But before I had time to settle myself with American *Vogue,* Paige herself appeared, in a black outfit, complete with phone headset.

"Hold my calls. I'll take it from here, Tiffany," she said, ushering me into her office with some urgency. She gestured for me to sit down, then poured me a large decaf coffee from her own personal machine and got straight to it.

"Melissa, I really appreciate your making time for me. And you're busy, so I won't waste it — here's the thing," she said, tapping the empty desk with her pen. "As you know, I'm working with your friend, Ric Spencer."

She paused and smiled before I could point out that "friend" was rather overstating things. Paige had a lovely smile. I smiled back without even thinking.

"I love your dress," she added. "So cute! Anyway, I was really impressed with how you handled Ric's . . . communication malfunction at the party. I don't know if you realized, but Lucy Powell is quite an influential arts writer, and —"

"Oh, it was nothing, really. But, before we

start, Paige, I have to —"

She tipped her head to one side. "To be honest? I'm surprised you didn't know about Ric's success over here — he's hot. He's spent the last year working on this film, and let me tell you, Melissa, when it opens, Ric is going to be seriously big. I mean, front of *Vanity Fair* big. The fold-over cover edition."

"Wow," I said, struggling to equate this with the puking Goth with the low nylon tolerance I'd known. "*That* big, eh?"

"*Oh,* yes. So, listen to me, Ric's got the looks, he's got the talent, he's got the best management in New York, but . . ." She let her voice trail away and raised her palms to heaven.

"But? . . ." I repeated.

"But he hasn't got the . . . *tseychel.* You know?" Paige blinked rapidly.

"Oh," I said. The *what?*

"Yip. And you need that. You need to be able to *charm* people into loving you, and there's just . . . he can't do it," she finished briskly. "I mean, you never have to tell Colin Firth to stop staring at interviewer's tits, do you?"

"Well . . ."

"And I'll level with you here, Melissa, I'm

thinking that's how I want to pitch Ric. Mr. Darcy. You know, he's got this great public school background, he's got these brooding features, like he's got this crumbling stately pile that's falling into the sea because his family spent the inheritance on gambling, then dueled each other to death — that sort of feel. You know? I'm talking lakes. I'm talking vintage cars in the drive, I'm talking *class*."

"I see," I said. It sounded to me rather as if Paige was describing my own hellish family.

"I mean, is that right?" Paige looked over the top of her winged spectacles. "I'll level with you. I don't know what sort of background he has." She threw her hands in the air again. "Ric won't tell me. I have to drag details out of him" — she made scarily convincing clawing gestures as she said this — "and all it says on his resumé is that he was expelled from three schools and loves Wilkie Collins." She coughed. "His *old* resumé. Obviously I've worked on that with him since."

"Mmm." I could understand that omission. A certain proportion of the public schoolboys I knew, mostly the ones who didn't work in the City or the armed forces, vehemently denied they'd ever been near a

262

blazer, let alone a prep school. Being posh was career death in the London arts world. Bobsy Parkin's brother Clement ran a T-shirt company in Clerkenwell, and you'd think he'd grown up in a squat in Hackney. Especially now that he insisted on being called DJ CP.

"Ric's a man of few words," Paige went on, "and when he does speak, it's . . . kind of hard to make out what he's saying. He *sounds* quite posh. But of course, when he's *acting*, he's fine! Beautiful articulation. He was in two episodes of *Grey's Anatomy*, and oh, my God! The way he described symptoms? I'd love to have a doctor like that. The only episodes I've ever understood. Ever. Period!"

Her hands now made chop-chop gestures. I was getting terrible manicure envy. New York grooming was on a whole new level, even for me. I folded my hands into one another.

"It sounds like you've got everything under control," I said nervously. "I can't think what you'd need —"

"I need *you*, Melissa," barked Paige passionately. "I want you to come on board and help Ric make it here in the U.S. I'm thinking in terms of a . . . personality makeover." She broke out a wide and very white smile.

"Nothing too radical. Just, ah, encourage him to speak up, and be polite."

I scrutinized Paige, trying to work out what she wasn't telling me. I might be naive on occasion, but I'm not daft, and there seemed to be a few gaps here.

For one thing, he was an actor! On television! Generally, actors did what they wanted and got away with murder. Wasn't it one of the perks of the job?

Secondly, I was beginning to wonder, queasily, if I hadn't rather overstated my own business in an effort to keep up my end at the party. Did she imagine I was one of those *executive* makeover people? Had Cindy somehow found out about my agency and put Paige up to *testing* me?

I gulped.

Then there was Godric himself. If he'd turned up at my office wanting advice on smartening himself up for the Fulham meat market, I'd have considered it a tough assignment. But Paige wanted me to sort him out to international publicity standards!

No, I couldn't do it. It was asking for total humiliation. Not to mention the fact that Jonathan had asked me so sweetly to have a break from work.

I took a deep breath. Saying no wasn't one of my strong points.

"Paige, you know I'm terribly flattered that you think I could help out here, but don't you have all sorts of specialists you could be employing?" I protested.

Paige pushed her glasses back up on her nose and looked at me. "But I want *you.*"

"Well, that's awfully kind of you to —"

"Melissa, let me level with you."

This was the third leveling we'd had. Things were pretty flat between us by now.

"I need someone *discreet.* Ric's at a delicate stage in his career, and I'm loving his naturalness. Everyone's loving his naturalness. I don't want any gossip about *coaching* to impact that. And what could be more natural than to have someone like you, someone well-spoken, from his own jolly homeland, just reminding him, by being there, how he should be behaving?"

I could see where she was coming from. Despite myself, I was starting to be tempted by the idea of working with someone who was about to be famous. I mean, how good would it be for the agency's reputation in London when I got back, not to mention the gossip I could dangle in front of Gabi?

I wrestled with my conscience as Paige's singsong tones lapped gently at my ear. Maybe this could even be the start of a legitimate business in New York — okay, so

265

Godric was a bloke, but really this *was* life coaching, not pretending to be anyone's girlfriend, and that was what Jonathan had had such a problem with, wasn't it?

I began to soften to the idea despite the alarm bells going off in some distant part of my brain. How badly could it go if I just saw Godric for coffee and put him straight about a few things?

". . . favor for a friend?" Paige gave me a meaningful look, and I realized I should have been listening harder. As usual.

"Um, well, yes, I suppose so," I said automatically.

"Melissa, I am *so* thrilled!" she exclaimed.

I panicked. What had I just agreed to? She was acting like I'd offered to marry him.

"Well, maybe if Ric and I meet for a coffee and see how it goes from there?"

"Fabulous. Fabulous," gushed Paige, and she jabbed a button on her phone, adjusting her headset so she could talk into it. "Would you excuse me one second?"

I nodded.

"Hello, Tiffany, is he here yet?"

Paige invited Ric here already? Before she knew I was going to say yes?

Confident.

Paige's brow furrowed. "Tiffany, sweetie, you're mumbling. You can't mumble. It wastes my time and it makes you sound dumb," she said in a gentle, but steely, voice. "Well, where is he? Have you called him?"

I tried not to meet Paige's sharp eyes, fixing my attention instead out of her huge window. All I could see was a lot of other windows, in the looped arches of the building across the street.

"He's *what? What?* Tiffany, sweetie, I don't want to be hearing that!" Paige's face darkened, and I sensed that beneath the smiles was a heart of pure aluminum. "Keep paging!"

"Well, I had hoped to have him here," she said to me. "I need you to meet with him ASAP. The publicists are on my case, wanting to set up interviews, and I need to have him good and prepped."

"Right," I said. "Well, I'll just —"

Paige held up a hand. "Would you hang around here for a half hour? He can't be far away. I told him ten thirty."

I smiled politely. "Paige, I'm meeting Jonathan for lunch —"

"A half hour." And now she wasn't beaming so fully. In fact, her eyes had gone a little glinty. "Thirty minutes, Melissa. That's all I'm asking. I thought you'd understand how time-sensitive these things are." She paused, then added, "Did you say you ran your own business?" as if she'd heard wrong.

Something in me caviled at that.

"Well, half an hour. I really do have to go after that. But if it's all the same to you, I'll wait in the café across the street," I added. "I have some calls to make." I paused too. "I need to check in with my assistants at the office."

I smiled to underline that this was my final offer, and Paige was smart enough to nod curtly. "You have your cell phone switched on?"

"Not during a meeting," I replied. "That would be terribly bad manners."

Paige beamed. "Oh, you! Well, could you turn it back on now?"

"Naturally."

Not that I was going to answer it on the first ring, though.

When I'd settled myself into a corner seat in Starbucks with a bucket of cappuccino and a slab of blueberry coffee cake that tasted too good to be as low-fat as it claimed, I turned my phone back on, and immediately it ding-donged with new messages.

"Mel, it's Gabi. I can't find Allegra. She's not been in all day, she won't answer her phone, and she's left me a note to pick up her bloody car from the garage. Can you have a word with her? She's . . . [sound of a door banging] Oh, hello. What time do you call this? [muffled response] I don't *care* what your barrister says! I'm on the phone to Melissa right now, actually. Do you want to talk to her? No? And you can put that down. You can . . . [not-so-muffled crash]"

I closed my eyes and massaged my forehead.

"Hello, Melissa." My eyes snapped open. It was an American voice. "It's Bonnie here, checking that you're still okay for lunch on Thursday? I have a friend, Irene, who's planning to make a trip to Scotland this fall, and she's simply dying to meet you. Do you remember, you were telling me about some marvelous hotel you knew in Edinburgh? Could you perhaps let me know the details, so I can pass them on?"

God, what had I told her? By that stage in the evening, I'd barely been registering names, let alone recalling advice. I made a note to call Bonnie back.

I looked at my watch and tried to work out what time it was in London. Half-four-ish. I should probably give them a ring, just to check that things were okay.

I dialed the office number, but to my

surprise, instead of Gabi answering, the answering machine cut in and I heard my own voice.

"You've reached the Little Lady Agency. I'm afraid we can't take your call right now, but if you leave your number and a short message, we'll call you straight back."

At least Allegra hadn't taken it upon herself to change the message, I told myself. But where were they? I'd told them they could do shopping appointments as long as one of them stayed to answer the phone.

There were a couple of bleeps, then a worried-sounding man's voice said, "Marks and Spencer's have stopped making their Breathe-Easy socks. I can't wear any other kind. This is Julian Hervey. Please call me back. Um, cheers."

I made a note.

"Hello, Honey. It's Arlo Donaldson here. Look, I'll get to the point — I've been invited to a shoot up in Scotland, and the host's new girlfriend is the woman I, er, had to jilt last year. You might remember — you phoned up as my mother and told her I'd taken religious orders? Daisy? With the nose? Um, well, thing is, it's frightfully good shooting, and there's a decent still up there too, so I rather want to go, so could you, er, advise? Thanks very much."

I shook my head in disbelief.

"Hello. Melissa? It's Roger. Listen, have you thought any more about this Hunt Ball? I won't tell Remington. I'm . . . I'm . . . Look, I don't mind paying you double." His voice sounded quite desperate, and I could hear music in the background. Miserable student music. He must really be missing Nelson, I thought. "I've been getting calls from Celia and . . . Oh, just ring me, woman."

I sighed and scribbled "Call Roger" on my notebook. I'd have to get tough.

The answering machine gave me the option to delete my messages. I paused, before leaving them on. Hadn't the girls listened to the machine? What were they playing at? What if someone had had a frightful emergency and needed immediate advice?

As I was jotting down the next couple of messages, both from clients who refused to believe I wasn't in London, I let my eyes wander around the room. New Yorkers were, on the whole, not so different from Londoners, really. Soho, NY, had much in common with Soho, W1: trendy black-framed glasses, strange clothes, laptop bags, people wearing sunglasses indoors . . .

My eyes stopped wandering as they fell on a familiar figure in shades.

Godric.

He was chugging back espresso while reading a thin book, very intently. I assumed, from his black clothing and existentialist demeanor, that it was something in the original French — Camus, or Sartre, or something. Emery had gone through a phase like that. Although in her case the books had been chosen because, being short, they'd taken up less space in her handbag.

As I watched, his phone rang, two people turned to glare at him, and he sent it to Busy.

Honestly. Lateness I could forgive if one had to rush one's grandmother to hospital, or rescue a puppy from a burning house, but not just because one had reached a gripping argument for free will.

I got up and moved purposefully across the café, slipping onto the easy chair opposite his. "Hello, Godric," I chirruped. "Aren't you meant to be in a meeting right now?"

He looked up, bewildered, realized it was me, and let his shoulders slump down into ennui mode again.

"Maybe, maybe not," he said defensively. Then he looked up and added, "How do you know that, anyway?"

The phone rang again, and we both stared at it. Godric sent it to Busy once again.

"Because you're having the meeting with me," I said firmly.

"Why?"

"Godric, would you take off your sunglasses? I know it's sunny outside, but it's rather rude to the person you're talking to."

"I need them for privacy reasons," he sulked. "Don't want to be recognized."

"Please? It makes an enormous difference."

He huffed, but removed them.

"Thank you!" I said. "Gosh, now I see you properly, you've hardly changed!"

He hadn't, actually. The ludicrously long, dark eyelashes and round brown eyes were just the same as I remembered from when he'd been advancing on me in the props cupboard.

I could see why Paige was so sure teenage girls everywhere would be squealing in excitement over him.

"Can we go over to Paige's office, please? I have another lunch appointment today, and I don't want to be late."

"Do we have to?" Godric managed to sound both bored and annoyed at the same time. "I'm busy too."

"Doing what?" I enquired sweetly.

"Researching."

I looked at his book. He was reading *James and the Giant Peach*.

"I'm an *actor*," he snotted in response to my raised eyebrow. "You wouldn't understand."

If I hadn't been so hot and on edge from my own meeting with Paige, perhaps I'd have been more intimidated by his attitude, but there were limits to how long I was prepared to hang around waiting for anyone.

"Well?" I said, gathering my notebooks together and pushing my chair back. "Shall we go over there now? Sooner we do it, the sooner we get out, and we can both carry on with our busy days."

Godric regarded me sullenly. "What if I don't want to go?"

I stopped. "Godric, it's a business meeting. About your business."

"Then it's my *business* whether I go or not, surely? Not any of yours."

"In that case, I'll just have to invoice Paige for three wasted hours of my time, which I'm sure she'll dock from whatever you're earning."

That seemed to galvanize him into action, and in ten minutes all three of us were back in Paige's office, setting up an appointment for Godric's — or Ric's, as I now supposed

I had to call him — new set of publicity photographs. And somehow, I found myself agreeing to "pop along" with him, just to hold his hand and keep him calm.

"But I don't need anyone to look after me," protested Godric, in appalled tones. "What do you think I am? A baby or something?"

"Work with me here," said Paige lightly. "Okay? We don't want a repeat of the Balthazar incident, do we?"

And they shared a look of such mutual distaste that even I shrank back in my chair.

"I need a slash," announced Godric, shoving back his chair and shuffling out of the room in high dudgeon.

Paige shot me a quizzical look.

"He needs to visit the bathroom," I explained.

"Cute! Listen, I can't believe you got him over here," Paige marveled. "How did you do it?"

"I just told him we had to go," I said. "And he came."

She clasped her hands together. "You are so good! I told you — I can't get him to do anything, but he's responding to you!"

"It's all in the tone," I said, vaguely aware that Mummy had said exactly the same thing to me when she'd been detailing how to bring Braveheart to heel.

I had a grim feeling Godric was going to need more than chicken scraps and ear tickling, however.

TWELVE

"So what are you up to today?" Jonathan said, raising his voice to make himself heard over the plaintive sound of a histrionic dog being ignored in a box.

It felt awfully cruel but we were following my (okay, my mother's) strict instructions to disregard Braveheart's outrage at being placed in the crate of doom while we ate our breakfast, to teach him firstly that his crate was a fun place to be, and secondly, that only human beings had breakfast on the breakfast table.

Easier said than done, when Braveheart was emoting like Barbra Streisand.

In desperation, I spun round in my chair and tried The Look. The one I gave idiot boys like Jem Wilde when they messed around with mustache bleaching creams in Harvey Nichols's beauty hall.

To my surprise, and his, Braveheart shut up.

"Hey! Melissa, you haven't lost your touch!" Jonathan pointed at me and clicked his fingers in delight — an annoying game-show-host tic I thought I'd cured him of when he first moved to London.

I gave him The Look, and he stopped too and stared at his fingers.

"Sorry," I said. "Force of habit."

"So, what are you up to today?" Jonathan bit into his whole-grain bagel. "I'm really sorry about missing lunch yesterday," he added for the ninth time.

"Jonathan! Honestly! I don't mind," I replied, also for the ninth time.

He looked at me apologetically across the table. "I thought Lori had canceled, but apparently the Schultzes had flown back to New York specially to make the viewing, so I just had —"

"Forget it," I insisted. "It's not your fault you're in demand." I tried not to think about what I'd said to Karen about men who kept you waiting. "I met up with one of Bonnie's friends from the party instead. Blythe? Her niece is planning to go to Europe during her winter vacation, so she wanted my advice about where she should stay, what she should see." And, more to the point, which shops she should visit.

"Well, I'm glad you're making friends," he said, sticking his fingers into his hair. It messed up the neat morning style. "Just wish it could have been me, not Blythe, getting the benefit of your restaurant tips. Anyway, I've asked Lori to help you out with any arrangements you'd like to make — you know, if you want to take a boat ride, or go up in a helicopter, or something like that."

"Oooh, lovely!" It wasn't the same as him taking me, though. But looking on the bright side, Lori seemed to know quite a lot about sample sales. She'd already e-mailed me links to about ten.

As if he could read my mind, Jonathan added, "You know, I wish I could be showing you around myself, but work is just . . . insane." He shrugged helplessly.

"I understand." His diary in London had always been ridiculous. "Why don't we go out for dinner tonight?" I suggested. "Let's make an early reservation, and you'll have to leave work by seven."

"Great idea. Where?"

"Somewhere that's special to you." I hesitated, not wanting to say *but not somewhere you used to go with your ex-wife.* "Somewhere with a great view," I added quickly, before he could say something about getting Lori to check out the Zagat Guide.

"Well, I know just the place." Jonathan shot me a wicked smile, then checked his watch. "The walker should be here to get Braveheart at half past eight. I've asked that he stay there all day, until we get home. Better than being cooped up here in his box, don't you think?"

I looked over at Braveheart, who had set up a low-level whimpering, with his head on his paws. I'd misjudged him: He had more emotional range than Barbra Streisand. "And what'll happen to him there?"

"Guess he'll be in a bigger box there, with some other dogs." Jonathan started to pack up his papers. He kissed me on the top of my head. "Mmm, Melissa. You smell delicious."

He swept my hair over one shoulder and kissed the nape of my neck. Little tingles ran up and down my spine.

"Do you smell this nice all the way down?" Jonathan enquired into my neck.

Braveheart started yapping crossly, and Jonathan broke off with a vexed sigh.

"I'll take him with me today," I said, impulsively. "He obviously needs more attention, and he really needs to learn who's boss."

"Shouldn't that be *me?*" asked Jonathan with a wry grin. "Anyway, I'll leave it up to you — after all, you're the one with the magic touch when it comes to that mutt. I was telling Kurt about how you'd tamed the beast, and he wants to talk to you about his sister's dachshund. Keeps mauling her Manolos." He winked. "Now if you need a job in New York, that might be something to think about?"

Emboldened by this, I decided to come clean about my meeting with Paige and Godric. I was a rotten liar, and I hated the idea of not being up-front with Jonathan.

"Well, actually, I'm sort of trying to explore that avenue myself," I said. "With people, obviously, not dogs. Training, sort of."

Jonathan looked surprised. "I thought we agreed you were on vacation."

"Yes, I know, but I, er, I've sort of got a freelance job."

Jonathan's surprise turned to suspicion. "Which is?"

I took a deep breath. "You remember the actor we met at Bonnie's party?"

He nodded warily. "Hard to forget Ric Spencer."

"Yes, well, Paige has asked me to pop along to a photo shoot he's doing today, to

281

keep an eye on him, as it were."

"In what way, 'keeping an eye on him'?"

"Just . . . keeping an eye on him. Making sure he looks okay in the pictures. Trying to get a smile out of him. Stopping him from insulting the photographer so badly he walks out."

I laughed merrily.

"Melissa, that sounds like a hell of a lot of work," said Jonathan, less merrily. "The guy is a moron. I mean, I know he's British and a" — his face twisted up very slightly — "a *friend,* and you feel some kind of obligation, but come on . . . this is Paige's job."

"No, it's not!" I said. "It'll be fun. It's just for an hour or so this morning, and I'll get to see Central Park, and maybe get some top gossip for Gabi, and . . ."

"It's just a for today?" he demanded, fixing me with a firm look.

"I haven't agreed to anything," I hedged. "Exactly."

"Ding!" went Nelson's lie detector in my head.

"Well, okay, just do this, then tell Paige to hire him some kind of therapist," said Jonathan. "I mean it. I don't want you spending your vacation stressing yourself out with morons. Is Paige paying you for? . . ."

Before he could go on, his Blackberry

bleeped with a message and his brow furrowed as he read it. "Oh, Christ," he muttered, under his breath. "Not again."

"Trouble?"

It was his turn to look a little evasive. "Nothing I can't handle. Listen, honey, I've got to make tracks. Call Lori if there's anything you need," he said. "She's more than happy to help. I'm going to be pretty tied up all day, but I'll let you know about dinner. We'll work out the logistics later, okay?"

I smiled and gave him a kiss good-bye. Then another one, in the hallway by his antique hat-stand, then another, on the tree-shaded doorstep. Jonathan was the best kisser I'd ever kissed, bar none. It was all in the way he held me, carefully but firmly, as if I were a fragile ornament, then kissed me like I was anything but.

Maybe it was a good thing he was so busy, or else we'd never leave the house.

Braveheart and I set off in the direction of Central Park, with me feeding him snippets of organic chicken breast and heaping him with praise every block or so, as per instructions. I had to admit that when Braveheart was behaving, he looked pretty cute. While I was wearing a simple cotton dress and a large hat to keep the sun off my face, he was sporting an outrageously expensive tartan dog collar and Tiffany dog tag, with his fur gleaming in the sun like fresh ice cream after his wash and brush-up at Karen's yesterday. Frankly, Braveheart looked more Park Avenue than I did, and he was walking along like he knew it.

We walked twenty blocks, then, in order to preserve my final shreds of composure, we took a taxi.

While we were stuck in traffic, I took the opportunity to call the agency again. If I went onto answering machine again, I told myself, then I'd really have to get tough.

Fortunately, after six rings, the phone was snatched up at the other end.

". . . All right, I'll bloody get it then. What?" barked a clearly peeved voice.

"Allegra!" I gasped. "What if I were a client?"

There was a clunk and a tussle, and then Gabi came on the line. "Hello, Mel!" she said too brightly. "How's the Big Apple?"

Braveheart growled up at me from the floor of the cab.

"It's all wonderful," I said. "But listen, where were you two yesterday?"

"Here?"

"But I called at about half four and got

the answering machine." I tried to keep my voice light.

There was a faint pause, in which I distinctly heard Allegra say, "What is she, the lunch police? Tell her to mind her own bloody business."

That was too much.

"That's exactly what I *am* doing!" I roared down the phone. "Tell her I said that, Gabi!"

"Oh, yesterday? Um, well, Allegra was out most of the afternoon . . ."

"Doing your shopping!" Allegra yelled in the background.

"And I . . . must have been in the loo. Did you leave a message?"

"No," I said. "And you hadn't checked the messages."

I could tell we were now nearing Central Park, so I grabbed my notebook out of my bag. "Listen, this is what I want you to do. Tell Julian Hervey I know where to get his socks but remind him to use that special foot spray I found for him, then tell Arlo Donaldson that if he wants to go to that shoot, he'll just have to find himself a dog collar and pretend to have joined some obscure religious sect that allows him to carry on an apparently normal life."

There was a pause at the other end. "You

285

might want to listen to the messages first," I said.

"Okay," said Gabi contritely. "Sorry."

"Oh," I added, "almost forgot — ring Roger and tell him it's definitely not on about the Hunt Ball. He wants me to go with him as Honey and he won't take no for an answer. If he won't take it from you, get Allegra to tell him."

"Right," said Gabi. "Socks, dog collar, no to Roger. Anything else?"

"Not at the moment," I said. "But, Gabi —"

"Byeeee!" said Gabi and hung up.

I found Godric lurking by the entrance nearest the John Lennon Strawberry Fields garden, as prearranged by Paige so we'd "feel at home!" He was smoking a cigarette furtively and wearing dark glasses, a dark cotton turtleneck, and a dark pair of trousers, despite the heat. He looked like a cartoon Frenchman.

Even as I was waving at him and he was shuffling in response, my mobile rang, and a wave of guilt hit me because I assumed it was Jonathan. But it wasn't. It was Paige.

"Are you there? You're with him, right?" she demanded without preamble.

"Yes, I'm here," I said.

"Good, because he *cannot* be on his own."

"Why?" I asked, regarding Godric curiously. "Is he liable to run off?"

Paige laughed as if I were being deliberately obtuse. "Oh, you're funny! No, he's liable to be mobbed by fans, Melissa. He needs someone with him to make sure there are no *incidents*."

Absolutely no one was clamoring to mob Godric, as far as I could see.

"Well, I'm here now," I said. "There's no sign of the photographer, though."

Godric looked as if he was about to slope off into the park, so I raised a warning finger at him. To my surprise, he stayed put. While it was working, I raised another finger at Braveheart, who obediently sat down and eyed my handbag.

"Now, Ric's had lots of pictures done before, and we just can't get them right. I told him to bring them with him so you can get an idea." She clicked something in the background — her pen? Her knuckles? I couldn't tell. "I keep telling him, I'm okay with a bit of smoldering, but I need some smiles! I need charm! He just does this . . . face. I don't know how to describe it. You'll see. He never does it when he's working, for some reason. Just when he's in an expensive photo session. He's costing us, so

287

I'd appreciate it if you could control things a little."

"Um, but what do you mean by that? Roughly?"

Paige clicked again.

"Just . . . talk to him. So he knows what to project. These pictures, they're going to go out to casting agents, for all sorts of different jobs. So I wanna see Hugh Grant, but I need Hugh Jackman as well. Know what I'm saying? I need Ralph Fiennes, but also the young Richard Burton. I need some *range*."

I looked at Godric, who was indeed toting a leather portfolio under one scrawny arm. The raw material didn't look promising. "Okay," I said. "I'll do my best."

"Great," said Paige, over the sound of the phone ringing again. "Should only take an hour or two! Tiffany! Tiffany! Don't mumble at me!"

I rang off to save her the bother of hanging up on me.

"Morning, Godric!" I said, walking over to him. "How are you today?"

"Is that your dog?" he demanded. "I can't *stand* yappy little dogs." He bent down to Braveheart's level. "They should be put on spits and *eaten!*"

Braveheart paused then snapped at his nose with precision timing, and Godric leaped back with a yelp.

"Godric, this is Braveheart. Braveheart, this is Ric Spencer. Right, well, now you two have got to know each other," I said, tugging at the leash. "Is that your portfolio?"

"Yes. It's shit." Godric handed it over and I flipped through the photographs inside.

Paige was right: They all bore the hallmarks of very expensive lighting and artistry, but Godric was projecting variations on the same emotion in every single one of them. Acute awkwardness.

Admittedly he'd really gotten "awkward" nailed — even in black Armani, leaning against a glass wall, he looked like a teenager waiting outside an STD clinic. I carried on flipping through the glossy photographs. Then, right at the end, were some photos of him on stage, in the sort of frilly white shirt that even Allegra would have rejected as too attention-seeking. It could have been a different person.

"Wow!" I exclaimed, pulling them out. "What's this?"

Godric leaned over. "Oh, that. I was in a production of *Dracula* up in Edinburgh, couple of years ago. I was Jonathan Harker. Got some good reviews, actually."

"I bet." In these photos, Godric looked rather foxy, with his dark hair flopping into his eyes and his face animated with terror. I think it was terror, anyway. There was a seven-foot bat behind him.

"So how come you can't do *that* in *these?*" I asked, shaking the other photos. "Eh?"

Surliness returned to his face like a cloud. "Not an effing model, am I? Can't stand all that poncing around. It's a waste of time."

Before I could give him a brisk lecture about how making an effort for an hour could help his career no end, a large man with two shouldersful of bags hoved into view.

"Ric Spencer?" he asked.

"Yeah," said Godric without removing his shades.

"Dwight Kramer. First up, let me tell you — I loved you in *Grey's Anatomy,*" said the photographer, unpacking one of his bags. "When you gave up your kidney? My wife cried so much I thought she was ill. No, I gotta be honest" — he clapped a hand over his chest to demonstrate manly emotion — "we *both* cried, man."

"Jesus," muttered Godric, staring at his feet. "I didn't think anyone with a brain still watched it."

Dwight boggled.

I nudged Godric hard and spoke quickly to cover the man's confusion. "Hello,

Dwight, I'm Melissa. I'm, er, a friend of Ric's. From home. In London."

"Pleased to meet you, Melissa!" We shook hands warmly. "Do you have any particular ideas for this shoot?" asked Dwight. "Any special angles? I'm very open to direction."

"Don't make me look like a prick," Godric mumbled. "If you can manage that. It's about me, right, not about what a great artist you are."

I swallowed. I'd only been in New York a few days, but it had really struck me how much more accommodating people were here, even when they didn't necessarily mean it. I kept reading how New Yorkers were meant to be fearsomely rude, but compared to London, where you could literally go into labor on the Tube only to have people tut about you for not moving down the carriage, the general air of friendliness was noticeable. It might have been something to do with the tipping culture, but even so, I *liked* being wished a nice day.

So, although I knew by London standards that Godric was just being a bit grumpy, by American standards, he was edging toward sectionable rudeness.

"Why don't we have a walk farther into the park?" I suggested, hoping that moving out of the sun might sweeten Godric up a bit.

"I'm cool with that," said Dwight agreeably, and we set off.

I hung back a bit to let Godric shuffle along ahead, with his hands in his pockets.

Braveheart was trotting at my heels now, nosing my bag and looking cute. I felt a surge of warmth toward him. If Jonathan couldn't be with me during the day, then Braveheart was the next best thing. We were *sharing* him.

"Ric always like that?" asked Dwight.

"Oh, God, no. Sorry about that. He's rather tired," I confided. "You know what these actors are like. Up all night rehearsing, learning lines . . ."

"Drinking," added Dwight, with a wink.

"Goodness, certainly not!" I protested, Paige's words about polishing Godric up into a Ye Olde English Gentleman Actor ringing in my head. "He's really not like that at all. Ric's terribly serious about his acting. He reads and reads and . . . he's just jet-lagged."

As I said this, two lady joggers swerved to avoid Ric, who was shuffling like a Dementor down the middle of the path.

"Did you see that?" Dwight asked. "Did you see who that was?"

I craned my neck round, but they'd gone. "No?"

"That was Reese Witherspoon. With a trainer, I guess. You never know who you'll run into, walking their dogs or what have you."

"Really?"

"Oh, yeah. Well, you got all the stars in those apartments over there." And Dwight proceeded to reel off a list of famous people who lived nearby, and then another list of what his photographer friends had caught them doing on camera.

After a while, Dwight found a nice quiet corner of the park where the light was falling beautifully through the trees. I sat down on a bench and watched while he set up the shot, moving Godric backward and forward, trying to coax him into showing some of his famous dramatic sensitivity.

But as soon as Dwight raised his camera to his eye, Godric's face instinctively rearranged itself into the awkward photograph face much beloved of self-conscious men all over Britain: eyebrows aloft, strange, apologetic smile that suggested some gastric indiscretion, coupled with a gentle hunching of the shoulders. He did it every time: Dwight would talk, Godric would listen, stare into the distance, then look back with

exactly the same expression. It was like trying to make a teddy bear sit up: Things
looked hopeful until you moved your hands,
then it slumped down again into the same
lifeless hunch.

The charade went on for another twenty
minutes, with similar results. Or rather, lack
of results. It was interesting for me, though:
Sitting comfortably in the shade, I could
watch the stream of New Yorkers walking
their dogs, Rollerblading, jogging, arguing,
eating their lunch, sunbathing, with the
Manhattan skyline rising above the trees
behind them like a film set. Some of the
passersby, I noticed, even glanced at Ric as
if they recognized him. But then again, they
might just have been wondering who the
grumpy bloke being photographed was.

Eventually, I could see that Dwight was
struggling, while Ric's face reddened in the
sun. "Shall we go and get a drink?" I called
over.

Gratefully, they followed me back onto
the main path, and we wandered further
into the park, where I insisted we stop at an
ice-cream cart. Godric initially refused, then
succumbed to a Good Humor bar, which
he ate with incongruous enthusiasm for a
man dressed head to toe in black.

"You take the little fella to one of the

Central Park dog runs?" asked Dwight, nodding at Braveheart, who had now grown tired of being obedient and cute and was charging at passersby.

"I don't, no," I said. According to Cindy's notes, Braveheart was a member of no fewer than three private dog runs, one of which even offered single-sex walking hours.

He laughed. "Gotta get on the right dog run, hey?"

I started to say that he wasn't mine, but as I looked down, I realized that Braveheart's extending leash had extended so far that I couldn't actually see him. There were bushes in the way and only his red leash vanishing into them.

My heart sank. "Braveheart!" I called, quietly at first, trying to ravel the leash back in. "Come! Come here!"

I turned to Dwight. "Sorry about this. He's frightfully stubborn."

"Can't you control that thing?" demanded Godric loftily. "I mean, how hard is it to control an animal you could easily stick on a barbecue? Surely he weighs less than your ludicrous handbag?"

Godric was really starting to get on my nerves. He had absolutely no reason to be so rude, especially to people who were trying to help him.

I got up to wind in the leash before I could succumb and tell Godric just where to get off. It went round a waste-bin, through a bush, and at last I spotted him.

"Braveheart!" I yelled furiously. He was over by a tree, enthusiastically mounting a spaniel who didn't seem to know quite what was going on.

Her owner, however, did, and he seemed pretty livid.

"What the hell are you doing?" he screamed, flapping his hands at the dogs. "What the hell? Get off! Get off! Oh, my God! Call the police!"

Braveheart flashed him an "oh, do just leave us to it" look that my father would have been proud of and carried on thrashing away.

Well, that was it. It was one thing being shown up by the rudeness of a recalcitrant semi-client, but to be shown up by my own dog?

"Braveheart!" I thundered, bright red with nine different types of embarrassment. "Braveheart! This behavior is *utterly* unacceptable! Come here *right now! Right now!*"

Dwight and Godric flinched at the steel in my voice.

"Christ," I heard Godric mumble. "Maggie effing Thatcher or what?"

With one final thrust, Braveheart dismounted and trotted over to me, leaving the spaniel swaying slightly. I bent down to his level and gave him my Grade One Look of Severe Displeasure, complete with the Strict Finger of Disappointment. "Never, *never* do that again," I hissed, "or I will tan your sorry Scottish hide from here to Aberdeen, pedigree or no pedigree!"

I was pleased to see him quail and lie down in groveling supplication.

I stood up and prepared to grovel myself to the owner. Never actually having owned a dog myself, I wasn't sure what the correct procedure was. Did I offer to pay for the morning-after pill, or something? Should I insist that Braveheart marry her?

"Hello. Gosh, I'm terribly, terribly sorry. If it's any consolation," I said, trying to be wry, "he does have an excellent pedigree. And wonderful taste in bitches too! What a lovely dog you have. What's she called?"

The man looked outraged. "His name is King Charles."

I blanched. "Oh, heavens, I do apologize. Um . . ."

"Your freakin' dog has just assaulted my show champion, in broad daylight, and you're sayin' sorry?" His voice was getting higher and higher, and I wondered if he was maybe taking this a little too personally. "How do I know what kind of filthy diseases —"

"Now, hang on a moment," I said. "Braveheart's a pedigree terrier — he has a *sheaf* of papers from the American Kennel Club!"

But the man was pointing and stepping nearer. Invading my space, as Gabi would have said.

I kind of wished Gabi was here now. She had no problems about settling disputes in public.

"Women like you are what spoil these parks for proper dog lovers," he spat. "Coming here with your stupid little dogs and your attitude — oh, I'm too busy to train him! That's for someone else to do." He stopped flapping his hands around in imitation of some Park Avenue dog owner and stepped even nearer, the better to jab his finger at me. "Maybe if you spent less time sitting on your fat ass, which, may I add, is about to bust out of that dress. Don't you *have* stairmasters in Britain? Maybe if you spent more time running in the park with your dog instead of sitting there eating ice cream . . ."

I flinched at that. I mean, criticize the dog, by all means, but —

"What did you say?"

I turned round. Out of nowhere, Godric was now standing right next to the angry man. I suddenly realized how tall Godric was — he stood a good head over Angry Dog Man and, as if to emphasize his outrage, he'd even removed his shades. And he looked surprisingly tough.

Not that Angry Dog Man seemed worried. "Who're you?"

"What did you say to this lady?" demanded Godric. Somewhat distractedly, I noticed that his diction was absolutely crystal clear. No sign of a mumble whatsoever.

"That your little doggie?" the man sneered. "Well, now it all makes sense."

"Godric, just leave it," I quailed, aware of a crowd gathering a safe distance away. I hate being shouted at. "I'm sure once we've all calmed down, we can —"

"I *am* freakin' calm, lady!" shrieked Angry Dog Man. "You're the one with the problem!"

"Don't speak to her like that," said Godric ominously.

"What?"

"I *said,* don't speak to her like that." Honestly, you could have heard him on the other side of the park. "Are you stupid, or just ill-mannered? Don't you *know* how to behave toward a lady?"

"Godric, listen, please don't —"

"Will you *can* it, you fat bitch?" Angry Dog Man snapped, and then he seemed to hurtle sideways as Godric's fist connected with his jaw and sent him reeling.

The crowd gasped. To my horror, I heard the rattle of camera shutters. Spinning round to tell Dwight that this wasn't really the time, I realized that it wasn't just him taking pictures — there was another photographer there too, and they were jostling each other for position as Godric and Angry Dog Man rolled around, punching each other.

Oh, God, this was dreadful! A whole range of horrors ran through my head — Godric's famous face maimed, Godric in court, Paige suing me . . .

I racked my brains for what celebrities were meant to do in this situation but all I could think of were pictures of Sean Penn brawling with the paparazzi while Madonna put a bag over her head. Clearly that wasn't going to cut it here, so I yanked the top off the bottle of tepid mineral water in my handbag, hurled it over the pair of them to shock them into breaking it up, then turned to put my hands over the camera lenses.

"Quick, quick!" I shouted, in a desperate attempt to distract them. "The dogs are getting away!"

That, at least, was true — the spaniel was making a break for it, with Braveheart in hot pursuit. Angry Dog Man struggled to his feet, glaring furiously between Godric, who had the classic public school slap-and-roll fight technique down pat, and his vanishing show champion. With a fearsome growl, he set off after the dog, jabbing his fist.

"I'm coming back!" he yelled, pointing at us. "Don't think this is over! I know who you are! I'm coming back!"

I dragged Godric to his feet and brushed the grass off his shirt. My heart was still pounding with shock, and I was glad to have some briskness to hide behind. Manners are the corset of the soul, I find.

"That was terribly chivalrous of you, Godric, but next time you want to defend a lady's honor," I said, brushing hard, "can you please check for paparazzi?"

"I don't care how fat your arse is," muttered Godric, returning to his usual semi-intelligible mumble. "He had no right to talk to you like that. It was out of line. Can't stand it when people are rude. Makes me . . . mad. Effing American yob."

But he looked quietly pleased with himself, and I couldn't help feeling flattered, in an uncommonly medieval way, even though I was really very angry with him about behaving like that.

Still, no one had ever defended my honor before. I mean, apart from Nelson. And never with *fists*.

"Oh, my God," said Dwight. "You want to see *these*."

We spun round. He proffered his camera, showing us the images on the digital screen: close-ups of Godric's face, doing enraged, surprised, defensive, and, finally, quite chuffed.

"Aren't they great?" he enthused. "I mean, yeah, extreme way to get them, but hey! It worked. There's got to be five, six great shots there."

But it wasn't those photographs I was worried about. I was more concerned about the ones in the camera of the photographer who was now heading off at high speed toward the nearest exit.

THIRTEEN

They say that nothing spoils your appetite like a guilty conscience, and I can confirm this is true. In my experience — and believe me, I generally make Augustus Gloop look picky — extreme desire also renders me less than peckish, so a combination of the two meant that Jonathan's promised romantic dinner was off to a bad start before the food even arrived.

He'd gone to some effort to make up for missing lunch the day before: He'd picked me up in a cab at half-six, postponing appointments on his phone as we'd gone, then he'd refused to tell me where we were going. I think he might have made the cab drive round the city for a bit to confuse me — which he needn't have bothered doing, because I'd had no idea where we were anyway — until we'd ended up at a rickety-looking jetty, down by the East River, next to a five-lane intersection-and-bridge combo.

"Um, is it some kind of special seafood place?" I hazarded, not wanting to sound disappointed.

"Not really." He was scanning the quay-side, then he suddenly strode off, pulling me by the hand after him. "Here we are!"

We were standing in front of a little landing deck, with the gangplank extended into the launch. I looked uncertainly at a small tugboat bobbing in the choppy waters. It was a two-level tourist contraption, with rails around the top, and it didn't look all that seaworthy to me. Underneath it, the river was churning away ominously.

"Get in!" Jonathan handed me up and over the gangplank, gesturing for me to go up the stairs to the front of the top deck. We were the only people on the boat, and when the captain fastened the chain behind us, he hurled the mooring rope and plank onto the deck behind us with carefree abandon. With a lurch, the little boat set off.

The view, though, took my mind off any impending seasickness at once. I leaned against the front rails and watched the skyscrapers and riverside office blocks pass by in a glittering collage of glass and steel, brick and marble. The sun was setting behind them, sending fingers of orange light through the spaces, picking out flat panes of glass and frosted curlicues like multicolored jewels, shifting with every new wave that lifted and dropped us.

Jonathan stood behind me, holding onto the rails to keep me steady, and I leaned back happily into his chest, feeling his chin tuck protectively over my head.

"I keep forgetting the city's so close to the water's edge," I said, the stress of the morning vanishing as the wind blew strands of hair around my face. "It's so beautiful."

"Isn't it? I love this. You remember when you took me on the London Eye and told me how proud you felt of London when you saw it all spread out underneath? Well, this is my favorite view of Manhattan. From the river, with no people in the way. In the evening, preferably." He lifted his hand and sketched a line along the jagged row of skyscrapers. "All those windows, all those offices and apartments . . . I love looking at them, and imagining what those buildings have seen going down this river over the years, you know? The ships, the people, the seasons. We can come and go, but this all stays pretty much the same. I like that. Buildings. They're kind of . . . comforting."

I didn't say anything, but I smiled and relaxed back against him.

Jonathan tucked his head tenderly into my neck. "I want to share all of *my* New York with you, Melissa. My house, my friends, my life." He paused. "It's not just about where you live, what you have. It's about who you're with. I know you get that, and I can't tell you what it means to me."

"I know," I said, quavering just a little at the responsibility involved there. But could I ever really share friends who'd known him so much longer? And how was I meant to share them with Cindy? "But . . ."

He leaned back so his arms were round me once again, and we were both looking out at the skyline scrolling along in front of us. "Don't say anything," he said, putting one finger over my lips. "Let's just enjoy this view."

And we crossed the river in silence, alone on the little boat, surrounded by our thoughts. I felt so happy, wrapped up in Jonathan's arms, that I barely even noticed how we were pitching up and down on the wash, until we reached the restaurant on the other side and I nearly slipped off the gangplank in my high heels.

It wasn't just some seafood place. The menu was about a meter square, there were three waiters to our table alone, and the piano player switched to playing selections from *West Side Story* when we walked in, almost as if Jonathan had arranged it.

"This okay?" he asked.

"Absolutely!" I said.

We held hands until the starters came, then we talked about New York, about London, about his new colleagues, about my sightseeing, about Braveheart. We even touched, again, on Cindy, obliquely.

"I haven't talked like this for the longest time," said Jonathan suddenly.

I put my fork down in readiness. I have a terrible habit of having my mouth full at inopportune moments.

"You know why?" he went on. "Trust. It's so great to have trust."

I smiled nervously. "Good."

"I know I sometimes tease you for being a little bit . . . innocent," he said, stroking the inside of my wrist, "but I love that you're so open with me. I can trust you absolutely."

"Well, of course," I said. "What's the point otherwise?"

"And I hope you trust me?" he added. "You'd tell me if there was anything on your mind, wouldn't you? Anything you weren't happy about?"

I bit my lip and nodded hard.

In the candlelight, I could see that Jonathan's face was wreathed in smiles. He looked so happy. Relaxed, even.

Across the water, the lights of Manhattan had come on, and they were glowing through the gathering evening dusk. The Empire State Building was lit up in red and blue, and I could see the Chrysler Building rising elegantly over the peaks and spires of the dark city.

It was perfect.

Now wasn't the time to admit my stupid, immature Cindy fears, or tell him about today's Godric fiasco.

"Melissa," said Jonathan quietly, pushing his fingers through mine. "You know I love you, don't you?"

My head snapped up to look at him. It was the first time he'd said it. In my chest, my heart swooped and dived like a swallow.

"I do!" I said. "I mean, I love you too."

And undemonstrative Jonathan leaned over the table and kissed me on the lips. He tasted delicious.

I wasn't telling him anything after that, believe me.

The next morning, I didn't exactly spring out of bed, due to the crashing champagne headache pinning me to the Egyptian cotton pillows. But Jonathan was already in the shower when I pried my eyes open, and he was singing selections from *High Society.* He had, I noted distantly, rather a good voice.

I stumbled out of bed and into the other bathroom, where I splashed water on my face to wake up. When I looked nearly human, with Jonathan still bellowing away next door, I pulled on my linen trousers, a T-shirt, and shades, and took Braveheart out for his morning constitutional. Okay, so I also took the sneaky opportunity to check my mobile out of Jonathan's earshot for business arising at home.

Not that I had anything to hide. I just didn't want to flaunt it in front of him. Even so, it felt a little like calling a secret boyfriend.

There were three texts and a couple of messages. One from Nelson ("Do not get in unlicensed cabs!"), one from Gabi ("Best place for men's shirts with extra long arms?") and one from Allegra ("Gabi nightmare. Please sack."). As I was reading that one, another arrived, this time from Gabi ("Tell yr sis office opens at 10!! Not 3!! Fed up with slacking! Can I fire her?").

Oh, God. Were they doing this in front of

clients? I shook myself. Why was I surprised? The main thing was that they were actually in the office. Yesterday's phone call would have reminded them that I was keeping an eye on them from a distance.

My fingers itched to ring Roger to check that Gabi had called him back.

No. I took a deep breath. I was meant to be on holiday. On *holiday*.

Anyway, according to Gabi's cunning plan, in about six days' time I was going to fly back to London to deal with some pretend family crisis. I could deal with any ructions then. I knew Gabi and Allegra were never going to be best mates, but they might settle down if I left them to work things out. Stranger things had happened.

I fired off quick responses to each message and picked up the gossipy papers that weren't filled with dry financial news (i.e., the ones that Jonathan didn't already get). I also grabbed a coffee to jump-start my morning personality before I had to talk to Jonathan, and, after a brief power struggle near some pigeons, Braveheart and I returned home, feeling really rather New York-y.

Jonathan was sorting through the previous day's mail at the table and beamed approvingly at me when we walked in.

"You know what I *love* about you?" he asked.

"My gin and tonics?" I suggested, stuffing Braveheart in his crate with some chicken and MooMoo.

"Well, that too. But mainly I love the way you look so gorgeous first thing in the morning!"

I peered at him. "Do you have your contact lenses in, darling?"

He nodded. "Of course I do! You just look . . . *natural.* Like a peach. That's nice. Not like these women who have to spend hours and hours plastering themselves with makeup and mascara and what have you, before they'll even step outside."

My initial beam of pleasure faded slightly into wanness. Was that a compliment or a ghost dig at Cindy? The two weren't mutually exclusive, I was beginning to realize.

"Hey! You picked up the tabloids? Homesick for celebrities falling out of nightclubs and showing their panties?" Jonathan asked. C'mon, let's see. You want more coffee? Here, let me get you some."

I gave him the *New York Post,* while I flicked through *Star* magazine, and we shoveled up our granola contentedly.

I paused, as the comforting warmth of

solid food spread over me. This was what I'd come over for, I thought happily. Little moments like this, sharing breakfast with The Man I Loved. I wasn't saying that the expensive dinners and armfuls of roses weren't amazing, but it was the small intimacies, seeing how precisely Jonathan spread butter on his bagel, how he dissolved exactly half a lump of sugar in his espresso, that —

"Oh ho, Melissa!" said Jonathan suddenly, peering up over the paper with a mock-disapproving look on his face. Or was it real disapproval? It was so hard to tell. "Oh dear, oh dear, oh dear."

"What?" I put my coffee cup down. "Oh, God, it's not Allegra, is it? Tell me it's nothing to do with her court case."

Jonathan looked puzzled. "Why would anyone care about Allegra? No, it's that *friend* of yours."

"Which friend? Not Nelson?"

Jonathan pretended to look disapproving. "No. Your ex."

"*Orlando?*" I spluttered.

He frowned. "Who?"

"Let me see," I said, pulling the paper away from him.

To my horror, on Page Six was a blurry shot of Ric pounding Angry Dog Man, with a large black Letterbox of Privacy over his eyes.

My flowered skirt, meanwhile, was clearly visible in the background, accessorized with a retractable dog leash and no dog. I looked shocked, and rather stupid. Well, the portion of my face that my hat wasn't concealing looked shocked. Thank heavens for small mercies.

Gosh. There really was quite a lot of that skirt. Angry Dog Man might have had a point about the size of my rear end.

"Oh, it's *Godric*," I exclaimed. "I thought . . ." I trailed off as the full implications rolled over my brain like molten tarmac.

Godric. Oh, hell.

" 'Which rising Hollywood star-to-be was seeing stars in Central Park yesterday morning?' " Jonathan read aloud. " 'His agent, noted industry tigress Paige Drogan, was quick to leap to the hotheaded hotshot's defense. "As I understand it, there was a lady's honor at stake and my client isn't ashamed of his good old-fashioned English manners." ' " He looked up. "That is Ric Spencer, right?"

"Um, yes," I said uncomfortably.

"Wow. We're Page Six celebrities once removed!" " 'The British bruiser refused to identify the lady in question,' " Jonathan read on, " 'but we'd love to know what the unfortunate dog lover said to offend him quite so much.' " His voice slowed down, and he raised his eyes from the paper. "Melissa, that's *you* in the background, isn't it? That's the dress you were wearing yesterday."

I drew in a deep breath. There really wasn't any point in lying — after all, hadn't I told Jonathan where I'd been?

"It is, yes," I admitted. "It happened while we were doing that photo shoot I was telling you about."

"So why didn't you mention anything about the fight last night? And the cameras? And the noted industry tigress?"

My stomach tightened with tension, and, even though I had absolutely no reason to, I felt terribly guilty all of a sudden.

"Oh, God, because it was all so embarrassing, and we were having such a lovely dinner! I thought I'd managed to convince the photographer that it was a silly misunderstanding, and . . ." I spread my hands. "What can I say? I felt ridiculous. I hoped it would blow over."

Jonathan opened his mouth to speak, then closed it again. "Don't keep secrets from me," he said.

"It's not a secret!" I protested. "I told you

I was meeting Godric yesterday —"

"You didn't say you were going to end up in the *Post*."

"How could I?" I protested. "I had no idea! You think I wanted that to happen? I . . . I'm *mortified*."

"Mortified, why?" said Jonathan coolly.

"Because I was meant to be keeping an eye on him, and he ends up in the papers!" I said, without thinking.

He gave me a level stare. "Not because my friends might see this and wonder what you're doing being defended by another man? A good-looking Hollywood actor man?"

"No!"

"Oh, yeah, I forgot. Who just happens to be an ex-boyfriend of yours?"

Jonathan said all this in a very light, adult way, but I could tell from his face that he wasn't entirely joking.

"Oh, don't be so silly!" I burst out. "He's not an *ex!* We had a brief snog, in a *cupboard,* when we were both at school! That's years ago! Anyway, why on earth would I be . . ." I trailed off. I hadn't actually told Jonathan that Godric and I had ever been an item before. Damn.

Jonathan sighed. "Melissa, tell me the truth. Has Paige hired you to pretend to be this jerk's girlfriend? Because I can kind of understand why he might have trouble getting a real one."

"No!" I insisted. "Jonathan, I gave you my word that I'd never do that again. All that is absolutely, definitely in the past. Paige just wants someone to act as a sort of . . . manners coach for Godric."

A thick silence fell over the kitchen table.

"And that is all," I added aloud.

"I don't mean to get heavy with you here." Jonathan looked wounded, but patient. "But I've been meaning to say this to you for a while. You might not be putting on a wig and pretending to be *Ric's girlfriend,* but, as far as I'm concerned, there's not much difference. I know you. You get *involved* with these guys. You *care* about them. And . . . I don't know. I worry about people taking advantage of you." He hesitated, seeing me bridle.

"And call me a jealous, mean, possessive boyfriend," Jonathan went on quickly, "but I only want you caring and getting involved with *me.* You want to advise Blythe on her travel plans, or run seminars for ladies about how to organize baby showers, that's fine. In my opinion, you could make a real success out of an agency like that here." He paused so I could see how serious he was.

"In fact, I think you should give it some thought."

I swallowed. "Really? But everyone's so well organized already. I don't —"

Jonathan topped up my coffee. "No such thing as being too organized in New York. And it's something you do so well — that garden party you threw for me when I first arrived in London was fabulous. Bonnie's already telling everyone you're London's most fashionable etiquette expert — you'd have women lining up for your authentic British advice on showers and such."

"Well . . ."

He looked at me across the table. "But do me a favor and leave the hopeless guys out of it, okay?"

"It's not *like* that!" I said. "If Godric was a useless, rude woman who needed some help presenting herself, would you still have a problem with my helping out?"

Jonathan thought about that for a moment. "I don't know. I think women are just as capable of forming crushes on you as men are, to be frank." He cut me a teasing look.

"I don't think so," I said haughtily. "You're moving the goalposts."

"Is that a fact? How far do you think your

goalposts could move?" He lifted an eyebrow, and I had to look down into my granola to retain my haughtiness.

Okay. So, it was his house. I was in his country. They were his friends, and he did have a position to keep up. And it would hardly make me look like the ideal new girlfriend if I kept being photographed with Godric.

What I did in *London,* though, was definitely my own business.

"Fine," I said. "I'll talk to Paige and tell her I can't see Godric again. But honestly, Jonathan, you're so wrong about Godric. He's not a sex symbol at all. He's just this hopelessly shy idiot who read too much Arthurian legend when he was young and thinks that women should —"

"Nu-uh!" said Jonathan, raising his finger to stop me. "Don't tell me that. I want to go into the office today and tell everyone that my girlfriend is hanging with Ric Spencer!"

"Jonathan, I'd be surprised if they even know who he is."

"They will now," he said, tucking the paper into his briefcase. "He's a hotheaded hotshot from Hollywood."

"He's a fat-headed fuck-wit from Fulham, more like."

"Well, you are the hotline to the gossip, honey."

I thought Jonathan had let it go, and I was pouring myself another coffee when he added, as an afterthought, "So what did this guy say about you? To get such a beating from a geek you kissed ten years ago?" Jonathan tipped his head to one side. "I mean, the girls at work will need to know that."

"The man made some personal remarks about my weight," I said stiffly. "And implied that Braveheart was out of control."

"Well, he deserved all he got then," said Jonathan, folding up the paper. "Right, I need to scoot. Give me a ring if you have coffee with any more Hollywood actors, okay? Got to get my story straight for the reporters." He paused. "I intend to be a red-blooded realtor from . . ." His brow creased.

"We'll work on it," I said.

When Jonathan left, with me promising that I'd definitely go to the Metropolitan Museum of Art today, I readied myself for some quality groveling.

That preparation involved, in addition to rehearsing my apology to Paige for propelling her client into murky publicity waters, ironing a proper dress, putting my hair in proper rollers, and finding some proper hosiery. I needed as much reinforcement as I could manage, and in times of crisis I'd always derived enormous support from knowing that I was wearing the right shoes and underwear.

As Braveheart and I set off through Greenwich Village toward Paige's, I kept telling myself that I hadn't done anything wrong. But if I was being completely honest, I was rather cross that I hadn't contained the situation as well as I'd have liked. I hated that feeling of leaving a job half done.

Particularly when I knew I *could* have done it so much better. Had I been properly assigned to it. In my professional Honey Blennerhesket capacity.

I stopped outside Dean & DeLuca's and looked at myself sternly in the glass. I saw a tallish, dark-haired girl in a tight-around-the-bosom '50s frock, gripping her handbag and frowning. Without thinking, I put a hand to my hair and, for a second, wished I had my blond wig to slip on. I knew where I was when I was Honey.

Melissa, I reminded myself. You're perfectly capable of dealing with this as *Melissa*. Honey is just a state of mind. That wig does not have magic powers. And Jonathan's right. Maybe it is time to stop blurring the lines in your life.

I pushed the frown off my forehead with my spare hand. And before Braveheart could follow his twitching black nose toward the gourmet foodstuffs, I swept us both off to Paige's office.

To my surprise, Braveheart was ushered in with great cooing and fussing and given a bowl of water by Tiffany, the receptionist, while I sat on the black leather sofa and ran through my apology again in my head. Not too effusive, I told myself. Retain pride. You weren't actually *told* what to do at the photo shoot.

"Melissa," said Paige shortly, appearing from nowhere.

"Hello, Paige," I said, pulling myself together.

"Come in." She nodded her head toward her office.

"I won't take up too much of your time, Paige," I started, once I'd sat down. "I've come to apologize for the fiasco yesterday. It was entirely my fault — well, the fault of Jonathan's dog, which I know I should have had under proper control, but even so, Ric —"

"Melissa," said Paige, holding up both her forefingers, then moving them from side to side, as if she was playing with an invisible cat's cradle. Then she pointed them at me. "Stop you there."

"Sorry," I said, rather thrown by the fact that Paige didn't seem as raging mad as I'd expected.

"*I* should be apologizing to *you,*" she began. "In fact, I thought that's what you were here for! Let me assure you right now that New York is not like this at all! What must you think of us, getting you into a fight in your first week in the city! Oh, my God!" she laughed. "Isn't that just the most awful thing? I hope you haven't put that on your postcards home! Hi, Mom! Today I was nearly beaten up in Central Park and was rescued by a film star! Well, hey, come to think of it — maybe you should!"

"Um, actually, no," I said. In my immediate mortification at the bad publicity, I hadn't even considered that I should have been angry about it. Still, it had been sort of my fault. . . .

Paige leaned forward in her seat, as if we were suddenly old friends again. "Ric is a tricky customer," she said. "Don't you think? But, you know, he's a genius, and sometimes you have to cut them a little slack. *However,* I can see we've got a problem here, and I'm asking you, as a fellow Brit — what can we do? What's the best way to help him out?"

"I can see how he comes across badly," I agreed. "But he's really not as rude as he makes out, not intentionally. I mean, I think he's more . . . shy than anything else? Lacking in social confidence?"

"Like a rough diamond, you mean?" Paige looked eager for my opinion. I felt quite flattered.

"Yes! I mean, does he have a girlfriend, for instance?"

She hesitated. "I get the feeling there was one, quite recently, back in England. He refuses to discuss his private life. Says it's none of my effing business." She laughed hollowly. "Ric! So discreet!"

"Well, then." I sank back in my chair, feeling vindicated. "Maybe you should help him find one. She'll knock all this flouncing and showing off on the head. No decent girl wants to be seen out and about with a man who insults everyone he meets."

Paige seemed to think for a moment.

"Not that I'm offering to do *that!*" I added without thinking. "I've completely given *that* up for Lent!"

At once her eyebrows shot up, and she leaned back in her seat.

Oops. That had been a stupid thing to say. Given that Paige didn't know about my secret agency past, it must have sounded plain bizarre.

"So, er, I can only apologize for the fracas in the park," I said hurriedly, "but, ah . . ."

Paige said nothing but carried on staring at me, a smile on her lips, as if she was thinking hard about what to say next.

I faltered. It was very unsettling.

"Melissa, the incident in the park wasn't ideal. I mean, I can't pitch Ric as a charming English gentleman if he's got a black eye and a reputation for brawling, now, can I?"

She said this with a fabulously warm smile, as if she just couldn't stop seeing the funny side, and I found myself smiling back with relief.

"But I've had two calls already this morning from casting directors who've never shown any interest in Ric whatsoever — until now. Go figure, huh? So, hey! Let's turn this negative into a positive!"

Light began to dawn, and I was fascinated, despite myself, by how pragmatic Paige was being, right before my very eyes.

"I'm thinking Mr. Knightley . . . extreme," she said meaningfully.

"What?"

"Yup! Dangerous! Like one of those poets. A real actor, uncompromising, passionate, fiery . . ."

"Paige, that sounds amazing. Best of luck!"

"Melissa, I need you." She looked at me with serious eyes. "I need you to help me with this."

"No, no," I said, but already she was reeling me in. I could feel it.

"Wouldn't you love to be involved with something so exciting? Don't you want to help a . . . *friend* at a really crucial time in his career?

"Hey, I know you're on *vacation* and everything, but what kind of agent would I be if I didn't grab skills like yours when they come along? I mean, wouldn't you say you have a great understanding of how men should present themselves? And we can make it totally worth your while in terms of financial compensation, if you know what I'm saying here. If you could just be there with him when I can't be, just make sure he comes across . . . as we discussed just now."

Jonathan would freak out.

"Jonathan will freak out," I said firmly.

"Jonathan's a businessman," she replied. "Come *on!* He wouldn't let a chance like this slip past, just for the sake of a little holiday. And he's always telling people what a star you are."

"You think?" I said uncertainly. I couldn't quite get used to the fact that these people had all known Jonathan much longer than I had. Besides, the teeny amount I was seeing of him during the day meant that I could practically rehearse the Ring Cycle with Godric and he'd never know.

"Sure!" She wagged her finger again. "He *loves* women who can do their own thing. Independence, you know? It's the secret of healthy relationships. But to be serious a second, Melissa, you know what? I think it was Fate that we bumped into each other at that party. Ric needs you right now. I need you. And it could really be the start of something for you too."

Oh, *God*. Maybe I did owe Godric a favor for getting me out of that awful fight in the park. And I did feel a certain patriotic responsibility to arm him with at least a few useful social tips.

"Okay," I said firmly. "But I can't be photographed with him again. You must understand that Jonathan's privacy comes way before Godric's reputation." I paused to let it sink in and gave her a diluted version of The Look. "Way before."

"I understand completely," she said and gave me a smile that reminded me uncomfortably of Allegra.

FOURTEEN

As the days went on, I fielded more and more enquiries from Gabi and Allegra, each bitching about the other or asking disturbingly obvious questions. "Is a waxing voucher an acceptable wedding gift?" "Can stepcousins marry?" "Who refills the petty-cash box?" That sort of thing. Despite my repeated promises to Jonathan that, yes, I was keeping the office at arm's length, and, yes, I was putting my vacation time with him first, I found myself breaking my resolve to step away from the drama.

If I'm being completely honest, one morning I snuck out of bed at 4.30 a.m., just to phone the office to see if they were there — at 9:30 a.m. English time.

They weren't.

They weren't there at 5 a.m./10 a.m., either, but I couldn't keep checking after that, because Jonathan got up at 6 a.m. most mornings, and I didn't want him to find me snoring over my mobile at the kitchen table, listening to my own outgoing message.

I also didn't mention to Jonathan that I'd done a couple of shopping sprees at Banana Republic for one Ollie Ross, a client who claimed normal shirts gave him "gibbon shoulders," and that I'd FedExed a whole box of dental hygiene products back to the office for tactful distribution to clients.

I'd been telling Bonnie about the international etiquette notes I was putting together for my father, and she'd insisted on taking me out for lunch with some of her professional friends, so I could get some details "straight from the horse's mouth."

"And you can tell us all how we should make proper cucumber sandwiches!" she'd added gaily. "I know Diana's been dying to ask you about the time your father went to a garden party at Buckingham Palace — Jonathan was telling us about that when we saw him last."

I sincerely hoped that Jonathan hadn't mentioned the part about Daddy aiming a swift kick at a corgi when it tried to cock its leg against a trestle table and collapsing an entire table of scones, and then blaming Emery.

"Oh, I think one sandwich is very like

another," I'd murmured vaguely and taken down the details for the restaurant.

The weather in New York wasn't showing any signs of cooling off, but I was finally coming to grips with the geography, if not the heat. I was still never sure how long to allow to get anywhere, though, and as my cab crawled forward in the traffic jam on my way to the Upper East Side, I started to feel the familiar panic that I'd be late for lunch — a lunch with people who'd been assured that my manners were impeccable.

Feeling the sweat prickling under my arms, I watched the minutes tick by while my linen skirt rumpled in front of my eyes.

"Traffic, huh?" the cab driver yelled in my direction. "This bad in London?"

"Almost," I said.

I looked out the window at the shops to get my bearings. The restaurant was on 70th and Lexington. From what I remembered from the subway map, there was a stop not too far from there. It would be loads quicker just to hop on a train, surely?

Not to mention how cool it would be to tell Jonathan that I'd successfully conquered the subway system and still arrived at lunch without a hair out of place.

"Can I get out here?" I asked, digging in my bag for my wallet.

■ ■ ■ ■

Outside the blissful air-conditioning of the cab, the air was thick and muggy, but I set off briskly in what I hoped was the right direction. After a few blocks, it became clear that it wasn't the right direction, but I squared my shoulders, ignoring the protests from my blistered heels, and set off again, this time slightly more quickly.

Finally, I spotted a subway sign and gratefully trotted down the stairs into the cool station below.

Now, I don't pretend to be a genius, but something about the New York subway map sent my brain into slow motion. The numbers, and the colors, and the express thing and the local thing . . . how could it be more complicated than the London underground when it was practically all in straight lines?

I stared in bewilderment at the map until a couple of sweet French tourists took pity on me and helped me onto a train.

Obviously, either my French was worse than I thought or they had even less idea where they were going than I did, because half an hour later, I was somewhere else entirely and the bearded man sitting opposite me was cleaning out his ears with

Q-tips and muttering secretively into a shopping bag.

To cut a very long story short, after a frantic phone call to Karen, who calmed me down and guided me practically all the way there at regular intervals, I finally arrived at the restaurant, just over twenty minutes late.

I didn't even want to find a shop window to check out my reflection because I could feel exactly how grim I must look. My hair was sticking to my forehead, my feet were in agony, and my lovely linen frock looked more like a paper Chinese lantern than an elegant shift.

Still, I thought, pushing open the restaurant door, *if I can just slide in here quietly, I can make some emergency adjustments in the ladies' loos, think up some hilarious yet plausible reason for the delay, and rejoin the party with minimum fuss.*

I smoothed down my skirt, pushed my hair out of my eyes with my sunglasses, and approached the maitre d'.

"Hello," I said, fanning myself with a self-deprecating flap of the hand. "So wonderfully cool in here!"

The maitre d' stared down his nose at me.

"Um, there should be a reservation under the name of Hegel?" I added quickly. "Bonnie Hegel?"

He glanced down at the reservations book, then back up. "Ms. Hegel has arrived, yes. Can I take her a message?"

I hesitated. Did he think I was Bonnie's household help or something? "I was rather hoping you could take me!" I said with a winning smile. "I'm one of her lunch party."

The maitre d' shot me a look of pure disbelief and sniffed so emphatically that I could see right up his nose.

"Perhaps I should take a note to Ms. Hegel. Just to be? . . ." His voice trailed off and he cast a pointed look at my hem. Which I noticed now had started to come undone.

Now, one thing I've learned from hanging out with men like Roger Trumpet is that you simply can't make assumptions about people from their clothes alone. Roger might smell like something his cat slept on, but his family owns half of Herefordshire and a significant portion of the Isle of Wight.

For all this man knew, I could be a famous English actress going incognito! Besides, I was a customer. And *every* customer deserved to be treated with courtesy.

I pulled up my spine, and suddenly my dress looked a whole lot better.

"I do hope Bonnie won't mind that I'm a little late," I said confidently, "but my driver simply wasn't getting me here quickly enough, so I thought I'd walk and enjoy your lovely Manhattan architecture. But as you can see" — and now my voice was reaching quite glacial heights of cut-glassness — "I need to freshen up before I join the party. So if you could direct me to the ladies' powder room, I'd be most grateful."

And I fixed him with the special Honey look that I saved for snotty shop assistants who claimed "they didn't stock . . . *such big sizes*" and clients' mothers who told their sons off in public.

He blinked twice, then, without letting his gaze leave my face, he gestured for an underling to direct me downstairs.

"Thank you so much," I said pleasantly and stalked off to the loos.

The ladies' loos were just as chilly and elegant as the rest of the restaurant. Once safely inside the cubicle, I scrabbled in my bag for my emergency needle and thread and soon had my hem tacked up. I was biting the thread and wondering what on earth I could do to rescue my hair when the door opened and I heard a pair of high heels click-clack in.

I slipped off my shoes, squirted them with fresh cologne, and checked my watch. I was now twenty-three minutes late.

Obviously the woman outside hadn't seen my locked door, because I heard her start to mutter, "Step up to the plate, Sally, step up to the plate, Sally." Then she stopped, and, to my embarrassment, I caught the sound of a deep sob.

I waited for a moment to give her a chance to leave without seeing me.

Twenty-four minutes. Oh, God, I really couldn't be much later.

I flushed the loo to warn her I was on my way out, paused, then pushed open the door.

When she saw me in the mirror, she hastily began powdering her nose with a gold compact, but it was clear that she'd been crying. A mobile phone was out on the counter, noticeably not ringing. I knew that feeling.

I washed my hands and met her gaze in the mirror. She was about my age, but with the sort of impeccable middle-aged style that only very rich young women can pull off: dark bobbed hair, a triple strand of pearls, and perfect "no-makeup" makeup, now slightly smudged. I tried an encouraging smile as I made what adjustments I could to my crumpled appearance.

"If it got this hot in London, I think we'd probably have to close the entire city down!"

I said, to break the awkward moment.

She turned her huge brown eyes on me. "You're from London?"

I nodded.

"Gosh, could I ask you something?" She bit her perfect pink lip with small white teeth.

"Please do!" I said, trying not to look at my watch.

"What's the best way to get a British woman on your side? Like, what can I do to really let her know that I'm a good person?" There was the faintest tremor of hysteria in her voice, and she gripped the side of the sink. "And that my daughter is a *really* good person also?"

"Ah, well, if I knew the answer to that I wouldn't have been sacked quite so often!" I said, then, seeing the tight cords of desperation spring up in her neck, I added, "I think the key is not to try too hard, really."

The lady stared at me as if I were barking mad. "I'm talking about St. Perpetua . . . I'm talking about a very prestigious school here in Manhattan. I've gone *beyond* trying. The headmistress is British, and she is simply impossible to please. We've donated, we've had influential friends write letters on our behalf, I've pulled every string I own to get Tom Ford to redesign the uniform, and still she said no! Can you believe that? She turned down Tom Ford! She said she preferred the sacks the girls wear already!"

"Well, yes. Unflattering skirts are a big part of a traditional English education," I said with feeling.

Her face lit up. "Maybe you know her — Bridget Collins?"

I shook my head.

"She used to run a girls' house at Eton." She sighed. "And I thought the Park Avenue set were snobby."

"I don't think there is a girls' house at Eton," I said firmly. "Not last time I looked, anyway."

"Oh. Maybe I got that wrong," she said doubtfully. "The kids all come out with lovely English accents, though. Maybe I should send Julia to rowing lessons as well as fencing? We've even been watching *Doctor Who* on cable, to get her started."

"If you really want to impress this woman, stop trying immediately." I hadn't meant my tone to sound so nannyish. It just came out like that. This headmistress sounded awfully like the Head Witch at my alma mater, compulsory curtseys and all. "You should take Julia along to the interview, explain to this Miss Collins just what a promising and delightful child she is, and leave it at that! If you want to be very English, you could even refuse to *talk* about how promising and delightful she is."

"Really?"

"Yes," I said, warming to my theme. "Tell her you do rather hope there'll be a spot for Julia, since you've heard quite good things about St. Perpetua, but you're talking to some prep schools in England too, let her know you've got connections, but don't tell her what they are. Go all modest. That'll put the wind up her much more than name-dropping . . ." I arched an eyebrow meaningfully. "You might call her on the Eton thing, if it comes to that."

"Okay," said the woman, suddenly looking much more cheery. "I see . . ."

I glanced at my watch and frowned apologetically. "I'd love to help more, but I really am frightfully late for lunch already. I'm so sorry."

"Oh, I'm late too," she said as we hastily freshened up our lipstick. "I had to drop off some homemade rose-hip jam at the school. Guess I shouldn't have bothered, huh?"

"Don't ask if the school meals are organic," I advised, smacking my lips. "Tell her you think kids should eat really awful school food so they learn to appreciate home cooking. I mean, you don't have to believe it," I added hastily, as her jaw dropped. "But she'll be so shocked, she'll think you went somewhere really ghastly in England yourself."

"You know, you've made me feel so much better," she replied. "I've been dreading lunch with the girls today — my friends all have acceptances for their kids already, and I know they're going to ask about Julia. The girls mean well, but . . ." She made a lemon-sucking face.

"I know," I sympathized. "Sometimes women can make you feel even worse when they're trying to be nice. God, is that the time? I'm meeting some of my boyfriend's friends for the first time, but I got totally lost on the subway, so I'm probably already into negative approval rating."

Her eyes widened. "You're having lunch with Bonnie? You're Melissa?"

I nodded, and she extended her hand. "Sally Chandler."

"Melissa Romney-Jones."

She shook my hand enthusiastically, then looked stricken.

"Don't worry," I said before Sally could speak, "I won't breathe a word. If you sit next to me, I can give you a whole stack of names to drop to this headmistress woman, if you like." I paused, then met her gaze in the mirror. "As long as you don't tell anyone how terrible I looked when I came in?"

"Of course I won't!" Sally thought for a second, then said, "How about I tell everyone we were both early, and I hauled you away to see the school and then we got talking so we were both late — that okay?"

"That sounds brilliant," I said, smiling, and we headed off upstairs.

After Sally made our excuses with such charm that I almost started to believe her myself, lunch turned out to be a thoroughly enjoyable experience, if a little like being grilled by four very kindly interviewers. We covered pretty much everything — where I grew up, what the point of Victoria Beckham was, whether Prince William would go bald like his father, whether anyone still used cockney rhyming slang outside East Enders, that sort of thing. When the conversation started to veer dangerously toward the topic of schools in New York, I managed to relax Sally's tense neck by asking their opinions on American business etiquette, and the reams of useful hints and tips they'd given me were still spread all over the kitchen table when Jonathan and I sat down for breakfast the following day.

"You sure this isn't just . . . busy work?"

he asked, looking over my copious notes on business gifts. "Your dad really needs to know how to greet an" — he peered at the paper — "an Uzbeki divorcée?"

"Of course he does," I replied, snatching it from him. "Don't be so cynical."

I wasn't sure what busy work was, but it sounded like one of Jonathan's technical office terms, and I didn't want to appear any less professional than I already did in New York. Anyway, it *was* keeping me busy. I'd e-mailed Daddy several reams of notes, but so far he hadn't gotten back to me on it, merely reminding me to invoice him so he could clear it with the Olympic people.

"Bonnie was very helpful," I said. "I had no idea about this 'no white shoes after Labor Day' business, for a start."

Jonathan tipped his head to one side. "I'm sure Bonnie learned plenty from you about dealing with rude waiters, though. You should talk to her about your ideas for a New York Little Lady Agency . . ."

I raised my eyebrows. "Don't you mean *your* ideas?"

He shrugged. "Our ideas, then. I bet she could give you a list of brides who'd give their right arm to have you shepherding them through their wedding plans."

"Ah, well, since you mention it," I said,

not wanting to get back into the tricky wedding ground, "I did help out one of Bonnie's friends — she needed some advice about dealing with the awful English headmistress at the school she's trying to get her daughter into. She's going to call me to let me know if my advice worked."

Jonathan looked so thrilled that he almost did a little point and click. "See? There's another thing you could do. Manners coaching for kids. Upper East Side mothers would love the benefit of your boarding-school wisdom."

I blanched slightly. It hadn't been about that — it had been about dealing with the *head,* surely? I was *hopeless* with children. Especially high-achieving ones. "No, actually, it was more about helping her get over this dreadful woman. I mean, I wouldn't have the first idea how to help children get into New York schools . . ."

But Jonathan was gazing at me with such delight that I ground to a halt.

"Think about it," he said, interpreting my silence as agreement. "Yes?"

"Okay," I replied and poured myself some coffee.

I had plenty of time to get Daddy's notes straight, since Jonathan's insane schedule seemed to have redoubled even since I'd arrived. He'd stopped promising to try to make lunch since the day I'd turned up at his office as prearranged, having teetered up Fifth Avenue in peep-toe sandals, weaving under the weight of a full picnic basket, only to have Lori confess, pinkly, that he'd had to slip "out with a client." Lori and I had ended up eating my delicious deli picnic together in the elegant boardroom, and while we'd been discussing the best ways of cutting off toxic exes, she'd rather let slip that the client who'd demanded Jonathan's presence had, in fact, been Cindy.

Then she'd been so overcome with professional confusion that I'd asked her to explain the subway map to me, just to spare her her blushes.

Though I hadn't said as much to Lori, I'd had my suspicions. Jonathan wouldn't talk about the apartment sale. He brushed off any polite enquiries about how it was going with a "let's not bring that problem into *this* house," but I'd heard him outside one evening on his mobile, yelling and kicking the iron railings in a most un-Jonathan-like fashion. Since his expertise as a realtor was proven every day by his packed schedule and the apartment was fabulous, that only left Cindy as the fly in the ointment.

■ ■ ■ ■

Two days later, Jonathan brought me breakfast in bed and announced he had Big News.

"Now, I hope you don't have any plans set for today, because I'm taking the afternoon off," said Jonathan, and he raised his eyebrows to indicate that I should make some appreciative gesture.

"I should think so too. What's the point of being in charge if you can't take the afternoon off?" I glared at Braveheart, who was trying to slink onto the bed, and he scuttled off to his basket in the corner of the room. "What do you have planned?"

"It's a surprise!" Jonathan beamed with pleasure. "You have to meet me outside the Met at one thirty."

"We're going to the Met?"

"No! Even better than that."

"Should I wear anything in particular?"

"Nope." He finished off his strong coffee, then winked. "Just your very nicest —" He opened his mouth, then stopped himself. "— summer dress," he finished instead.

"Well, of course I'll wear a summer dress," I said, confused. Sometimes it felt like there was a whole other FM station of innuendo that I simply couldn't pick up, with my poor

AM brain. "What else would I wear?"

Jonathan flashed me a wicked look and shoved a stack of papers into his briefcase. "It's not so much the dress as the . . . Oh, never mind." He dropped a kiss on my head. "Don't get into trouble. I'll see you later."

I had slapped on my factor 30 sunscreen and was preparing to take Braveheart for a walk when my phone rang.

"Hello, Melissa? It's Sally."

"Oh, hello!" I said, shutting the door and sitting down on the nearest kitchen chair. Braveheart's eyebrows knitted in irritation, but I ignored him. "How did things go at the school?"

"Um, I haven't actually had the interview yet."

"Really? I thought it was this week."

"Yes." Pause. "It's this morning." Pause. "I was wondering if you could come with me."

"Come with you?"

"Well, yes. I'm so sorry to spring this on you, but I just know I won't be able to say all those things you told me to, and I was thinking that if you just came along . . ."

I sighed. "Sally, that'll make things worse. You're meant to be looking like you're not bothered. Unless . . ." A thought was beginning to stir in my mind. "Unless I come along as someone else."

"Would you?" she said eagerly.

I looked at Braveheart. He glared back at me.

"It's always easier to do these things as someone else," I said breezily.

"Do I look okay?" Sally asked me for the tenth time as we sat waiting for our appointment.

"You look . . . just right," I said, because she did. She was wearing an adorable little twinset, toning skirt, and a headband. Everything gleamed expensively.

I, on the other hand, was wearing a Marks and Spencer's sundress with a cardigan, and the ballet flats I'd brought to wear on the plane in case my feet swelled up. Not my finest sartorial hour, but more to the point, I looked as if I'd just stepped off the Fulham Road. For once, looking authentically English and ungroomed was the whole point.

"Now remember," I said in an undertone, "I am Julia's English governess, this is my first job in Manhattan, which is why she's never heard of me before, and I used to work with two very famous celebrity children, but you couldn't possibly say who."

"Why not?" said Sally. "Surely I'd be dying to tell people!"

I looked stern. "Because it's part of my contract. Don't forget you're very lucky to have me."

Sally looked startled, then giggled. "Sure. I've got it."

"Ms. Chandler?" barked a woman's voice.

My head bounced up in a sudden jerk of nostalgia.

"Hello, Miss Collins." Sally leaped up and started shaking hands with a middle-aged woman in a tweed skirt. "It's so good of you to see Julia and me. We're so keen to —"

"And this is?" I boggled at the tweed skirt, accessorized with thick tights. She must be boiling, I thought automatically, then remembered that according to the school website, Miss Collins had taught at boarding schools all over Great Britain and therefore probably had no sense of hot or cold left.

"This is Julia's governess," gabbled Sally. "Um . . ."

Miss Collins waved away my extended hand. "Not interested. We've nearly finished with Julia now, so I just have to talk to you.

346

Step into my office. Come along! Chop, chop!"

She made to close the door in my face, but I smiled and stepped inside after Sally. I'm afraid to say I'd already taken "agin" her.

"We don't allow staff into interviews," she informed me.

"Since Mr. Chandler can't make the appointment, he's sent me to accompany Mrs. Chandler in his place," I replied smoothly.

Miss Collins looked outraged. "He couldn't come? And he sent the *governess?*" She turned her attention to Sally. "This isn't the sort of commitment we expect from our parents, Mrs. Chandler."

"Anthony's away on business in Thailand," stammered Sally. "I'm so sorry, I mean, he tried to arrange for video conferencing, but —"

"So, in the end, he sent me," I said calmly. "After all, who better to ask questions about an English-style school than someone who actually went to one?"

Miss Collins's eyes narrowed, but she appeared to set me aside for later and motioned for us to sit down in the hard chairs opposite her desk.

"We weren't terribly impressed with Julia's exam results," she said — rudely, I thought.

"She seems behind in certain subjects, and as you must be aware, our standards here are exceptionally demanding. Her reading level, for instance —"

"She can get tutoring," insisted Sally. "We're prepared to commit to whatever extracurricular —"

I coughed discreetly, and Sally's head swiveled. "I mean . . . ," she stammered, then raised her eyebrows helplessly at me.

"Do you have something you wish to say?" Miss Collins demanded icily.

"Only that Julia is a most delightful, articulate child." This wasn't a total fib. She was a sweetie, if somewhat on the quiet side. Sally hadn't stopped talking about Julia and her myriad accomplishments since I'd met them that morning — even when poor Julia had been there. "She'd be an asset to any school! Julia's coming along just fine at her own pace — not like some of those poor little hot-house poppets one sees."

I met Miss Collins's eye, and she seemed surprised that I wasn't cowering.

"She can speak basic German!" added Sally. "And she's top of her ballet class!"

Julia was also five years old. I hoped she had one or two friends, as well.

I nudged Sally with my foot, and she pushed her velvet headband back nervously.

"I understand that St. Perpetua is a marvelous school," I said casually, as if we were discussing the relative merits of SUVs. "Lovely children, *wonderful* results. And how charming is your sweet herb garden? Do the children garden? I do hope so!"

Miss Collins looked faintly mollified, then regained her nasty expression. "We are in the position of being able to pick and choose our girls."

"Well, quite! Jolly good! But, naturally, Mrs. Chandler does have other options in mind."

I don't know who looked more shocked: Sally or Miss Collins.

Sally, fortunately, recovered first. "Um, why don't you explain, Melissa? You are, after all, the expert."

"Well, Julia and I have flown over to London to interview at Pembridge Hall and Norland Place . . ." I nodded knowingly. "Of course, you'll be familiar with both those excellent prep schools. Mrs. Chandler tells me you used to run the *girls'* house at Eton?"

Miss Collins suddenly looked panicked, as if she'd been caught out in a fib. "Ah, no, not exactly, I, er . . . I used to, ah . . ."

"Didn't realize they'd started letting girls in. One of my greatest friends went to

Eton," I went on cheerfully. "When were you there? His name is Nelson Barber? He wasn't bad at rowing — rowed for Great Britain at junior level or something like that."

"Before my time, perhaps," mumbled Miss Collins. "So, do you, ah, are you still in touch with . . ." She trailed off, paralyzed by an English inability to ask a direct question about whom one knows but at the same time clearly nervous about the undercover Mary Poppins smiling back over the desk.

"Oh, I keep my eyes and ears open!" I reassured her. "I find the grapevine extends over the Atlantic pretty well! Awfully small world, isn't it?"

Miss Collins gave Sally a very shifty look, and I was pretty certain from that point onward that Julia would be picking up her boater and sacklike uniform as soon as the school outfitters opened.

"Melissa is a fount of knowledge about all things English," said Sally, suddenly finding her voice. "I wonder who else you both know?"

There was a knock on the door, and Miss Collins was saved from having to come up with an answer by the arrival of Julia, who was sporting a dazed expression, as if she'd just completed a steeplechase while answering general knowledge questions in French. Her white kneesocks were starting to wrinkle down, but she still smiled politely, shook hands, and sat down with her knees clamped together.

My heart went out to the poor little mite. She deserved a nicer school. Or, if she had to go to this one, she deserved not to be scared by the power-mad bossy-boots behind the desk. I imagined a swift look at Miss Collins's CV would reveal some interesting details. Her vowels were already sounding much less Pimlico than they had when we'd been ushered in, and I wasn't sure that the crest hanging over her desk really was from Cambridge University. I'd have to ask Roger.

"Well," I said, with a sideways glance at Sally, "I think someone here looks about ready for an ice cream, doesn't she?"

"Julia doesn't eat dairy," said Sally automatically, as Julia nodded. "It's —"

I laughed gaily. "I always say hard work deserves rewards, don't you think, Miss Collins? You'll be in touch, I expect? Marvelous! Now, come on, Julia — socks up! Good girl!"

I shepherded her out in a convincingly nannyish manner, leaving Sally to wind up dealings with Miss Collins. From what I could hear, suddenly Sally seemed to be do-ing most of the talking.

Outside, the three of us strolled down East Ninety-first Street toward Park Avenue until we were well out of sight of the school windows.

Then Sally turned round, her face shining with glee, and gave me a big hug. "Thank you thank you thank you! You were fabu-lous!" she cried. "Did you act at school?"

"Not intentionally," I said. "Anyway, it was a pleasure to help. I hope it works out for you." I smiled at Julia. "For you both."

Julia smiled, then rolled her eyes, out of her mother's sight.

Five was a different age over here, clearly.

"Well, you don't know how much you've helped us. Really. We're so grateful." Sally gave me a critical once-over. "And I mean — God, you really got into part for me. I'm so sorry to drag you out looking like this! Can I call my hair stylist and book you in so you don't have to go round town in such a state?"

I waved a dismissive hand over my comfy dress. "Oh, you know. Good to look authen-tic. I have to go home and change, in any case — I've got a lunch date."

"With Jonathan?" Sally's eyes went round and gooey. "Oh, he's a lovely guy."

I nodded, strongly suspecting my eyes had gone gooey too.

Braveheart and I arrived at the steps of the Met at one thirty on the dot, but there was no sign of Jonathan among the crowds of tourists milling around.

The sun was scorching hot, so I sat down on the steps in a small patch of shade, arranged my full cotton skirt so my knickers weren't on show, and waited for him. Braveheart sat at my feet and panted, lolling his big white fluffy head. I scratched him behind the ears, and he made an appreciative growling noise.

Jonathan still hadn't appeared by quarter to. It was very unlike him to be so late and not call, I thought, checking my phone in case he'd left a message. But he hadn't.

As I was looking at it, a text arrived with an incongruously English doorbell noise. A couple of tourists looked round, startled.

"Where best place emergency lawyer?"

It was from Allegra. Since she was already lawyered up to the gills with the finest nitpickers money could buy, I assumed it was a query on behalf of a client, possibly one who'd done something too humiliating to run past the family solicitor. I texted her the details of a friend of Nelson's, who specialized in getting dodgy solicitors off the hook, then resumed my scanning of the crowd for Jonathan's red hair.

The phone ding-donged again.

"Not big enough. Need QC."

Crikey. It must be serious. I was texting Allegra with firm instructions that it wasn't her job to start initiating legal proceedings or egging anyone else on into complicated law suits, when the phone rang.

"Hello, Melissa? It's Lori speaking."

"Hello, Lori," I said. "Are you calling to tell me Jonathan's in a meeting?"

"How did you know?" she asked very seriously. "I am. He's in conference with . . ." She hesitated. "With a client, and he's just called me to say he can't get away. He's very sorry and has asked me to send you a car. It should be with you . . . now."

I looked up, and indeed there was a black Lincoln Town Car idling on the other side of Fifth Avenue, complete with driver looking up and down the pavement.

"I can see it." I hauled myself to my feet. Braveheart woke up with a snort of disgust.

"Jonathan will be there as soon as he can. He's really sorry. I've given the driver directions and a map for you."

Trying not to think about what Lori had let slip over our boardroom picnic, I trotted

354

down the steps, established that it was in fact my car, and got into the back with Braveheart as the driver held the door open.

We'd only gone a few blocks when the car pulled to a stop and the driver got out to open my door again.

"Central Park, ma'am," he said. "I was told to direct you to the boathouse."

Jonathan had sent a car to drive me just a few blocks to Central Park? I got out, feeling embarrassed.

"I could have walked!" I said to the driver. "Honestly!"

But he just smiled politely and gave me a map of the park, prepared by Lori, with directions printed out to the Loeb Boathouse.

Choosing as much shade as we could, Braveheart and I strolled through the park to the beautiful boathouse, where I ordered a pot of tea for myself in the restaurant and a bowl of water for him. And we waited for Jonathan.

And waited.

And waited.

We waited so long that I'd made a fresh list of to-dos, jotted down some new ideas for the agency, filed my nails, sent three texts to Gabi insisting that she find out what on earth Allegra needed legal recommendations for, drunk two pots of tea and made so many notes in my little book that the wait staff were probably starting to mutter among themselves about restaurant inspectors.

Every thirty minutes or so, I'd get a call from poor Lori, apologizing for the delay. Even though I assured her that I was having a lovely time just people watching, I couldn't help feeling tetchy. Then cross, then hurt, then plain worried.

In the end, I caved and phoned Gabi.

"Is it, er, unreasonable to call the police if your date is two and a half hours late?" I asked.

"Depends where your date's meant to be," she said. From the sound of the background noise, she was in a bar. A bar where people were laughing and getting drunk.

"He's out with a client," I quavered. "Lori won't tell me anything more than that."

"Cindy?" said Gabi immediately.

"I don't know!" I felt sick.

"You think she's stabbed him in their empty apartment and set fire to the evidence? Or that he's stabbed *her* and is clinically dismembering the corpse and constructing a watertight alibi based on train times?"

"Gabi! That's not helping!"

I could hear her giggling. And I could also hear *male* giggling. I heard her say, muffled, "It's Mel. Yeah, he's stood her up. I *know!*"

"Who are you with?" I demanded. "And where are you?"

"I'm in Hush," she giggled, then went as serious as she could after, I estimated, three cocktails. "Look, take Auntie Gabi's advice and go home. That'll teach him to leave you hanging around. He's an . . . idiot. No man should keep you waiting, Mel, specially one as lucky to have you as he is. Dr. No needs to learn to get his priorities straight . . ."

Her voice was rising in a bit of a tirade, but at that point I spotted Jonathan's red hair glinting in the sun as he jogged rather awkwardly down the path, and I rose to make sure it was him.

"Gabi! It's okay! I can see him. Call you later!" I said, hanging up as quickly as I could.

With an attention-seeking volley of yapping, Braveheart confirmed that it was Jonathan.

"Shh!" I hissed to him as heads turned. "Don't look so *keen.*"

Jonathan bounded up to my table and leaned on it, breathing heavily. It only took him a few moments to get his breath back;

he did, after all, play competitive racket sports three times a week.

"Hello, darling," I said, biting back the urge to say, *Have you been with Cindy?*

"Melissa, I can't apologize enough," he said, wiping the back of his hand across his pale brow, now flushed with heat and exertion. Possibly a touch of mortification too. "You must be seriously razzed. I've been trying to get away for the last ninety minutes, but it was just impossible. I am *so* sorry."

"It's fine," I said, surprised at how calm I sounded. "Lori kept me up to date with your progress."

"I'm sorry," he said, spreading his hands apologetically. "I hate to keep you waiting."

I was smiling sunnily, but my panic was simmering into crossness. If I'd kept him waiting because I'd been at work, he'd probably have played his "who comes first?" hurt card and canceled me. And I'd have told him, up front, who I was seeing . . .

Stop it, I told myself.

"You brought the dog?" he asked quizzically. "Thought we established that he wasn't safe in parks?"

"Of course he is." I fondled Braveheart's white ears. "A dog isn't an *accessory*. It's a part of the family. If you want him to behave well, you have to show him, not just bring him out of the doggy nursery when you feel like looking like a dog owner."

"Okay, okay," he said, regarding Braveheart with suspicion. "But tell him to behave."

"You tell him."

"I don't think he gets my accent," said Jonathan. "That or he just doesn't like sharing you with me."

I looked up, straight into Jonathan's eyes. "Well, these days I see much more of him than I do of you."

Jonathan bit his lower lip and looked guilty. He shoved a hand through his hair, messing up the neatly gelled waves. "Guess I deserved that."

"Kind of. But you're here now, so let's enjoy this glorious afternoon," I said, getting to my feet. "Where are we going?"

He offered his arm to me. "The plan was to walk romantically through the park until we chanced upon the boating lake, then you were going to be all amazed at the beautiful lake in the middle of the city, and I was going to suggest going for a row in one of the boats." He smiled wryly. "That was the plan, anyway."

Poor Jonathan. I knew how he felt about his plans.

I'm arm-in-arm with the man of my dreams, the sun is shining and getting less hot by the moment, and I'm wearing a dress that makes me feel like Gina Lollobrigida, I told myself. There was no point in spoiling that combination of positive things by being moody. None at all.

"Oh, look!" I gasped, turning in pretend surprise at the lake, then turning back to him. "Jonathan! I never knew there was this great big *pond* in the middle of New York City!"

"No?" he replied, playing along. "Do you want to go for a paddle?"

"I certainly would," I said, allowing him to lead off toward the rental hut.

Jonathan let me pick out the boat, helped me and Braveheart in, then rowed us out into the middle of the lake with long, sure strokes.

"I used to row at Princeton," he explained unnecessarily as we cruised past less professionally manned craft. "Made the first boat for a season."

I made appreciative noises. Rowers, in my experience, were disturbing. They had a bloody-mindedness rarely achieved by rugby players, and barely even understood by cricketers. Cricket might be a little complicated, but at least it had the virtue of being arranged around food and drink breaks. Rowing was just shouting and pain barriers and eight men thinking as one.

"I can row too," I said, not wanting to sound weedy. "Not like *boat race* rowing, though. Dinghies, like these. Nelson taught me to row his inflatable when we were out sailing."

"Really?" Jonathan feathered a little, to maneuver round another couple, then let us drift gently to a halt.

"Mmm. Mainly so he could stay aboard the sailboat and shout while Roger and I went ashore for supplies, I think."

"Well, you can row us back."

"Erm . . . okay." *We should probably set off in about ten minutes then,* I thought, but didn't say anything.

With an easy gesture, Jonathan pulled in his oars and reached for his briefcase. He triumphantly produced two champagne flutes and a chilled bottle of champagne and set them on the spare seat. "Somewhere, in the middle of town, there is a Zabar's hamper, in a taxi, going round and round trying to find me. I hope Lori's caught up with it and taken it home. This is all I could fit in my briefcase. I hope you don't mind drinking on an empty stomach?"

I was charmed. "Not in the slightest! That's just lovely."

And it was lovely too. The sun was fading gently in the sky and dancing on the ripples made by other, distant boats. It felt a little cooler in the park, and I could see the very tops of the ornate apartment buildings on Central Park West rising gracefully above the green trees, but there were no grating sounds of traffic — just faint splashes and birdsong.

"Thank you," I said as Jonathan handed me a flute. It was still so cold that beads of moisture clung round the glass.

"Flutes, yes?" he said, with a raised eyebrow. "You see? I listen to your improving words."

I smiled, as a warm glow spread through me. God, it was so nice to have in-jokes that didn't involve me falling over something or being shown up by a family member. He was talking about the party where we'd met: the welcome party I'd arranged at Dean & Daniels. I'd told him his saucer-shaped champagne glasses were tacky, and amazingly, from that choice piece of snobbery, he'd decided to hire me as his pretend girlfriend.

"You know, it's exactly fifteen months since we met," he said, gently chinking his glass against mine. "That was the first thing you taught me, and I haven't stopped learning since. To you."

"Oh, no . . . ," I demurred, chinking my glass and leaning forward to let him tip up my chin with his finger and kiss me very gently on the lips. He couldn't really kiss me any more energetically anyway, on account of the boat and the glasses, but it was quite a sexy kiss all the same.

"What have I got to teach you?" I sighed, leaning back and admiring him in his neatly rolled shirtsleeves. "You don't need fixing up. You don't need to be told where to buy decent shoes. You don't need to be told not to take a girl to an all-you-can-eat restaurant." I smiled, drunk on a moment of pure happiness. "I mean, look at you. You don't need someone holding your hand while you buy a fabulous suit like that, do you?"

"Well, I do have a good tailor." Jonathan sipped his champagne. "And I get help from the shopper when I go to Saks —"

"But that's the point," I said euphorically. "You go to Saks! You just carry on with your own marvelous taste."

He pulled a face. "Melissa, I'm not really as organized as you think. You're the organizer."

"Darling, if you want to think that, it's

fine with me," I said, stretching out my white legs in the last of the sunshine.

Braveheart was asleep, his nose on his paws, worn out by his walk through the park. His granddad-white eyebrows flickered as he slept, as if he were chasing other dogs in his sleep.

"There's a dog who knows how to relax," observed Jonathan.

"Yes, well, you should take some tips." I looked up at Jonathan before he could set off apologizing again. "I'm not cross about waiting, Jonathan, but you had the afternoon off. You *have* to take time off. How else will they understand how much they really need you?"

He sighed. "Look, I know. I *know.* You don't need to tell me. You think I'd rather be at work when I could be here with you? Huh? But things are really frantic right now, and I need to prove myself, what with the promotion and everything."

"But you did!" I goggled at him. "You flew back from London, you're working all hours . . . What more do they need you to do?"

"Justify my salary, I guess." He raked a hand through his hair. "I know Lisa is lining me up to take over, not now, maybe not for five years, but there's only one other guy between me and her. And she owns the whole business, all sixty offices. *And* the ones in London. *And* Chicago. *And* L.A. And between you and me, we're looking into buying a Parisian operation too, so . . ." He shrugged again, but there was a flash of panic behind his studied nonchalance. "I can't screw up."

"You won't," I said, patting his leg reassuringly. "But, honestly, darling, you need the odd afternoon off. I don't want you having a heart attack or getting high blood pressure." I looked at him with my mock-stern expression. "I've seen what stress can do to estate agents, don't forget."

Jonathan flicked a cheeky glance at me. "Melissa, don't look at me like that. Not if you want to keep this boat stable." He loosened his collar. "If anything's messing with my blood pressure, it's you."

I blushed and tried not to let him see how flattered I was. "Oh, come on, you're a workaholic," I said. "Admit it."

"Well, actually, no. I'm not, really. It hasn't always been like this," he replied, topping up our glasses. We were drifting a little now, but with nothing to bump into, I didn't mind. "I mean, I've always been a hard worker, always wanted to get on, have security. But to tell you the God's honest truth, when things started going . . . a little

365

awry with Cindy, that was when I put in serious hours at work. And I mean serious hours. Getting in before seven, staying until eleven . . ."

I felt the familiar prickling of curiosity and intimidation that Cindy inspired. "Just because of . . . problems at home?" I ventured, unable to resist. What was she doing? Throwing plates at him?

He sighed. "Yeah. Kind of stupid really, since she wasn't getting home until eleven herself. Now, Cindy — she *is* a workaholic. She was the youngest director her company ever had, internationally. She was literally running her department before she was twenty-six."

My stomach crept a little as the perfectly coiffed Ghost of Cindy materialized in the boat between us. Her hair, unlike mine, was not frizzing in the humidity. Neither was she perspiring beneath her cardigan. Still, I needed to grasp the nettle here. I needed to show him I wasn't afraid to talk about her.

Even though I . . . was, rather.

"What exactly does she do again?" I asked casually.

"Oh, God, Cindy works in *advertising*," Jonathan groaned. "The sales side, not the creative, but she goes on about it like she's Van Gogh crossed with Donald Trump. She runs international marketing campaigns, really big money operations. She's good at what she does, but it's a very unpleasant industry. If you're not in by seven, you might find someone else sitting at your desk tomorrow morning, you know? They want complete commitment, especially from women.

"You don't mind me telling you this?" he asked suddenly. "You don't mind hearing? . . ."

"No, no!" I said quickly. "I want to know."

"I'd understand if you wanted to, you know . . ." He made a walling-off gesture with his hand.

I shook my head. As my mother was wont to mutter, better to know all than to guess half. "No, honestly. Go ahead."

"Okay." Jonathan coughed self-consciously, as if he was working out how best to present things. "Well, um, at first, it wasn't too bad," he began. "We were both working hard to pay the bills, meeting our goals. All our friends are kind of *driven,* as you've no doubt noticed, so it wasn't like we were any different. But after a few years, it got to be like a competition — who was spending less time at home. She was out all the time because she was working, and I was out . . ." He hesitated. "I was out because when Cindy was in, she was so wired and hypercritical that I'd rather have been anywhere else than sharing a take-out dinner with her. It was always takeout, by the way. She doesn't cook."

"Oh," I said. No wonder the poor man got so excited the one time I offered to roast a chicken. "Stress can make people say things they don't mean, though. That's why you have to relax."

"Yeah, well, I kind of put the arguing down to the stress of work, but then we argued on vacation too. The vacations were also competitive — safaris and skiing and God knows what else. I just wanted to go back to my parents' place in Boston, you know, kick back with a few beers, but . . ." He rolled his eyes. "Cindy didn't *do* kicking back. Unless it was some kind of new gym class. And my mother never forgave her for the time she gave my entire family dental work for Christmas."

I flinched. "So your mother must be thrilled she's lost a daughter-in-law and gained a daughter-in-law right back."

That raised a raw smile. "Yeah. Not. The only good thing is that Cindy refuses to leave New York for Thanksgiving so it'll be Brendan missing out on mom's turkey this year, and not me."

"Darling," I said, taking his hand. It was easy to be generous to Cindy from a distance, but inside I felt very jumbled up. I felt nervous, and out of my depth, and very, very sorry for him. Suddenly I wasn't sure this was something I could fix. This was the most he'd ever told me about his marriage, and far from being the bitter divorce, he sounded sad, as if he'd lost something precious. I wondered why he'd never told me these things before.

Out here on the glittering stretch of water, there was a lovely, private, peaceful stillness, even though I knew we were in the heart of the city. I searched my mind for the right thing to say, found nothing, and squeezed Jonathan's hand tighter between mine.

Eventually, he lifted his head and looked me straight in the eye. "What I'm trying to say is that even if we both ended up workaholics, I think only Cindy was *born* one. I was made into one." He paused. "So there's an outside chance you can *un* make me."

"But she'll have to slow down now she's had Parker, surely?" I said. "I mean, on a biological level at least."

"Melissa, she was back in the office *five days* after the birth."

"And Brendan? . . ."

Jonathan nodded. "He's looking after Parker. He writes screenplays, freelance. I know it's pointless to torment yourself with "what ifs," but I do sometimes wonder why she couldn't find time in her schedule for childbirth when she was married to me . . ." He didn't finish but stared hard at a duck paddling past with three ducklings in a line behind it.

If Gabi could see him now, I thought fiercely, she'd never call him Dr. No again. He didn't look so executive now in his bespoke shirt — he looked heartbreakingly vulnerable. Who in their right mind wouldn't want to have children with this handsome, successful, caring man?

"Don't!" I said. "Whatever you're thinking, stop it! Because I bet it had nothing to do with you at all!"

I had to bite my tongue to stop myself from saying that Cindy, in my opinion, was exactly the sort of premiere league cow who thought she could get away with seeing both Brendan and Jonathan just so long as she kept her diary straight. Getting pregnant by Brendan probably hadn't been so much a romantic decision to celebrate their love as a scheduling slipup that had forced her into an emergency merger.

I supposed, grudgingly, that at least she hadn't tried to pass Parker off as Jonathan's.

Whether that was noble or just doubly cow-
ish, I didn't know.

Or maybe, added a prurient voice, it said
more than I wanted to know about the
regularity of their sex life.

Ding!

It says everything you want to know, I
reminded myself. *If you were being honest.*

"Well, all I can say is that I'm glad she's
moved on," I said firmly.

I looked at him closely when he didn't
reply at once.

In fact, he was staring at Braveheart a bit
too hard.

My heart was hammering in my chest.
Frankly, I could have done without Cindy
popping up in our lovely romantic rowboat,
like a stingray with perfect teeth, but I had
to know.

"Jonathan?" I repeated.

He sighed. "Yes. Yes, she's moved on. But
she's . . . It was okay when I was in London,
because she literally couldn't get hold of me
there, except by phone. And you don't
always have to answer the phone. Now,
though . . ." He pressed his lips together.
"I'm telling you this because I don't want
you to get the idea that I'm hiding anything.
I haven't told you *before,* because I saw how
you acted when we visited the old apart-

371

ment. I thought I could contain her. Which was pretty dumb. Cindy is not easily containable."

"Oh." What else could I say?

"She blows hot and cold — first, she wants me to sell the flat, then I can't get hold of her to sign documents. She makes a big deal about changing her will so I'm not even mentioned, then phones me five times in one day to check I've got the number of the best interior designer for Jane Street."

I swallowed. *Well, you did ask to hear this,* I reminded myself.

"She's a control freak," I said flatly.

"You got it. Look at Braveheart. She moved heaven and earth to get that dog and now she's dumped him on me, just at a time when I *really* don't need a puppy around the place, you know?" He fiddled with his glass. "And the constant calls to check I'm meeting her care guidelines. I mean, *Jesus.*"

"Calm down, Jonathan. I'm dealing with the dog," I said firmly.

How often has she been ringing him? And why hasn't he said so? And why is he still so wound up about her — one minute sad, the next livid?

"I know. I know." He sighed. "But if we could just make a clean break . . . you know, when you've been together as long as we

372

were, the hardest things to divide up are your friends. I can hardly ask her to stop seeing Bonnie and Kurt, and God knows it's pretty petty to start bickering over who's known who the longest. Or making a rota of parties we can go to."

"Oh, I know," I sympathized. This I *did* know about. "Whenever Daddy threatens to divorce my mother, she reminds him that she'd get the accountant, the wine merchant, and the cleaning lady. And he soon backs off."

Oops. Their anniversary. I'd nearly forgotten. I only just stopped myself mentioning it out loud. Not a good moment.

I looked at the empty bottle. I'd drunk half and didn't feel in the least bit puddled. Ex-wives had a very sobering effect.

"Of course, she's very curious about *you,*" he went on. "She pretends not to be, but I know she's pumping everyone for details."

"Really," I said. "Well, actually, I know. She told Jennifer I was a blond teen temptress called Happy."

Jonathan grimaced. "Sorry about that."

"Don't be. Let her think whatever she likes. I'm meeting your friends, and I hope they'll make up their own minds." I screwed up the last of my courage and tried to make it sound casual. "Listen, should I meet her? Wouldn't that get it out of the way? For all of us?"

"That's very sweet of you," said Jonathan. "But you're only here for a little while and I don't want to spoil your visit by letting Cindy create her own miniseries. Besides, you're so right — let her stew." He smiled. "Even if they're singing your praises — which I know they are — it's only half the story."

I smiled at the compliment, but inside I was less certain.

"I just don't want you to feel . . . I don't know, intimidated by her," he went on.

"I'm not!"

Ding!

He fiddled with his signet ring, as if he were searching for the right words. "Believe me, *I* have moved on." He looked up so I could see the sincerity in his gray eyes. "And I hope — for Brendan's sake, for Parker's sake — that she has. But I can't help worrying that she'll continue meddling in my life — *our* life — *because she can.* She's that sort of woman. *And,* to be frank with you, that's why I'm a little wary of Paige Drogan, people who're still very friendly with Cindy. People who have nothing better to do than mess up situations just for the hell of it. So what I guess I'm saying is . . . Melissa?"

I was still tingling at the way he'd said "our life." *Our* life.

"Mmm?"

He opened his mouth to speak, then closed it again and smiled. When Jonathan smiled, the worry lines vanished and his eyes glittered with boyish mischief. They would still look boyish when he was seventy. I melted inside.

"Melissa," he said. "Here we are in Central Park, talking about my nightmare ex-wife, when all I want to do is sit here and look at you. Maybe get you to say something every now and again in your very alluring accent." He took my hand again, turned it over, and traced the lines on my palm with a ticklish-light touch. "Sometimes I look at you, and I can't believe you're really mine." He raised my hand so he could press my palm against his lips, and looked over the top of it. "Lucky me."

"That's funny," I said in a wobbly voice, "because I frequently have the same thought."

We smiled, and the bright light made us both squint.

"Don't fly away when your job here is done, Mary Poppins," he said unexpectedly, in a truly atrocious Dick van Dyke cockney accent.

"Gor blimey no, guv'nor." I kissed the tip of his nose. "Plenty of work still to do here. Now, shall I row us back, or would you like me to summon some cartoon animals to take the oars?"

Jonathan sat back with a laugh. "I am more than happy to watch you, Miss Mary."

"Fine!" I said. "Prepare to be impressed."

We went round in one huge circle for about twenty minutes, during which time Braveheart deigned to wake up and started getting feisty with the ducks, so Jonathan took one oar, while I took the other, and together we rowed the boat back.

It took a long, long time, but I think it was the happiest hour of exercise I've ever taken.

FIFTEEN

My parents' wedding anniversary was in three days' time, which I reckoned was close enough to risk buying a card. I was in Kate's Paperie, a vast temple to stationery-based politeness, staring at a "Wow! You Made It To Your 35th Anniversary, Parents!" card and wondering if it was sarcastic enough, when my phone rang and I discovered I needn't worry about posting it in time. I could deliver it by hand. I could also dispense with my plan to invent a crisis I'd have to fly back for: My father was thoughtfully providing a real one.

"I need you back here in London," announced my father, without bothering to enquire about the weather or the state of the exchange rate. "Tout de suite."

"Daddy, I might be busy," I tried.

He snorted rudely in response. "I'm not asking as your father, I am summoning you *as your employer.*"

I wrinkled my brow, trying to work out what he meant, but then I remembered the Olympic etiquette stuff.

"I thought you'd forgotten about that," I protested. "I mean, I've sent you three very long e-mails, covering forms of address for everyone from the Pope to Tongan dignitaries, and I haven't had any acknowledgment from you or your secretary that you even *got* them."

"Claudia's not . . . My secretaries are far too busy," he said evasively. "They can't be wasting their time chitchatting."

I stared longingly at a huge display of Thank You notes. Manners were so much easier when you could just buy a year's worth of polite sentiments and dispatch them at intervals. I wondered if I could place bulk orders for my family.

"I need you back here by Friday lunchtime," Daddy bellowed. "So you'd better get cracking."

"But that's the day after tomorrow! I can't just . . ."

"For Pete's sake, Melissa, you're on holiday! What have you got to rush away from? An urgent appointment with a bagel? If you weren't prepared to take this assignment seriously, you should never have taken it on," he reminded me censoriously.

I didn't remember being given much of a choice. Besides, why did he need me there in person? All right, so I was looking for an excuse to go back and check up on Gabi and Allegra, but I wasn't at all sure I wanted to stumble into one of Daddy's labyrinthine plots *for real.*

"Oh, I know your game! Are you trying to get me to pay for your tickets?" he demanded when I didn't respond instantly. "Is that what this churlish show of reluctance is about?"

My mouth opened and shut like a fish. "Well . . ."

He tutted, as if I were attempting some audacious street robbery, then said, "I might be able to arrange something. But get yourself back here. And make sure you're wearing something smart."

"But I always look smart," I objected.

Daddy made another derisive noise, then added, as an afterthought, "And fetch something nice back from Duty Free for your mother. It's our anniversary at the weekend. Fifty quid, preferably under, and don't try to smuggle anything back through the wrong channel. We've only just got your sister out of the clutches of the boys in blue."

"Oh, that's good news!" I said, relieved.

"And Lars?"

"I can't talk about this now," he said abruptly. "I will see you on Friday."

And he hung up.

When I explained this turn of events to Jonathan over a pot of tea and some shortbread I'd knocked up according to Nelson's recipe, he took it with his customary sangfroid. In his line of business, jetting hither and thither wasn't such a big deal. He was also inspecting the latest missive from his bathroom designers, so I only had about forty percent of his attention anyway.

"It means I'm going to miss Wentworth's Labor Day house party," I said, looking at my diary sadly. "I really wanted to see the Hamptons, too."

"Always next year," said Jonathan.

I tried not to reveal my secret delight at this throwaway comment. "You'll still go, won't you? And you'll let Wentworth know how sorry I am to miss it?"

"Sure. Won't be much fun without you, though."

"I'll send a postcard from London."

"You have checked your father's booked your ticket?"

I nodded. "The lovely Claudia e-mailed the details. Business class return."

"Hey. That's nice of the old man."

"I very much doubt he'll be paying for it," I said heavily. I'd gotten my mother a huge bag of multicolored wools and fancy needles from a shop I'd found on Sullivan Street; I doubted very much that Daddy would end up paying for that either, but at least Mummy wouldn't be unwrapping another silk negligee in the wrong size. With someone else's monogram on the breast.

"I'm just sorry I can't go with you." Jonathan gave me a rueful grimace. "Would have been quite fun to test out those new business-class beds BA does. Still, I'll get some of this work out of the way, so when you get back, I can give you my full attention."

That made me feel slightly better.

Thanks to the luxurious seat on the plane and the lavish toiletries bag supplied therein, not to mention the use of the business-class spa on arrival, I caught a taxi to Victoria feeling positively refreshed. I had time to fit in a quick visit to the agency before the afternoon meeting with Daddy — and, actually, when you put it like that, I felt like I almost deserved my business-class luggage tag.

I felt a rush of affection for London as I

walked down the street, noticing all the things I'd missed without realizing: parking meters, discarded copies of *Metro*, Pret a Manger. Maybe a touch of trepidation too, in case I ran into a queue of disgruntled clients hammering on the door and demanding their money back. Still, I reminded myself nervously, I shouldn't be too mean to Gabi and Allegra. There had been a lot to pick up, and they'd probably been trying their best.

I waved at the beauty therapists in the discreet salon on the ground floor and checked my bag for the presents I'd brought from Bloomingdale's. I hoped Gabi was in before Allegra, not just because her present was significantly nicer but also because I could get a reasonably accurate version of the previous fortnight's events. If I encountered Allegra first, it would take at least half an hour of intense chat about herself before she'd even consider getting round to what she'd been up to at work.

In fact, I needn't have worried, because when I reached the second floor, I found the agency door locked, a stack of mail on the table outside, and no sign of either of them.

Frowning, I checked my watch. Ten past ten. Where were they? I could hear the telephone ringing, and I let myself in as fast as I could get the key in the lock.

Once inside, I nearly dropped the mail in shock and had to steady myself against the leather couch.

For a start, the leather couch wasn't where I'd left it. It was on the other side of the room, where the desk had been. The desk was up against the opposite wall and looked as if a small but savage land battle had been fought on it recently. All my lovely pictures had been taken down, and there were shopping bags and discarded coffee cups everywhere. Worst of all, the dressmaker's dummy was wearing some kind of rugby shirt.

My knees felt like buckling, but the phone was still ringing, so I pulled myself together and answered it.

"The Little Lady Agency. How can I help you?" I said smoothly, running my eyes around the office. Thank God I'd come back!

"This is Thomasina Kendall," said a clipped voice. "Can I speak to whoever organized my son's christening present on behalf of Patrick Gough?"

Patrick Gough? The name didn't ring any bells. It must have been something the girls had sorted out while I'd been away.

Oh *God.*

"I'm terribly sorry," I apologized, searching around for the absent desk diary, "but I think one of my assistants was looking after that for Patrick, and they're not in the office at the moment. Was there a problem? Is there something I can deal with for you?"

"No," said Thomasina Kendall. "I need to speak to whomever it was *directly.*"

I fervently hoped it had been something simple, like Gabi leaving the price tag on a silver rattle, rather than Allegra giving a newborn baby a replica Aztec sacrificial knife.

I opened the drawer, saw a pair of boxer shorts draped over everything from the desktop, and closed it again. Then I closed my eyes too, for good measure.

"I am *so* sorry, Mrs. Kendall. If you give me a contact number, I'll ask her to call you the instant she comes in."

"If you could." She rattled off a series of numbers at which she could be contacted throughout the day. Whatever it was she needed to talk to them about, clearly it couldn't wait.

I put down the phone, feeling ill. *Calm down,* I told myself, trying to find three positive aspects of the gloomy situation facing me. Three positive things and the rest wouldn't look half so bad.

384

One, the phone hadn't been cut off.

Two, Gabi and Allegra had clearly been doing *something*.

And, three, I could always tidy up. Everything would look a hundred times better after thirty minutes' intensive tidying up.

I opened my eyes, sank back into my familiar carved oak office chair, and surveyed the confusion: no biscuits in the glass barrel, five dying bunches of flowers on the shelves, magazines ditched everywhere, and, bafflingly, one size five red stiletto discarded on top of the filing cabinet. There was a lingering smell in the air that I couldn't quite pinpoint. It smelled like . . . gunpowder.

In twelve days, Gabi and Allegra had turned my office into a fifth-form common room. And that was only the mess I could *see*. A shudder ran through my blood.

I couldn't stand it any longer. I yanked open my desk drawer and rummaged around until I found the photograph of me and Jonathan, absent from its pride of place by the phone, then set it firmly on the desk. Then, as my momentum picked up, I pushed back my chair, grabbed the nearest three magazines and dumped them in the bin, followed by all the paper coffee cups, plastic bags, and discarded bits of clothing.

Breathing deeply, I hung the pictures back on the wall — I could already hear Allegra whining about having to look at such cheap art — and started to tidy the bookshelves with cross, jerky movements.

And, honestly, I *hate* tidying up. I really wasn't tidying it out of a neat-freak inability to endure a badly stacked pile of books (as Nelson would have confirmed, had he been there); until the office was back to the way I'd left it, I'd feel unsettled. As if I'd been burgled.

Just as I was tottering unsteadily about the place with the vacuum cleaner, like one of those unhinged sitcom housewives Hoovering in high heels at 3 a.m., the door opened and Gabi rushed in, with two big Hamleys bags balancing her small frame. She wasn't, as I'd carefully hinted in my instruction file, wearing a skirt and pretty heels but her jeans, a black cotton shirt, and a pair of gold sneakers.

"Oh, my God, you're back!" she gasped. Then she rearranged her face into an unconvincingly confident smile and exclaimed, "Oh, my God! You're *back!*"

I turned off the vacuum cleaner. We both watched as a red casino chip whirled and then sank back into the gray dust of the transparent chamber. Somewhere in my head, I registered that it was for £500.

"When did you fly in?" asked Gabi quickly. "You must be really jet-lagged. Can I make you a coffee? I've got some more biscuits in here somewhere . . . Not telling tales, but I've been here and out again already this morning, because I had to collect a present that Allegra was supposed to have sorted out yesterday, before she felt tired and had to go to Calmia to have her chakras rebalanced. Oh, I see you've . . . er . . ." She trailed off and looked at me, and the shell-shocked expression currently freezing my face. "Sorry," she said contritely. "I was planning to do the cleaning today. Honest."

I took a deep breath. Much better to know the whole story than to guess half. Why was I thinking that so often these days?

"Just tell me," I said, "without any exaggeration *or* explanation, what's been going on while I've been away?"

"With what?" Gabi hedged.

"Well, you could start with why the desk is on the other side of the room? Why there's a shoe on the filing cabinet? Why there are sixteen messages on the answering machine? What you've done to Thomasina Kendall's son? Why no one was here when . . ." I stopped, hearing my voice rising with each question, and I pressed my lips together, breathing into my stomach to calm myself down. It wasn't like me to be so shouty, either. Tidying up *and* shouting. Blimey, I was turning into an office manager.

I let out all the pent-up breath in a big sigh and felt marginally better. But not much. "Maybe I will have that cup of coffee."

"God, Mel," said Gabi, turning on the coffee machine, "you've only been in New York two weeks and already you're barking orders at me like Jonathan. Take a chill pill. Sit down, will you? Have you had a good time?"

"I've had a fantastic time," I said, but I wasn't going to be sidetracked until I heard what needed to be sorted out here. "But come on, give me the bad news. Before Allegra gets in."

Gabi tossed her head dismissively. "Chuh. In that case, we've got time for a minute-by-minute account of the past twelve days for both of us. And I thought I had a bad attitude about time-keeping. It's her fault the place is in this mess."

"Really?" I gave Gabi my best "now, is that the whole truth?" look.

"It is!" she insisted. "The police were here yesterday! She claimed she was too trauma-

tized to tidy up after they'd searched it, and
—"

I held up my hand as my heart sank into
my stomach-flattening pants. "Stop there.
Slowly, please. The *police* were here?"

Gabi nodded. "They're done searching
her place, and your mum's place, and they
still haven't found whatever it is they're
looking for, so when they found out Allegra
was here, suddenly we had Scotland Yard
knocking on the door. They fingerprinted
everything, even your dressmaking dummy."
She sniffed. "You can still smell it, can't
you?"

I sank my head onto my forearms on the
desk.

Police! In my office.

No. I couldn't think of three positive
things to say about that.

In fact, I couldn't think of one.

A grim thought occurred to me, and I sat
bolt upright. "God in heaven. Tell me they
didn't —"

"Nope, they didn't find anything here,
either," added Gabi cheerfully. "But
they had a good laugh watching your home
movies of Tristram Hart-Mossop leching
at you in Selfridges. And I got some
very interesting gossip about one of them
who knows the protection officers at

Downing Street. Apparently, Cherie has this
—"

"Don't tell me," I yelped. "Just tell me
some nice encouraging things until I get my
composure back."

"Okay," said Gabi, heaping ground coffee
into the filter. She took a look at me, and
added an extra scoop. "I've spoken to some
awfully worried young posh blokes, who are
all having hernias because you're in New
York." She put her head on one side curiously. "What is it you do to these people?
Some of them sound desperate. You can tell
me, Allegra's not here."

"Nothing, really," I said, feeling mollified.
"I just . . . Well, it's not all just shopping,
you know. It's the talking, and, er, listening."

Gabi looked baffled. "But half of them
never say anything."

"Oh, it's all about giving them a bosom to
cry on. I mean, a shoulder. To cry on."

"Well, that might be closer to the truth
than you know," said Gabi, turning on the
coffee machine. "Your bosom could bring a
grown man to tears."

"And what exactly do you mean by that?"
I demanded.

"Oh . . . never mind. If you look on the
desk, there's a list of messages. Do you

mind having your coffee black? We're out of milk."

"That's all right." I moved the invoice files and the mail file to one side. So I could see Gabi better over the desk, I also moved the large cardboard box that had been dumped there.

"What's this?" I asked, peering in. "Is it those breath fresheners I sent over? I thought we could slip some in with each invoice. Then no one can take it personally."

"Ah, no, they're in the storeroom. You don't need to see that," said Gabi quickly. "That's just . . . just nothing."

She swooped to take the box away, but I swooped it in the opposite direction first and held the box away from her.

"So what's in here then?" I asked, reaching inside. My hand made contact with a whole load of soft things. "Don't tell me you've taken up knitting socks for Nelson?" I asked, pulling one out.

When I saw what it was, I nearly hurled it straight back in. "Argh!"

Gabi sighed.

"What in the name of all that's holy is this?" I shook it at her, then peered more closely. It seemed to be a knitted toy dog, except it had six legs and one ear much longer than the other, and it was knitted from a strange green mohair, which gave it a fuzzy halo. There was also a tumor on its back, bulging obscenely, but not quite as obscenely as its red tongue, which lolled out at some length. The whole thing looked radioactive.

"Is it a dog?" I asked incredulously. "A camel? An . . . anteater? I mean, *what?*"

I dropped it onto the desk with a shudder and looked at Gabi for some explanation.

She opened her mouth, then closed it again and shrugged.

Silently, I reached into the box and pulled out a cat, created in a luminous rainbow stripe, sporting a tail that was three times as long as its body and massive ears that bent in different directions. For some reason, there were three of them. It also had terrifying human-shaped eyes sewn onto its head in green wool, complete with *Clockwork Orange* eyelashes and staring pupils.

I put it next to the dog. They made a fearsome couple. In fact, just looking at them brought back vague stirrings of childhood nightmares.

I giggled nervously. "Gabi, did my mother send these?"

She nodded. "There are lots."

I peered into the box and vaguely made

out a tangle of legs, heads, tails, and torsos, all in different colors. A child could end up with lifelong issues if they woke up with something like that next to them on the pillow.

"Mummy must have been very busy," I said, trying to think of a positive observation to make.

"She's knitting away her stress," explained Gabi. "I had a very interesting chat with her on the phone. Apparently, there's been a bit of bother with —"

"Gabi," I said firmly. "One catastrophe at a time."

She rolled her eyes in a manner that hardly befitted her recent "Nelson makes me feel like a *lady*" posturings. "Look, it hasn't been a total disaster while you've been swanning round New York," she snapped. "If you look in the invoice file, you'll see that it hasn't all been police raids and shopping. Some of us have been doing some work."

I bit my tongue and opened the box file. "I know," I apologized. I had no right to yell at Gabi. Coping with Allegra was a full-time job for most people. "I'm sorry. I know you've been working hard, and I do appreciate it."

"We have. Well, I have." Gabi poured me

some coffee and brought it over to the desk. I noticed, as she put the cup and saucer down, that she surreptitiously moved the box of mutant toys to somewhere out of my line of vision.

"Oh, come here and give me a hug," I said, pushing my chair back and going over to embrace her. "I've really missed you."

"I've missed you too," she said, hugging me back, and I was relieved. It was horrible being cross with Gabi — I wasn't cut out for ball-breaking, and to be honest, I was quite glad about that.

"So," I said, "what's in the Hamleys bags?" I peered but couldn't see inside. "I love Hamleys. I could spend all day in there!"

Gabi looked shifty, and at that moment, the door swung open and Allegra shimmered in. When she saw me, a ghost of a double take flitted across her face, then vanished behind her usual expression of barely concealed impatience.

"Hello, Melissa," she said. "Ah, splendid, you've made coffee, Gabi. Black, three sugars, please."

"I made coffee for *Melissa*," said Gabi through gritted teeth.

"Biscuits?" Allegra held out her hand toward Gabi expectantly.

"Allegra, this isn't a café!" I protested. "And Gabi isn't here to furnish you with *elevenses*." I took a deliberate look at my watch. "As it now is."

Allegra shot Gabi a filthy look. "Well, she's keen enough to provide . . ."

"In my bag," snapped Gabi, quickly. "There are some Bahlsen chocolate wafers."

"Excellent," said Allegra with a vulpine smile.

I looked between the pair of them. They were fixing each other with the sort of death-looks I'd last seen in the St. Cathal's Junior Common Room circa 1987.

"So," I said, trying to keep the atmosphere noncombative for as long as possible, "Gabi was just telling me about the presents she'd got in Hamleys this morning. Isn't it just the most fun place to shop for other people? Did you find my christening present checklist?"

"I did, thank you. It was most helpful," said Gabi pointedly. "I bought a train set, after *looking around* for *half an hour* and reading your notes really carefully."

Allegra tossed her head and helped herself to another biscuit.

I looked first at Gabi, then at Allegra, but couldn't for the life of me work out what was going on. Honestly, it was like being at a tennis match, only with an invisible ball. Not only could you not see what was going on, but it was impossible to tell who was winning.

I pulled myself together. After all, I was the one in charge here.

"Anyway, getting back to business," I said briskly, "maybe one of you can tell me what the problem is with Thomasina Kendall?"

"You little snitch!" hissed Allegra, at the same time as Gabi snapped, "I said nothing, so don't even think of blaming me!"

I banged my hands on the desk to get their attention. "Stop it! Stop it right now! Allegra! Tell me what you sent that poor child!"

Allegra heaved in a long breath through her long nose. "Did Gabi tell you that the police have been here, harassing me?"

"She did, yes, but that's —"

"And that I've been incredibly stressed and busy, complying with their impertinent demands? I've had to provide bank statements and —"

"Allegra!" I said fiercely, trying to ignore the fact that her job, for which she was being paid more than *me,* clearly came some way down her list of must-dos. "Get to the point. Police. Why?"

Gabi looked impressed. Then a bit scared.

"I, unlike some people, have been too busy with personal tragedy to trail around Hamleys looking at tacky geegaws for over-indulged brats," Allegra informed me. "And since I was anxious to meet the deadline for posting the present to this ridiculous child . . ."

"Who has two minor royals for godparents," added Gabi.

"Is that kind of thing impressive in Mill Hill?" sneered Allegra. "I wouldn't know."

I closed my eyes and placed my palms over my eyelids. Tea bags would only ruin my eyeliner, and I needed that in place for Daddy's meeting.

"Because I *knew* he would be inundated with exactly that sort of boring, mass-produced rubbish, I sent him a beautiful, unique piece of art, which any child of taste would treasure forever," she finished, with a distinct note of smugness. "I fail to see the problem. Gabi and I will have to agree to differ about what constitutes a thoughtful gift."

"Well, in that case, you should have booked him some therapy sessions, for when he's able to talk!" interrupted Gabi furiously. "*If* he ever manages to gain the power of speech!"

A ghastly idea was beginning to solidify

in my head.

"Allegra," I said, trying to keep the panic out of my voice, "just tell me. What did you send?"

She made a dismissive gesture toward my desk. "A couple of those toys Mummy's been knitting. A cat, I think, and a giraffe." She paused. "Or it could have just been a leopard with a long neck. Whatever. The child'll adore it."

The blood drained from my face as I saw my reputation as a telepathic gift-giver evaporate in a hot gust of nanny gossip. "Allegra, please tell me this is your idea of a joke."

"I've got the train set right here," Gabi interrupted. "We can wrap it up now, and courier it over there, and say there's been an awful mistake, and —"

"No, it's too late for that," I groaned. "The child's traumatized mother is already on the warpath."

"Oh, how preposterous!" Allegra waved her hand. "Silly woman probably prefers those dreadful silver teething rings."

"Allegra!" I howled. "How many times do I have to say this? It isn't about what *you* think is the right thing to do, it's about listening to the client and helping *them* decide!"

"I did try to stop her," said Gabi. "But she flounced out."

"Oh, shut up, Gabi," snapped Allegra. "I suppose you haven't told her about your little outing last weekend?"

Gabi shot Allegra a dirty look. "That's hardly the same thing."

Allegra arched her plucked eyebrow. "No?"

The phone rang, interrupting this horrendous double act, and I picked it up crossly.

"Good morning, the Little Lady Agency?"

There was a familiar nasal squelch. "Ah, the lovely Mel! Wasn't expecting to hear your dulcet tones."

"Hello, Roger," I said. This was all I needed.

Allegra gave Gabi a triumphant smirk, and Gabi scowled back.

"Can I speak to Gabi, please?" he said. "If she's there."

"She is here, Roger," I said, gesturing to Gabi. "We're in the middle of a meeting, actually —"

"I won't keep you then. Anyway, how are you?" he enquired suavely. "Enjoying New York?"

"Very much," I said, confused by his cordiality. Last time we'd spoken, he'd been virtually Neanderthal. "Listen, I'm sure we'll catch up soon, Roger, but in the meantime, here's Gabi."

I mouthed "Keep it brief" at her as I handed over the phone, then leaned over to Allegra.

"You will phone Mrs. Kendall and apologize for sending those revolting toys," I hissed. "I know Mummy's very stressed right now, and I'm sure when she gets less tense she'll make lovely animals with the right number of appendages, but those things would scare an experienced adult, let alone a child."

"Shh!" said Allegra, pointing at Gabi.

I turned back, bewildered, to see Gabi looking most discomfited, twisting the phone cord around her finger and keeping her eyes fixed on me.

"No, that's fine," she said carefully. "I'm glad it went well."

"*What* went well, I wonder?" muttered Allegra with malicious glee.

"No, I don't think there's any need to speak to . . . Well, I don't know, Roger. I thought we agreed that . . ."

Gabi looked at me. Panic and guilt were written all over her face.

I held out my hand for the telephone.

"If that's all you called about, Roger, we're

in the middle of a meeting right now," she said quickly. "So maybe we can talk about this later."

"Give me the phone," I said. "I'd like a word."

Gabi turned her gaze to me. "Here's Melissa," she said and handed me the receiver.

"Roger," I said heavily.

"Hello again! Jolly decent of Gabi to leap into the breach, if you ask me," Roger chuckled. "I can quite see why you might not be up to it, but in the humble opinion of R. Trumpet, Esq., Gabi makes quite the blond bombshell too!"

I said nothing, but from Gabi's reaction, my face was probably speaking for me.

"Have to say, there was quite an awkward moment during the dancing, when Gabs got a bit carried away in the Gay Gordons and brought all eight of us down, arse over tip," he went on, less jovially. "I didn't realize that Moira Sutton really did have a false leg, but, generally, you know, no one noticed. And, mmm, I should probably tell you that the aged mama was a bit narky about your comments about Celia's get-up — well, I say 'your' . . . ." He chortled at the memory, which was obviously tickling him no end.

I glared at Gabi. I'd spent hours buttering up Lady Trumpet that weekend at Trumpet Manor. *Hours.* Not to mention learning all the complicated country dances required for her parties. That was the whole point about the pretend girlfriend dates: it wasn't just about the dress and the wig. It was about talking to the datee's friends, bolstering his confidence, probing delicately, then laying subtle foundations for him to springboard into better things.

Allegra and Gabi were bickering again, under their breath. It seemed to be about the biscuits.

"So what were you calling about, Roger?" I enquired. "Because sadly, I don't think Gabi will be making any more outings in that capacity."

"Shame," said Roger. "We got on rather well. Anyway, I was ringing to ask about whether she was going to invoice me through the office, or whether she'd do it for cash. You know, freelance."

I glared at Gabi. "I think she'll be invoicing through the office," I said. "And perhaps making a charity donation."

"Rarely?" exclaimed Roger. He meant "really," but his inner Sloane mangled his vowels in moments of extreme surprise.

"Yes, rarely," I said. "The Lifeboats, I

should think. Would you excuse me, Roger? I'm right in the middle of debriefing Gabi and Allegra."

I hung up the phone on Roger's snorts. It rang again immediately, but I sent the call to the answering machine.

Gabi looked shocked. It went totally against my office efficiency grain to let a phone call go unanswered.

Instead, I folded my arms and glared at the pair of them in silence until the bickering petered out.

"I'm terribly disappointed in you two," I said, drawing up my spine until the garters on my stockings stretched. "I didn't ask you to do very much. I didn't make any outrageous demands. In fact, I only asked you to follow some very simple instructions, and you deliberately ignored them. I'm especially disappointed in you, Gabi," I said, turning to her.

She bowed her dark head, contritely.

"Bring me the wig, please," I said.

She got to her feet and went over to the filing cabinet. I swallowed my distress that she'd just stuffed it in under *w* for wig. The wig held a sacred place in my heart. I'd built up my business with the help of that wig, and whatever Nelson might say in teasing, I remained in awe of its powers.

Honestly, I thought, this was almost more than I could stand. Between these two running riot with my reputation, and Jonathan intimating that I should be organizing tea party classes, and Paige Drogan playing me like a cheap fiddle, I was hardly the Honey Blennerhesket who'd waltzed around London in this very wig, charming all in her path with verve and élan.

Honey, I knew, would not be putting up with this. But then, Honey didn't have to live with any of these people, whereas I did.

Gabi put the wig in front of me on the desk and sat down.

I smoothed out the soft hair until it was shiny and sleek again, then opened my big handbag and put it safely inside.

"I'm taking this back with me," I informed them. "If you can't be trusted."

"Oh, for heaven's sake, Melissa, stop acting like some religious martyr," snapped Allegra. "No one's impressed."

I turned on her, furious. "Don't talk me to me about being impressed! If you think you're getting paid for the rest of this month, you can start by turning up before eleven o'clock in the morning! I am sick and tired of people underestimating how hard it is to do this job," I fumed. "And I thought you two might understand.

But you don't, and that makes me really rather *sad*."

I realized that tears were rising in my throat, and I stopped midrant. Obviously the flight had affected me more than I'd thought. Or maybe it was something else. I blinked rapidly.

The phone rang again, and this time I picked it up as a reflex reaction.

"The Little Lady Agency?"

Allegra and Gabi both flinched this time, in guilty anticipation.

There was a nervous cough. "Ees Franco? The father of Inez, the daily cleeeaner of Meester Ralph Waterstone? Plis inforrrrm Allegra that my daughter ees being investigated by the social servicessss. I hope she ees happy! But we haf frrriends, and we knows wherrre you leeve! Mother of God!" Then the phone slammed down.

"She was an illegal immigrant," whined Allegra before I'd even opened my mouth. "What was I meant to do?"

"You were only meant to tell her to clean the loo with a different cloth than the one she uses on the sink!" snapped Gabi.

"Shut up!" I yelled, raising my hands. "Shut up! Shut up! Shut up!"

That finally shut them up. They probably thought I was about to have a seizure. It certainly felt like that from where I was sitting.

"I need to have a look through the diary and the mail," I went on, after a pregnant pause. "Gabi, would you walk round to Baker and Spice and get us some cake. Allegra, kindly call Mrs. Kendall, explain about the mix-up, apologize like you've never apologized before, send that train set, and then . . ." I hesitated. "Then just go and do something else for the rest of the day, please. I'm sure you've got plenty to occupy you."

She gave me a pitying look, as if I'd been the one causing trouble. "Those of us with full lives do, Melissa. I'll see you later." And she swept out. I was surprised not to hear a clap of thunder and lightning as she left the building, although we did hear the front door slam with a ferocity that probably ruined several relaxation treatments in the salon below.

"Mel?" asked Gabi tentatively.

"Can you give me ten minutes?" I said, trying a brave smile. "I just need a moment to see the funny side. I mean, I know there is a funny side. But I'm just having a temporary sense-of-humor failure."

"Sure," she said. "I'll go and get those cakes."

And she spun on her heel and scurried out without even asking for petty cash.

Sixteen

I couldn't stay mad at Gabi for long. She knew me too well, for one thing, and, besides, there was something about my office that always calmed me down. The lilac walls, I think. In the sensible hour Gabi took to walk to Elizabeth Street and back again, I'd made eight brisk phone calls of apology for services rendered (or not, in three instances), replied to five letters, and opened all the mail, while taking deep breaths and listening to Ella Fitzgerald.

I also allowed myself to try on the wig. Just seeing myself in the bathroom mirror with that long caramel fringe falling into my eyes made me feel more in control of everything. A strange peace fell over my shoulders, along with the additional hair, and I knew I could tackle anything. Hadn't I conquered my own shyness, and built up a successful business, all on my own? In this very wig?

Then I took it off, in case one of them came back unexpectedly.

Smoothing out a few knotty problems was actually rather invigorating, and the jet lag soon fell away as my brain negotiated the familiar steps of London social routines once more.

For instance, I spoke to poor Toby Henderson *before* he'd had time to give his entire wardrobe to the nearest charity shop, as advised by Gabi and Allegra, and I managed to soothe his shell-shocked ego back to semioperational state. In a stroke of inspiration, I looked up his measurements, still on his file card from our trip to Austin Reed last year, and suggested doing some shopping for him, online, when I was back in New York.

At half twelve, the office door edged open, and Gabi's dark curls appeared nervously round it; she found me in a surprisingly good mood, considering the horrors I was unearthing.

"Just think," I said over the phone to Toby, motioning for Gabi to sit, "you won't have to go into a changing room, and I know how much you hate that. I know. I *know* — *not* the most hygienic places . . . no, you won't have to deal with Allegra again. I promise. Ever. Yes, on my honor."

Gabi made some fresh coffee, rather self-consciously.

"Or Gabi," I added, in response to Toby's question. "Actually, she *does* have a boy-friend. No, I don't think she talks to him quite like that though . . ."

Gabi started to make an outraged face, then remembered she was meant to be contrite, and stopped.

"Toby, I'm terribly sorry, but I have to go," I said, as he began to unload his new hair-loss agony. "But I think I saw something exactly for that kind of problem in Duane Reade, this super American drug-store, so why don't you write me a nice long e-mail, and I'll sort it all out for you by the end of the week?"

That seemed to cheer him up, and I crossed his name off my list with some relief. It was the last one, apart from Roger Trumpet, with whom I intended to have a *very* long chat, but not over the phone.

"Well," I said, as Gabi put a cup of coffee and a slice of chocolate cake in front of me. "That's that cleared up. And you might like to know that Piers Saunders isn't going to sue us, after all."

"Sorry," she said immediately. "But he should have known Allegra wasn't a real skin specialist —"

I held up a "Stop!" hand. "Gabi, come on — if these people had *any* idea what they were doing, they wouldn't be calling us in the first place. I know you and Allegra don't have much sympathy for dithering men, but, for my sake, can you try? This is my livelihood you're dealing with, not to mention their feelings."

Gabi cast her eyes down for a moment, then looked up, unable to disguise her unquenchable thirst for gossip.

"So, you *are* coming back then? Jonathan hasn't proposed now he's finally lured you over there?"

I blushed. "Yes! And no. He hasn't. Come on, Gabi, it's only been a *fortnight.*"

"But it's going all right?" She added a meaningful look.

"Yes," I said, busying myself with my pencil pot.

"He's making more time for you now?"

I hesitated. "Um, yes. Sort of. And the house is amazing! The master bedroom has two bathrooms."

Gabi kicked off her shoes and tucked her feet under her on the sofa, balancing her cup and saucer on the arm — until she saw my expression and placed them carefully on the side table next to her.

"Well, go on then," she said encouragingly.

"Spill. What kind of house has the King of Realtors chosen for his domain?"

After I described Jonathan's house in Greenwich Village in sufficient detail to satisfy her, Gabi asked, "So he's sold the huge apartment on Park Avenue that he had with . . . Cindy."

"Yes," I said. Gabi was the sort of PA who made her job interesting by raiding the HR files like she was on an MI5 intelligence mission. "He's selling it right now."

"He's selling it? You mean, as in *he's* . . ."

I nodded.

Gabi widened her eyes. "That's so typical! And you tell me he's not a control freak?"

"No, Gabi, it's not like that — Cindy instructed him! She's driving him round the bend about it . . ." I stopped. We were getting onto quite thin ice now.

Gabi's eyes narrowed again. "I see. How convenient for her. To have her ex over a barrel and on the end of a string. No wonder you're worried. Did you find out if that's where he was the other day, when he was late for your lunch meeting?"

Suddenly I didn't really want to talk about it anymore.

"Um, he didn't say where he was." I forked some cake in half, trying to ignore her very perceptive observation. Any minute now my lurking fears about Cindy would spill out. Then there'd be no packing them away again. In desperation, I tried the distraction technique that worked so well on Braveheart. "Did you know in New York, they say "I don't care" instead of "I don't mind"? I couldn't work out why people were being so rude to me when I was trying to be nice . . ."

"Really?" Gabi's expression suddenly turned serious. "Did you get my Kiehl's stuff? Because if you haven't, I've just been reading about a new cleanser you can only get in New York . . ."

For a good ten minutes, every time Gabi's mouth opened to ask another question about Cindy I told her about Karen and her speed-dating adventures, and how breathtaking Grand Central Station was, and the supercheap OPI nail varnish, and the bus maps that you needed to have A-level Maths to figure out, and how weirdly hard it was to buy postage stamps. For variation, I also filled her in on Braveheart, Jonathan's romantic boating trip, and the frosting-tastic Magnolia Bakery on Bleecker Street.

"And do they love your accent?" she demanded. "Do you tell them your father is a Right Honorable Gentleman?"

"No! I do not." I paused. "I'm not telling anyone very much about me, to be honest."

"Not even about your agency?"

"Especially not that." I hesitated. This wasn't going to play well in Gabi's eyes either, I knew it. "Jonathan wants me to softpedal the whole agency thing. Because it comes across wrong to Americans," I added, seeing the outrage on her face. "The fact that it's *men,* and me, and you know. And I don't want to show him up or anything. Everyone's so easily offended over there — they keep asking me if I mind them smoking, or drinking wine, or talking about religion . . ." I stopped, as a positive thing occurred to me. "The good thing is, I never miss any of their jokes, not like I do here. I always know when to get my hearty laugh ready, because they check first that I won't be offended by the punch line."

"Thoughtful," said Gabi dryly. "So, come on — you haven't met Cindy?"

"No," I admitted. Even though I didn't really want to talk about it, something inside was urging me to get it off my chest, now I was here with one of my own friends. "Jonathan and I had a really good talk about her, and he doesn't want me to spoil my trip by meeting her."

"How thoughtful of him," said Gabi sarcastically.

"Don't say it like you don't believe me. Plus, he doesn't want to see her any more than he has to. Apparently, she's acting up about their apartment."

"And not just because his new girlfriend is in town?"

I bit my lip, but it was too late. The floodgates were opening, sweeping away all the lovely things I wanted to remember. "Oh, Gabi, I feel like she's there all the time, but in a negative way. Like, when we meet people, I can see them looking me over, to see if I've got anything in common with her. And Jonathan's always telling me how he loves the fact that I'm *not* pushy, and *not* plastered in makeup, and *not* this, that or the other . . ."

"But I thought it was all done and dusted, with the divorce. You told me last *year* that he . . ."

"I don't think it's that simple," I said unhappily. And I *was* shocked at how unhappy I felt, now that I thought about it.

I knew I should tell Gabi about what that Jennifer woman had said at Kurt and Bonnie's party, about the "rebound girl." But suddenly, a familiar old mortification started to creep back into my stomach, and I wondered if that's what they were *all* saying.

Maybe even saying to him *this weekend,* over drinks at Wentworth's country place, while I was away.

"Mel?" said Gabi. "You're . . . you're not crying, are you?"

I shook my head. "I was really excited when I flew in," I said sadly. "Now . . . I'm not so much."

Gabi got up and came to sit on the edge of the desk so she could put her arm round me. "Listen," she said firmly. "Cindy sounds like a nightmare. But you've known that for ages. And Jonathan is very clearly nuts about you. Who wouldn't be? You're beautiful, and clever, you run your own business, and you can sew bias-cut skirts. What more could a corporate weasel like Jonathan want?"

"So why does he want me to run stupid tea party seminars?" I exploded.

There was a pause, then Gabi said, "No. Back up. You've lost me."

"Oh, it's just a conversation we had over dinner. He thinks I could set up another Little Lady Agency in New York, but organizing tea parties for brides, and new mothers, and sweet sixteens. Etiquette stuff, you know."

"But Mel, more weddings?" asked Gabi anxiously. "I mean, Emery's wedding was fab, but it nearly killed you."

I shrugged. "I don't *want* to do weddings. But I get the feeling that's what Jonathan thinks I should be doing. I mean, I wouldn't be short of work — I've already spent one lunch helping one of his friends organize a fortieth birthday party." I paused. "Themed around *Pride and Prejudice*."

"Well, to be fair," said Gabi, "you are the only woman I know with her own corsets."

I gazed helplessly at her. "But is it really awful of me not to want to do weddings and stuff all the time? Even if Jonathan wants me to? Be honest. I don't like brides. I don't like what all that white does to women's brains. And I prefer dealing with men. They're just so much more straightforward."

Gabi gave me a "well, duh" look. "Which is probably exactly why Jonathan doesn't want you doing it. He's scared you'll run off with someone better. Running off with a groom would *really* wreck your business."

"Don't be ridiculous!" I scoffed. "The whole *point* is that those men need help buying their own socks, and he's practically perfect!"

"Maybe he doesn't see it like that." Gabi paused. "I mean, not being funny or anything, but maybe he's still sore about Cindy running off with his less thrusting and dynamic brother? That's got to hurt, when you're Mr. Perfect."

I ate some cake. Jonathan *was* obviously still sore about his marriage breakdown, but that only proved how much he still felt about Cindy. Not good.

"I just don't understand why he's being like this when he's always been so gung-ho about my so-called 'business savvy.' " I put bunny ears around it, in case Gabi thought I'd lost all remaining traces of irony.

"Has he come straight out and told you to pack in the agency here?"

I wriggled. "No. But we haven't really discussed what's going to happen . . . next. I didn't want to look pushy. I've only been in New York ten minutes. But he has made it pretty clear that I'm not supposed to do anything, you know, Agencyish, while I'm over there, and it's hard to know whether he genuinely wants me to have a rest, or whether he's more bothered than he lets on about people finding out how we met, or whether it's some kind of test to see if I can leave work alone, and . . ."

I was about to add *and focus my attention on him,* when I realized how selfish that made Jonathan sound. I closed my mouth on that thought. I knew that wasn't what he meant.

Gabi peered at me closely. "And you have been working, haven't you?"

Honestly, she could read me like a book. I really had to learn how to be more poker-faced. "Sort of. Actually, no. No! Well, yes."

Gabi giggled. "Oh, dear, Mel. Dr. No doesn't like being disobeyed. It's not programmed into his circuitry."

"I didn't do it on purpose!" I protested. "I just got . . . niced into it."

She wagged her finger. "And that, Melissa, is your Achilles' heel. The *nice.* God Almighty. And it was a man, too, wasn't it? Go on, tell Auntie Gabi. I have this odd feeling that Jonathan's funny moods are about to fall into place."

With a growing sense of panic, I confessed all about Godric, and Paige maneuvering me into looking after him, and the photo in the paper, and how I was meant to be spinning his rudeness into some kind of persona. Back in London the whole thing suddenly looked like a disaster waiting to happen. No. A disaster that was actually *happening.*

"And I don't even know what she *wants me to do!*" I wailed. "How on earth am I meant to make him look *dangerous,* Gabi? I'm used to smoothing down rough edges, not roughing them up. I mean, the only bad boys I've been out with were bad in the 'sometimes don't brush my teeth for three days' kind of bad."

Gabi tapped her fingers against her jawline. "Well, Orlando von Borsch was bad. He had slip-on shoes. And he broke your heart."

"I don't think that's quite what Paige is after."

"Isn't it? Getting a gullible MP's daughter to arrange his tax investigation while he perfects his tan on board HMS *Saucy Sue* or wherever he was, using the pneumatic Lady Tiziana Buckeridge as a human lounge chair . . ."

"Gabi! Stop it!" I glared at her. "Thank you for your sage advice. But had you met Godric Ponsonby, you'd realize how he isn't even in Orlando's league. Anyway," I added, "Orlando is all in the past for me. I have more self-respect these days. Now tell me, what can I do with Godric to keep Paige happy? Just so I can get out of this mess before Jonathan really kicks off."

She pulled her lower lip sternly over her top one. "I think you should tell this agent that your boyfriend has instructed you, in no uncertain terms, that your ingenuity is strictly off limits, and that you can have no more to do with this project of deception."

"You think?" I sighed. "I mean, you're

right. I should. But Paige is kind of scary and —"

"Of *course* I don't think you should tell her that!" roared Gabi. "Jesus! I know you never had much of a sense of irony, Mel, but are they draining it out of you, or something?" She slid off the desk and refilled our coffee cups. "If you prove to Jonathan how well you can handle this, he won't have a leg to stand on about making you do boring wedding parties. Much better that you just do it, then pretend that it took you so little effort that you didn't even remember to tell him about it."

"Exactly!" I said, relieved that it had been Gabi who'd said that.

"Right. Okay, you want that kind of up-market living, downtown connections bad boy thing, yeah? Well . . ." She thought. "Get him a BMW from somewhere, one of those classic old-school M ones, and some really English suits, from Oliver James or someone like that. As English as possible. Tell him to pay for everything in cash — it looks good and secretive. Has he got a ring? Great. Get a bigger one. One really big diamond ring on his little finger, and one of those big camel coats he can wear over his shoulders . . ."

"Gabi, it's September?" I said faintly. "It's

still quite warm out there . . ."

"He needs some personal pain and suffering in his past," she steamed on. "And some women who've broken his heart, but who he'd do anything for, even now. No kids though," she added, "that just looks careless. What's his girlfriend history?"

"Paige thinks there was one girl a while ago who dumped him," I admitted, my mind filling with Godric's pasty gloom. "But apart from that, I don't know. It's hard to imagine him with a woman."

"Hmm. Well, find out. Then make some up."

"Gabi, I don't know if Godric can pull this off! He's just not that confident. He comes across arsey, but I know he's just shy. You know, like Roger. I can't even see him wearing *jewelry.*"

Gabi looked disbelieving. "He's an actor, isn't he?"

"Well, yes." I stopped as light belatedly dawned on my thick head. "But this is perfect, because he can just *act* the part. Ace!" I bounced up off my seat and gave her a big hug. "God, I knew you'd work it out for me! I *knew* it was a good idea to come back!"

Gabi squeezed me. "Well, if you're anything like you were first thing today, then you should be flying back for weekends. Jeez." She held me at arm's length. "Talk about stroppy. Don't do that again. I was scared."

"Sorry. But, you know . . ." I didn't want to admit how much better I felt after just a few hours in the office. In my own office. Being me. Not Jonathan's girlfriend, or Cindy's replacement, or even Braveheart's wrangler.

"Listen to me," said Gabi. "Don't let Jonathan make you give up what you love doing best. And don't let anyone make you think you're not blond enough or skinny enough or overachieving enough. Because you're perfect as you are."

I hadn't said any of that. So how on earth did she know that was what I was thinking?

"Gabi," I said hesitantly, "do you reckon sometimes obstacles are there to make you want something more?"

Gabi's face softened. "Within reason. There's no point climbing and climbing over obstacles if you're too knackered to enjoy the view, you know?"

I nodded, and we shared a long pause.

"So, anyway, how long have we got you in London for?" she asked, going over to the machine to make more coffee. "And, more to the point, how long are you staying?"

"Um, I'll fly back after the weekend," I said. "And I suppose I'll be staying in New York until Nelson's flat's finished. How's that coming along, by the way?"

"Erm, fine. Fine." I noticed Gabi make a surreptitious note on the back of her hand. "I have it all under control. And," she added, before I could speak, "I will keep a really close eye on everything here while you're away. I promise."

Gabi put the biscuits down and rubbed her hands together expectantly. "So, have you got a picture of this Godric lad, then?" she asked. "If you're hanging out with film stars, I need to know what they look like."

I turned on the office computer to find Godric's official website, and I found Ric Spencer.com, complete with his new head-shots. While Gabi was swooning over them, I realized, to my shock, that it was almost time for me to leave for Daddy's meeting.

"Mel, he's sex on a stick!" she said. "Why did you never introduce me? He's a fox!"

"Because I haven't seen him since I was seventeen. Besides, you've got your own fox to be considering."

"My fox who never writes, who never phones, not even a carrier pigeon," replied Gabi mournfully.

"Well, I haven't heard from him either, if

it makes you feel any better," I said, not feeling up to tackling the Nelson/Gabi issue just yet. "Why don't you e-mail Godric your ideas?" I suggested. "Saves me time, and you can have a nice little correspondence."

"Can I?" she asked, eyes lighting up.

"Yes, but let me see your e-mail first, okay?" I insisted. "Now I don't know where Allegra's gone to, but I want that apology out of her, if it's the last thing I do."

"Leave it to me," said Gabi.

Crossing London after being in New York felt rather odd. The streets were winding, for a start, and weren't laid out *logically.* The meeting was taking place at the antediluvian members' club my father belonged to, and as I walked down Piccadilly, en route to Pall Mall, I was struck as never before by the ornamentation on the building facades. Fortnum and Mason nearly brought me out in a proud patriotic rash. It was all so . . . old!

Daddy was lurking in the fusty reception area, ready to pluck me from the disapproving eyes of the doorman. It was not an establishment that readily welcomed women, or indeed any aspect of the twenty-first century, which was why my father liked it so much.

"She's my secretary," he explained, hustling me past the front desk.

"You could just have said I was your daughter," I protested, under my breath. "There's no shame in that!"

"For the purposes of today, you are my secretary. Got that?" he hissed, as he propelled me past an oak door and into a paneled meeting room, where two besuited men in very minimalist European spectacles were sitting in stunned silence in front of a presentation plate of cheese in various shades of orange, while Allegra regarded them with her steeliest gaze. She had changed, I noticed, into a sharp black pencil skirt and matching jacket, accessorized with a lapel brooch that looked like a stainless-steel chrysanthemum. Her long black hair hung in a shiny curtain down her back, and her lips were exactly the same color as a red Ferrari. She looked like a wildly sexed up Goth version of Honey.

The anti-Honey.

I shuddered, as the thunder clapped in my head.

Before I could say *Why are you here?* Daddy moved swiftly to cut me off.

"Always late, eh? These women! What *can* one do?" he tutted blokishly to the first of the two men, and Allegra snarled something

426

in what might have been Swedish but could easily have been her clearing her throat.

"Anyway, now that my assistant has finally laid her hands on that vital paperwork, let's get down to business! As you know, gentlemen, there will be a significant tender for cheese at the Games — we'll need that plastic stuff for the Continental breakfasts, plus regional specialities for lunch buffets, as well as a selection of quality cheeses for the formal dinners," he rolled on.

Then he paused, while Allegra cackled away in tongues. "Melissa, take it down, take it down!"

"But my shorthand is rubbish!" I whispered. "I failed my exams twice."

He leaned very close to me, so close I could smell the Jarlsberg on his breath. "Just pretend then. And do try to smile. You might at least *look* authentic."

And so this bizarre meeting passed. Since Daddy had spent the best part of his parliamentary life chasing various EU cheese freebies round the five-star hotels of Europe, I should have known he'd find a way to shoehorn his cheese interests into his new line of work. Sadly, the delights of Cheddar weren't enough to stave off the jet lag creeping up on me. I literally had three functioning minutes left on my brain meter when

Daddy abruptly drew things to a close, swept Sven and Ullick off to a boys-only drinking session, and unceremoniously booted me and Allegra out into Pall Mall. It was drizzling, but warm at the same time — a meteorological treat only London could offer. Like a monsoon without the excitement factor.

"What was that about?" I demanded as we walked in the direction of Green Park tube.

"Oh, I don't ask," said Allegra. "I think we had to make an appearance at some point. For the sake of his invoices."

I stopped walking and stared at her. "What do you mean?"

Allegra didn't stop. "Oh, I expect he's putting us on his expenses. Two secretaries, three secretaries . . . every little bit counts."

Was this a scam, after all? That cash going into my account for Allegra's salary — *was* that Daddy's money? But surely I'd be getting more than twenty percent of it, if that had been true. I batted the thought away.

Allegra was some way off now, and I had to hurry to catch up with her.

"How's Lars?" I asked, panting slightly. "I hear things are moving on with the investigation? I meant to ask earlier, but . . ."

Allegra turned to me with a disgusted

expression. "Do you think I *care?* That little shit. He sent me flowers, you know. From the police station! Like I would be impressed!"

I decided I didn't want to go down that road either. Allegra didn't offer many conversational avenues in this sort of mood. "Well, just so long as you know what you're doing. And you're okay."

She didn't even dignify that with a response.

I steeled myself. "Allegra, you will speak to Mrs. Kendall, won't you? Those toys were . . . most unsuitable for the poor little chap."

"Are you going home for the weekend?" she demanded, ignoring me.

"Um, yes, I suppose so. It's Mummy and Daddy's —"

"I know! Give them this from me," she said, reaching into her bag and shoving a small giftbox at me. I recognized it as one of the emergency scented candles I kept in my office present drawer. "If they're still together by the weekend. I've seen Daddy's *real* secretary." She pulled a very descriptive face. "Apparently, she used to be a rhythmic gymnast. Still is, by the look of her. I had to make an appointment for Daddy with his chiropractor before you arrived."

And she stalked off toward Cork Street
without a backward glance.

Seventeen

Jonathan met me at JFK on Tuesday night and drove me back to Jane Street.

"How was home?" he asked as we crossed the bridge back into Manhattan. I was still transfixed by the glittering skyline. I didn't think I'd ever get used to its film-set grandeur, no matter how long I spent in New York City.

"Oh, er, quite pleasant, actually."

"Parents on drugs?"

"Parents not there."

"But I thought . . ."

"Yes, well, I thought too. I only saw them for a few hours. Emery had booked them on a mini-vacation to Venice six months ago and forgotten to tell them. William called while we were having dinner, to tell them a cab was on its way. They only made the plane on the final call."

"What a shame," said Jonathan.

"Not really," I said. "Two hours goes a

long way with my family." My parents had an up-and-down relationship, but the ups tended to be as dramatic and vocal as the downs, which didn't make "home on an anniversary weekend" an ideal place for a child reluctant to end up in therapy.

"Anything happen while I was away?" I asked, to push that lurid thought away.

"I didn't go to Wentworth's after all — I stayed in town and got some work done instead. Braveheart's been foul. He's furious with me for letting you leave the country. Bonnie needs you to help her with some bridal shower gift she has to buy. Sally Chandler sent you an enormous basket of Jo Malone stuff because Julia got into St. Perpetua's."

"Oh, good!" I exclaimed, pleased.

"And finally, Paige wants us to go and see that idiot Godric in whatever play he's in off-off-off-Broadway."

Jonathan took his eyes off the driving for a moment. "You want to go?" he asked, as though we'd been offered front-row seats at an autopsy.

"I'd quite like to see Godric act," I said. "And maybe you should too. It might improve your opinion of him."

Jonathan leaned out the window to pay the bridge toll. "Unless he's working really hard and acting the part of a civilized intelligent human being, I doubt that. What else?"

"Sold your apartment?" I asked. I tried to sound casual, but it was much easier to promise Gabi that I'd be tough about Cindy than it was to do it, now I was back in New York without a safety net.

"Almost," he said.

"Problems with the buyers?"

Jonathan's face turned stony, and I knew he was concealing extreme annoyance. His voice, though, remained light, which only made me more edgy. "Problems with the co-seller, I regret to say. I'm going to have to get lawyers involved if she doesn't stop messing around."

"Oh," I said, sinking back into my seat. "You think she will?"

"I intend to make her," replied Jonathan grimly, and I let the subject drop.

"Now, do nothing today," Jonathan said the next morning as he stood on the doorstep so our heads were the same height. "Go . . . shopping or something. Visit a museum, go to a movie." He leaned forward to kiss me, quickly, in case anyone was watching.

"I will," I promised.

"Great," he said. "I might be late because

433

of my fund-raiser meeting, but don't forget we're having dinner at Gramercy Tavern tonight with some people."

More people? I'd met most of Jonathan's friends now — some of them more than once, thanks to Bonnie's enthusiastic lunching habits. I'd rather hoped for a quiet dinner in together on my first night back. But all I said was, "Lovely!"

When I'd fed Braveheart, and read the papers, and looked at my guidebooks, I found my thoughts straying back to work despite my best tourist intentions. Which was pretty inevitable, since I'd just seen how much damage Gabi and Allegra could wreak on my business in a matter of days.

Besides, I told myself, I needed to talk to Gabi about some problems I'd spotted with Nelson's flat when I'd popped in to check up on the builders. I poured myself another cup of coffee from Jonathan's drip machine and dialed the agency number.

Again, there was no reply. Where were those two? Was Allegra translating something for Daddy somewhere else? And was she getting paid twice? The more I thought about it, the fishier it got. Honestly, they were all such shameless scammers.

I heard my own outgoing message, then

accessed the new voice mails. From the extended bleeping, there seemed to be quite a few.

"What ho, Gabs, Roger here. Lunch today okay for you? I've booked at Foxtrot Oscar. Hope Mel isn't too cut up. Got a bit of an ear-bashing from her at the weekend. Think living with Remington's gone to her head a bit. So, um, probably best not to tell her about the other night, eh?"

What?

Roger blethered on some more in an unrecognizably chummy manner, then rang off.

My brow creased. Roger? Surely Gabi couldn't have been drinking in Hush the other night with *Roger? Could* she? Surely they didn't let men dressed like him in?

The next message was from Tristram Hart-Mossop's mother, Olympia. "Good morning. This is Olympia Hart-Mossop, Tristram Hart-Mossop's mother," she announced, in case I couldn't make the connection myself. "I need to make an appointment with you to, ah, discuss certain new developments regarding my son. He's very, ah, anxious to ascertain when the transmission date of his makeover show will be, as his school friends intend to organize some kind of party around it."

Oops.

"So if you could call me back," she wound up nervously, "that would put all our minds at rest. He's hectoring me about buying a new outfit for the event. A new outfit," she repeated, in wonderment. "Apparently several young ladies are keen to attend. Ah, yes. Thank you. Good-bye!"

I picked at a blueberry minimuffin (made specially for me by Concetta as a treat for my return). Transmission dates. I should have thought of that. Maybe Paige would have a good explanation I could borrow, for shows that didn't get made. I made a note to ring her back — I didn't want Tristram to lose face, not now when he was on the road to superstuddom.

Once I'd checked the office landline, I called the answering service on my own office cell phone and was immediately pleased I had.

"Hello, Mel," said a familiar voice, backed with what sounded like seagulls. "It's Nelson. I knew you'd be checking your voice mail, even though you're not meant to be, so I thought I'd say hello. We're having a great time, weather's pretty grim, but that just makes it more fun. Not that I'm letting anyone put themselves at risk," he added predictably. "That would be silly. Well. Not

436

unless they've really annoyed me." I could hear clanking and swooshing in the background. For an engineless ship, it was very noisy. "Anyway, just ringing to remind you not to buy any of those knock-off handbags, like the one you got in Turin that gave you a rash, and don't forget my deli list. GET OFF THAT MAST, TARIQ! AND WHERE IS YOUR REGULATION JACKET? So, yes, some granola and . . ."

A piercing emergency whistle — presumably the one around his own neck — ended Nelson's call, and I felt a little bit bereft. Although I wouldn't have admitted it, especially not to him, I did worry. Awful things happened at sea, even to capable sailors like Nelson — storms, leaks, falling off the boat.

Besides, I thought in a small voice, it would have been kind of nice to have him scoff rudely, in his inimitable fashion, at my worries about Cindy.

I bit my lip. But what if he hadn't scoffed?

Braveheart pushed his china dish toward me across the floor with his black leathery nose, as if to say, *Fill her up, lady.*

"You've eaten once this morning," I pointed out.

He fixed me with his licorice eyes and quivered with apparent starvation.

I buckled. "Okay. I suppose you are getting twice as much exercise as normal."

He wagged his whole body with pleasure as I shook out a few dog biscuits, then shoved his nose into the dish.

Pulling my mind back to practicalities, I accessed a frantic message from Jem Wilde, who needed to know what black tie casual entailed on an invitation and whether that meant he could wear his dinner jacket with his snowboarding shorts. I scribbled a note to e-mail him as soon as possible with the news that no, it wasn't "kind of cool," it was kind of insane.

And the final message was from Daddy. I knew that just from the first breath he took before launching into his message.

"Melissa. I've called this agency three times now and Allegra hasn't answered the phone. I know you'll be checking your own messages even if she isn't, and I need to get hold of her. The silly mare phoned your mother, talking about applying for a mortgage, and we don't want that, do we?"

Why not? I wondered. The rest of us had to apply for mortgages.

But Daddy was frothing on. "The last thing that silly girl needs — and the last thing I bloody need, come to that — is some nosy parker bank clerk poking through sensitive financial documents. . . . Good God! I swear you three do these things just to bring on my early demise. Do I need to tell you I am on holiday with your poor mother, and I'm still forced to deal with the cretinous shenanigans of her children? Hmm?"

With an odd, almost euphorically druglike detachment, I watched Braveheart stuffing his face and getting crumbs over his freshly groomed beard. None of the above was actually my problem for once. Allegra, Daddy, Lars . . .

Then I remembered that Allegra's salary went through my books, and normal service was resumed.

I had equally bad luck in getting hold of Allegra. Just as I was lying down on Jonathan's big brass bed to relax for a while and flick through a New York recipe book I'd bought for Nelson, my mobile rang again.

I grabbed it, in case Allegra had deigned to return my call.

"Hey, Melissa," grunted a familiar voice. "You about?"

It was Godric. I hadn't actually spoken to him since I'd gotten back, which made me feel a little guilty. I was sort of getting used to his grumpy company. He reminded me, in some ways, of a very hung-over Nelson.

"Speak up, Godric," I said. I could barely hear him for the sound of a car revving in the street below. "I'm . . ." I flipped the book shut. "I'm working."

"Right," he said, not sounding remotely bothered. "Well, I got your list of suggestions."

"Did you?" I'd asked Gabi to forward them to my e-mail account before she sent them, and so far I'd had nothing from her, so . . .

"You've *read* them?" I repeated more fiercely.

"Yeah, your partner sent them to me."

Partner, was it now?

"Right, well, I didn't have time to, um, conference with my *partner,* so maybe we should just have a quick run through them before you actually —"

"I'm not doing anything right now," he said, "if you're about. And not busy."

My practiced ear discerned a note of genuine hope beneath the apparent schoolboy disinterest. No matter what Jonathan said, I couldn't just *drop* Godric. That would be rude *and* unprofessional.

The engine continued revving in the street. I gave in and peered out the window. A huge black car was blocking the street, much to the annoyance of a couple of dog-walkers and an old lady who was trying to get past on her bicycle.

"You'll have to speak up, Godric, I can hardly hear you. Some idiot outside . . ." I put a finger in my ear. "Where are you?"

"I said, you want to go out for a coffee?"

Again, the studied casualness. He obviously had something he really wanted to show me.

I checked my watch. I wasn't meeting Jonathan until six, so I had plenty of time.

"Well, all right," I said. "But I have to be back by three. I'm going out for dinner tonight."

"Aces. Come on down."

"What?"

"I'm outside."

I went back to the window. I couldn't see inside the car since it had those "look at me! No, *don't* look at me!" celebrity tinted windows, but Godric obviously saw me, because he started honking the horn. The woman on the bicycle looked up at the window, and I ducked down in shame.

"I'll be right there," I said, grabbing my bag.

Outside, I avoided the gazes of passersby and slid gratefully into the cavernous interior of Godric's car. I didn't like to say "This is yours?" because wherever I placed the stress in the sentence it sounded faintly insulting. It felt as if I were sitting inside a very pricey black leather handbag. Things glittered at me, and the bits that weren't leather or glittering were sort of dull black. It all smelled wildly expensive.

"So, you've bought yourself a —," I started to say, but he lifted a silencing hand.

I found that men seemed to acquire a whole new personality as soon as they were installed behind the wheel of something with an engine bigger than a lawn mower — a personality borrowed largely from films. Whereas Nelson turned into one of the camp stunt drivers from *The Italian Job*, Godric seemed to be channeling Tom Cruise in *Days of Thunder*. Or was it some kind of gangsta rapper? Whatever it was, he'd donned a new pair of black sunglasses. They were somehow . . . blingier than his usual ones.

Then he spoiled the effect by pulling them down his nose so he could peer at me in a rather Nelson-ish manner. "Have you done up your seat belt?" he enquired pointedly.

"Well, yes, but . . ."

The monosyllabic gangsta returned. "Okay, let's go," Godric snarled, flooring the accelerator. I was jerked forward, then flung back in my seat so hard that my head actually hit the headrest, and from the cavalcade of horns around us, I guessed we were lucky not to have collided with anything else.

I swallowed as Godric made appreciative noises over the sound of the engine. The trick was not to let them feel your fear. I'd learned that at Pony Club.

"So, er, where d'you fancy going then?" asked Godric, running out of attitude.

"Wherever you want!" I managed to gasp. "I don't know Manhattan very well."

With a cautious stab in the direction of the minimalist controls, he buzzed down the windows and turned on the stereo in one movement. Bon Jovi blasted out at tooth-rattling volume, mid-synth solo.

"Woooaargh! Livin' on a praaaa-yeeeer!" he yelled, making a death metal horn symbol with a broad smile. "Rockin'!"

I hesitated, then smiled back. Actually, it was kind of endearing to see Godric like this. Trying so hard to be cool, failing so dismally, but seemingly enjoying himself too much to care.

"I took your advice about making myself look cooler," he went on. "You did say to buy an M6, didn't you?"

"Well, yes!" I said. Gabi was the expert, not me. Buildings flashed by at a worrying rate. "It's, er . . . It's very impressive. Do you want to slow down a little?"

"Nope!" Godric straightened his arms against the multifunction steering wheel. "This is the most fun I've had since . . . well, since ages." Then he remembered he was meant to be looking dangerous, and he snarled at me.

It was so hopeless that we both giggled.

We roared through the streets, leaving a trail of Bon Jovi and exhaust fumes behind us. Once I got over the initial stomach-lurch every time Godric changed lanes, I started to enjoy myself — after all, it wasn't often one was swept through New York by a film star, albeit a rather unfinished one.

We left the brownstones behind us, and the buildings got taller as we headed toward midtown.

"You okay there?" Godric enquired. "Comfortable? Not scared?"

I smiled, pleased to see him enjoying himself. He was quite a good driver, to be fair to him, and it was a pretty fabulous car. "I feel perfectly safe in your hands, Godric!"

A strange look crossed his face at the compliment, and it seemed to send him back into his usual round-shouldered diffidence. "Uh, thanks, Mel."

"Quite capable hands they seem to be too!" I added cheerfully. "Are you going to take me on a bit of a joy ride? Scream if you want to go faster, and all that?" I pushed a random button and felt my seat move in on me, gripping my waist in a surprisingly intimate way, for a car. "Oooh! Godric!" I giggled. "Something's vibrating! I'm getting all . . . tingly! Wow! What else can this car do? Make you breakfast?"

Godric made a choking noise, and I looked over. He'd gone very pink and seemed to be fidgeting suddenly with his trousers.

"Oh, God, sorry!" I exclaimed, jabbing at the buttons. "Have I made your seat vibrate too?"

"No," he croaked. "It's just that . . . I, um . . ." He looked at me, and I noticed that despite the air con he was perspiring. I made a mental note to introduce some linen to his wardrobe. "Thanks-for-coming-out-with-me-it-was-jolly-decent-of-you-know-how-busy-you-are-and-everything-so-nice-to-have-some-time-alone-with-you-and —," he gabbled, and for a moment, it sounded almost as if he was trying to flirt with me, albeit in a very ham-fisted manner.

Surely not! I patted his knee jovially. "Eyes

on the road, Godric. You don't want to be a James Dean kind of film star, now, do you?"

That seemed to snap him back into his mean and moody actor mode, and after a few blocks, I noticed that he was speeding up and getting quite chancy with the red lights. I hoped he wasn't doing it to impress me.

"Godric, don't you think you should keep an eye on the speedo?" I asked. "I mean, it would be awful to get a ticket on your maiden voyage."

He grunted in response and looked in the rearview mirror for what seemed like the first time.

"What's the matter?" I asked. "Is there something? . . ."

When he didn't reply, I looked out the rear window and saw that someone was following us, very close.

"Gosh, they should back off," I said, turning round in my seat. "American drivers are so inconsiderate, don't you find? The cars are so huge they don't even consider what a shunt would feel like."

Godric didn't take my hint, though. His mind seemed elsewhere. "So, you think this is a sexy car, then? Like the look of the backseat?" he asked.

I twisted round. The backseat was larger

than most sofas I'd known. "Blimey! You could sleep on that! With a friend!"

When I twisted back, Godric snapped his head round very quickly, almost as if he'd been trying to look down my top. I tugged my cardigan together where it had started to gape.

"Did you know, you can see right down your . . . ," Godric began conversationally.

"That doesn't mean you have to *look*," I snapped. "So, did you get your first pay-check for the film, then?"

"Er, sort of."

The other car was getting very near. I hoped they weren't carjackers. I'd read about that sort of thing.

"Why don't you just let him past?" I suggested. "Pull over?"

"Melissa, I have a British driving license," Godric informed me darkly. "If he wants to get past, he can indicate. That's the way it works. Fair's fair."

I looked round again. The car behind was now so close that I could see two men in the front seats, both wearing rather sinister-looking shades. If they got any closer, they'd be able to change the CD in the player. As I looked, one smiled at me, and it wasn't nice. At all.

My skin went cold. Could they have

something to do with Allegra? Could they somehow have found out I was here? Could Allegra be mixed up, somehow, with . . . the Mafia?

I grabbed Godric's arm. "For Pete's sake, this isn't the time for your ridiculous right and wrong games! Pull over, just pull over."

"No way!" he snarled.

Then the passenger in the car behind slammed a revolving light on top of the car and turned on the siren.

I swiveled as far as my seat belt would allow. "Godric!" I roared. "It's the police! I am *telling* you now — pull over!"

A broad smile broke across his face. "Excellent! Let's go!"

I couldn't believe this. We were in a car chase. Godric really did only galvanize himself in make-believe situations.

As we roared through the streets, my mind raced equally quickly, trying to establish some kind of defense. A thought occurred to me. "Godric, tell me honestly," I said in my very firmest tone. "Do you have any idea why the police would have been following us? Before you started jumping lights. Godric!" I snapped, as he squirmed pleasurably. This wasn't the time to discover his Supernanny fixation. "Quickly!"

He huffed and reslumped his shoulders.

"It might be something to do with the dealer bloke."

My heart sank. "You are talking about *car* dealers here?"

"Yes!"

"Well, what about him?"

Godric gave a familiar sullen shrug, and any residual vestiges of film star vanished as the more familiar overgrown adolescent re-appeared. "I think I might have left him at the gas station."

The police car was now trying to overtake us, to head us off.

"What?" I shrieked. "You *left* him?"

"Yeah," grunted Godric. "He was boring the pants off me, with his boring car dealer spiel, so when he stopped to put some *gas* in it, I thought I'd just take it round the block a few times on my own, see what you thought, then take it back." He paused. "Only I got lost."

I covered my face with my hands for a few seconds, but when I removed them, every-thing was still there. Including the siren.

"Pull over!" I said firmly. "Pull over now!"

"I'm not very good with left-hand drive cars," he whined.

"Do it, or I'll do it for you!"

Godric lurched to a halt, nearly taking out a street sweeper.

"Right," I said, thinking quickly. I had maybe thirty seconds. "Don't say a word. Leave this to me."

"What are you going to say?"

"I don't know yet. Let's see how mad they are."

We got a rough idea of how mad they were when both policemen leaped out of the car and started yelling at us through a loud-speaker.

"Get out of the car and put your hands on the roof! Don't try any sudden movements! We are armed, repeat armed."

Godric and I stared at each other.

Then to my absolute horror, he frowned. The same affronted English gent frown that I'd seen before he'd punched the man in Central Park. "This is absolutely outrageous!" he said. "Armed police? How unnecessary is that? And you've done nothing wrong!"

Before I could stop him, he swung the door open, shouting, "This is police harassment, you bastards!"

"Noooo!" I yelled, jumping out as fast as I could. How much worse could this get?

The nearest officer made a grab for Godric and started to cuff him. "Thought you could just stroll into a car dealership with your fancy British accent and steal a hundred-thousand-dollar car, huh? I am arresting you —"

"No, wait!" I protested. "Do you know who he is?"

"Nope," said the other policeman. "Hugh Grant? Bono? Don't make no difference — it's still theft."

"I am going to get my agent onto you," Godric was fulminating, his face turning red and white with rage. "And she is going to sue your *arse* off!"

"Go right ahead, sir. We look forward to receiving her call. In the meantime —"

"But this is Ric Spencer, the actor! The Hollywood actor? And he didn't steal the car," I insisted, as the other one started to approach me with a pair of cuffs. "He was, um, taking it for a test drive . . ."

"We know that, miss. We received the call from the carjackee."

I swallowed. "Yes, well, he was taking it for a test drive as part of his research for a new role he's playing in an upcoming movie with, er, Keira Knightley, in which Ric here —"

"Still theft."

"Yes, but I was getting to that . . ." I stalled, as the cuffs got nearer and my mind got blanker.

"Would you hold out your hands for me,

please, miss?" enquired the second policeman.

I couldn't help notice how nicely he asked. However, with Gabi's words about being niced into things still fresh in my mind, I absently lifted my wrists out of reach and went on, "When he saw me walking down the road." I paused and raised my eyebrows with a big smile, as if I was about to begin the most hilarious cocktail party anecdote.

To my amazement, it seemed to work. Both policemen, and Godric, tipped their heads in lovely "do go on" encouragement.

"Right, well, I was walking down Fifth Avenue, just, you know, looking at the shops, when I realized I was being followed! By a big man. I could see him in the shop windows behind me, and I'm sure he followed me into the Gap, anyway, I was just walking along, and I'd got to about, er, Thirty-ninth Street," I elaborated randomly, "when I saw Godric in the car, so I waved at him, and at that exact moment, I felt someone try to steal my handbag!"

I clapped a hand on my maidenly chest for emphasis.

"I didn't know what to do! I mean, I'd read all your very helpful New York guidelines about what to do if you think you're being mugged —"

"We do advise you to hand over your bag, miss," the policeman reminded me. "Not steal a car to chase the offender."

"Oh, well, normally I would have let him have it!" I improvised. "But I have some very confidential documents in here, pertaining to some work I'm doing on behalf of my father, who is a key figure in the British Olympic committee. And so, you see, I was concerned about letting my bag go."

I cannot tell you how much it pained me to use my father as a bargaining tool. But it had suddenly occurred to me that being arrested in the company of the man Jonathan had specifically not wanted me to get involved with looked very bad.

The first policeman removed his sunglasses and rubbed his forehead, as if he was having trouble working out if I was lying, or merely insane. "So you're saying you were being trailed because your father is some kind of British . . . politician? And this guy is a Hollywood actor? Anything else we should know?"

I opened my eyes very wide and tried to look disarming. "I know it seems rather far-fetched, Officer, but yes. I've had to have special police training at home, to avoid kidnap."

"And you're saying you just ran into this

guy?" he went on, suspiciously. "On the street? How do you two know each other again?"

"Friend of a friend," I said, at the same time as Godric said, "She's my *girlfriend!*"

I glared at him. "Godric, I'm not your girlfriend. That isn't going to help."

He looked back at me guiltily. "Okay, then, an *ex*-girlfriend."

I stroked Godric's arm sympathetically. He couldn't have had that many exes if he regarded a hopeless fumble in a cupboard as at all significant. "Darling, it was very nice and everything, and of course it's awfully exciting to say I snogged a famous Hollywood star, but I don't think —"

"Can it," snapped the second, still shaded, officer. "I don't need to know your romantic arrangements."

"There's no need for that!" said Godric testily.

"Now, come on, Godric," I said. "I really don't think —"

"You simply *cannot* harass us like this!" fumed Godric, Englishly. "How were we to know that you operate test drives as if perfectly innocent customers were potential thieves? I'll have you know that in London, the dealers are decent enough people to let you take the car around the block yourself without ringing the police to —"

"That's enough! Get in the car!"

"— have you hauled in like a common criminal. And another thing, this car did not have cruise control as advertised!"

I felt cold steel snap around my wrists. "Get in the car!" barked the policeman.

For the first time, I became aware of the people stopping and staring on the pavement, and I began to die inside, very slowly.

As I was shoved into the patrol car, I saw Godric attempt to take a swing at the officer, only to lose his balance, at which point the other policeman neatly tipped him into the other side.

We sat next to each other, temporarily silenced by the air-conditioning, which was positively glacial.

"Do you think they bought it?" demanded Godric in a not-very-hushed undertone.

I glared at him, temporarily too cross to speak.

"Brilliant," he said, settling back into his seat as we roared off. "I've always wanted to be a political prisoner."

I hope you won't mind if I draw a veil over the intervening three hours at the police station. Godric and I were allowed to make calls, and while the police were checking out our story, I called home.

The phone rang and rang, and suddenly I remembered that there was no one there! They were on Emery's anniversary mini-vacation.

Cold sweat prickled my skin.

Just as I thought I was about to burst into tears, the phone was picked up at the other end.

"Hello," husked a heavily accented voice, "I'm really just burgling this house, so I'm afraid I can't help you with any enquiries you might have."

"Granny!" I almost sobbed with relief.

"Melissa! Darling!" she cried, in her more familiar Park Lane tones. "How lovely to hear from you! Where are you calling from?"

"A police station in New York."

"Gracious, how racy!"

"Listen," I gabbled, dropping my voice. "I need you to cover for me. I can't explain now, but there's been an awful misunderstanding. I've . . . I've been arrested with, um, an old school friend who borrowed a car for a test drive, but the garage called the police and said he'd stolen it so I've told them he saved me from a stalker, and was on the way to take it back."

"And?" said Granny. "What do you need me to do? Sounds like you've got it covered.

Jolly well done, darling. Your father would be proud. Your very first international fib."

"I don't think they believe me!" I wailed. "I mean, who would?"

"Let me speak to someone, Melissa," she said calmly. "We'll soon have this cleared up."

I had some misgivings about letting Granny take the reins, since she was even more imaginative than Daddy, but she must have said something, because half an hour later, Godric and I were chucked out of the cells, without even having our fingerprints taken.

"I understand you've had some trouble in the past, ma'am," said the arresting officer. "You should have said. We take press intrusion very seriously in New York."

"Um, well, quite," I mumbled.

He cut me a cheeky glance. "So, off the record, you got any good stories?"

I looked bewildered. "About? . . ."

"About dating Wills?"

Godric stared at me. His call to Paige hadn't gotten results like that, and she was supposed to know everyone in New York.

"You dated Prince William? I never knew that," he gawked, then added, rather unnecessarily, in my opinion, "you dirty cradle-snatcher!"

"Um, I don't talk about it. All in the past," I muttered. *Granny.* Honestly.

After a brief lecture about wasting police time, and the rules for testing new cars in New York, we were free to go.

"God, I should tell Paige about your brush with royalty," said Godric. "She'll be —"

"Godric," I snapped. "Do not, under any circumstances, tell anyone. Especially not Paige. Just be grateful we are out of here."

"But . . ."

I stopped walking and grabbed him by the hands. I really didn't want this getting out. Too many people would have too many field days. In my father's case, a jamboree.

"Please, Godric," I said, squeezing his hands hard. "Can this be our little secret? Please?"

He looked down at me with a noble glint in his dark eyes and squeezed my hands back. "If that's what you want, Melissa," he said gruffly. "Then it's our secret. On my honor."

Our eyes met. I knew that Godric, with his dramatic fixations, would take it as a matter of principle not to tell. Flooded with relief, I leaned up and planted a kiss on his stubbly cheek. "Thanks!" I said. "You're a real friend!"

"Nngh," choked Godric. He opened his

mouth to say something, but I put a finger over his lips to stop him.

"Say no more!" I shhed. I was wiping my lipstick off his cheek when I caught sight of a familiar form in the waiting room, where various disheveled and rough-looking people were congregating. A smart, be-suited form with very square shoulders and shiny shoes I could see from twenty feet away.

"Oh, bollocks," I murmured, letting go of Godric's hands as panic returned to my bloodstream.

"So, what are you up to tonight?" asked Godric conversationally.

Any chance of covering this up vanished like steam off a latte.

"Do you want to come and see my play?" he blethered on. "It's not very good, but you know, it passes the time. And there's a party next week, actually, that you could come to? Paige wants me to take you." He pulled a face. "It's like she doesn't trust me out on my own or something."

I didn't think it would help Godric's confidence to confirm that.

"But I'd still quite like you to come anyway. If you wanted to," Godric finished, in a smaller voice, but I wasn't listening.

"Jonathan!" I said, trying to sound as if I

got arrested all the time. Well, it was worth making one small attempt to bluff it out. The adrenaline of talking my way out of the crisis, seasoned with the sheer horror of brushing with the law, was making my voice frightfully English.

"Melissa," said Jonathan through very tight lips. "I realize you've got some kind of television fixation going on, but couldn't you have limited your research to *The Kids from Fame* and skipped *NYPD Blue*?"

I let out a tinkly social laugh, but I knew that this show of levity from Jonathan was for Godric's benefit. Underneath his polite smile, he looked seriously rattled.

"I'm glad to see you've found the funny side to all this, but I still need to speak to the officer in charge," he said. "Would you excuse me, Mr. Spencer?" And he moved away, toward the enquiry desk, ignoring the line of people.

"No, honestly, there's no need!" I said, grabbing his arm.

"There most certainly is." He disengaged me firmly. "While I admire your grace in adversity, Melissa, might I remind you that you've just suffered both an abduction attempt and a false arrest? Of course I need to speak to someone. I need to know the facts. There may be consequences, legal consequences, actually. Not to mention security issues." He banged on the desk. "Hello?"

"But Jonathan, really . . ." I chewed my lip. Oh, God. This was why I tried not to tell fibs. I just couldn't handle them once they were out of the bag. "How did you know about the, er, abduction attempt?"

He turned back, concern drawing deep lines around his mouth. "Paige called me. She explained how Ric here got you out of a tight spot with some man who'd been following you and —" Jonathan ran a hand through his hair. "Good Lord, Melissa! You really shouldn't be carrying politically sensitive documents! What was your father thinking? It's not your job, you don't have protection, and you're on holiday!" He turned back to the desk. "Can I get some attention here?"

Godric opened his mouth, and I glared at him. A cold chill ran over my skin, and for once it had nothing to do with the air-conditioning.

"If I don't talk to someone in the next thirty seconds, I am calling my lawyer!" bellowed Jonathan.

"Jonathan," I said, pulling at his arm. "Please? Can we just go home? I feel an utter fool. I should have been more careful

461

with my bag." Actually, I had to get a grip on my accent; I was starting to sound like Miss Marple. "I've certainly learned a lesson. Honestly. Handbag strap *firmly* across my body from now on."

Jonathan paused in his slamming of the desk to give me a patient look.

I inspected my feet. "I . . . I might just have been paranoid. And I'd really rather not make a big deal about it, you know . . . the newspapers and everything?"

"Melissa! Get your priorities sorted out! I don't care about your stupid father, but I do care if you're being intimidated on the streets of this city!"

"Jonathan, I just want to *go home!*"

"But —" He saw the pleading look in my eyes and gave up. "Fine. Let's get you home. I can deal with this later."

Part of me bridled a little at the fact that he felt obliged to deal with it at any time when I'd dealt with it already, but that part was swamped by the relief I felt as he ushered me out of there, back onto the street, his strong arm protectively around my shoulders.

"I'll, er, get a cab," said Godric, who, deprived of his car, had shed his gangsta swagger and reverted to his usual dank persona.

"Thank you," said Jonathan stiffly. "I appreciate your taking care of Melissa." And he shook Godric's hand twice, then gave him an equally awkward slap on the back. "Call me if you decide to take any further action about the arrest situation. I can recommend an attorney."

"Cheers," mumbled Godric. "I'll see you around, Mel," he added with a hopeful look in my direction.

"Oh, I shouldn't think so!" I said brightly. "Maybe at that premiere of yours!"

Spotting a vacant taxi approaching, I managed to make it stop, for the first time since I'd been in New York. The tension must have made me look positively native.

EIGHTEEN

Jonathan said nothing for several blocks. And that was worse than being yelled at by the police officer.

Eventually, I could bear the silence no longer. "Jonathan," I burst out, "please believe me, I honestly didn't know that . . ."

He ran a finger around his collar and loosened his tie. "What?"

"Godric," I said. "I really did just bump into him. I wasn't, you know, *improving* him or anything . . ."

Jonathan looked at me strangely. "Did I even suggest that you were? Interesting that you're more concerned about that than about being arrested. Or stalked! Look, I can see there was . . . an element of confusion about the whole incident, but as long as you're all right, that's all I care about. Melissa, honey," he said more quietly, putting his finger on my chin to turn my face gently to his, "I was really worried about

464

you. Paige called me herself. She said you were with this Ric idiot and you were in a police station, that you were being *stalked*. What was I meant to think?"

I caught my breath. It hadn't properly occurred to me how serious it must have looked from the outside.

"Honestly, Jonathan, Godric borrowed the car for a test drive, he did what you can sometimes do in England and drove around on his own for a bit, and the dealer called the police."

Jonathan drew in a deep breath. "Whatever. Tell me about this stalker."

I hesitated. Why had it been so much easier to lie to the police than it was to tell Jonathan the truth? "I tried to explain that there'd been a misunderstanding. They wouldn't listen. And Godric got . . . aggressive, and they must have got the wrong idea. So I . . . I tried to use my initiative."

His face clouded. "Don't tell me. You *invented* the stalker?"

"Yes," I said quickly, to get it over with. "But I didn't invent Prince William. Granny did that, to make it look like the man following me was a press photographer," I paused. "I suppose at least she didn't say I was dating Kate Moss."

Jonathan blew out the breath in his cheeks

and sank back into his seat.

There was a short pause in which he seemed to be considering his response. "I'm not mad at you," he said carefully. "I could never be mad at you. Not even for . . . lying to a policeman."

Was I imagining a hint of a laugh there? Surely not.

"But . . ." He exhaled again. "This stepping in to fix Ric's little theft problem — it's *working*, Melissa. You made up the story to get this guy off the hook! Why couldn't you just have said he'd picked you up in the car, you'd had no idea it wasn't his, and let him talk his way out of it?"

"I couldn't! I couldn't just stand by and let him —"

"Deal with it himself?"

That was a good point.

Jonathan pressed on. "Or let his agent deal with it? The agent who gets paid to look after him? Who is more than equipped to —"

"All right!" I flustered. "You've made your point. But I owed him a favor! He got *me* out of trouble in the park when Braveheart attacked that other dog and that ghastly man went ballistic with me."

"And I guess he's a friend," said Jonathan obliquely.

466

What was that supposed to mean? "Yes. He's a friend."

There was an awkward pause, where I wasn't sure what to say.

"Melissa, you have a big heart and it's one of the things I love about you," sighed Jonathan. "But . . ." He raised his eyebrows, then dropped them. "Enough with the fixing, already. Leave it. Please. I'm really not going to tell you again. Just concentrate on relaxing. Enjoying New York. Being with me." He gave me his serious look, the one that seemed to see straight through to my lingerie. "Next time I catch you Honey-ing, you're on the first plane back. I mean it, Miss Romney-Jones."

"Okay."

"Okay," he said and made a "drawing a line" gesture with his hands. "End of afternoon. Let's start again with this evening."

Jonathan and I arrived at Gramercy Tavern at seven fifteen on the dot. He was looking dashing in a cream linen suit, and I was wearing one of my slinky Honey silk dresses.

He caught me drawing a deep breath as we got out of the cab and almost laughed.

"Hey! Relax!" he said, slipping his arm round my waist. "It's just dinner with a few friends."

The maitre d' greeted us warmly, and as we made our way toward the bar, a man called out, "Jonathan! Hey, man!"

Another man in a suit, sitting next to another man in a suit, sitting next to two women, also in suits, sitting next to Kurt and Bonnie Hegel, waved at us, and Jonathan steered me toward them with a discreet hand on the back.

They all looked like they'd come straight from work, and suddenly I felt overdressed, not underdressed. God. Was I ever going to get this right?

I smiled and got ready to concentrate on remembering their names. When I got closer, I realized to my horror that one of the women in suits was Jennifer with the Flapping Tongue from Bonnie's party.

Okay. *Rise above it, rise above it,* I told myself frantically. *She's more embarrassed than you.*

"Melissa! Hi!" gushed Bonnie, engulfing me in her usual embrace of bones. "You look absolutely stunning! You look like Catherine Zeta Jones!"

"Hello, Bonnie," I said when she released me. "What a gorgeous jacket."

"You see!" she stage-whispered to the two women next to her, directing a huge smile my way. "You see? Isn't she a darling?"

468

"Hey, Melissa!"

I was delighted to see Wentworth's friendly face. "Hello!" I said, greeting him with a kiss." I was so sorry to miss your Labor Day weekend party!"

"Not as sorry as I was," he said, kissing my cheek. "It wasn't the same without you and Jon."

Kurt appeared at my elbow. "Now, do you know everyone else here? Have you met Steve? He was at Princeton with Jonathan."

"And this is my wife, Diana," Steve added. "We're all set to give birth in eleven and a half weeks!"

"Hello, Melissa," cooed Diana, flicking back her coppery fringe to see me better. She had one of those precision-cut messy bobs that fell back into place perfectly every time she moved her head.

I gulped. I'd barely even noticed she was pregnant. Everyone here was so *fit.*

"So you're back in New York!" observed Steve.

"Seems so," said Jonathan.

"Oh, you are *so* London these days!" shrieked Bonnie. " 'Seems so,' " she repeated in deadpan tones. "Come *on!*"

"Jonathan, I need to drag you aside for a moment," said Steve. "Yeah, yeah, okay, I know!" He raised his hands against the barrage of *Friends*-style bantering that ensued. "But I'm looking at this apartment, and I need the inside line from the man here about the board."

"Melissa, I refuse to have you listen to that awful property talk," said Bonnie, taking me by the arm and patting the spare seat next to her. "Let's get you a drink. Champagne, isn't it?"

She signalled to the waiter, then turned back to me.

"So, tell me, how are you finding everything?"

Everyone asked me that, all the time, as if I were the first English person to set foot in Manhattan since the Mayflower landed, and I was never sure what to say: "It's all so big!" was clichéd but true. And they were being nice, and I wanted to be nice back, so I could hardly say, *Why are you all so obsessed with dental products?* or *What's with the sales tax on coffee?*

Bonnie and Diana were looking at me eagerly.

"It's all so big!" I caroled. "And the subway map makes no sense whatsoever."

"Oh, you are funny. Let me come with you one morning," said Bonnie indulgently. "I'll show you how it works."

"Thank you," I said as my flute of champagne arrived with about seven different dishes of nuts and nibbles. About two seconds later, the black-clad form of Jennifer materialized and placed itself on the seat next to mine. The breasts did not move during this maneuver.

Bonnie and Diana exchanged glances.

"Hello, Jennifer," I said, to show there were no hard feelings.

"I'm so sorry," said Jennifer in a big rush. "I have to apologize. I've been carrying around this . . . this awful tumor of guilt." And she scrunched her hands up to demonstrate the tumor-ness of her guilt. "My thoughtlessness must have made you feel insecure and humiliated, and you must believe me when I assure you that *no one* was in any way discussing you, or you and Jonathan, or you, Jonathan, and Cindy . . ."

"Or Jonathan, Cindy, and Brendan," put in Diana.

"Or *any* combination of the above," said Bonnie firmly.

"I am so mortified." Jennifer put a hand to her string-of-pearls area. "Can you forgive me? I so want us to be friends. Jonathan is a wonderful, dear old friend of mine, and any woman he chooses to spend his life with is a woman I really want to get to know."

"Well . . . ," started Diana, but Bonnie shut her down with a look.

Good going, Bonnie, I thought approvingly.

Jennifer now had a Hand of Appeal on my knee, which was taking it a little far. Call me old-fashioned, but there's a time and a place for a hand on the knee, and this wasn't it. But she looked genuinely mortified, and something about her reminded me of Gabi. The Botkier handbag, maybe.

"Really, there's no need," I said. "Please let's just wipe it from our minds. I'm always putting my foot in it. And now you've met me you know I'm not blond — and not even that young!"

"Really? How old are you?" she asked rather directly.

"Oh, er, twenty-eight?" I stammered.

Jennifer cocked her head. "Really?"

"So, let me just get this straight, was that someone else?" Diana butted in. "I definitely heard Jonathan dated a blond girl."

"I think wires were crossed," I said firmly, before Bonnie could start complicating matters.

"Well, I appreciate your graciousness," said Jennifer. "I don't think I could be so kind." She sighed. "The British have beautiful manners. It's like . . . they're just born with a natural grasp of etiquette."

I thought of Godric. And Roger. And Gabi. And Prince Philip.

Though he was, of course, technically Greek.

"I wouldn't go that far," I demurred. "The accent covers a multitude of sins. And it doesn't wash at home, sadly."

"But you do have great manners," said Bonnie. "I noticed that when we were over there. All the little kids say please and thank you. It's adorable."

I wondered where in London Kurt and Bonnie had been staying. "Well, I suppose we do get it drilled into us," I said. "Thank you for saying so."

"Oh. My. God!" exclaimed Jennifer, as if she'd just had a marvelous idea. "You could run classes in it here! I've seen things like that on the internet. You get to spend a week in a stately home in the UK, and learn all about flower arranging, and the aristocracy, and how to curtsey properly."

"Really?" I hoped my father never stumbled on that website. She nodded. "Oh, yah. The HR department at the agency I work for? The head of PR went on a course so she'd know how to deal with some of our British clients. She can make scones now." Her brow furrowed. "Scoones? Scones? Scornes?"

"Whichever you like. Lovely!" I said, because I honestly couldn't think of anything else to add, apart from *Did Jonathan tell you to tell me this?*

After we chatted a bit about New York shopping techniques, the various boarding schools I'd attended, and Prince Charles, who had visited Kurt's firm and charmed everyone by eating a digestive biscuit *right there in front of them,* Diana said, "Oh, Melissa, you know what would be so cool?" She shot a quick look across at Bonnie.

"What?" I played along, emboldened by the second glass of champagne and the warm girls-together atmosphere.

"If you could organize my baby shower!"

Now I *knew* Jonathan must have put them up to it.

"Oh, I don't think I *could,* sorry. I mean, I don't know what they are," I said apologetically. "We don't have them in England. A pipe of port for a boy, and a charm bracelet for a girl, and that's about it, really."

Diana wrinkled her brow as far as it would wrinkle, which wasn't far. "A pipe? Of port? But, no, the shower — that's just a lovely, lovely afternoon where the mom-to-be gets together with her closest friends and spends some quality time with them, and receives beautiful gifts for the baby."

Bonnie nodded. "It's a very special event. The grandmothers-to-be attend too, and it's a lovely bonding time for everyone, in the dizzy whirlwind of the whole birth experience!" She waved her hands around to demonstrate the whirlwind effect.

"And it would be so fabulous if you could do it like a traditional British tea party!" added Diana. "You know, like one of those nursery teas you read about in books!"

"Well, yes, that would be lovely," I said, feeling hemmed in. "But I'm sure there's a tradition about who arranges it? Isn't it meant to be your best friend, or your chief bridesmaid or something?"

Jennifer, Diana, and Bonnie all drew in a sharp breath and cast their eyes down at the cocktail nibbles.

"Oh, I'm terribly sorry," I said quickly. "Have I? . . ."

Bonnie glanced quickly at the others, and assumed the mantle of responsibility. "Diana's matron of honor was *Cindy*," she said.

"Don't get me wrong, I love Cindy," Diana added, a little too quickly. "But — ha, ha! — I don't want her round my baby!"

"Not without *close* supervision!" Jennifer chimed in.

"And of course she's run off her feet with

Parker, so I doubt if she could anyway," Bonnie explained. A nanosecond too late.

"Oh," I said.

All four of us looked at our empty glasses.

The abrupt silence allowed the conversation from the other end of the table to cut in.

"So what are the home-owning differences over there, Jonathan?" Kurt had his earnest interviewing voice on. "Would you say that the UK property market would be affected by the introduction of a co-op board arrangement in state-owned apartment buildings?"

Jonathan's eyes were glazed like a week-old cod, but he was still making polite nodding gestures. When he caught me looking in his direction, Jonathan moved his eyebrow in his familiar, near-imperceptible "it's just you and me in this room and no one else" way, and my heart melted.

I knew nothing about baby showers. I didn't even like babies all that much. But if it would get me some brownie points with Jonathan, when he was making such an effort for me, then, fine, I'd do it. I really wanted this to work. I really, *really* did.

And if it would show up Cindy in the process, well . . . that was just a bonus.

"Oh, I'm honored that you've asked me!"

I said brightly. "What a lovely way to get to know New York better. I'd love to help out. Let's get together over coffee this week and I can give you some ideas, Diana."

"Oh, my God! Oh, my God!" she said, clapping her hands together so hard that her bob bounced. And then fell back into perfect place.

"Really, it's a pleasure," I said as Jennifer and Bonnie joined in the raptures so genuinely that I did start to feel that maybe I could turn things around. Maybe, if I just tried really hard, I could fit in with Jonathan's friends. Maybe . . .

"Melissa?" said Diana, suddenly very serious.

"Yes?"

She smiled angelically. "Baby says thank you."

If I hadn't grabbed my wineglass, I honestly think she would have placed my hand on her tiny pregnant stomach for confirmation.

I smiled, nervously.

NINETEEN

Immersing myself in Diana's plans, however, wasn't enough to save me from an excruciating scene when the news about Godric's little adventure became public knowledge.

Ironically — or perhaps not — it was my father who broke it.

He called me on my mobile as Jonathan and I were having a rare conversation over an early cup of coffee before he went off to work, about what he could do to the house. We were sharing a box of fresh blueberry muffins. The flowers he'd brought home the previous evening were on the table between us. Even Braveheart was behaving himself. I should have known such domestic bliss couldn't last.

"Melissa!" Daddy roared. "You sly dog!"

"What?"

"Dating Prince William! I'd never have guessed! He doesn't seem the type to go for older women."

Jonathan raised his eyebrows enquiringly.

"Wrong number," I lied.

"It's in the papers, you know," Daddy went on, less gleefully.

"What?" I demanded, turning cold. "How?"

"Oh, Melissa . . . Anyway, what were you doing with that film star chap? And in a *BMW,* for heaven's sake. Were there no British cars he could have pinched?"

I glanced over at Jonathan to see if he'd heard. The expression on his face suggested he had. Daddy was certainly bellowing loud enough. He sounded quite refreshed.

"My father," I mouthed apologetically.

Jonathan was getting up from the table.

"Don't leave yet," I said, panicking.

"I'm not leaving. I'm just going out for the papers," he replied.

"Anyway," Daddy went on, "does this mean you've ditched that stuffed-shirt Yank?"

I pressed the phone to my chest. "Jonathan! Wait!"

Jonathan looked impassive. "I don't want to interrupt your family call. Back soon."

I slumped in my chair as the front door slammed behind him.

"Why are you ringing?" I asked Daddy

tetchily. "Just to have a laugh at me? And before you ask, I didn't tell them that. Granny did. She seemed to think it would help."

"Your mother's very upset. It's bad for her image to have a daughter who gets involved in police chases."

I stared out the window. It had come to something when New York felt more normal than London. "*Which* image?"

"You haven't seen *Country Life*?"

"No, funnily enough, I haven't been in a dentist's waiting room recently."

Then I remembered about Mummy and the journalist and the pots of jam. Oh, *God.* One family crisis at a time, I thought, pushing the image out of my head.

"Ah, well, you'll see soon enough. Now listen, if you get a call today from anyone from London as a result of your carryings-on, I want you to tell them that Red Leicester cheese makes your hair shine, and you eat three ounces every day. Got that?"

"Fine," I said dully and hung up.

Jonathan was not pleased. Despite his polite amusement, I could tell he was furious underneath.

"Ex-girlfriend of the heir to the throne, current girlfriend of a Hollywood film star

. . . I should be flattered you're having breakfast with me at all," he said as he slapped the papers down on the table.

"But —"

"Melissa, this really isn't great news." He looked at me, his eyes now the color of steel.

"I know!" I wailed. "But I wasn't . . ."

My voice trailed away as we both stared at the evidence to the contrary.

Nothing — and I mean, *nothing* — I said could make him see it was just wild press exaggeration. It didn't even stop him sweeping off to work on time. If only he'd expressed his anger, I could have dealt with it. Biblical disappointment was so much worse.

And that wasn't the half of it. I still had to tackle Paige. She was meant to have contained all this. She'd *promised* me she would!

With a very heavy heart, I went upstairs to dress myself into some kind of dignity. Despite the heat, I pulled on stockings and garters, a smart summer dress and heels, then applied my most serious makeup.

I gazed at my finished reflection in the round dressing-table mirror, rehearsing my disappointment. Stern disappointment. "How *could* you, Paige?" I started.

No, not firm enough.

"Paige, you've let me down, you've let Ric

down, and most of all, you've let yourself down . . ."

I stared at myself. There was something missing. I just looked too *guilty.*

I sank onto the bed. Other people would have probably snorted some cocaine or something at this point. Or had a drink. Or . . .

My eyes moved toward my overnight bag.

No. I shook myself. No, that was a very slippery slope.

Just quickly. Just for a moment or two.

No!

But I was already halfway across the room, sliding back the zipper, feeling about feverishly for the forbidden bag.

And then, before I knew it, the wig was on my head, the blond fringe was falling into my eyes, and staring out of the mirror was Honey, her eyes positively gleaming with ire.

"Paige." I paused and gave myself a devastating glare of dismay. "Darling, what happened? I'm simply bewildered! I thought you knew everyone and could do anything!" Rueful shake of the fringe. "Oh, dear . . ."

Without warning, a deafening volley of outraged barking broke my attention, and I was horrified to see that not only was Braveheart on the bed, now strictly forbidden, but also that he was preparing to launch himself at my head.

"No!" I roared as he and I tussled in a very undignified manner, his sharp little teeth locked firmly around a thick hank of real hair. "Braveheart! Get off!"

Breathlessly, I managed to remove him from my hair, real and fake, and stowed the wig well out of sight under my spare evening slip. Braveheart retreated suspiciously to the corner, where he set up a defensive growling toward the wardrobe.

"You're quite right," I said to him, brushing myself down. "I don't need the wig, now, do I? No," I repeated, more to myself, though, than him. "No, I don't."

Erupting at Paige Drogan might not change the fact that my picture was right there next to Godric's more animated headshot, plus illustrative, insinuating copy, but it would make me feel as if it wasn't all my fault.

"Ms. Drogan is unavailable this morning," Tiffany informed me without moving her telephone headset.

"Then I'll wait," I said, settling myself into the uncomfortable chair. I ignored the tempting range of glossy periodicals on offer, choosing instead to stare straight ahead at Tiffany until she was unnerved enough to make a few discreet calls.

Paige came hopping out of her office, beaming with delight.

"Melissa! Just the person I wanted to see! Come on in!"

I stalked in after her and closed the door.

"I can't stay long," I said, trying to summon up the imperious tone I'd found when I'd been be-wigged. "But I needed to see you about this awful business in the papers."

"Hey, it's not so awful, Melissa," said Paige, tipping her head to one side. "In fact, it's exactly what I asked you to do! You made him look like a real knight on a white charger, rescuing you like that!"

"Paige, he was about to be arrested for car theft!"

"Well, even that wouldn't have been totally bad news," she conceded happily. "Ric Spencer is impulsive! He's gotta-have-it!" She looked over her glasses. "I tell you, in six months' time, BMW will be begging him to steal their cars. So well done, honey!"

"Listen," I said furiously, "it might be great for Ric, but it's not great for *me*. I told you Jonathan wasn't keen on me seeing Ric at all — and now the papers are making out I'm his girlfriend! I thought we had an understanding that *nothing of that nature* would happen. I thought you'd be able to keep details like that *out* of the papers."

Paige looked surprised. "What can I say? People draw their own conclusions."

"Yes, that I'm cheating on my boyfriend with some actor!"

"With some film star," she corrected me.

"I'm sorry, Paige," I said firmly, "but this simply isn't on. I can't have anything more to do with Godric. Jonathan means an awful lot to me, and I won't risk hurting him, not for anything." I paused. "I'm surprised you don't care about how he feels. He's your friend, isn't he?"

Paige's surprise turned slightly patronizing. "Melissa, Jonathan's a professional. We're all professionals here. Maybe it's different in London" — she pronounced London as if she really meant Chipping Snodbury — "but I think he understands that I need to work for my client. I thought *you* understood that too, in your line of work?"

"Obviously not," I said with a smile I didn't feel. She had no idea what my line of work was, not really. "Never mind! It's been a fascinating experience." I stood up and offered her my hand to shake. "Let me know when the retraction runs, won't you, so I can show Jonathan?"

"What?"

"The correction that Godric and I *aren't* dating."

Paige shook her head sadly at me. "Honey, you have a lot to learn about the ways of the world."

I was so furious with Paige, but proud of myself for actually losing my temper, that I took myself down to the Magnolia Bakery and bought the biggest, sickliest cupcake they had. I'd had smaller birthday cakes as a child.

I was licking the last of the blue icing off the paper when my phone rang.

"Melissa, it's Godric."

Oh, great.

"Hello, Godric," I said heavily. "How are you?"

"Shit. Do you want to have a cup of tea?"

"I'm kind of busy," I fibbed, then paused, feeling a sudden twinge of sneakiness. It was all very well yelling at Paige, but she wasn't the one saddled with a hermit's personality in an actor's body. Godric sounded even glummer than usual, which was saying something. It was only fair to say good-bye in person. And if I was completely honest with myself, being with Godric meant I could just be me. Melissa "Melons" Romney-Jones. That was quite a big temptation right now.

"Go on. Please," he said unexpectedly. "I'll pay."

"Are you *feeling* all right?" I asked.

Godric sighed and made strange noises over the phone, which I assumed was nose clearing. I sincerely hoped it wasn't manly sniffling. "Just feeling a bit . . . I'm fine. Shut *up*, all right?"

I was so used to men employing rudeness to disguise distress that I didn't take offense. "Listen, I know where we can get a nice cup of tea," I said soothingly. "And some treacle tart." No one, but no one, can feel miserable in front of a plate of treacle tart and a pot of tea.

I gave him directions to Tea and Sympathy on Greenwich Avenue. If I was going to remove Godric's one English crutch in New York, I needed a strong cup of tea to do it with.

"Godric, is something up?" I asked, once we were installed in a corner table with a pot of Tetley's (three bags) between us. I insisted on a corner table and kept my shades and sunhat on, just in case anyone could be bothered to recognize us.

He paused momentarily in his gradual transference of the contents of the sugar bowl into his teacup.

"No," he lied, with a glare. "Didn't anyone tell you not to be so nosy?"

"Frequently," I replied briskly. "But you look ill. And I don't want to catch anything. Does Paige know? I'm sure she has a doctor you could see. I'm sure she won't want your upcoming promotion plans ruined."

That got the cat out of the bag. At the mention of his big film, Godric flaked visibly.

"Shut up," he whined, then looked hopeful. "Do you think I look ill? You know, now you mention it, I haven't had a dump in a few days. Maybe I need someone to nurse me?"

"Stop that right now," I said, topping up his tea. "There's no point malingering. We all have to do things we don't want to, from time to time. It's called having a job."

"But I'm an *actor!*"

"That's still a job, last time I checked. Now, what's the problem?"

He heaved a sigh. "You know that party I told you about, at the end of the week? I really don't fancy going. Paige says I have to. Something to do with corporate sponsors." He looked up at me hopefully. "I don't suppose? . . ."

"Not on your life," I said. "Godric, you

have to understand, I really can't risk that sort of thing happening again, even if it's totally innocent. I have to think of Jonathan."

He looked at me with his big sad eyes, and I felt a twinge of something, possibly remorse.

"Come on, Godric," I said gently, "you have to get over it. There'll be lots of compulsory parties in your career."

"It wouldn't be so bad if I had someone to *go with* to these effing awful wank-fests," he whined. "At least I'd have someone to *talk* to. About something other than *everyone else there*."

God, this shyness masquerading as misanthropy was wearing.

"Well," I said practically, "can't you call someone? A friend?"

"Don't have any friends here."

"What about someone in London, then? Surely Paige can arrange for them to come over. No . . . old girlfriends, perhaps?"

Godric looked agonized. "Shut up. How's Jonathan, you know, about the car . . . incident?"

"He's not as mad as I would be if it were me," I said carefully.

"It wouldn't surprise me if Paige fed them all that information herself," he grumbled.

"I mean, the police can't release details like that, can they, if there's no arrest made?"

I looked up at him. "No." I frowned. "That's right. It must have been her."

"The sly cow," said Godric. "I felt bad about that, you know. And we were really starting to have a good time together, weren't we?"

"Um, yes. Yes, I suppose we were."

Godric stared into his teacup. "I haven't had such a good time with . . . with anyone for ages. Cheers. For bailing me out. Appreciate it."

He gave me an awkward pat on the arm. There was something about his expression that I found oddly touching. Even if he was socially prehensile, I felt like Godric and I had started to get to know each other, and, more than that, I'd helped him. Sad to say, it was quite heartwarming.

Then, of course, he had to go and spoil it by saying something bloke-ish.

"You know, Melissa," said Godric, leaning over the tablecloth so I could see his chest hair poking out of his Aertex shirt, "you're a game girl."

I shrank back as if he'd scalded me. The last time someone had called me game, I'd been in the dining room of the Savoy, wearing my wig and stockings, and my dining companion had erroneously assumed I was the pudding course. He'd also been over sixty with some kind of thyroid problem, but I'd had no compunction about setting him straight.

"Don't say that," I said, and my voice came out rather snappy.

"Why not?" Godric raised his eyebrows. "You should be flattered!"

"Godric," I said firmly. "To a woman, being called game is . . . well, it's practically short for being *on* the game. You know," I dropped my voice, "being a *hooker.*"

"I *know* what *that* means," he grunted, "but I totally disagree! Being game means you're up for it, you know, not too high maintenance. Men *love* game girls," he went on. "They're great fun! You know, resourceful. Like you were when we got nicked. Shows a bit of spirit!"

And on he went: drinking games, shenanigans in parks, reckless driving, cross-dressing . . .

All of a sudden, I could see exactly why Jonathan didn't want me hanging out with Godric, or indeed standing in for anyone else's girlfriend.

It made me look *game.*

The cold fingers of fear gripped me around the neck, where my nice girl pearls should have been. Why had I never seen it like this before?

I didn't want to be a "game" girl. Game girls never got married. Game girls ended up alone at fifty-five with nine "boisterous" Labradors, running the Pony Club trials with red noses and hearty handshakes, always being invited to other people's Christmas lunches and never coming "because of the dogs," then spending the day swilling back a bottle of Baileys and weeping over a rerun of *National Velvet.* No one, in short, ever fell in love with a game girl.

I sat speechless as my future unfolded before me in the tearoom like some hideous Charles Dickens vision, while Godric worked himself up into a froth about some up-for-it lass who'd once mounted one of the lions in Trafalgar Square while wearing only a policeman's helmet.

". . . and of course, all that is just. Incredibly. Sexy." Godric finished with a slurp of tea to disguise the fact that he'd just said the word sexy.

"Listen, Godric," I said. "It's one thing to think of a girl as game *in your head,* but don't ever say it aloud unless you want to split up with her. I once . . ." I hesitated, but then steeled myself. "I once had a boyfriend who thought it was the height of compliments to tell me I was game. He used to wear Gucci loafers and get me to pick up his dry cleaning too."

"Really?" Godric looked as if he wasn't sure whether to disapprove of that or not. "And what happened?"

"Well, we split up when he ran off with someone else. But that's not the point," I added. "I should have known from the moment that Orlando told me that "all boys love a game girl" that he was only after one thing."

Godric's brow had darkened.

"I mean, I did adore him," I went on, encouraged by his apparent disapproval. "He was awfully charming. Very handsome, and frightfully good at . . ." I shook myself. Now wasn't the time to be thinking about *that*. "But now I realize that a man like Jonathan . . . what? What are you looking at me like that for?"

"Orlando?" Godric demanded. "Orlando what?"

"Oh, you won't know him," I said. "He's not an actor."

"I'm not just an actor," huffed Godric. "Orlando *what?*"

"Orlando who?" I corrected him. "Orlando von Borsch. His father's one of the stuffed olive von Borsches. He's one hundred percent cast-iron Euro-trash. Well, one hundred percent gold-plated Euro-trash, actually. You might have seen him in —"

"I know exactly who he is." Godric's face looked like thunder. "He copped off with Kirst — With my girlfriend at Crazy Larry's so-called nightclub before I flew out to do this stupid film, and that was the last I saw of her."

"Oh, that's terrible!" I said with a rush of fellow feeling. "Poor you! What was her name?"

"Kirsty," he said reluctantly. "Kirsty Carruthers. Do you know her?"

I shook my head. "No, sorry."

Godric turned his head away like a wounded animal. "I'm over it now. I mean, if she's seriously impressed by someone so creepy he virtually slithers into the room on his stomach, she's welcome."

I slipped my hand across the table and squeezed his thumb. So this was the girlfriend that Paige had meant. No wonder Godric was such a miserable sod. Despite his stroppy behavior, I knew Godric was rather like Braveheart; all snap and no bite.

Well, okay, Braveheart had a nasty nip. And I'd seen Godric's left hook fell a passerby *and* get us arrested.

But *apart* from that, I realized in an

unexpected flash of insight, they both just did it to avoid being nice to people because they were scared of being hurt again. Braveheart didn't ask to be a bratty, tug-of-love latch-key pet. Godric was obviously reliving every single time he'd been dumped at school. Which couldn't have been that often.

I blinked at my own ghastly Oprah-style psychoanalysis. Two more weeks in New York, and I'd have my own chat show.

"I'm not saying we were in *love* or anything," mumbled Godric. "But I was, erm, pretty keen on Kirsty. And I thought she liked me. Just goes to show." He hesitated, then raised his puppy-dog eyes. "You're a woman, Mel — I mean, just between us, you know, it wouldn't be because I asked her to? . . ."

"Asked her to what?" I prompted, my mind filling with lurid possibilities as he flushed painfully. "What? Spit it out."

Godric stared at me, horrified. "No! I didn't ask her *that!* Christ almighty!"

I blinked. I really had no idea what he was talking about. "Then what?" I prompted.

"Iron my shirt," he mumbled into his chest.

I sighed. If that was the most outrageous thing he'd suggested, then no wonder Orlando had slimed her off her feet. "No,

Godric. I don't think that'll be it. But, chin up! You're about to be a big film star!" I said encouragingly. "Stupid old Kirsty, eh? Forget the whole sorry affair. This time next month, you'll have women beating down your door."

Godric flinched.

"Most men would love that," I pointed out. "Beautiful model types with long legs and perfect teeth. You don't get that in West London."

"I'd rather have a game girl with fat legs and a nice smile," he muttered under his breath. "Like you."

"Don't be silly," I said briskly. "Now, do you want some more crumpets? I think these are better than the ones we get at home."

"Melissa," said Godric suddenly, grabbing my other hand. "Please come to the party with me! You have no idea what it's like! Everyone coming up to you, and saying how much shorter you look in real life, and offering you drugs you have no idea how to take, and asking about people you're meant to know . . ." His eyes were wild and staring. I wondered if he really was ill. "Please come. Just for half an hour. Please."

"But Godric, no. I *can't*. I promised . . ."

Inside my head, a terrible struggle was

raging between my conscience, which was now painfully aware of exactly why Jonathan didn't want me pretending to be other people's girlfriends, and my other conscience, which couldn't let a fellow shy Brit down in his hour of need. I felt a certain kinship with Godric, even more so now that I knew we were both victims of the Orlando von Borsch charm-Panzer.

"Please, Melissa," he said, and his voice had the authentic note of gruff, English-bloke embarrassment at having to ask his mate's sister for a date. "I need you to."

Wheels were starting to turn in my head, albeit very slowly. There was a way round this — a way that would kill a few birds with the one stone. It was rather a riskily chucked stone, though.

"Before I decide anything, have you got Kirsty's phone number?"

Godric started to pretend that he'd discarded it straight away, but I raised a commanding finger and he dug about in his jacket pocket for his mobile.

"You're not going to phone her, are you?" he said as I wrote it down in my notebook.

"I don't know," I said, and snapped it shut. "I haven't decided. Now, how about those crumpets?"

TWENTY

Sometimes, it feels as though Fate is right on your side, blowing wind into your sails and generally speeding your plans through as a personal priority. Frequently, however, just as the harbor's hoving into view you discover that actually the reason you are speeding along is that Fate has cut your anchor and the harbor wall is heading up fast . . . But I'm getting a little ahead of myself here.

Three things happened that made me believe that for once, I'd come up with a seriously clever little plan, with side benefits all round. I phoned Kirsty, I spoke to Paige, and my sister Emery invited me for dinner.

First things first.

Kirsty, when I got hold of her, could not have been more thrilled to hear from me, especially when I told her I was a friend of Godric's, trying to arrange a surprise for him.

(True! No ding!)

"He's in New York? I've been desperate to get hold of him for months!" she squealed. "But his phone isn't working and he won't answer his e-mails." Then the bubbles dropped out of her voice. "Has he? . . . You're not organizing . . . an *engagement* party or something?"

"Good heavens, no," I said. "Not at all. Between you and me, I think he's still completely nuts about some girl in London, but of course he's far too gentlemanly to name names."

Then it all came tumbling out: the blissful six months of happy hour cocktails and Italian cinema, then the row about some stupid chance remark about a previous boyfriend's new car, her snogging Orlando out of drunken pique, and Godric seeing it as the biggest betrayal since Samson and Delilah, and him refusing to take her calls, and her regretting it almost immediately (but not that immediately, because I seem to recall some mention of antibiotics), and then him going off to the States "on some job" and not leaving any details.

"And I wish I knew where he was, just so I can say sorry," she finished up, miserably. "Is he still acting? Did he get any work over there?"

It was rather sweet, I thought, that she still wanted him even without knowing he was about to be a huge film star. If she wanted Godric in his original state, then it must be love.

"Yes, he's doing rather well," I said. "So, do you think you could come? It's awfully short notice, sorry."

"I'd clear my diary for Godders," she said fervently. "Um, I'm not sure about flights though." She paused discreetly. "I'll have to check my, er, my diary."

"Oh, if you can come, I can arrange the tickets from this end," I assured her.

"You can?"

"Yes," I said, feeling like a fairy god-mother. "I can."

Well, maybe a fairy godmother in the venge-ful, unpredictable Allegra Svensson sense.

By the third week in September, the weather had cooled off sufficiently for me to button myself into a new fitted suit I'd bought at Saks, which had just the right amount of sauce, coupled with just the right amount of nanny-ness. Finished off with a new pair of black leather pumps, I felt far more like myself than I had in ages, wig or no wig. As I strode through the jostling crowds on Broome Street toward Paige's office, I smiled at everyone I passed, even if they did give me funny looks.

Tiffany didn't bother to pretend Paige was busy when I walked in. She couldn't, since I'd called to make an appointment and had refused, in a very polite way, of course, to get off the line till I'd gotten one.

"Melissa," said Paige coolly, as I sat down. "What can I do for you?"

"I have a great story for you, Paige," I said. "For Godric."

She put her fingers together. "I'm listening."

"I think I can reunite Godric with his very sweet English girlfriend," I said. "I don't know anything about her, but she knows my flatmate's brother from some real tennis club or other, and Woolfe's frightfully picky about who he hangs out with."

"Is she pretty?"

"That doesn't matter," I said sternly. "What matters is that she and Godric sound very star-crossed, and having her around might make him less of a growling dog and more of a malleable charmer-in-the-making."

Paige tipped her head to one side and pressed a button on her phone set. "Tell me more."

I explained how I could arrange for Miss

X and Godric to "bump into each other" at a party and leave the rest up to fate and cocktails.

"But," I added, "I'll do this on the following conditions. One, you pay for her tickets over here, plus a decent hotel, and two, you do not, under any circumstances, tell anyone from the press, until they're sure it'll work out. If it doesn't work out, you are not allowed to sell some Ric Spencer Heartbreak story, either."

Paige squinted at me. "And why would I do that?"

I looked at her firmly and wished I had my tortoiseshell-winged Honey glasses to peer over. "Paige, Jonathan thinks so highly of you. You're a very tight-knit group of friends, too. Honestly, you lot are so lucky to have a social circle like that, even now."

"And?"

"And . . ." I sighed. "It would be really *awkward* if Jonathan found out that you were the person behind all the stories in the papers about me and Godric. I mean, he'd wonder what sort of friend would make his girlfriend look like a two-timing slapper!"

Paige looked shifty. "I don't know where he'd get that idea from."

"I know! Fancy the police passing on all

those details!" I shook my head. "He might even wonder if you were doing it on purpose to drive some kind of wedge between me and him — and I know you'd hate the very idea of that!" I added gaily. "Putting your client before your friends. Crikey!"

We sat there in silence for a moment, the atmosphere balanced precariously on a knife-edge.

For one heart-stopping second it occurred to me that maybe Cindy *had* told Paige to do all this — wasn't she her friend from college, not Jonathan's? I battled down the rising panic.

But then Paige obviously weighed the benefits against the blackmail and sprang back to life. "Melissa, that's a charming plan you've come up with!" she cooed. "It would be an awesome thing for us to do for Ric. But . . . ah, I don't see quite why we should have to stand tickets for this girl?"

I pretended to pause, then beamed as if an idea had just occurred to me. "We never did agree on a fee, did we, for the time I spent with Ric? Why don't you get the tickets and we'll call it quits?" I waited a beat. "Better make them business class, actually. I daren't tell you what my day rates are in London!"

Paige managed a smile. "I'll get Tiffany

straight onto it. Can she call you for details?"

"Absolutely," I said, allowing myself to smile. It was a nice thing to do.

And that balanced the books in my head.

When I got home from all this machinating, I got a call from Emery.

I took a moment to establish it was her, as usual. When I answered the phone there was a protracted pause, as if between her dialing and me picking up she'd forgotten who she'd called. Emery always made calls as if she was on ring-back and it was her phone that had rung, not mine.

Emery the Memory, Granny sometimes called her.

"Melissa?" she murmured uncertainly.

"Hello, Emery," I said. "How are you?"

"Mmm," she said. "I'm in New York on Friday, and I was wondering whether you were about for a spot of dinner? And I do mean a spot. I've found an amazing new macrobiotic place where they bring you all your food in tiny paint palettes and syringes. Doesn't that sound brilliant?"

My heart skipped. Perfect! I could tell Jonathan I was meeting Emery for dinner, leave an hour earlier, prep Godric for his big moment at the party, then leave in time to meet her.

"Just you," she added. "William's not coming — he's away in Europe on business, so I thought I'd have a weekend shopping and so on. We could have a girls' night! Without Allegra!"

If Emery had had any idea how perfectly she was fitting into my plans, she'd have been astonished. I don't think any member of my family had ever been so unwittingly accommodating.

"That sounds brilliant," I said. "I'm putting it in my diary right now."

We were still chatting — or rather she was telling me at long and gusting length about her new yoga teacher (I think), and I was trying to get off the phone, when the door opened and Jonathan wandered in.

"Emery," I mouthed, and he pulled a face.

"Give her my love," he mouthed, backing away so I couldn't put him on.

I wrapped up the conversation as quickly as was polite, made arrangements to meet her on Friday, then went to find him. He was going through the mail with a frown on his pale forehead.

"To what do I owe this early pleasure?" I asked, slipping my arms round him happily.

"Client canceled on me. Wanted to re-arrange. So I thought I'd pop back and see you." He took a step back and regarded me with a critical eye. "And I'm glad I did. New suit?"

I nodded, and twirled, so he could see my seamed stockings.

"I like it," he said, hooking his eyebrow sexily. "Makes me feel . . . kind of nostalgic. What did Emery want?"

"Dinner on Friday. She's in town for the weekend."

Jonathan paused, and for a second, I thought I caught a glimpse of furtiveness about him, which was most out of character. "Sorry, sweetie, but I can't make it. I have to meet with a client, and Friday evening's the only time . . . they can do it."

I batted him with a gourmet pizza leaflet. "You weren't invited! It was just me and her. Sisters only."

He looked relieved. "I won't expect you back early then."

"Well, I wouldn't go that far," I said. "But I appreciate the thought! Anyway, enough about Emery. What shall we do now?" I slid my arms under his jacket and pressed myself up against the fine fabric of his shirt. "How about a backward evening? Start in bed, then get dressed and go out to eat?"

Jonathan grinned, pushed the hair out of my eyes, tipped me backward and kissed me, holding my head in the palm of his hand as if we were swing dancers.

I giggled. That was another side of Jonathan Gabi didn't know — the old romantic who loved Hollywood musicals as much as I did. Who could dance properly.

This was more like it, I thought happily, returning his kiss with upside-down enthusiasm.

Then he swung me upward again. "Much as I'd love to take you upstairs and unpeel you out of that delicious suit, I can't stay. I've got another client in an hour, then I might be late."

My heart sank. "But we were going to go out for dinner tonight, weren't we? Just the two of us!" We'd only been out on our own three times since I'd arrived, though I managed to bite my tongue on that.

Jonathan sighed and scratched his ear. "I'm sorry, honey. Really I am. That's why I came all the way downtown now, so I could see you for half an hour." He stroked my jaw ruefully with his finger, circling around my lips. "I'll try to get back as soon as I can. You appreciate how much I'd rather be with you, don't you? Listen, instead of going out, how about we phone out for sushi and watch *Singing in the Rain*? How about that?"

I looked at him, trying hard not to listen to the hissy little voices in my head.

"Okay," I said. He was trying. I knew he was. "But don't be late."

I could have gone out and walked the dogs with Karen, and gotten the latest about her latest speed-dating adventures, but to be honest, I really didn't feel like talking to anyone. Instead, I passed the rest of the afternoon drifting listlessly through Bloomingdale's without buying anything, then at half five, I took the subway back to the Village and wandered home, taking even more time than normal to inspect all the wrought-iron porches and overflowing window boxes.

As I washed my hair in Jonathan's huge bath and soaked in deep bubbles, I came up with positive after positive after positive about my situation, but somehow I just couldn't bounce myself into a better mood.

Not even drinking almost an entire bottle of Jonathan's Fine Wine improved my outlook. All I could think of was how Jonathan put his clients way before our relationship. Clients who might or might not have been his glamorous ex-wife, who probably didn't even *drink* and definitely didn't haul herself onto tables to do the twist, only to have them collapse under her.

I grabbed the phone off the coffee table. I just wasn't seeing things properly. What I needed was to tell someone just what a great time I was having. That would soon put things in perspective.

My fingers hesitated over the keypad. But who would be up at this hour? It would be . . . half twelve. Half twelve. Hmm.

Gabi. But she might be out — with someone. I didn't want to negotiate that minefield. That required total sobriety.

I couldn't phone my family, not unless I wanted to hear how much worse things could be.

That left one person who would have no qualms about putting me straight about how lucky I was. I pulled out my diary and started dialing the number Nelson had given me. Okay, he'd said emergencies, but it was typical of him to be all headmasterly about it. I knew he'd love a call.

I listened to the phone ring. Technology was amazing, I thought, sloshing the last of the wine into the huge glass. Somewhere out in the ocean, Nelson was bobbing around in his hammock, probably taking a night watch right now, steering the ship with one of those great big wheels. . . .

"What?" barked a familiar voice over the line. "What's happened? Are you okay?"

The alcohol, I think, triggered a warm rush of happiness at the sound of his voice. "Nelson!" I cried, stretching out my pedicured toes. "It's *me!*"

"I know it's you," he said. "No one else has this number DON'T YANK IT ABOUT! TREAT IT WITH RESPECT!"

I blinked. "What are you doing?"

"I'm supervising the night watch. Yannick is steering the course and Leah is DON'T PLAY WITH THAT IT'S NOT A TOY!"

"Oh. I see. Are you busy?"

Either Nelson heaved a huge sarcastic sigh over the phone, or there was some serious interference. "I'm in charge of an eight-hundred-tonne square rigger, Melissa, but apart from that, not really. So, I take it this is a social call and not some 'get me out of jail' panic?"

I looked around the room. Just talking to Nelson seemed to bring a little bit of my London life into the room. He sounded like home.

"Melissa? Are you still there? Having a good time?"

"Um, yes!" I hauled myself back, feeling a slight dizziness. Maybe I was drunker than I thought. "I'm having a *great* time! Jonathan's been taking me round the city, introducing me to all his friends, and he's put his secretary totally at my disposal, so Lori's been booking me into spas and tearooms and what have you . . ."

"Lovely!" said Nelson. "ARE YOU CHEWING?"

"No!" I replied, startled.

"Not you, YOU," he roared. "NO GUM ON THIS SHIP, YANNICK!" There was a slight pause in which I thought I could hear a seagull. "OR TOBACCO, NO! I DON'T CARE IF IT IS HISTORICALLY AC-CURATE!"

"Nelson, there's really no need to shout quite so —"

"IF YOU WANT HISTORICAL AC-CURACY I CAN LASH YOU TO THE YARDARM FOR A FEW HOURS, IF YOU WANT? So, have you been shopping then?"

"God, yes, I've been to Macy's, Bloom-ingdale's, Henri Bendel, where I met a gor-geous denim advisor called Seth who told me I had a cute ass, can you believe that?"

"Yes."

"And I've had a cupcake at the Magnolia Bakery, which wasn't as nice as your sponge, you'll be pleased to hear, and I've been to the street where that Led Zeppelin album cover was photographed, and . . ."

My voice cracked, and I stopped. To my surprise, tears were bulging along my eyelids. "I. . . ."

"I'M GOING BELOWDECKS NOW SO YOU'D BETTER CONCENTRATE, THE PAIR OF YOU. I THINK YOU'VE BOTH SEEN *TITANIC,* YES?" bellowed Nelson. "Hang on, Mel, I'll be right with you I SAW THAT, YANNICK!"

I quickly wiped away the tears with the back of my hand. "I'm having a great time, Nelson, really."

There was a pause, the sound of non-marking-sole shoes on wooden floors, and I could tell he was now inside.

"Ding!" he said gently.

A huge lump rose up in my throat as I imagined his big blond bear hug engulfing me.

"Come on. What's up?" he said.

"I don't know!" I sobbed. "I . . . don't know!"

"Melissa, you know I love you and your funny ways, but can we keep the amateur dramatics to a minimum? International mobile rates are outrageous, for both of us. Now, what's happened? Things not working out with Remington?"

"Things are working out," I gulped. "I just . . . he's never here. He's working *all the time,* and I think he's spending most of that overtime with Cindy."

"Why would he be with Cindy, for crying out loud?"

"He's selling their apartment. Didn't Gabi tell you?"

"Gabi? I haven't spoken to her recently. Listen, have you told him any of this? How you feel?"

I shook my head. "No."

Nelson made a familiar "ungh!" noise of despair that made homesickness bloom in my stomach like a bright red flower. "Well, why not, for crying out loud? I did flick through all those stupid magazines you left in the loo — even *Roger* knows talking is meant to be the solution to all relationship ills!"

"I don't want him to think I'm being whiny!" I whined. "I don't want him to think I'm not enjoying myself!"

"But it doesn't sound like you are."

"I *am*." I paused. "It's just . . . not quite turning out the way I thought it would."

Nelson paused too. Then he put into words what I was thinking. "New York, or Jonathan?"

"Both," I said in a small voice.

"Oh," said Nelson. He coughed. "Why do I get the feeling you're not telling me

513

the whole story?"

"Because you'd probably shout at me?"

He laughed, and over the shifting, whistling air between us, he suddenly felt very close. "Go on then, you stupid woman. In no more than two hundred words, please."

So I told him. Godric, Paige, the police, Cindy, Bonnie, everything. Even Braveheart.

"Right," he said, when I'd forced out the last agonizing word. "I think you need to talk to him about this Cindy business. But that's all it'll be — business."

"You think?" It was easy for him to say that.

"Mel, I don't know Jonathan as well as you do, but he doesn't seem the type to treat his new girlfriend the way his wife treated him, now, does he?"

"No."

"I'm not saying she might not be trying to wind him up, but the best thing you can do is just be yourself. The woman he fell in love with." There was a painful grinding noise.

"Was that the ship?" I asked urgently. "Nelson? Are you sinking?"

"No, that was me. I can't believe you're making me say these things."

"I feel so much better for talking to you,

Nelson," I said, and I meant it.

"Good, because you know how much I . . . THIS IS THE OFFICERS' MESS! GET BACK ON DECK! WHAT DO YOU MEAN THE CAPSTAN CAME OFF IN YOUR HANDS? IT'S TITANIUM!"

I sensed our conversation had drawn to a natural close, an impression reinforced, worryingly, by the connection being lost.

I sat back on the sofa in the warm darkness and digested Nelson's pearls of wisdom.

Be the woman Jonathan fell in love with.

But that woman had been an organizer, a fixer, a stitcher-up of people's problems. I couldn't help it if I ended up caring about them. That was who I *was.*

And I was starting to wonder if, despite his protestations to the contrary, Jonathan really was in love with Honey, the beautifully constructed end result, and not Melissa, the woman paddling furiously beneath Honey's swanlike elegance.

But I'd sworn that from now on, I'd be myself and not hide behind Honey. Maybe between them, Gabi and Nelson were right. If I stitched Godric's problems up, Jonathan would see that that was where my strengths lay. He'd be proud of me.

Just thinking about taking an active stance

made me feel better. Then I knocked over the side table with the wine on it and was scrubbing at the handwoven rug with table salt when Jonathan finally arrived home, bearing sushi and a very small La Perla bag.

TWENTY-ONE

Godric's party was being held in one of those trendy bars that are so small and in-the-know that you can't find them the first three times you walk past, and then when you manage to remember to take a friend back there, hoping to wow them with your connections, it's closed down and moved on.

I wasn't at all sure I had the right clothes with me for a party involving media types and actors. Trendy was never part of my wardrobe repertoire at the best of times, and anything I'd bought so far in New York (on the advice of the nice salesgirls who understood about dressing to impress) was designed to look expensively understated, or understatedly expensive. In other words, everything I had was awfully Upper East Side, and I needed something a little more Meat Packing District. As it were.

In the end I opted for my simplest black

dress and a pair of polka-dot Roman Holiday sandals. That looked pretty good on its own, as I let myself out of the house into the early evening warmth. But in my handbag I had my own special magic wand, which I knew would transform everything.

Believe me, I'd *agonized* about whether to wear the wig. I knew Jonathan had a huge problem with it, but, I reasoned, surely it was better to disguise myself completely, just in case there were any photographers around. They'd already snapped me with Godric as myself, so more pictures of brunette Melissa-the-MP's-daughter would just add fuel to the fire. Some random blond, on the other hand, would be merely another party guest.

I stood in the loo at the Starbucks on Sixth and Waverley, gazing at myself as I adjusted my illicit blond hair so the fringe hung into my eyes, and a shiver of guilt, heavily laced with excitement, ran through me. The blond hair was like a gorgeous gilt picture frame around my face, casting a sexy glow over my skin. My eyes seemed to darken and open up, seeming more black than dark brown. There was an element of shock in there, too.

Honey.

I was Honey again.

I fluttered my eyelashes at myself, then reached for my makeup bag. There was something about that curtain of light-reflecting hair that demanded more drama in my face. Carefully, I traced another layer of dark liner along my upper lids, then a touch more mascara. Then a quick flush of pink shimmer along my cheekbones. Then another final round of mascara.

I stood back to admire the effect. Suddenly the dress looked effortlessly chic, almost don't-care-ish. Maybe it was the way I was standing now, hips out. With my dark eyes smoldering out from beneath my fringe, and my lips barely glossed, I looked like Brigitte Bardot.

"Wow," I said, without thinking. How on earth could Jonathan prefer Melissa to this?

Thinking about Jonathan brought me round very quickly, and I checked my watch.

I'd promised Godric I would stay for exactly forty minutes at the party, including that bit at the beginning when no one's arrived, and the ten minutes it takes to extricate oneself. I absolutely *had* to be out of there by eight thirty, even if the party had barely gotten going by then. The shrieky little voices of my conscience were scarcely allowing this as it was.

Since the restaurant Emery wanted to try

was only a few blocks away from the party venue, I'd told her to meet me outside at eight, to be on the safe side. I'd never known her to be less than an hour late for anything.

When Godric shuffled into Starbucks ten minutes later, he walked straight past my table, then failed to spot me when he turned round and scanned the place with a surly eye.

I raised a discreet hand, not wanting to draw too much attention to myself.

Godric's boggling reaction, however, did that for me.

"Hay caramba!" he bellowed. "Melissa!"

I nodded for him to sit and to stop his adolescent "phwoarr!" gestures. "Quick tip," I hissed. "Don't walk into a date venue and scan the room like that. Makes you look stood up before you've even *been* stood up. And don't forget — you're a film star now."

He was still gawking at me as if I were a two-headed calf. "Effing hell, Mel," he gasped. "You look . . . you look like a model. Not a skinny model, you know, one of those decent-sized ones. Like Sophie Dahl or something. Before she got scrawny."

"Thank you," I said. "I'd stop there if I were you."

"Can we go?" he said, leaping to his feet.

"Let's go now."

He tugged my chair out for me while I was still on it. While I admired his strength, it probably wasn't a habit he ought to develop.

"I thought you didn't want to go to this do," I protested. Honestly, I'd never seen him so enthusiastic.

"I do now," he said and smiled. It was the first time I'd seen Godric smile, and, really, the effect was transformational. His entire face changed from that of a constipated teddy bear to that of a, well, quite an attractive teddy bear.

"Okay then," I said. "Let's go."

The enthusiasm lasted until we got to the club, and then it wavered at the sight of three extraordinarily cool people sloping wearily down the stairs, as if they were en route to a hemorrhoid clinic.

Godric stopped. "I'm wearing all the wrong things," he grunted forlornly. "I look like a geek."

"You look fine," I said. He wasn't looking too bad at all: deep green shirt, dark jeans with no obvious logo, jacket just on the right side of smart-casual. All of it seemed to fit properly too. If Kirsty had fancied him in London, she was definitely going to go for it here.

"Here." I checked that no one was about, then undid one button on his shirt, dug around in my bag for my grooming cream, and ran some through his hair so it looked glossed rather than greased. Then, for a final touch, I pulled off one of my green-glass cocktail rings and shoved it onto his little finger as a tribute to Gabi's Urban Gangsta advice, more than anything.

"What the hell is that?" demanded Godric, staring at it as if it had been some kind of obscenity.

"It's a talking point," I said. "Right, you've got thirty-nine minutes remaining. For the next thirty-nine minutes, you absolutely *can't* refer to me as Melissa. Not even when you're talking to me. You don't know who's listening. And if you see a camera, you *have* to tell me."

"What should I call you then?" he asked.

"Honey," I said firmly.

Well, it was too late now to make up a whole new identity. At least I'd remember to answer to Honey.

I pushed aside a flutter of misgiving. This was about giving Ric a boost. After I'd zhouzed up his personality and introduced him to my surprise guest, he'd be fine on his own, I knew it.

"Let's go, Ric Spencer," I said.

The funny thing about that wig was that it let me saunter into places I'd normally feel awkward in, even with my usual breezy attitude to social events. The shoes I was wearing also helped with the sauntering. Walking is so much easier in high heels, I find. It makes you use your whole body.

Downstairs, the room was very dark, made even darker by bloodred wall hangings and the red lightbulbs glowing inside huge paper shades above us. I blinked, trying to make out where the bar was. Adding to the Stygian effect were the hordes of black-clad people packing the side tables and what I now realized was underfloor lighting beneath maroon glass tiles. It was like being in a kidney, if kidneys had very loud sound systems and a free bar.

As I hovered, looking for a seat, a waitress passed with a huge tray of vodka shots of various colors in one hand and a tray of empty glasses in the other. Without even breaking chat, people grabbed fresh glasses and replaced old ones as she passed. When I turned back to Godric, he was throwing one blue drink down his neck and preparing a yellow one to follow it.

"Actors," he explained, with a gasp. "You need a couple too."

"No, thanks." As a sop to my conscience,

I'd made a vow not to let a drop past my lips. Besides, I needed to concentrate. People were already starting to look our way.

"See?" grunted Godric. "They're looking at us, wondering who you are." For once, though, he sounded almost pleased.

"Godric, they're looking at you, you idiot. You've just been in a play here. They know your film's coming out. Honestly . . ."

His eyes were scanning the place, and before he could toss back his urine-colored shot, a short, dark man in a black vest sidled up.

"Ric! How you doing?"

"Er, fine. Um, Ivan, this is Honey — Honey, this is Ivan Mueller."

"Hi! Hi!" Ivan was shaking my hand before I knew it. "Don't you have a second name?"

"No," I said, "just Honey."

"Cute!" he exclaimed and paused significantly.

"Ivan was the stage manager for a production of *Three Sisters* I was in last year," Godric supplied, in the manner of someone having their teeth pulled.

"And I *loved* working with him!" exclaimed Ivan theatrically. "We had a ball, didn't we, Ric?"

Godric shrugged.

"We did," Ivan confirmed. "Sooooo . . . What are you doing at the moment?"

"A short run of *The Real Inspector Hound*," grunted Godric. "It's okay."

"It's marvelous!" I added, in a deep coo. "Ric's had some rather good notices, haven't you, darling?"

Godric straightened up a bit. "Well, yeah. S'pose so."

Ivan pulled a face that suggested profound internal excitement.

"Are you working on something right now?" I asked politely.

"Am I? Oh, my Lord!" he exclaimed with a flourish of the shoulders, and launching into a long-winded litany of dismay and lack of professionalism, illuminated by unsubtle glances around the room at various miscreants seated in distant and not-so-distant corners.

Godric looked constipated throughout, but I was rather intrigued. I even recognized some of the names Ivan was throwing about like so much indiscreet confetti. It was, as Ivan assured me, a disgustingly incestuous business.

". . . and my partner Raj is a makeup artist, and what he sees, let me tell you, Honey, certain ladies would not want to be made common knowledge," he said, finally pausing for breath with an arch look over my shoulder. "Ooh, look who's just walked in! The poor thing! I have to fly. So nice to meet you, darling!" He gave me one of those showbiz air kisses, then bestowed another one on Godric, who flinched. "And look at you, all sexed up!" he added, as if noticing him for the first time. He nodded at me, "You suit him, Honey! See you soon!"

And Ivan vanished back into the crowd. I realized the room had filled up with people, in the intervening minutes, like seawater running into a sand castle. Godric and I were marooned at the edge of the room.

I checked my watch nervously. Where was Kirsty? I'd given her very specific instructions, but as she'd only flown in that afternoon, I hadn't been able to pick her up and sort her out myself. I hoped Paige hadn't somehow managed to intercept her.

"See what I mean?" whined Godric. "It's insufferable." But he looked quietly pleased at the same time. "I mean, he knows exactly what I'm doing right now. I know exactly what he's doing. But everyone always effing asks. It happens at all these parties — I hate actors."

"But you're doing really well!" I said encouragingly.

"Only cause you're here." He gave me

another intense look. "I really appreciate you coming. I've been —"

"You're going to have to learn how to do this on your own, you know, Godric," I said quickly. "Just pretend to be one of the characters you play, um, like . . ." My mind went blank.

"Can we sit down?" he said suddenly. "I feel a bit . . . seasick. It's these effing walls."

I steered him toward a table that had conveniently just become vacant, and he sank into a red velvet chair, long legs buckling beneath him.

"It's not easy when you're shy," I said, determined to get at least one useful lesson across. "But you just have to pretend to be someone else. It works, I promise you. And then when you realize you can do it as yourself, you're away."

I did mean all this, honestly. But there was a little voice at the back of my head, reminding me that I did it so much better when I was Honey. She didn't worry about what people thought, or whether she was living up to expectations.

"It's funny, isn't it," said Godric. He sounded quite pissed already.

"What is?"

"We're both here, pretending to be other people. You're a blond woman called Honey, and I'm a film actor called Ric."

I snapped my attention back to the evening and checked my watch surreptitiously. We only had fifteen minutes left.

"Yes. That's very true."

"And yet . . ." Godric waggled a finger. "And yet, only we know that underneath it, you're Melons the wardrobe mistress, and I'm Godric the geek." His face fell. "But in real life, you're still pretty gorgeous, albeit not quite as sexy as you are right now, whereas I'm just the sort of guy who does A-level Latin. And gets dumped."

Men, in my experience, are far, far worse at fishing for compliments than women.

"Oh, nonsense!" I said. "You're a *very* talented actor. My friend Gabi thinks you're sex on a stick." I paused. "That's a direct quote, by the way. It's not a term I'd normally use to describe men."

Godric looked at me with huge, tipsy, baby-seal eyes. "And how would you describe me?"

"I'd say you were . . . a very handsome, talented actor." Where was Kirsty? I searched the room for a tallish, thinish, English-ish girl. Argh. I could have done with her e-mailing me another photograph. Presumably she wouldn't be wearing dressage clothes when she arrived in the bar.

"You said the talented actor bit before," pouted Godric.

"I know," I stalled. "But personally, I find the talented bit as sexy as the . . . as anything else." God, this was a delicate one. Godric was staring at me, but swaying gently. I tried not to notice how much better than normal he looked this evening. Almost . . . eligible.

I shook myself. "I mean, Jonathan is gorgeous," I went on, "but I find the way he's so professional and clever, and good at ordering wine, just as sexy as his lovely strong hands. And you're such a versatile actor — women love men who can *do* things. Honestly, Godric. And stop being so grumpy with people. I know you're shy, but it's coming across as rudeness. To the point of your having some kind of *problem.*"

"Jonathan's not here, though, is he?" He paused. "Again."

I met Godric's dark-lashed eyes. I don't think he'd meant to be so perceptive, but he'd really managed to hit a nerve. I swallowed. Godric did have huge brown eyes. Chocolate brown eyes, in fact.

"No," I said. "He isn't. But that's not the point."

Godric looked deep into his drink, then downed it, grabbed two more from a passing tray. Without thinking, I grabbed one too and tossed it back.

We both gasped, then stared at each other. Uncomfortable things were happening. Uncomfortable things that I really wanted to put down to the drink, and the dark room, and the . . .

Godric broke the spell by burping, then shifted a little closer to me. "Mel, I mean, Honey," he said with a hint of a slur, "there's something I need to tell you."

"Ah, well, no, there's something I need to tell *you!*" I said quickly. There was no point making it a surprise. He'd recognize her far quicker than I would. "Mind if I go first?"

"I always like a lady to go first," he said with a leer. Then he looked confused, then went back to the leer.

I ignored all of it.

"I've phoned Kirsty and had a little chat about Orlando, and about you!" I said. "Are you cross?"

He was staring at me. He was actually staring at my chest, so I clapped my hands loudly in front of his face, at which point he rather blearily transferred his gaze to my eyes.

"You phoned Kirsty?"

"I did. I told her I was ringing because I needed to get something back from Orlando, and someone had given me this number. Bit of a fib, but, anyway, it turns out they split up ages and ages ago!" I beamed. "Isn't that great? She's too ashamed to call you, because of what happened. But I said you weren't bothered."

"I'm not bothered," he said.

"Well, no, of course you're not, because you've been so busy with your career and . . . What do you mean, you're not bothered?"

"I'm over Kirsty," said Godric loftily. "She means nothing to me anymore."

"Oh, Godric, don't say that," I cried. "She sounds lovely! We had such a nice chat, and she says she misses you, and feels awful about falling for a . . . Godric." I looked at him sharply. "Your hand's on my knee."

"I know," he said, with an Elvis-ish curl of the lip. "For the time being."

I removed it and replaced it where we could both see it, on the table. Godric stared at it, as if it belonged to someone else.

"So I got to chatting with Kirsty," I went on quickly. "And it turns out she's in New York at the moment! Isn't that a coincidence! She's come all the way . . . Godric! Are you listening to me?"

"Melissa," said Godric. "I have fallen, in

love, with you."

I stared at him in shock.

"You're what I need in this stupid, pretenshss, world of wankers," he slurred, his eyes suddenly full of emotion. "A good, solid game girl with proper tits. And nice strong legs."

"Well, I'm awfully flattered," I gabbled, "but really, I think you're just transferring your feelings for . . ."

He tried to put a finger sexily on my lips, but it went into my eye instead. With some effort, he placed it correctly. "Don't think," he said. "Jus' feel."

And then he lunged.

I would love to be able to say, snootily, that being kissed by Godric Ponsonby was like being assaulted by a dishwasher on economy cycle, but to my acute surprise, it was actually not an unpleasant experience.

He smelled very clean, underneath the rubbing alcohol aroma of the vodka, which is a trait I've always found rather sweet in overgrown public school boys: big date equals comprehensive bath. And his lips were soft, he'd shaved, and he didn't attempt to lick the inside of my mouth.

All in all, it was about nine hundred percent better than our previous encounter in the wardrobe cupboard.

But it was completely and utterly inappropriate, and after a few, um, seconds, I fought him off.

"*No*, Godric," I said firmly, as if I'd been talking to Braveheart.

"But why? Isn't it meant to be? Us meeting again after all these years?" he demanded. "Don't you think it's fate?"

I looked deep into his eyes. I hated saying no, especially when I'd just realized how fond I was of the surly brute, and how I'd hate to hurt his feelings, but . . . "No! Godric, it's not," I said. "I love Jonathan. I do. I love him."

He said nothing but widened his eyes fearfully, and when I followed his gaze, I realized why.

"Kirsty?" I said, recovering as fast as I could.

Kirsty, as indeed it was, was standing right next to our table, the living embodiment of what Gabi derisively called the "Sloane Square Ski, Surf and Sand Club." She had long, ruler-straight blond hair parted in the middle, skinny leg jeans tucked into high boots, and a pair of wide, pale eyes that were gazing at us and filling up with water faster than a leaky dinghy.

"Kirsty? Is it you?" I cried with joy. "Hello! It's Melissa!" I leaped up from my seat and shook her limp, somewhat damp hand.

Her lip, frosted with pink gloss, wobbled. "What were you . . ."

"Did you know Godric's in a simply *enormous* film? No? Well, he was talking me through his big romantic scene at the end — look, I'm sure he'll show you too. Apparently, there's a special way you have to kiss on camera, so you don't actually have to *kiss* the actress, if you know what I mean," I improvised wildly. "Godric?"

Godric and Kirsty were staring at each other. I couldn't work out quite what the stares were leading up to: tears, a fight, a reconciliation? I looked from one to the other.

Nope. No idea. That was the trouble with certain types of posh people, I'd found. Too much stiff upper lip eventually freezes your entire face. Aristocratic Botox.

"Shall I get you a drink, Kirsty?" I enquired. "I'm just about to leave for dinner."

At this point, Godric seemed to regalvanize himself. "Is he going to join us?" he demanded.

"Who?"

"Jonathan?"

"I'm not having dinner with Jonathan," I began. "I'm seeing my sister."

Godric's brow creased. "So what's he doing here?"

I spun round.

Sure enough, standing at the top of the stairs leading down into the main bar area, was Jonathan. And he wasn't alone. Standing next to him, mouth opening and closing in midyap, was a beanpole of a blond woman in a silver sheath dress.

Cindy.

My blood froze.

Honestly, it really did. It felt like it had set, thick and sluggish, like jelly in my veins.

Before I could move, Jonathan's eyes, rolling in annoyance at whatever Cindy was ranting about, met mine. He was standing beneath one of the only illuminated areas of the whole venue, all the better to make out the look of surprise, then extreme annoyance, then disgust that crossed his face.

I felt physically sick.

"Oh, *Christ,*" I moaned. Had he seen Godric fall on my neck? That must have looked so incriminating from a distance.

"What?" demanded Godric. "What now?"

I opened my mouth to tell him, but the words wouldn't come. It was as if I were seeing the whole thing from Jonathan's perspective: the deliberate disobeying of his request, the lying about where I was, and,

535

worst of all, the wearing of the wig.

I put my hand to my head to yank it off but stopped. What was the point? I was so busted. The best I could do was to stick to the truth: that this was a last favor for Godric and I was only wearing the wig so as *not* to embarrass Jonathan.

Then again, rallied a voice in my head, what the hell was he doing here with Cindy, when he was meant to be with a client? He'd *lied* to me! And if he'd lied, there must be something to hide!

Fury and guilt make a pretty noxious emotional cocktail. I felt even more sick, and if I hadn't been clinging onto the table, I think my legs would have buckled entirely.

But rather than let them come to me, I decided to face the problem head-on.

"Would you excuse me?" I said to Godric and Kirsty, took a deep breath, and walked over to meet them by an aggressive display of black thistles.

"Hello, Jonathan," I said, trying to sound merry. "Shh! I'm in disguise."

"Melissa," he replied, his face a study in granite. "Melissa, this is Cindy. Cindy, this is Melissa Romney-Jones."

Cindy up close was no less smooth and hard than Cindy at a distance. She was, however, very hard to describe: She looked

airbrushed from blow-dried head to pedicured toe. She certainly didn't look like
someone who'd recently seen a baby, let
alone given birth.

"So you're Melissa?" she drawled, as if it
would never have dawned on her that it
could be me. "They *said* you were a . . .
blond."

I dragged up all the pride I could, under
the circumstances.

"I'm not usually," I said in a friendly tone
that didn't quite come off, "but I'm right in
the middle of a secret operation right now.
I'm acting as Cupid for my old friend Godric and his estranged girlfriend, and I don't
want anyone to know it's me. Hence the
wig."

Jonathan's face turned gray with anger.

I met his eyes stoutly. I wasn't sure he had
much right to get mad about a little thing
like a wig, when he was there with his ex-
wife. That *totally* moved the goalposts.

"You are?" Cindy looked frankly skepti-
cal. "How . . . accommodating. And is it
working, Godric?" she added. "Are you rec-
onciled?"

Godric, in full honorable-knight-of-the-
realm mode, had stomped up behind me
and was glowering at Jonathan. He favored
Cindy with an extreme scowl. "We were

about to leave, actually."

Kirsty wisely said nothing. Her saucer-sized eyes were widening into dinner-plates. She was probably wondering if she'd been flown in to be in some reality TV show.

"I'd take that as a yes, Melissa!" said Cindy. "Congrats! Is it one of your specialties, reuniting estranged lovers?"

She said this with a significant glance at Jonathan.

My stomach turned. "No, this was just a one-off. And I was about to leave myself, to meet my sister for dinner," I gabbled. "She's probably outside right now."

"Really?" said Jonathan, his voice dripping with sarcasm. "Will she recognize you? Or is she in disguise too?"

I tried a tinkly laugh. "Oh, Jonathan. Didn't you see her outside?"

Bloody hell. It would have to be Emery I was meeting, the woman so vague she couldn't remember her PIN number, even when it was the year of her own birth. The chances of her being in the right area, let alone on time, were slim.

"No," said Jonathan, "we didn't."

"Emery?" demanded Godric, who wasn't quick at the best of times. "You're meeting Emery?"

"Yes!" I insisted. Godric's vocal tic of

habitual disbelief was hardly helping my case. "I didn't mention it in case you still . . . in case you still had feelings, or something." I held up a hand before he could say anything.

"But why would I have feelings for *Emery?*" demanded Godric. "I only ever fancied *you!*"

"Ten years ago!" I added, as Kirsty looked aghast. "Ten years ago! Ah ha ha ha!"

Godric opened his mouth, but I glared so hard at him, I swear pictures fell off the wall.

Cindy smirked. "Well, they do say true love never dies. Don't they, Jon?"

"I wouldn't know," he said through tight lips.

She nudged him, flashing me a "men!" eyebrow hike. "Come on, honey. You're the romantic. Remember Antigua?"

I felt an odd cocktail of emotions churn in my stomach: fear, depression, inadequacy, but also rage. Why hadn't Jonathan told me he was seeing *her* this evening? How many other times had he seen her without saying?

And what were they going to talk about when I left? Antigua?

I drew myself up to my full height.

"Anyway, I can see you're fully occupied this evening, Jonathan," I said. "Is Cindy your client, or . . ." I swallowed. "Or is this a social occasion?"

Cindy glanced at Jonathan. "Business or pleasure, Jon? Huh?" She looked back at me. "Let's say a bit of both."

"Cindy's company is sponsoring the production," Jonathan explained tightly.

"Yes, I had to come along this evening, and since Jonathan wanted to" — she paused just long enough for me to think she was making up an excuse — "meet to discuss the apartment sale, I thought we might as well meet here."

I turned to him.

"That's right," he said tonelessly.

Something snapped inside me and sank like a stone, deep into the pit of my stomach.

"Well, in that case, I won't keep you from your discussions," I said. "Good night, Godric, Kirsty. I hope you have a lovely evening. I made a reservation for you at Cipriani's. So nice to meet you, Cindy."

And I swept out.

TWENTY-TWO

Of course, who should I run into at the top of the steps but Emery, a mere ten minutes late for the first time in twenty-odd years.

I resisted the temptation to drag her downstairs and show her off as evidence. It was too late for that.

"Melissa?" she said, peering at me on the street. "Melissa?"

"Yes, it's me," I said, "it's just a wig."

"Suits you," she said. "You look like Mummy. If she was younger, and a bit fatter. And sort of . . . crosser."

"That's not the wig," I said. "Come on, I need a drink."

We ended up not in the fancy restaurant Emery had booked — since she hadn't remembered to write down the address — but in a simple Italian place, where we ordered large bowls of pasta and some red wine.

I let everything tumble out, and Emery

listened with a wise expression on her face. I knew it didn't necessarily mean she'd come out with anything wise, but Em had always been very good at sympathy. Years of weeping over orphaned lambs and First World War poets had seen to that.

"How do you manage?" I asked her. "With William's ex?"

"Oh, it's very simple," she said. "I never see her. Well, of course, Laurie's dead, which helps, but you mean Gwendolyn?"

I nodded. I didn't have the energy to do much else.

"I just pretend she doesn't exist," said Emery serenely. "I tell myself she's a fictional character who sends us Christmas cards."

"But what about Valentino?" Valentino was William's five-year-old son.

Emery widened her eyes. "William won't let me meet him. He doesn't want lines to be crossed."

I paused, my spaghetti dripping on my napkin. "You're telling me that *William* wants you to pretend Gwendolyn and Valentino don't exist?"

"Mmm. His therapist says it's easier for him to keep things in boxes than it would be to try to make us all into a collage. Separate pages, you see. I think it's rather a good idea. I find it much easier to put Daddy on a separate page, since he's in another country from me." She smiled pensively. "Actually, I've just about put him in a different book."

"Em, I don't think that's so healthy."

"You want to have this other woman floating in and out of your life *forever?*" asked Emery with unusual sharpness.

I thought about that for a moment. "I'd rather have her where I can see her, than go mad wondering where she's lurking," I said.

Emery kicked me affectionately under the table. "Poor Mel," she said. "Have you thought about going blond permanently? It rather suits you."

I sighed, and pushed my pasta away.

Emery had to leave to get back to her hotel in time for her late-night meditation routine, so I wandered slowly back through the streets of the West Village to Jonathan's house, my wig curled up in my bag like a dirty secret, my own hair lank and dark. Like I felt.

When I reached Washington Square, I sat on the steps of one of the elegant town houses and sank my head into my hands. The lamps were all lit in the park, and people were still playing chess, walking their dogs for the last time, and strolling back from their nights out, full and happy.

An awful heaviness filled my chest, pinning me to the spot. Nothing could feel worse than this. I'd had some pretty grim moments in the past, but nothing that had paralyzed me so completely. It was like being trapped in quicksand; the more I tried to explain, the more guilty I looked, and the more Jonathan would realize he'd made a mistake. I'd let him down. Even if it had been for a very good reason, I'd still let him down.

Cindy popped up in my imagination, all poofy hair and gimlet eyes. She'd looked so proprietorial there, virtually hanging onto Jonathan's arm. And if he'd just been meeting her to discuss their apartment, why hadn't he told me? It wasn't like I didn't *know* he was selling it. If he thought I was more likely to fly off the handle about him meeting her than I was about him *pretending he wasn't,* then he obviously didn't know me very well at all.

My eyes filled with tears, and I wished I was sitting on my own front door steps. More than anything I wished I was at home.

And so I called the one person I knew who'd tell me what I should do, or else tell me to snap out of it.

The phone rang three times and was then answered very abruptly.

"What now?" sighed Nelson. "THAT'S NOT WHAT I CALL A SHEET KNOT, LEANNE! DO YOU WANT THIS SHIP TO CRASH INTO ROCKS AND SPLINTER INTO MATCHSTICKS BECAUSE OF YOUR NAILS? AGAIN, PLEASE!"

"You were wrong!" I wailed. "I took your advice and I've really messed things up with Jonathan. I think . . . I think I'll have to come home!"

Nelson sighed, and I heard him order some minion to take over. I think I even heard the minion say, "Aye, aye, Cap'n," but that might have been underprivileged urchin cheek.

"Right, quickly, please, and don't leave anything out," he said, but his voice was more gentle than his words.

I tried to explain as quickly and as simply as I could.

"Right," he said eventually. "I assume you did all this out of your usual misguided desire to help everyone apart from yourself? And to prove to Remington Steele that you were just as capable in New York as you are here?"

"Yes! I don't humiliate myself for *fun*, you know!"

"That's not what I meant," he sighed. "And you know it. Okay, first of all, don't come home."

My heart sank. "Ever?"

"No! Don't come home *now*, like you've done something wrong. You're not having an affair, you're not working on the side, and you're not lying to him. If you come home it'll be like admitting you are. You'll just have to wait for him to calm down, then explain that you weren't doing the pretend girlfriend stuff as a job, you were helping out a friend. Okay, you should have told him, but you know, control freakery and all that. Pretty bad show."

"You think?" I said doubtfully. "But it'll be unbearable. He's furious."

"Melissa," sighed Nelson. "If this paragon of estate agency ends up marrying you, it won't be the last time you'll do something so daft that he'll be speechless with fury. But if he has anything about him, he'll also realize that you did it for the very best reasons, and if he loves you, he'll see why that's far more important than some wifey who just follows orders."

Tears started to slide down my cheeks again, but I managed a weak smile through them.

"Thank you," I said. "I know you don't

like him very much."

"It's not that. I, er, don't really think I'm . . ." Nelson decided not to go on with whatever he had in mind but instead said, "Look, Melissa, it's really very simple — ask yourself, what would your granny do? She's bound to have been in a similar situation. Why don't you phone her?"

"No," I said, looking out over the park railings. "No, I don't need to do that. I just wanted to . . . talk to you."

"Jolly good," he said gruffly.

I sighed. "I might be hurrying back sooner than you think. There doesn't seem much point in staying if Jonathan doesn't . . ."

I swallowed rather than put the awful thought into words.

"Melissa, sometimes men are their own worst enemies," said Nelson, with unexpected tenderness. "When it comes to . . . *feelings*."

"What do you mean?"

"I mean, we don't always express ourselves as well as we could. Or at the right time. We don't have the same verbal diarrhea as you women do, frankly."

"And your point is?" I bristled.

"I'm just saying . . ." His voice — or the telephone line — went crackly. "You lot like to waffle on about how you feel the entire time, like relationships require some kind of perpetual football commentary. Men are usually waiting for the right moment." Nelson paused. "And we're never sure when that right moment is. That doesn't mean we're not feeling it."

Light dawned. That sounded exactly like Jonathan. He always wanted everything to be perfect. I just needed to make him see that with me it didn't have to be perfect all the time. Or, more to the point, that it probably never would be.

"Oh, Nelson, you're so right!" I exclaimed rapturously. "You always are! Honestly, you're the best friend a girl could ever, ever want!"

There was a distant crashing at the other end of the line that I assumed was Nelson being distracted by some onboard disaster. "Is that the sail falling off?" I asked helpfully.

Nelson sighed. "No, it's Dean Bradley falling over on deck again. I told him those soles weren't seaworthy. Look, much as I'd love to sit and hear you snivel transatlantically, I have a deck inspection to supervise and you have a boyfriend to make up with. Am I going to see you in a few weeks?"

"I'll be on the dockside with my hanky, Cap'n," I assured him.

"Yes, well, make sure you have your adoring American there too," he replied, and was then cut off amid clanking background noises.

I hoped the urchins hadn't decided to punish him for unauthorized use of a mobile phone. Those cabin-boys in Hornblower novels could be vicious.

I put my phone back in my bag and sat for a moment, pulling myself together. I had to go back and try to fix what I'd broken, even if it turned out to be unfixable. Never let it be said that I ran away from my own problems, or tried to pretend that someone else's didn't exist. At least then I'd know.

I was still fighting the temptation to phone British Airways and get on the first flight home when I walked up the front steps. Maybe Jonathan had been right; I didn't have the same understanding of the way New York worked as I did of London. It was like hearing a familiar song sung in a different language; when you tried to join in, it didn't sound in tune.

But I kept Nelson's words in the forefront of my mind and made myself walk back into the house, where Jonathan sat on the leather sofa, staring blankly into space. The room was dark, with only the street light filtering through the trees outside, dappling the faded walls. He still hadn't made a wallpaper/paint decision.

I went to turn on the main light, then stopped.

Braveheart saw me walk in and launched himself through the room, his claws skittering on the wooden floorboards. I picked him up as he tried to lick my face.

This wasn't helping my dignified speech, but it gave me something to hold on to.

"Jonathan, I'm sorry," I began. "I know I've done something you didn't want me to do. I had no intention of hurting you, or embarrassing you — that's why I wore the wig. So no one would know it was me."

He turned round, and I was shocked at the stoniness of his face, which made the presidents on Mount Rushmore seem positively festive. It was the expression he wore when he didn't want anyone to see what he'd been feeling; the last time I'd seen him look this grim was when he'd been telling me about his divorce from Cindy, way back before we'd started dating properly.

"It's not *about* the damn wig. Although why you think no one would recognize you in it is yet another manifestation of this weird lack of esteem thing you have and . . . You just don't get it, do you?"

"I do!" I protested. "I understand *perfectly.* You don't want me to show you up! You didn't want me to be working in New York! And I swear to you, I *wasn't* — I was honestly just doing a favor for a friend who —"

"Happens to be in love with you?"

"Don't be ridiculous. That was the vodka talking. Anyway, not all exes are mad and out for revenge," I said pointedly. "I'm good friends with, well, nearly all of my exes. Godric's just —"

Jonathan raised an eyebrow. "How are you still so naive?" he demanded.

"I'd rather be naive than cynical!" I protested hotly. "Jonathan, I *am* sorry. I really am. I had no intention of showing you up. I have so many chances to make you happy, and I only had to do this one small thing for Godric. I was *only there* to make sure he met up with *Kirsty,* his ex, so they could reconcile, and you have so much confidence, so much . . . aplomb, and he has none. And I know how he feels."

"Melissa, Ric is a film star," said Jonathan. "If he can't walk into a party on his own, he's going to have something of a career problem." He shook his head. "But *why* can't you see how that makes me feel? Arriving at a party, only to find my girlfriend wrapped around some pinup?"

"You're not jealous of Godric, are you?" I asked, shocked. "I mean, there's nothing to be jealous *of!*"

"No?" A flash of vulnerability broke through the granite for a second. "When he was hanging off your neck, was that just acting?"

"I'm not going to dignify that with a response," I retorted. "Have I made a big deal about you selling your flat for Cindy? Letting her carry on interfering in your life? Have I made a big deal about you escorting her to a *party,* while telling me you were out with a client? How do you think I felt about that?"

Jonathan's head whipped up. "Melissa, I —"

"For your information, I felt *terrible,*" I said. "Not just because that's not how I wanted to meet her but because she *knew* you'd lied to me. Some girls would have gone absolutely berserk about that, but I haven't. Because I trust you. And I thought you trusted me."

A terrible silence fell.

"I thought I could," said Jonathan quietly, his face suddenly very sad. My heart cracked. "Maybe you're not the one with the problem."

"Jonathan!" I said, hurling myself across the room like Braveheart, and kneeling on the sofa next to him. "Don't be silly! Of course you can trust me!"

For an awful second, I thought he was going to push me away, but he slid an arm around my waist so that I fell into his lap, then he hugged me hard for a few minutes, while neither of us spoke.

Finally, he drew a deep breath. "I didn't mention it because I didn't want you worrying. Look, from now on I'll tell you whenever Cindy calls. You can see all the cell phone bills."

"I'm not a little girl," I replied. "I can cope with the idea that she's around."

"Yeah, well, maybe I can't." He looked at me. "If it makes you feel better, I'll ask her not to come to the fund-raiser at the Met next week."

Jonathan had been working on this fund-raiser for months now; apparently charitable volunteering was a significant element of his new role. From the papers I'd seen, it was something between a state opening of Parliament and the New Year's Ball in Vienna.

"She's hosting a table," he went on, pained, "but if it makes you feel better —"

"No," I said. I wasn't running scared of

her. I was a St. Cathal's girl. "She's part of your past. But she doesn't have to be more than a bit player in your future."

Jonathan looked at me with what I hoped was admiration, and I seized the moment.

"But, Jonathan, we're not going to *have* a future if you don't make some more time for me," I said bravely. "I've hardly seen you. I didn't fly all the way over here to hang out with your dog and your secretary and your dog walker and your cleaner and your college friends, agreeable though they all are."

"Honey, you know how busy I've —"

"I do know. But you're the boss. And I'm going to have to go back to London before too long." I gazed up at him. "Then you'll be wishing you'd spent the afternoon viewing *me* instead of chasing phone calls in the office. Even Saks gets kind of lonely when you're on your own all day."

"I didn't realize you were lonely." He sighed. "Guess when you put it like that, it sounds so simple."

"That's because it is."

"Yes, well, your front elevations are a darn sight more attractive than most of my current portfolio." Jonathan twisted my hair round his fingers, sliding them into the ringlets he'd made. "It's not a case of choosing between you or work, Melissa. You should know that. Don't ask me for something you know I can't deliver."

My throat tightened. That wasn't what I wanted to hear. But Jonathan hadn't finished.

"But, yeah, I take your point. I haven't made enough free time for you, and that's more my loss than yours. I'm going to fix that." He lifted my chin so I could see from his serious gray eyes that he meant what he said. "And if I do that for you, will you? . . ."

I flinched, not wanting to hear him say it. "Don't. I've learned my lesson. No more man management."

"Don't look so whipped." Jonathan traced the lines of my face, up over my cheeks, around my nose. "There are plenty other ways you can do your thing in New York without wearing yourself out dealing with idiots like Ric, you know."

"Like what?"

"Well, like this baby shower you're planning for Diana. You'll do an awesome job with that. She knows so many people in Manhattan, I'm sure you wouldn't have a minute to spare if you wanted to set yourself up advising women on that type of event."

Visions of endless gift registries filled my

head. I really didn't want to hear Jonathan's party planning plans again, but right then I'd have agreed to become Braveheart's full-time PA. I could see he was trying. I wanted to try too.

"Let's enjoy the rest of your time here," said Jonathan softly. "Please?"

"Right," I said. At least he wanted me to *stay*. He was even looking ahead to my working. Surely that was good? "Well, I could certainly do that, I suppose. Yes. I could definitely do that."

"Melissa, you make me so happy." With one strong movement, Jonathan lifted me up into his lap and snuggled me into his chest.

I relaxed completely, as powerful relief chemicals flooded my system, sweeping away any awkward little protesting voices in my head. I felt as though I'd slid right to the edge of the precipice, seen the terrifying drop at the edge, and somehow managed to cling on.

"We're good then?" he murmured into my hair.

"Yes," I said, inhaling his familiar warm smell. "We're good."

TWENTY-THREE

If Jonathan's office was keeping him in a state of hypertension, then the additional organization he'd taken on for the charity fund-raiser was stretching even his extraordinary powers of organization to the limits.

He kept his promise, though, and carved out much more time for me than before, even calling me himself when he was running late, instead of getting Lori to do it. But even when we were sipping cocktails at The Carlyle, or strolling hand in hand through Central Park with Braveheart, I could tell his brain was always making lists, or working on logistical problems, and with only a few days to go until the big night, the little crease between his eyebrows deepened into a furrow.

I could hardly complain about Jonathan's preoccupation, though. I was pretty busy myself. Officially, I was consulting with Diana and her caterers about her baby shower, which was pleasant enough except for a troubling remark I overheard at the baby shower summit at Diana's Upper West Side apartment. As I walked back from the loo and paused in Diana's photo gallery to look at a picture of Jonathan and Cindy as they stood on a manicured lawn, smiling in their chinos with sweaters thrown over their shoulders — it could have been a Ralph Lauren ad — I heard Diana say, "You think she's up to all that social stuff Jonathan has to do now? I mean there's some serious heavy lifting there. Say what you like about Cindy, but she knew how to work a room. They were a team, you know? Melissa's got so much to catch up on . . ." I tried to shake that off. I wasn't half as naive as people seemed to think. In fact, unofficially, I was sneaking out of the house to make check-up calls to the office at least once a day. I still hadn't gotten an answer out of Allegra as to whether she'd apologized to that poor woman to whom she'd sent those knitted toys. After Gabi's and Allegra's little perfor-mance last time I was home, I didn't want them thinking that they weren't under constant supervision. I wanted a business to go home *to.*

And that was the weight on my mind: go-ing home. Somehow, Jonathan and I had managed to skirt the small matter of my return to England and indeed, what would happen after that. I was meant to be flying back three days after the fund-raiser, but it was impossible, of course, to think beyond *that* massive deadline. So now there were two elephants in our hallway: Cindy and The Future.

Could you blame me for enjoying my lattes where I could?

The morning of the fund-raiser rolled round all too soon. I woke up before my alarm, which was set for 5:30, and sat for a while in the kitchen, watching the light spread through the slatted shutters, over the wooden floor, as the sounds of the city waking up began to filter in along with the dawn. I hoped Jonathan wasn't going to let the designers plan the character out of this house. It had so much cobwebby charm in a city that was constantly cleaning and improving itself.

I wished, for a moment, that he'd let me do it for him. There had to be something I could do for him.

Then I felt a kiss on my hair.

"Couldn't sleep either, huh?" said Jonathan. He was already in his gym clothes and looked disgustingly awake.

I shook my head. "Darling, isn't it a bit early for a run?"

"No! Big day ahead! I thought I'd get my run in early, jog to work, then start with the arrangements by six. I need to make sure everyone's on track."

I goggled. So this was the full Dr. No mode. "At six in the morning?"

He nodded and started to pull on his trainers. "We start early here, Melissa." His head vanished beneath the table. "You got your salon appointments booked?" his voice floated up.

"Yup. Lori's done herself proud." I was spending no fewer than four hours at the Bliss Spa in Soho. "I'll be a different woman by the time you see me at the Met tonight."

He reemerged. "Don't be too different, please," he said, kissing my forehead. "I like the woman I've got just fine. You could go like that and still be the cutest one there." He checked his watch. "Okay, gotta go. Don't call me if you need anything . . ."

"Call Lori," I finished. "I know."

"Hey!" he said, as if it had just occurred to him. "I can take the dog!"

"I don't think he'll like it," I warned.

"No, it's a cool thing for us to do together," said Jonathan, approaching Braveheart's crate. "C'mon, little fella! Come for a jog with Daddy!"

A low growling emanated from the crate.

"Okay!" said Jonathan, as if he was making an executive decision. "Stay home and look after Mommy then!"

He clicked his fingers and pointed at me with a near-satanic energy for such an unearthly time of the morning, then jogged off.

I went back to bed but didn't get much sleep.

I was woken at nine, just as I'd finally dropped off, by a man from the florist's bearing a huge bunch of roses, and a smaller bunch of other flowers that on a normal day would have looked lavish. I tipped him the right money — having learned florist delivery tips as part of my never-ending research into the complexities of American tipping — and staggered to the table with the floral tributes.

The huge bunch of velvety crimson roses was from Jonathan. The card, in his handwriting, simply read, "Always." I allowed myself a moment just to stand and quiver with romance. He was, undoubtedly, the classiest man I had ever met.

The second bunch of freesias and lilies contained a card saying, "Orlando von

Borsch did us a favor! Love from Godric and Kirsty xx."

And that really did send me into the power shower singing.

Once dressed and invigorated by such early-morning efficiency, I called the builders at Nelson's house to check up on them. Gabi and Woolfe, predictably, hadn't been running the show with the necessary ferocity, so I told them I'd stupidly forgotten to unhook Nelson's hidden security webcams in the house — a handy trick I used to buck up slacking cleaners. Yes, I said, I could see Jason waving at me, and crikey! Would Dave please stop doing that?

I couldn't see them, of course. But builders are easy to second-guess.

Once I'd done that, even my usual to-do list was exhausted. I'd bought a new dress for the occasion, and as I had nothing else to do but get ready to wear it, I gave up and spent the rest of the morning browsing round the little vintage shops in the Village, buying presents to take home. I even called in at a bookstore and was flicking through the English magazines when I suddenly caught sight of *Country Life*.

Or rather, I caught sight of my mother, *Country Life* cover girl and new face of the Women's Institute.

Dumbstruck, I flipped through to the feature, where Mummy sat looking twenty years younger than she really was on her chaise longue, wearing a silky pair of Indian trousers, surrounded by pots and pots and pots of jam, gleaming like jewels on every available surface.

I squinted. Was that Allegra scowling in the background? She looked as if she'd been made over by a seriously determined stylist, in a pretty red dress and — heaven forfend — blusher. The caption read, "Belinda Romney-Jones, at home with just some of her year's produce, with etiquette expert daughter, Melissa."

Melissa?

Well, if Allegra was still under Swedish mafia surveillance, it was cheaper than plastic surgery, I guessed.

My eye skimmed the article with a mixture of pride and dread. "Mrs. Romney-Jones, wife of long-serving Tory MP, Martin . . . Keen home-maker . . . knitting . . . supporter of WI markets. . . . 'I've always loved making jam, ever since I planted our first quince tree!' "

Pride, horror, and bewilderment swirled up in me, and I couldn't read any more. I still bought the magazine though.

■ ■ ■ ■

By two, I was in Bliss, on the very last lap of my pampering, when the phone rang.

That was very bad in itself, I knew, as phones were verboten, but what made it worse was that it was Daddy.

Nobody knew how to puncture a relaxing mood like Daddy.

As usual, he didn't bother with *"Hello! How are you? We miss you"* or anything like that. He went straight in with, "I need to get time sheets from you for that research you're doing for me, in the next twenty-four hours. And don't bother adding extra hours onto them because I've got to get them past those bottom-feeders at Customs and Excise."

The Russian lady pummling the dead skin off my feet glowered upward. I felt got at from both ends.

"Yes, well, of course, I'd do that," I began, "but I don't have the —"

"Well, get them!" he squawked. "You have been putting all this through the Agency accounts, haven't you?"

"Yes!"

"Don't say yes like that! Your sister, it seems, has set up her own company to process her salary!"

"What?"

"Indeed! What? That's not what I need to hear when I've got Simon round here with some missive from the bank, your grandmother wafting around as if she's in a second-rate touring production of *Blithe Spirit,* and bloody Lars hanging about the place, cluttering up the drawing room with spearheads!"

"Oh, is Lars back?"

"He's *just going!*" Daddy bellowed, I think, toward Lars.

"And Mummy?" I tried, longing for one nice image to close the conversation on. "I saw her feature in *Country Life.* Happy anniversary, by the way. Did you have a nice time on your minibreak?"

Daddy took a long breath. "Melissa, your mother has barely stopped knitting for seven months now. When we plighted our troth, thirty-five years ago, I got Madame Butterfly. I did not marry your mother for her to turn into Madame bloody Defarge. And I resent the way she is constantly *armed.*"

"She's the face of the WI!" I added hopefully.

"Yes," he said. "That's the whole point."

I wished he could be nicer about her. It was never too late to make a fresh start, as I told my clients.

Then either he was cut off by a poor Manhattan signal (charitable explanation) or he hung up on me (usual explanation).

I sighed.

"Sorry," I said to Svetlana.

She glared at me. "Forty minutes it take, to get strrrress out of your feet."

We both looked down. They were jutting out of the water like a pair of Lars's prehistoric flint spearheads.

"Sorry," I said again.

It would have been nice to sweep into the Met on Jonathan's arm, but he was too busy attending to last-minute details to take me there himself. I could really have done with his reassurance early in the evening, since it was such a high-profile event, and I didn't want to turn up looking out of place.

Fortunately, Karen popped round to collect Braveheart for his overnight, and she gave me the sweetest confidence boost I could have wished for.

"Hi!" she called as she let herself in. "Sorry I'm running late, I had to call . . . Oh, Melissa!"

"Do I look okay?" I asked nervously, stepping away from the kitchen table so she could see my whole outfit at once. "I haven't

. . . gone overboard?"

"You look . . . like a princess," she said, putting her hands to her mouth. "Oh, my God, I'm going to cry!"

I did look rather glamorous, if I say so myself. The hairdresser had curled and pinned up my hair into full, glossy waves — a '50s style that went perfectly with my simple ruby-red dress, matching satin courts, and perfect manicure. The long, curving cut and strapless bodice reminded me of something Sophia Loren might have worn to the Oscars, and once I saw the satin gleaming voluptuously over my hips, I knew I had to have it. When you look divine even under changing room lights, you know you're onto something.

"If he doesn't propose tonight, there's something wrong with that guy!" she said, wagging her finger. "Where is he? Do I get to see him in his tux too?"

"No, sorry." I sighed and put my lipstick into my tiny evening purse. "Jonathan's there already. I had rather hoped he might . . ." I stopped, not wanting to sound whiny.

My face must have said more than I wanted to, though, because Karen grabbed my hands and said, "Aw, Melissa, it's his loss. If Mr. Riley didn't have a million things to do I bet he'd definitely want to be escorting you in. He's definitely going to want everyone to know you're with him!"

"You think?"

Karen's face softened. "Listen, remember when I was tearing my hair out over the speed-dating guys? And you told me successful men are always going to be busy, because, hey! That's why they're successful! Well, you were right. What's an hour here or there, over a lifetime?" She shook my hands as if I were a little girl. "Because I'm willing to bet that's what he's hoping for. A lifetime."

I looked at her, wishing I could be so confident.

"I've seen the way he looks at you," she added. "And that's when you're in your regular dress-down clothes. Tonight! Well . . ." She winked.

"Thank you," I said, finding a smile. "That makes me feel a whole lot better."

"Now you go and have a fabulous fairy-tale night," said Karen, picking Braveheart up before he could slobber over my skirts. She paused, Braveheart under one arm, and pointed at him quizzically. "You sure you don't need me to turn this one into a coach and horses for you?"

"No," I smiled. "I have a limousine waiting."

Karen clapped her other hand to her chest in pretend jealousy, and I floated out of the house, feeling exactly like Cinderella.

Lori had indeed arranged for a very swish limo to sweep me off to the Met, and it almost made up for my solo arrival, especially when I found a movie-star gardenia corsage on the backseat.

However, when the car drew away and I found myself looking up the long sweep of steps to the imposing entrance, I suddenly felt very nervous. Still, I'd told Godric to get on and do this sort of thing, hadn't I?

One, I told myself, arriving on my own means I can take my time and look at everything without being rushed past.

Two, no one will be looking at me with Jonathan and wondering why I'm not Cindy.

Three . . .

I took small steps up the red carpet, my stomach fluttering self-consciously.

I really wished Jonathan was here, just so I could tell him how speechless I was at the glamor of it all.

Three . . .

There was no three. I wished he was here.

I took my time going in because I wanted to savor the thrill of it all, stepping past the impassive stewards and making my way toward the entrance. Tiny lanterns lit the way into the splendid marble hall, where huge sprays of lilies and roses sat like giant peacocks, throwing their musky nighttime fragrance into the echoing air. Red ropes marked off the area for the party, and even though I was early, black-tied guests were already gathering, removing coats and cashmere shawls, taking long-stemmed flutes of champagne from huge trays before being ushered discreetly toward the Temple of Dendur, where the main event was taking place.

I handed in my little fake fur jacket and followed the flow of people, letting my spine lengthen and my walk swing. With no one watching me, I reveled in the sensation of walking on my high heels, clicking through the empty halls. Beyond the ropes, the museum was empty, and I felt a delicious giddiness at the idea of the silent halls and darkened rooms, waiting, deserted, while the glamorous guests ate and drank below.

The Temple of Dendur was a majestic room: an ancient arch, with the stone temple behind it, dwarfed by a swooping modern glass ceiling. It glowed with a strange light, and I felt rather self-conscious about mingling in such a dignified setting. It was rather like having a wine and cheese evening in a church, say. On a much grander scale, of course.

But mingling was on the menu, so I took a glass of champagne from a passing waiter and looked round for someone to mingle with.

"Melissa!" cried a familiar voice, and I turned to see Wentworth's friendly face smiling at me. He was looking very distinguished in his black tie. "You look . . . no, I don't think words can do you justice! You look gorgeous this evening."

"You look pretty wonderful yourself," I said, balancing my drink and kissing his cheek.

"Now, listen, Jonathan told me to look out for you and carry you off the moment you arrived, before everyone starting demanding your attention," Wentworth went on. "You know what he's like, still perfecting the final details, so I guess he won't notice if I keep you to myself for a moment or two, because I really need to ask your advice about what I should get my mother for her sixtieth birthday . . ."

As I reeled off a list of suggestions, I couldn't help scanning the crowd for Jonathan, and suddenly I spotted him, talking animatedly to an elderly couple in very fancy black tie, and my breath caught in my throat and my chest swelled with pride beneath my corset.

Jonathan was born to wear black tie. He looked so dignified, yet comfortable, in his dinner jacket; his hair was neat without being overdone, his hands were elegant without being manicured, and he carried the whole thing off with understated confidence.

While he talked, he turned his head discreetly, as if he was looking for something, and when he caught sight of me, looking for him, a smile broke across his face, like sunshine.

"So . . . yes, impractical but darling slippers," I finished up. Wentworth was making notes on his Blackberry. "Little embroidered Chinese ones — I saw some in Saks recently. Oh, look, here comes Jonathan!"

He excused himself from the conversation and made his way through the crowds of guests, gliding around the waiters with their broad trays of sparkling glasses. My lips tingled with excitement as he approached, and when he finally put his fingers on my bare arm, the hairs stood up on my skin.

"Damn," said Wentworth. "And I thought you wouldn't notice." He did a pretend shrug of regret, turning to me with his good-natured smile. "Thanks for the idea,

Melissa — and I'll see you two later, okay?"

And with a wink at Jonathan, he slipped away into the crowd of black suits.

"Hello," I said to Jonathan, suddenly feeling quite self-concious as I stood on my toes to kiss his cheek.

"You're here at last!" he murmured into my ear. "And you're the most spectacular exhibit in here. That dress is amazing."

"Too kind," I said.

"I can see you're busy working your famous charm on the guests, but could I beg a quick word?"

"Of course you can!" I murmured back. "As many as you like!"

"Oh, I only need a few," he said, and my heart skipped.

Jonathan put his hand in the small of my back and guided me away from the main crowd, out of the temple area and past a couple of dark-suited guards, who went to stop us, then, realizing it was Jonathan, nodded us through.

"The museum is supposed to be closed," he whispered as he took my hand to lead me quickly down the corridors. "We're not meant to be sneaking out like this, but I, ah . . . I spoke to some people. We don't have long," he added, "but there's something I want you to see."

Given the fact that his to-do list ran into several pages, I was amazed he could even spare two minutes to admire my hairdo, much less slip off for a private moment among the sarcophagi. My heart rate quickened, and not just because we were walking through the marble-floored halls so briskly that my high heels were only just keeping up with Jonathan's long strides.

Eventually, we passed through an area of what seemed like fairly standard cases of china and emerged, unexpectedly, in a drawing room.

An English drawing room, complete with wooden floorboards, mahogany sideboards, and three of those old mirrors, half-covered in tarnish, so the casual preener looks like she's got leprosy. It even smelled like a National Trust property. All it needed was a few bowls of very old potpourri and a retired lady sitting on a chair glowering at my stilettos, and I could have been in Great Chigley Manor House or somesuch.

Come to that, if there were two dogs, a lingering air of tension, and cigar smoke, plus some distant shouting, it could be chez Romney-Jones. The instant homesickness was startling.

"Good heavens," I said faintly. "It's like . . . being at home."

"I knew you'd like it!" beamed Jonathan. "Come on, we're not done yet!"

The thing was, I thought, as I followed him, I wasn't sure I *did* like it. What was this perfectly nice drawing room doing here, in New York? I had a sudden flash of how the Greeks must feel when they turn up at the British Museum and see great chunks of their own stuff displayed wholesale.

Barely able to contain his delight, Jonathan beckoned me through to a darker room, containing a huge, draped four-poster bed, with gorgeous old woven bedspreads falling in pleats around the base. It couldn't have been more English if it had had Union Jack curtains. Patriotism started to swell in my breast. Now that was what I called a bed of state.

"Wow!" I said. "How splendid!"

"Isn't it?" said Jonathan. He stood behind me and wrapped his arms around my waist so we could both admire the good solid bed. "I came here before Christmas last year, while I was going through all that . . . business with Cindy and the divorce. I love the Met for that. Whenever I feel tense, I like to come here, and I always see something that puts all the rest into perspective. Something beautiful, or peaceful, or just . . . special."

"I know just what you mean!" I said. "I

like to go and look at the wrought ironwork at the V&A. Sturdy but beautiful." I wondered if he was going to suggest some kind of romp. That would be taking risky sex to terrible extremes. Surely the four-poster was all alarmed?

"Well, when I came here, last December, I was very, very conflicted," Jonathan went on. He squeezed me. "But I'm not so conflicted now, I'm happy to say."

I couldn't help reading the label on the side of the bed. It had come from a stately home just down the road from Roger's mother's place! I felt a sharp pang of national pride. So it might have been given away fair and square to the Met, but all the same . . .

"I came here," Jonathan went on, "wondering if I was doing the right thing, and I saw this bed and you know what? I thought of you."

"Steady on!" I exclaimed in pretend horror.

Jonathan squeezed. "No, silly. I came here because I missed you, and London, and everything. The *comfort* of it made me think of you, and how comfortable you made me feel, like I wanted to tumble you into a bed like this, and close the curtains around us, and keep all the rest of the world out. It was totally English — solidly made, and honest, and such a thing of beauty. Like a fairy-tale bed, but made to last. And see? It's lasted five hundred years."

I held my breath, not quite sure where he was going with this.

"Melissa," said Jonathan, turning me round to face him. His expression was completely serious, and I thought I could detect a glimmer of nerves in his eyes. "I didn't believe I could ever be this happy. I want to draw those curtains around us forever, if you'll let me."

Then he hitched up one leg of his dinner trousers, dropped to one knee and looked up at me from the floor. "I appreciate that I should run this past your father first, but he's not answering his cell phone, and his secretary won't tell me where he is. Your grandmother gave me the go-ahead, though. So, Melissa . . ."

I swear I could not breathe, even if I wanted to.

". . . would you do me the great honor of becoming my wife?"

I opened my mouth to speak, but nothing came out. The tears had already started to slide down my face with giddy, champagne-bubble joy. I couldn't believe it. Literally. I tried to absorb what Jonathan had just said, and I couldn't make my brain acknowledge it was real. He was asking me to marry him!

And if I needed physical evidence, he had a small ring box in his hand, which he offered to me now.

"It's not the proper one," he said as I took it with shaky fingers, "because I know you'll want to go and pick out something together, but I thought you'd, you know, like to have something to show off tonight."

I opened the old-fashioned blue leather box and gasped when I saw the delicate little three-stone sapphire ring, nestled in the worn red velvet. It glittered in the low light. It was beautiful.

"My grandmother's," he explained. "An eternity ring my grandfather gave her for their golden wedding anniversary."

Kind of confident of him to have the ring right there, observed a detached voice in my head.

"Are you going to see if it fits?" he prompted. "I can have it altered. That's not a problem."

"But I haven't said yes yet," I said with as much solemnity as I could muster.

Panic widened Jonathan's eyes.

"Oh, don't be ridiculous," I said, dropping to my knees too with absolutely no regard for my sheer stockings. "Yes, of course, it's yes!"

"You don't know how happy that makes me!" he murmured as he cupped my face in his hands and kissed me.

We must have been the only couple in history to be just engaged, next to a four-poster bed, who ended up kissing passionately on the floor.

I must admit, the way Jonathan kissed me, I didn't really mind. He kissed the way men do in films: long, slow, deep kisses, always with his eyes closed.

"Oh, Melissa," said Jonathan, helping me up to my feet when we'd kissed long enough for pins and needles to be setting in. "This is the best night of my life." He put his arms round me and stroked my hair. The museum was so vast that we couldn't even hear the noise of the distant party. It was just us, and the great bed of state.

From that nice manor house down the road from Roger's.

I dragged my mind back to the present.

Jonathan nuzzled my neck, breathing in my perfume. "This is the beginning of our life together! Isn't it a great place to start it?"

"It is," I agreed. "In an English room, in an American museum."

What was wrong with me? I frowned at myself.

"You know," he mused, "I've thought about tonight so much, all the details . . ."

"You didn't think I'd say no, though, did you?" I said indulgently.

Jonathan looked blank for a second. "I meant the fund-raiser, but, um . . ."

I stared at him, taken aback.

"But yeah, of course I've been thinking about proposing to you too. I wasn't sure, actually, that you'd say yes." He recovered quickly, but not quite quickly enough.

"Well, I suppose tables and chairs are easier to arrange than people," I said, trying to make it come out lightly, but maybe I didn't quite manage it.

"Sometimes that's easier on the nerves!" said Jonathan, apparently missing the irony in my voice. He hugged me to him, so my nose filled up with the heady mix of Creed and laundered shirts and his own indefinable man smell, then he released me with a broad smile.

"Listen, we should be getting back to the party. They're going to start calling everyone in for dinner very soon and I want to . . . you know." He grinned. "Tell people. Shall we? . . ."

He extended a hand toward the door, and

automatically, I led the way out.

"So . . . when can you get your things shipped?" he asked, putting his arm around my waist as we walked back through the drawing room. Our footsteps rang loudly on the wooden floor. "Everything's in storage, right? You could just get it sent straight over from the holding company."

"I . . . I don't know," I said. "I suppose I could."

Not go back to Nelson's? At all?

"And then there's your agency to deal with, I guess," he went on, now in full organizational flow. "It seems to be running pretty well with Gabi and Allegra in charge, wouldn't you say? You feel happy letting those two carry on? Keep an eye on them via e-mail?"

"Jonathan, are you insane?" I laughed. "I wouldn't let those two run a scouts' jumble sale! No, that's just temporary!

"So you're going to close it down altogether? Okay, I can see the sense in that."

"I don't want to . . ." I stopped walking, as the reality of what I was saying dawned on me. "I don't want to close it down, not just like that."

Jonathan pulled a slightly impatient face, then smiled reasonably. "But, honey, why not? You can't be flying back and forth every couple of days, now, can you?"

"You fly back and forth!" I protested.

"Yes, but that's for business!"

"And what do you think my work is? People rely on me. I provide a service that people want! It's not so different from what you do."

I was trying hard to keep it light, but something about the strained patience in Jonathan's eyes was starting to tick me off.

"Come on, Melissa, it's very different. Anyway, it's not like you're really doing the same things you started out offering now that we're together, is it? Aren't you moving more into party planning and shopping advice and stuff like that?"

"No, it's not just about *parties* and *shopping* . . ."

"Face it, Melissa, you're just acting like a glorified nanny to these guys, and you know, I think that's kind of beneath your abilities. I mean, in terms of the value of your time? I didn't want to say so before, because I know you're *loyal* and *kind,* and I love that about you, but guys like Godric? They need professional help, and they need to shape up. And honey, I don't want to sound arrogant, but you won't *need* to work, once we're married." He took my hands. "I mean, that's the point about being run off my feet

— I'm pulling in a very decent salary now, and with bonuses . . ."

I stared at the ring on my finger, then looked up at Jonathan's face. I wanted to see the laughing boyfriend I'd rowed across the lake with, but in his dinner jacket, his hair smoothed neatly down, suddenly he looked much more grown-up than I felt. "But I want to work. I enjoy helping people."

"Then do what you've been doing for Diana!" he said, as if it were the most obvious answer in the world. "Run showers! You're so good at keeping people calm at stressful times like that, right? And she loves what you're doing for her baby shower. She can't stop telling everyone how cleverly you've arranged it all, and how sweet you've been with her mother, and Steve . . . I was so proud of you." He shook my hands to emphasize his pride, but suddenly I felt babied.

"Jonathan, I think we need to talk about this some more," I said, feeling the moment start to slide from under me.

"What's to talk about? You can't run your agency hands-on when you're living in New York, I don't want you to start doing the same thing over here . . ." He lifted his shoulders, then dropped them. "Anyway, I

583

was meaning to tell you — I've been rethinking the house plans?" He beamed, as if this was his trump card. "Forget the conversion. I think we need to make it one house. For the two of us. Two of us . . . for now?"

I gaped. Why was it that this was everything I'd ever dreamed of, and yet it felt so wrong?

Jonathan took my silence for emotional speechlessness and kissed me on the forehead. "Don't want to let Steve and Diana get too far ahead of us, huh?" He checked his watch and grimaced in apology. "Darling, I know this is an awful thing to say, but I really do need to get back to the event." He looked at me appealingly. "We can announce it! Most of our friends are here!"

Most of our friends. *Our* friends? What about Nelson? And Gabi? And Roger? How would my friendships feel when I was living in New York? And how would it be when all my friends were also friends with Cindy?

I started to feel sick.

"But Jonathan, this is important to me! My agency isn't just about shopping! It's about working out what's missing in people's lives, seeing what I can help to fix! I mean, take Godric," I said wildly. "It wasn't so much that he was rude, or mean — he just didn't have enough confidence to be himself! And I'm not saying I've waved a magic wand, but he needed someone to talk it out with and understand. And now look at him! He's got his girlfriend back, and everything!"

"Melissa, if you need men to fix, you can start with me," said Jonathan, and to my amazement, he said it with a straight face. "God knows I need someone to run my life for me, better than I do."

"But that's the whole point!" I wailed. "You *don't* need fixing! You're perfect just as you are! *Perfect!* And I can't be the sort of wife you need by your side at these things. . . ."

"Well, maybe I'm just better at faking it than you think. Why else do you think I've got a cleaner four days a week, and I never buy my own clothes? You ask Lori how perfect I am." He ran his hands through his hair impatiently. Clearly this wasn't going according to plan. "What sort of wife do you *think* I need?"

I searched Jonathan's face for some clue, but the stoniness had returned, shutting down any emotion.

I sighed, not wanting to give the answer I knew I had to, in all honesty. The reception was stuffed with immaculate, glossy women, working the room like a formation dance team of charm, devoting their whole lives to charity events, and networking, and having lunch with each other but not actually eating anything.

I thought of my mother, worn to a frazzle trying to maintain the social face of country Conservatism while the private face of knitting stress created deformed hippos. My father, driving her mad — driving *me* mad with his manipulations. I couldn't end up like that. Not with a man I loved as much as Jonathan.

But was Jonathan really the man I thought he was? Because he was glaring at me with an expression that seemed awfully Daddy-esque right now.

I wasn't just some *bed* he could ship out to New York, to be put in a museum to be admired and never slept in. I had a purpose in life!

I controlled myself as best I could. "You need a woman who can stand at your side at these events like a First Lady. A woman like one of the fund-raisers in there, someone who knows how to work the room and look perfect all the time. And I can *pretend* to be like that, if that's what you want," I said in a small voice, "but it's not really me. I don't look perfect all the time. That's

Honey. And I thought you didn't want Honey any more. I thought you wanted me."

Jonathan stared at me for a long minute, then exhaled slowly.

"Melissa. I do want you. But I've had one wife who put her whole life into her career, at the expense of everything else," he said, apparently ignoring what I'd just said. "At the expense of me, of our home, our family. Are you really telling me that you're weighing me in one basket and your damn agency in the other?"

I wanted to tell him that it wasn't about the agency, it was about me, and who I was. But if he couldn't see that — why should I have to tell him?

"Are you asking me to choose one or the other?" I demanded.

Because you asked him the very same question, and he couldn't choose.

And those missed lunches would add up to a lot of hours and days over the years, no matter what Karen said. Days, weeks, months of taking second place to a Blackberry . . .

We glared at each other, surrounded by cold marble statues. I was glad at least that I was in my very best black tie dress, because the tight corset and stockings at least made me hold my spine up tall.

"I guess I am," he said and rubbed his chin.

My heart broke inside my chest. I could feel it. But I struggled to muster up all my dignity. The situation demanded that I keep my head held high, even if everything inside was shattering into little pieces.

"You're asking me to leave my family and my friends, and move halfway across the world, to be surrounded by *your* friends, *your* ex-wife, *your* ex-wife's dog, and all the . . . *baggage* that goes with that," I said in a voice that didn't sound like mine. "And I would do that, Jonathan, because I love you. But you're asking me to give up the one thing I've found in life that I do really well, and come here with nothing of *me,* and honestly, that's impossible. I wouldn't be the woman you fell in love with. You would get frustrated with me. And it wouldn't work."

I made myself look at him, and the beautiful, familiar lines of his face made me ache, because I knew what I was saying was true, and it meant it was all ending. I'd walked across hot coals to get away from one controlling father in my life; I owed it to myself not to fall straight into being controlled again.

"I couldn't bear to have this turn sour," I

said, biting back the tears. "It's been too wonderful. I've never been so happy in my life. But you're right — I don't know New York. Maybe you need someone who does."

I struggled to remove the ring from my finger. It hurt as I dragged it over my knuckle, but not so much as it hurt inside.

"Here," I said. "I can't take this."

"You're breaking off our engagement?" said Jonathan faintly.

I raised my eyes to his, and now they were filled with hot tears. It only added to my misery to see his were too. "I have to," I said. "I couldn't bear to have you divorce me." I gulped. "I couldn't bear to have you realize you'd made another mistake."

And before he could speak, I turned on my heel and walked briskly down the corridor, leaving him standing there, as motionless as the marble statues.

I don't know how I found my way back, since the place was a maze of glass cases and roped-off areas, but somehow I was back at the coat-check, in a cloud of scented lilies and expensive ladies' perfume.

A steward tried to direct me toward the reception, but I mumbled that I didn't want to go in, and as I was stumbling out, my head down in case I saw Cindy, I bumped into a couple.

"Sorry," I started to say, as they cooed, "Melissa! Melissa!" at me.

Kurt and Bonnie Hegel.

Oh, God. Just what I didn't need.

"Melissa?" said Kurt, taking my arm. "Are you all right? You don't look all right. You look as if you've had a terrible shock. Do you want to sit down? Bonnie, don't you think she should sit down?"

"I'm okay! Honest!" I managed.

"Kurt, go and get a glass of water for Melissa. Go on!" She flapped him away, and peered at me with a professional rigor. "Are you *actually* okay?"

"Um, no, not really." I shook my head. "I've . . . I've had some bad news. I'm going to have to go home. Right away."

"Home to the Village? Listen, let me call my car service, we can have you back in no time." Bonnie got her tiny cell phone from her tiny clutch bag and had it to her ear before I could stop her. "Hello, yeah, I need a car from the Met to . . ." She looked over at me and whispered, "Where to, honey? I forget Jonathan's new address."

"To Kennedy airport, please," I said dully.

Bonnie's face registered such shock that I could see white all round her big green eyes. "Hold the car, I'll call back," she said without taking her gaze off me, and clicked the phone shut. "Where's Jonathan, does he know? Why isn't he taking you home? Jesus, he is so stupid about his priorities! Let me go and get him —"

"No, please," I said, stopping her. "He knows. He's busy, with the fund-raiser. It's going really well. I don't want to spoil it for him." God knows how I was keeping all this together, but my voice was turning posher by the moment. It must have been the Stiff Upper Lip coming out. "It's . . . a family matter. I have to fly back tonight. I should get to the airport."

"But your luggage?" Bonnie asked. "Don't you need to go home and pick up your stuff?"

It would look too weird if I refused. Besides, I could hardly sit all the way back to London in a cocktail dress, fancy under-wear, and stockings. I mean, there were dramatic gestures, and there were dramatic gestures.

Oh, and I'd need my passport.

"Don't worry," I said, dragging what remained of my self-control around me like the English royal armor that I'd just marched past. "I'll get a cab home. Um, if you could tell Jonathan I'll be fine, and . . ." I gulped as the self-control slipped. "Tell him I'm sorry for messing up his seating plan for dinner. At such short notice."

"Melissa, won't you let me help you?" Bonnie looked hard at me. "Because if anyone's said anything to you . . . even if it's Jonathan?" She pulled a face. "He can be kind of dumb sometimes, I know. Don't be fooled by that poker face."

I shook my head again as another little needle pricked my heart; they would always know him better than me. "No. No, it's nothing like that."

"I hear Cindy's here tonight," Bonnie went on. "Is that it? Is she being? . . ."

I didn't let her finish. I didn't want to hear whatever it was she had to say, and I could see Kurt returning with a glass of water and a first-aid official.

"Bonnie, you've been very kind, but I really must go now." I smiled at her. "Thank you."

And I took my fake fur jacket, ran down the beautiful steps, and managed to hail a cab first time. I guess the cocktail dress might have helped.

Part of me hoped that Jonathan would leap into a cab and follow me, just like in an old-fashioned movie, but the other part of me knew he'd give me a gentlemanly distance to recover myself. He gave me such a gentlemanly distance that when I turned my phone on at JFK, surrounded by my bags, he still hadn't left a message.

Twenty-Four

I tried really hard to find three positive things about my early arrival back in London, where the skies were a dull elephant-gray and a dank September chill hung in the air. I was in such a trance state that it actually wasn't so difficult to be objective about my situation; as soon as I stepped onto the tarmac at Heathrow and felt the rain soak through my open-toed sandals, it seemed as if the past few weeks, in all their Technicolor New York film set glory, had happened to someone else.

Whether I liked it or not, I was back, and the best remedy was manic busy-ness and a positive attitude that made Gabi demand to know what drugs you could buy in K-Mart. Never mind that I had to bite back tears every time I saw a small white dog. Leaving Braveheart stabbed my heart nearly as much as leaving Jonathan. He really did need me. Still, I'd made my choice. Doing the Right

Thing would be heaps more popular if it wasn't such a monumental pain in the arse to live with.

The first positive thing was that I was able to chivvy along the decorators putting the final touches to Nelson's flat. Well, they weren't really *final* touches, as it turned out — more halfway-through touches. Gabi hadn't been supervising the various workmen with the sort of rigor that builders require, even with Nelson's alarmingly specific plan of action at hand, whereas I needed a place to sleep and had nervous energy to spare. With Nelson due back in days and the new bath not yet plumbed in, let's just say that the project swiftly acquired an urgency usually seen in the latter stages of a television makeover show.

And that was the second positive thing; I would be able to meet Nelson at the quayside, to welcome him back off his voyage of charitable discovery.

Obviously, I had to drive Roger and Gabi there with me — with the accompanying emotional pea-souper that would suggest.

I offered Gabi the use of my car on the noble assumption that she'd want to share a private moment with her long-lost sailor boy, but she wriggled and looked shifty.

"Wouldn't it be nicer if we *all* went tomorrow?" she suggested. "I mean, Roger's missed him too, and so've you . . ."

We were sitting on the dust-sheeted sofa in Nelson's sitting room, waiting for the painters to come back off their lunch break.

"Gabi. Tell me the truth. Have you been seeing someone else while Nelson's been away?"

I didn't want to use the *R* word unless I absolutely had to.

She squirmed some more. "Well, not exactly . . . Anyway," she added, in a blatant subject change, "I thought it would be kind of insensitive to have a big emotional reunion, in light of current events."

"Have you been seeing someone else?" I repeated. "Because if you've been messing Nelson about, then . . ."

We stared at each other, gripped by sudden fear. The consequences were too ghastly to speak aloud, and we both knew it.

"I haven't been messing Nelson about," she said, fiddling with a set of paint cards. "But, um, I think perhaps I'd better have a quiet word with him when he gets off, or whatever you call it."

"Disembark. I think that would be a good idea," I said firmly. I was horribly torn between wanting to help, but then again, since I was so close to them both, I wasn't sure I even wanted to know the gory details. "Do you want to talk about it? I mean, you're sure? Nelson's . . ." I hesitated. Gabi had always maintained, erroneously, that I had a crush on Nelson myself, and I didn't want her to think I had vested interests in splitting them up now. I grabbed her hand. "I want you both to be happy."

She gave me an ambiguous half-smile, half-frown. "Mel, I know what I'm doing. You of all people should know how hard it is sometimes."

"It's not that I want everyone to be single, just because I am. I'd just hate to see him hurt," I said quietly. "Or see you hurt too."

"I know," said Gabi. She squeezed my hand back. "I know."

We arrived at Portsmouth docks after an arduous journey, during which Roger had provided a running commentary from the backseat, where I'd installed him with the map. I'd known where I was going, but that way he'd gotten to feel in charge of operations, while I'd gotten to tune him out with the radio, since only the front speakers worked.

Even so, he'd still managed to poke his nose into the conversation Gabi and I had been having about what still needed to be done on the flat.

"So are you in communication with Remington or what?" he'd bellowed as I parked. "What went wrong there? Been meaning to ask."

"Shut up, Roger," Gabi had said. "She doesn't want to talk about it."

"No," I said bravely. "No, we're not currently in communication. I thought it would be best to give him some space. It's . . . we separated over a nonnegotiable issue."

Roger had given me a hideous knowing wink in the rearview mirror that involved folding one half of his face into his neck. "Like *that,* was it?"

"Shut *up,* Roger," Gabi had said testily. "Are you deaf or just stupid?"

"Catch yourself on, girlfriend!" Roger had replied, in the most appalling North London accent I'd ever heard. "I'm only arksking!"

I'd looked at them suspiciously. This sort of familiar banter had had all the hallmarks of emotional involvement. Insofar as anyone could involve themselves emotionally with Roger Trumpet. Still, I'd thought, hadn't Gabi said she needed to be practical in relationships? And what could be more practical than the vast fortune Roger clearly wasn't spending on clothes and/or high living?

I locked the car and strode across the quayside, leaving Gabi to upbraid Roger in her own time. Nelson's ship was already in dock and his diminutive crew were being welcomed back by crowds of cheering parents as if they'd been at sea for years.

I looked about but couldn't see Nelson. Then, as I got nearer, I spotted him by a pile of sail bags, haranguing some poor parents about their gangling teenager. He was still in his full oceangoing regalia, which, I was sorry to see, didn't include a parrot, a three-cornered hat, or an eyepatch. As I watched, he finished whatever he was lecturing them about, the teenager gave him a sudden, sprawling hug, and the father shook his hand in that hearty way you only see in black-and-white films.

I was very touched, on Nelson's behalf. He really was the sort of man parents adored.

As they walked off, he spotted me and waved.

"Melissa!" he yelled happily.

"Hello, Nelson," I said, running over and throwing my arms around him. It was so nice to see him. At least some things in my life were where I'd left them. "Still got the two arms, I see! And both eyes!"

"Touch of beer scurvy, though," he said,

picking me up, staggering slightly, then putting me down again almost at once. "You might need to take me home via a pub."

"Er, no. You're going straight home for a bath!" I said. "Do you have any idea what you smell like?"

Roger and Gabi were now hoving into view, in full heated discussion mode.

"And I don't know why you made us come in Mel's car when you could have driven us in that Audi TT," he was moaning.

"Argh, *shut up,* Roger!" Gabi stopped when she saw us, straightened her shoulders, and tried to smile. "Hello, Nelson," she said. "Welcome home! Um, can I have a word?"

"Ship to shore, we have a problem," said Roger, holding his nose.

I grabbed his arm. If Gabi was dumping Nelson for this cretin, she really needed to get her head checked. "Roger, we're going to get some coffee."

Disregarding his gossip-hungry protests, I hauled him off to a mobile coffee wagon, where we got four cappuccinos and waited at a safe distance for the conversation to draw to a close. The wind off the open water was pretty chilly, as we sat on a low wall, warming our hands round the paper cups.

"What do you think she's saying to him?" asked Roger, slurping his coffee.

Honestly. Had he no shame? "I don't know. Didn't you discuss it with her first?"

"What? Why would she discuss it with me?"

I glared at him. "So you could get your story straight, I'd imagine. When did it happen? That Hunt Ball that I wouldn't go to? Did you think that just because she was wearing a wig she wasn't someone else's girlfriend?"

Roger's face turned crimson.

"I wouldn't say so in front of Gabi, but I think you've behaved pretty shabbily," I raged on. "Nelson's your best friend! What were you thinking? I hope you and Gabi are really serious about each other because —"

"For the love of God, Melissa, what makes you think I'm going out with Gabi?" roared Roger. "I'm not deaf! Or *stupid!*"

We stared at each other. I didn't know whether to be outraged on behalf of one best friend, or awash with relief for the other. Or both.

"Well, we might have had a bite to eat in London after that Ball affair," he conceded guiltily. "Took her to the Bluebird, you know. Cocktail or two. Three. She can certainly put them away, can't she? Talk

601

about hollow legs."

"So who *is* she seeing?" I demanded. "Don't deny it — I called her in a bar the other night, and she wasn't on her own."

Roger looked furtive, which gave him the air of a bloodhound that had done something it shouldn't, somewhere it shouldn't have been in the first place. "I, ah, I . . . if she hasn't told you, then . . ."

I'm afraid to say I held my cappuccino threateningly over his trousers.

"Aaron! She's got back with Aaron," he yelped.

Well, that made sense. Instead of the righteous anger I expected, I was surprised to feel a sudden warm glow of relief. I liked Aaron. He was funny, and sharp, and had the measure of Gabi. I hadn't entirely understood why they'd called off their engagement in the first place. Gabi and Aaron went together like Marks and Spencer. Or Boodle and Dunthorne. Or Fortnum and Mason.

Then I remembered Nelson's part in all this, and my heart jolted with sympathy. Poor Nelson! He'd come all the way back from sea to find he was dumped, before he'd even had a chance to get the kettle on.

"When did *that* happen?" I wailed.

"Oh, when Aaron called her to say that

he'd decided not to carry on with the pathology degree and go back to working in the City." Roger sniffed. "Apparently he sent her an entire car full of flowers and got down on one knee and begged her to marry him."

"She never said!"

"Well, she's still thinking about it."

"Why did no one tell me?" I stared out into the dock. "I can't believe she didn't tell me this."

"Um, she thought you'd go mad. What with her being with Nelson and all that."

"So she told *you?*"

"Yes? And what's wrong with that?" he huffed.

"Nothing," I said, and felt a sad sort of happiness run through me, like the cold wind coming in off the sea. I tucked my warm jacket closer around me. "Nothing wrong with that."

"I thought you'd be pleased I'd made a new friend." Roger sounded hurt. "Nelson's always droning on about how nice it is having a good girl friend like you. And Gabi and I . . . we get on. I know you don't approve, but I'm bloody glad she came to that do with me. Top night."

I put my arm through his and gave it a squeeze. That way I could show affection without having to look at whatever soppy face he was pulling. "I'm glad, Roger," I said. "I'm really glad."

As Nelson would have pointed out, there were strange and mysterious powers attached to the wig.

Over by the commemorative anchor, Nelson and Gabi seemed to have finished their little chat, and now they walked over to where Roger and I were sitting. He did not have his arm around her shoulders, and she was clinging onto her Paddington bag like a life raft.

I scanned Nelson's face for signs of distress, but he just seemed tanned and cheerful, as usual. Gabi, in fact, looked more churned up than he did.

"So," said Nelson, rubbing his hands, "who's for a pub lunch?"

"Is that it?" I hissed as Gabi and Roger led the way to the nearest pub. "It's all over and you're wondering whether you can get an organic steak and kidney pie?"

Nelson hung back a bit so we were well out of earshot. Then he slung one arm around my shoulders, as he was wont to do. "Melissa, between you and me, there were many reasons for my going on that voyage. I mean, obviously I wanted to help some young people experience the joys of proper sailing —"

"Yes, yes," I interrupted impatiently. "Sainthood, blah, blah, blah."

"And the flat did need tarting up. But . . ." He paused and turned to face me. "Promise you won't go off on one?"

"Of course I won't!"

He sighed. "Gabi is a great girl, and I know she's your best mate, but God in heaven . . . She was driving me insane, Mel. I don't know whether it was some kind of phase she was going through, but honestly, she wanted me to be this Mr. Darcy figure and boss her around and tell her what to do . . . it was *unnatural.* I didn't want to upset her, though, because I didn't want to cause trouble between you two. It could have been rather awkward."

I stared at him, flabbergasted. Just how long had this ailing relationship been propped up solely to spare my feelings?

"So you ran off to sea instead?" I said incredulously. "That's very English of you. Was the Foreign Legion not recruiting?"

"It seemed like the best thing to do." He shrugged his shoulders. "I mean, it played into her Jane Austen phase for a bit, the whole waving the hanky at the docks bit, but I knew the longer she was in London on her own, the more likely she was to get back with Aaron."

"And now she has."

"And now she has," he agreed. "Maybe it was just something she needed to do. Anyway, everyone's happy. She gets her Audi TT back, Aaron gets his soul mate back, I get my sofa to myself, and —"

"I get to share it with you," I ended dully.

Nelson exhaled. "Sorry, that was insensitive. Gabi mentioned —"

"The flat's lovely, though," I said, in a voice that was a little too high. "They put in all the plug sockets you asked for. And I've found you some new energy-saving lightbulbs."

He said nothing, but put his arm round me. "You're the only girl for me, Mel, you know that," he said, and he kissed me affectionately on the top of my head.

"And you're the only man for me," I replied, though my eyes were filling with happy-sad tears that I didn't let him see.

We carried on walking. "Tell me all about it later," he said. "I'll make you whatever you want for supper, and I'll even rub your disgusting feet."

Nelson might not have been much of a new man, but he knew how to make me feel better.

■ ■ ■ ■

The third positive aspect of my return to London was that I was able to attend my mother's "guest-list-only" first night show.

I know! I was pretty bewildered to hear about it too.

I wouldn't even have known it was happening had Allegra not chosen to grace the office with her presence shortly after my return.

"Oh, you're back," she said with scant interest as she swanned in with two large Smythsons bags and helped herself to a rum truffle from the huge box on the filing cabinet, sent as a thank-you from a gratefully rebarbered client.

"Yes, I am. I've been back for three days." I was in the middle of writing my etiquette column for *South West Now!* — specifically, a response to someone whose girlfriend had worse death breath than her cat. In my whirlwind of catching up, running the absent Allegra to earth had not been a priority. "What on earth have you bought from Smythsons? What have they got that comes in bags that big?"

"I need guest books, for the private show."

I rubbed my eyes gently, so as not to

smudge my winged eyeliner. "Allegra. You're not meant to be organizing private shows, unless it's for one of my clients. While Daddy's . . . while I'm paying you to work here, you work for *my* clients."

I'd given up trying to disentangle my father's Olympic scammery. Ignorance wasn't just bliss, it was a whole legal defense.

"It's Mummy's private show," she said disparagingly. "Anyway, she said to charge it to your agency. She'll have her agent negotiate the fee later."

"What?"

"Mummy is holding an exhibition," said Allegra impatiently.

"Of *what?*"

"Oh, do stop saying 'what,' Melissa. It makes you sound very thick. Her work, if you must know, has been snapped up by a London art agent who specializes in modern sculpture. Here, look at this."

She dug about in her bag and thrust a thick laminated invitation at me.

It featured a grotesque creature in shocking pink mohair. It could have been a cat, or a unicorn, but it had five legs, two and a half heads and either a horn or a very pointy ear in the middle of its forehead. Underneath were the details of Belinda Blennerhesket's private show party, due to take place on October 31st.

Hallowe'en. How appropriate.

"Why's she doing it under her maiden name?" I asked. This was some way down my list of questions, but it was the one least likely to throw Allegra into a froth of artistic outrage.

"She doesn't want Daddy taking the publicity spotlight for himself," she replied. "And I say, good for her. It's all her own work. Well, apart from the contract work she's put out to the local WI. They're rather confused, what with having to knit everything wrong and put in extra legs and so on, but if you ask me, Mummy's shown herself to be very enterprising. Fast as she knits them, I'm selling them. And not as *toys,* either," she added snottily. "As Art."

"But how? . . ." The mind boggled at the thought of Mummy doctoring knitting patterns, then handing them out at WI meetings. Mummy, more to the point, the WI poster girl! I sank my elbows onto the desk and rested my fuddled head.

Allegra smirked. "That child I sent the toys to? The one you went berserk about? Well, his mother runs a gallery in Cork Street, and she positively demanded to know where she could get more."

The smirk, already Daddy-like, increased as she said this, as if she'd known all along that the mother in question was connected to the art world's most fashionable players. I wished I knew for sure that this was untrue, but I didn't. Allegra was super-jammy like that. She didn't dress like the devil's handmaiden for nothing.

"I see," I said. "Well, that's marvelous news. I can't wait. What day is the thirty-first again?"

"Oh, you want to come?"

I stared at her. "*Yes*, Allegra. Since I was indirectly responsible for launching Mummy's new career."

She raised her plucked eyebrows. "Well, I'll have to see if I can get you on the guest list."

She was so getting a pay cut.

"Anyway," she said, as if she'd added telepathy to her list of spooky abilities. "I don't need your job. I have a new one."

"Really?"

"I'm acting as a marketing consultant to some very exclusive Scandinavian cheese importers."

Allegra. Cheese. Importing. There were a lot of holes in those cheeses. I hoped she wasn't planning to do anything funny with them.

"Daddy negotiated it for me," she went on, which only added to my suspicion. "So between that and the gallery, I don't know if I'll have time to help you out any more." She paused. "Sorry!"

"No, Allegra," I said, feeling the soothing rush of relief. "Thank you."

She swept out, snaffling another rum truffle, then paused at the door, where she turned round with what I assumed was a sympathetic look. "Still no news from what's-his-name?"

"No," I said. "And I don't want any news. I wrote to him explaining that it would be best if we didn't have any contact . . . for a while."

To be honest, I could barely remember what I'd written in that letter, despite taking thirty-seven attempts to get it right. I just knew that if I was going to cling onto my Doing The Right Thing stance, I couldn't so much as see Jonathan's handwriting, let alone him.

Allegra made a moue with her red lips. "Poor you."

"All for the best," I said and touch-typed fifteen lines of complete gibberish until she left.

Then I had a tearful moment, followed by four rum truffles in quick succession, and pulled myself together long enough to finish the article.

The days and weeks sped past in a numb blur of the ridiculous amount of work I'd taken on to distract myself from thinking about Jonathan. Mummy's private show was my first big social event since that awful last night in New York, and even getting ready for it opened up the festering wounds. I didn't want to wear anything that reminded me of the fund-raiser of doom at the Met, and as a result, I was still standing, sniveling, in my girdle when Nelson banged on the door and demanded to know if I was weaving my outfit from scratch.

All credit to him that he came into my room and virtually dressed me like a Barbie doll, in a not-at-all-awful outfit, while I moaned incoherently.

"Don't worry," he said, buttoning up my circle skirt. "It's Hallowe'en. Everyone will think you've come in costume."

"Cheers, Nelson."

"Can't have you letting the side down, can we?" Our gazes met in the mirror. Nelson's blond brows knit in brotherly concern. "I think you made the right decision, Mel. You can't live your life under someone else's rules. Feminism and all that. And I'll keep telling you so until you believe me."

"I suppose we're both dumped now," I said morosely.

"No," said Nelson, adding a jazzy scarf to my outfit. "I'm dumped. You're the dumper. Big difference. Now, come on. Roger and Gabi say they're coming round later to do ghost stories and apple bobbing. Never tell me again that you don't have a rich and varied social life."

Autumn was well under way in London, and we had to tramp through crisp fallen leaves to get to the bus stop. The coppers and golds and bronzes were like delicate little works of beaten metal against the mundane pavement slabs, but, like a very bad song, they only reminded me of Jonathan's hair.

I leaned my nose against the scratched glass of the bus window and sighed, making the window mist up. My mind seemed to think in terms of very bad song lyrics these days. I'd never get to feel his breath against my neck in the morning again. Never get to touch the pale gold hairs on his forearms, or trace the freckles on his back. Never hear his lecture about using Factor 40 sun cream to prevent sun damage . . .

Nelson heard me sigh and gave me a half-squeeze, half-nudge.

We were probably the only guests at the show who had come by public transport: The room was rammed with glittery bat-people in Allegra's image, all smoking with their cigarettes at shoulder-height, rubbing their noses and shrieking at their own jokes. I unwound my woolly scarf with some trepidation and handed it to the coat-check girl, who looked at if as if I'd handed her a dead badger.

"If it's going to be one of those evenings, let's not stay long," murmured Nelson, at the same moment that I leaned up to say exactly the same thing to him.

Around the perimeter of the gallery were glass cases containing Mummy's weird toys, illuminated with different-colored spot-lights, as if they needed any more freakish touches. I inspected the nearest tortoise/badger and recoiled in shock at how much they were asking for it. And according to the three red spots stuck on the caption, three people already wanted to buy it. Blimey.

"Don't look now, but someone's trying to get your attention," Nelson muttered in my ear.

My hopeful heart leaped up irrationally into my chest, in case, somehow, Jonathan had finally come for me. I spun round, smile already in place.

"Hello, darling!" said a familiar voice.

It wasn't Jonathan. It was Granny, looking regal in a floor-length silver velvet kaftan. A small diamond tiara nestled in her gray hair, managing to look offhand and deeply formal at the same time. She was also wearing a monocle, just for the sake of it. "Aren't these people awful! But you look lovely," she beamed.

"Hello," I said, trying not to sound too disappointed.

"Hoping I was someone else?" she said, tipping her head to one side.

"Sort of."

"Come with me, and let's get you a drink." And she steered us through the gibbering masses. "Now then, what's this I hear about you calling things off with your young man?"

"Do we have to talk about it? It's all anyone seems to ask me about these days."

"Well, we're worried about you." She pursed her lips.

"It's not helping. I can tell Mummy thinks I've lost my mind, and Gabi says she understands, but I don't think she does, and . . ." I raised my eyes to Granny's. "I thought you'd understand, though. I just can't believe that Jonathan, of all people, doesn't

615

get the fact that what I do with the agency is about helping people, not selling myself to them! I don't *want* to spend my days making shopping lists for rich women who could buy anything they needed. I want to feel like I'm making a practical difference to people."

"And you don't feel you can make a difference to him?"

"No," I said sadly. "He's perfect. From his perfect socks to his perfect scent."

Granny let out an amused little huff through her nose. "Darling, no one's perfect. Has it ever crossed your mind that he might be *trying* to be as perfect as possible so you don't feel you have to fix him too?"

"But I wouldn't mind . . ."

"Do think laterally, Melissa. You spend your days organizing useless chaps. Jonathan probably thinks that's the last thing you want to do when you come home. In fact, he probably thinks that the more organizing you have to do, the more you'll think of him as a client, not a boyfriend." She gave me a knowing look. "And he has his own very good reasons for not wanting you to think of him like that, now, doesn't he?"

I stared at her while she signaled at a waiter for fresh drinks.

Well, I thought, when you put it like that . . .

"He's always struck me as being a little insecure, you know," she went on, passing me a martini. "All those lists, that endless twitching, the obsession with his hair. His ridiculous Dictaphone." She gazed at me over her monocle. "There was no need to bring a Dictaphone to that shoot your father gave at New Year, darling, was there? It wasn't as though he was going to see any property that needed selling."

"No," I conceded. "And he's rather worried about doing enough at work —"

"And still quite cut up about his wife leaving him, I should imagine. Having to keep her under control and well away from you. Quite a juggle. I should know. And" — Granny gave me a friendly nudge — "probably not all that happy about his beautiful girlfriend hanging around with a famous ex."

I gave her a look. "His girlfriend who used to go out with *Prince William*. And Godric wasn't my ex."

She made a dismissive gesture with her free hand. "Oh, call your solicitor."

"Granny, I know what you're saying," I sighed, "but you're just making me feel as though I've made even more of a mistake."

I bit my lip as the truth of what she'd said sank in. "Poor Jonathan. I was so busy feeling inadequate myself to even think he might be too."

"Oh, darling, I'm not saying you made a mistake," she replied. "I think you did exactly the right thing — women who act like doormats to keep the peace only get chucked in the end for acting like doormats. No." She patted my cheek. "You did what you felt in your heart was right, and you'll never hear me tell you off for that. In fact," she added, draining her glass, "if he's got any sense he'll see that it's your spirit that makes you the girl you are. Besides, it's early days yet."

I wasn't so sure. "I told him not to call me," I said glumly. "And he's such a gentleman I know he won't. I mean," I added, "that's fine with me. I don't want him to call. It's over."

Granny arched her eyebrow. "Your mother dumped your father *four* times before they got married."

"And he didn't get the hint?"

"Well, they've been together ever since, haven't they?"

I had to concede that, despite their furious arguing, there did seem to be a spark between my parents. Not that I liked to examine that thought too closely. I must have looked particularly rueful, because Granny grabbed a passing martini off a tray and pressed it into my hand.

"Darling, I know your mother and Allegra aren't exactly an advert for married bliss," she said, "but there's a difference between compromising your independence and compromising yourself." She looked at me wisely. "Love's about giving up a little independence, darling. But that doesn't mean you have to stop being you."

"Well, that's fine," I grumped. "I suppose I'll know for next time. If there is a next time."

"Darling," said Granny, bestowing a kiss on my head. "There's always a next time. Take it from one who knows. Now, where did that waiter go? These martinis are hopeless. I think I might have to have a word."

Nelson and I sloped off by eight thirty, and as we turned the key in the front door, I felt the relief of being home sink into the very depths of my body. I eased off my shoes in readiness for a nice rub.

"Can't we cancel Roger and Gabi?" I asked as he pushed the door open. "I don't think I can cope with those two on top of Art."

"I can pretend you're dead drunk and miserable, if you want. That'll put Gabi off, but Roger's such a gossip-hound he'll probably insist on coming over. Oh, God, the lights have gone already," he groaned, feeling about for the switch. "Bloody cowboy electricians."

Eventually, he found a switch that worked and flicked it on, revealing Gabi and Roger sitting on the sofa wearing witch outfits and very convincing evil scowls.

"Surprise!" they said without much enthusiasm.

Nelson and I shrieked in shock.

The room was bedecked in cobwebs and fake spiders, with a huge applebobbing bucket in the middle of the new rug, plates of ghoulish black-currant jelly on the coffee table, and carved pumpkin heads on the television.

"Mwa-ha-ha-ha-ha!" added Roger, as an afterthought.

I clapped a hand to my racing heart. "Oh, my God, you gave me a fright."

"Give me that spare key," said Nelson, holding out his hand. "Right now. And you'd better hope that those cobwebs come off my brand-new skirting boards."

"You've had three trick or treaters already," Gabi informed him, peeling the keys reluctantly off her Tiffany keyring. "They wanted cash, or they were going to kick the headlights in on your car."

"Cash? What happened to sweets?"

"Inflation. You owe me fifteen quid." She turned on a table lamp and filled the room with a sinister red light. "I know you're a misery-guts at the moment, but we thought this might cheer you up."

"And it will!" I pulled off my coat. "I'm touched! Did you get spooky films?"

"Many," intoned Roger. "And Nelson's got a casserole in the oven."

"Brains and eye of newt ragout," said Nelson. "Just a little something I made earlier."

I smiled. "Then let the evil times commence!"

By eleven o'clock, we'd bobbed for apples, drunk Nelson's mulled wine, and freaked ourselves out with Gabi's tarot cards, and now all four of us were curled up on the two new sofas — my feet in Nelson's lap; Gabi and Roger's heads at opposite ends of theirs. We'd finished watching *The Others*, which Nelson and Roger had spoiled by pointing out the continuity errors, as was their wont, and now we were watching the equally horrific Selfridges video of Tristram Hart-Mossop quite blatantly ogling my cleavage while I demonstrated how cuff links worked. The shaky camera angles suggested how amusing Gabi was finding it, not to mention the salacious zooming in and out onto my straining shirt-buttons and Tristram's fidgeting trousers.

"Oh, my God," I gasped. "Gabi! Why didn't you *tell* me!"

"Because you look bloody great," she said, stuffing another handful of chocolate spiders in her mouth. "You've ruined that poor lad for ordinary Sloanes."

"Quite. We like women with a bit of meat on them, eh, Mel?" agreed Nelson, reaching over to wobble my stomach.

The doorbell rang downstairs as I was hauling myself up into a sitting position to protest. It carried on ringing, as if someone was leaning on the button.

Gabi and Roger groaned. "If it's those kids from before, tell them your car's barely worth new headlights," moaned Roger.

"What if it's my car?" demanded Nelson.

"Then *you* go down there," said Gabi, looking far too comfortable to move. "But take your checkbook."

"In my day it was apples and toffees, *if you were lucky*. What's going to happen to this generation of bloody awful kids when they need to get jobs?" Nelson opined

622

pompously, and I could tell this was the overture to a whole opera of pomposity. It had six acts and no intermission. I'd sat through it several times. Spending time on a ship with kids clearly hadn't improved his opinion of them.

"Oh, I'm just about up, I'll go," I said, heaving myself out of the sofa.

"Take this," said Gabi, throwing me her black tinsel witch's wig. "See if you can scare the little bastards off. Pretend you're Allegra."

I shuffled off toward the stairs, grabbing some chocolate spiders as I went, in case that might be enough. As a gesture to the evening, I was wearing my huge monster feet slippers I'd had since school, which made the stairs quite tricky, what with the wine and the lateness of the hour.

"I'm coming," I yelled as the ringing continued. When I got to the hallway, I pulled Gabi's wig on — backwards, to make it look like my head was the wrong way round, then pulled open the door with a cackle. "Ah ha ha ha ha har! A pox on you and all Satan's little wizards!"

I felt cold air, and a strange silence.

Oh, God, what if it was the police, about some damage to my car? Or Daddy?

I turned the wig round and tried to compose myself. *Really, Mel,* I thought, *leave the slapstick to Gabi and Roger.*

But there was no one there at the door.

I tsked loudly. "It's not big or clever, you know. Ringing the doorbell and running away!"

I leaned out to see if they were lurking by my car and realized that there *was* someone on the doorstep.

Braveheart.

He was wearing a chic tartan coat and gleaming brightly in the yellow streetlight. He was, to my amazement, sitting. And staying. And panting with his pink tongue out, a picture of self-satisfaction.

"New wig?" said a familiar voice. "I don't think I've seen that one."

I looked up, my heart pounding hard in my chest, and Jonathan stepped out of the shadows, wrapped up in a gray cashmere coat and a green scarf. His coat was smart, but his jawline was rough with stubble, and he looked less well groomed than usual.

"Hello," he said with an uncertain smile.

"Hello," I choked.

"Am I interrupting something?" He gestured toward my feet.

"Um, no. Just a little coven meeting," I gabbled, kicking off my slippers and chucking Gabi's wig onto the post table. "Smart casual, you know. Annual general meeting."

Jonathan scooped up Braveheart before he could run off, and he stepped up onto the second doorstep, so we were standing at more or less the same height. Braveheart licked Jonathan's nose, which spoiled his dramatic effect somewhat.

"I know you told me not to, but I had to come," he explained. "It was getting too much — the loss of appetite, the howling at night, the pining."

He paused.

"And the mutt missed you too," he added.

A broad smile split my face. Jonathan must have thought about that one all the way across the Atlantic.

"Well, I'm very pleased to see you both," I said, taking Braveheart out of his arms so I could shoo him upstairs.

Jonathan coughed. "Melissa, I'm afraid I have to do my speech now," he said. "Before I get distracted." He lifted his hand so I couldn't interrupt. "I've been thinking about nothing else since you walked out of the Met. I can't tell you how empty everything's felt. I totally respect the fact that you needed some space, but . . ." He pressed his lips together. "But I couldn't let you slip through my fingers like that! I *had* to see you, to tell you I made a mistake. First of all, you were right and I was wrong. It's not up to me what you do with your business. I should have known better than anyone how much it means to you to help people out. It wasn't that I didn't trust you . . ." He raised his eyes to mine, and they were bloodshot and weary. Somehow it only added a new vulnerability to those Ralph Lauren looks, and it melted my heart. "I didn't trust myself. Not to be jealous, or insecure, or to drive you away with my stupid insecurities."

"But you have no reason to be insecure," I said. "Not with *me*."

"I know that." He took my hands in his, and they were cold. I rubbed them with mine to warm them up. "I realize that now. That was the second apology. I shouldn't have tried to keep my communication with Cindy a secret. I got quite an ear-full on that score from Bonnie Hegel, I have to tell you. You have some serious fans in Manhattan. It wasn't that I didn't want you to know because something was going on. I was just scared, I guess, that somehow . . . she'd wreck things. Huh. I guess I did that on my own."

"No," I said. "You didn't. You just . . . gave us both something to think about."

Jonathan smiled wryly. "I don't know about that. But," he paused, "can't you understand how a guy like me might not quite believe his luck in having a girlfriend like you?"

"No," I almost laughed. "No, I can't!"

"Well, I'm telling you."

We both looked at each other, and my heart lifted inside my chest. He'd flown across the world to apologize, and he was doing it with such grace. And I could see in his hopeful, nervous eyes that he meant it. He wasn't just too good to be true, he *was* true.

Jonathan swallowed. "What if we just go for it — you think one of us might start believing it?"

"Maybe." I put his hands around my waist and pulled him nearer to me, so close I could feel the chill of the night air on the cashmere. "Maybe if we really concentrated on it. I might need some solid proof."

Jonathan's serious face twisted up into a grin, but he straightened it quickly.

"I think that can be arranged. And I'm sorry for not making that clear enough. You're right. I need to scale back on the work. You can keep your agency and run it as you think best and I can keep my Blackberry?" he murmured as his arms tightened around me and his nose approached mine. "I'm afraid we're both stuck with them, one way or another."

"I'm sure we can talk about it," I murmured back, tilting my head so my nose grazed his. "There's bound to be a compromise somewhere. And aren't you the expert negotiator?"

"Oh, I think I can be quite flexible." Jonathan's lips were touching mine, so lightly I could feel his breath on my mouth. "When I want something as much as I want you."

I let my body sink into his as our lips met, and our arms wrapped round each other, a warm spot in the cold draft of October wind. I didn't care about Nelson's yells to shut the front door to keep the heat in, or Braveheart's hysterical barking. I couldn't think about anything other than Jonathan.

We kissed until the moment was broken by Gabi screeching upstairs and Roger bellowing, "It's only a bloody dog with a wig on, Gabi!"

"I had to come back in any case," he said, disentangling himself. "I needed to call in at the Agency."

"Did you?" I said uncertainly. "What for?"

He was digging about in his pocket, then made a "Found it!" face as he pulled out a ring box. "Couple of things. First of all, I needed some advice on buying a ring . . .

May I?" He looked up with the ring in his hand, and I was touched to see a brief hesitation in his eyes.

"Please do," I said, as he slid it back onto my finger.

He looked at it critically. "I mean, it'll do for now. But we Americans like to make sure a woman looks engaged from a distance, know what I mean?"

I smiled. "This suits me fine, Jonathan. And the other thing?"

A satisfied sigh escaped from his lips as I turned the ring so the sapphires caught the light, as though he'd been tensed up until that moment. "I need to buy a bed for this new house I've got in the Village. A great big English four-poster bed. Preferably old? With curtains I can close? It's a great big house, you see . . . Gets kind of lonely, just me and the dog."

I smiled and slid my arms around his neck. I could hear the leaves rustling up and down the street in the wind. It would be even colder in Jane Street. Even more need to snuggle up. "That sounds rather cozy. I'd be *more* than happy to help you find one."

"Good," he said, and kissed me again.

ABOUT THE AUTHOR

Hester Browne was born in England's Lake District, read English at Trinity College, Cambridge, and lives in London. A former fiction editor, she made her own fiction debut with the critically acclaimed *New York Times* bestseller *The Little Lady Agency*. She is currently at work on her next novel, *The Little Lady and the Prince*.

The employees of Thorndike Press hope you have enjoyed this Large Print book. All our Thorndike and Wheeler Large Print titles are designed for easy reading, and all our books are made to last. Other Thorndike Press Large Print books are available at your library, through selected bookstores, or directly from us.

For information about titles, please call:
   (800) 223-1244

or visit our Web site at:
   www.gale.com/thorndike
   www.gale.com/wheeler

To share your comments, please write:
   Publisher
   Thorndike Press
   295 Kennedy Memorial Drive
   Waterville, ME 04901